To the Stars

To the Stars

— HOMEWORLD —

— WHEELWORLD —

— STARWORLD —

Harry Harrison

Nelson Doubleday, Inc.   Garden City, New York

HOMEWORLD
Copyright © 1980 by Harry Harrison

WHEELWORLD
Copyright © 1981 by Harry Harrison

STARWORLD
Copyright © 1981 by Harry Harrison

All rights reserved.

Published by arrangement with
Bantam Books, Inc.
666 Fifth Avenue
New York, New York 10019

Printed in the United States of America

Contents

To the Stars

HOMEWORLD

One

"It's a monstrosity, a bastard combination of antique piping, worn valves—and modern electronic technology. The whole thing should be blown up and built over from scratch."

"Not that bad, your honor, I think, not really that bad." Radcliffe rubbed his reddened nose with the back of his hand, looked up guiltily when he saw it streaked and wet. The tall engineer beside him had not noticed; Radcliffe wiped it surreptitiously on his trouser leg. "It works, we produce a fine spirit . . ."

"It works—but just barely." Jan Kulozik was tired and there was a sharp edge to his voice. "All of the packing glands should be replaced at once or it will blow itself up without any help from me. Look at those leaks, puddles of the stuff."

"I'll have it cleaned up at once, your honor."

"That's not what I mean. Stop the leaks in the first place. Do something constructive, man. That's an order."

"As you say, so shall it be done."

Radcliffe lowered his head obediently, trembling. Jan looked down on the man's balding head, the dusting of dandruff on the fringe of oily hair, and could feel only disgust. These people never learned. They could not think for themselves and even when ordered to do the correct thing made a mess of it half of the time. This manager was about as efficient as the collection of ancient fractioning columns, fermenting vats, and rusty pipes that made up this vegetable-fuel plant. It seemed a waste of time to install the automation controls.

Cold winter light from the tall windows barely outlined the

dark mechanical shapes inside the building; spotlights made pools
of yellow across the floor. One of the workmen shuffled into view,
paused, and groped through his pockets. The motion caught Jan's
eye.

"That man—stop!" he shouted.

The command was sudden, startling. The workman had not
known the engineer was there. He dropped the match—even before he had lit the joint—and it fell into the pool of liquid at his
feet. Sudden blue flame leaped high.

Jan shouldered the man aside roughly as he jumped for the fire
extinguisher, tearing it from the bracket, pounding the release as
he ran. The workman was stamping wildly at the pool of burning
alcohol which only served to spread the flame.

Foam coughed out of the extinguisher's mouth and Jan directed
it down, around. The fire was out in a moment, but the workman's trousers were smoldering. Jan whipped the foam across the
man's legs and then, in a fit of anger, up his legs, chest, splashing
and coating his face with a white blanket.

"You're an absolute fool, a total fool!"

Jan turned off the valve and threw the extinguisher down. The
workman was gasping and wiping his eyes; Jan looked on coldly.

"You know smoking is forbidden in here. You must have been
told often enough. And you're standing right under a *no smoking*
sign."

"I . . . I don't read so well, your honor." He choked and spat
out the bitter liquid.

"Not so well, or probably not at all. You're fired, get out of
here."

"No, please, your honor, don't say that," the man wailed, the
pain in his eyes forgotten, his mouth a gaping O of despair. "I've
worked hard—my family—the dole for years . . ."

"The dole for life," Jan said coldly, the anger drained away as
he looked at the man before him, on his knees in the foam. "Just
be happy that I'm not preferring sabotage charges."

The situation was almost impossible. Jan stamped away, unaware of the staring eyes of the manager and the silent workmen.
Just impossible. But better in the control room. Much better. He
could almost relax, smile, as he looked at the shining order of the
system he had installed. Cable conduits snaked in from all sides,
merging and joining together at the control unit. He pressed the
keys on the combination lock in sequence and the cover swung

open. Silent, smooth, and perfect. The microcomputer in the heart of the machine ran everything with infinite precision. The terminal hung in its holster from his belt. He unclipped it and plugged it into the computer, tapped out a message on the keys. The screen lit up in instant response. No problems, not here. Though of course that wasn't the case elsewhere in the plant. When he asked for a general condition report the lines of readout went marching by.

VALVE UNIT 376–L–9 LEAKING
VALVE UNIT 389–P–6 IN NEED OF REPLACEMENT
VALVE UNIT 429–P–8 LEAKING

It was all thoroughly depressing and he cleared the screen with a quick command. Behind him Radcliffe's voice spoke quietly, respectfully from the open door.

"Please excuse me, Engineer Kulozik, but it is about Simmons, the man you fired. He's a good worker."

"I don't think he's very good." The anger was drained now and Jan wanted to be reasonable about this. But firm. "There will be plenty of people queuing up for his job. Any one of them will do it as well—or better."

"He studied for years, your honor. Years. To get off the dole. That shows something."

"Lighting that match showed even more. I'm sorry. I'm not a cruel man. But I'm thinking of you and the others here. What would you do if he burned down *your* jobs. You're management, Radcliffe, and that's the way you must think. It may be hard, and look wrong from the outside, but it is the only thing to do. You agree, don't you?"

There was a slight hesitation, but the answer came.

"Of course. You're right. I'm sorry I bothered you. I'll get him out of here now. We can't have his kind around."

"That's the way to do it."

A soft buzz and a flashing red light from the control unit drew Jan's attention; Radcliffe hesitated in the doorway. The computer had found something wrong and wanted Jan to know about it, displaying the information.

VALVE UNIT 928–R–9 IS NOW INOPERATIVE IN PER-
MANENTLY OPEN CONDITION. IT HAS BEEN ISO-
LATED FOR REPLACEMENT.

"928-R. Sounds familiar." Jan tapped the information into his personal computer and nodded. "I thought so. That thing was supposed to have been replaced last week. Was the job completed?"

"I'll have to check the records." Radcliffe was pale.

"Don't bother. We both know it wasn't done. So get out of here and get a valve and we will do the job *now*."

Jan himself detached the motor drive unit, using a power wrench on the recalcitrant lugnuts. They were heavy with rust. Typical. It had apparently been too much effort to put some oil on them before they had been tightened. He stood aside and watched closely while the sweating proles struggled to get the old valve off, splashing through the runnels of liquid that ran from the pipe end. When the new unit had been fitted and tightened into place under his attentive eye—no second-rate job this time—he bolted on the motor drive. The work was done efficiently without any extra chatter and the workmen picked up their tools and left as soon as it was finished. Jan went back to control to open the blocked section and get the plant functioning again. Once more he had the condition report scroll by, then had a hard copy made. When it had emerged from the printer he dropped into a chair to go through it carefully, ticking off the items that seemed to need the most urgent attention. He was a tall, almost gangling man, in his late twenties. Women thought him good looking—a number had told him so—but he did not think it particularly important. They were nice but they had their place. Which was immediately after microcircuit engineering. Whenever he read he frowned so that an almost permanent crease was stamped between his eyes. He frowned even more now as he went through the list a second time—then burst into a wide grin.

"Done—just about done!"

What should have been a simple job here at the Walsoken Plant had stretched on and on. It had been autumn when he had arrived to make the control installation, along with Buchanan, a hydraulics engineer. But Buchanan had had the bad luck—good luck really—to be laid low by an attack of appendicitis and had been spirited away by ambulance copter never to return. Nor had his replacement ever arrived. Jan had found himself supervising the mechanical installation in addition to his own electronics and autumn had stretched into winter with no end in sight.

It was in sight now. All of the major installations and repairs had been done; the plant was up and running. And he was going to get out. For a few weeks at least—and the manager would just have to fend for himself.

"Radcliffe, get in here. I have some interesting news for you."

The words cracked from every loudspeaker in the building, rolled and echoed. Within seconds there was the sound of running footsteps and the panting manager came hurrying into the room.

"Yes . . . your honor?"

"I'm leaving. Today. Don't gape, man, I thought you would be pleased at the prospect. This antique vodka works is on line and should keep on running if you take care of all the maintenance on this list. I've hooked the computer through the network to fuel-concent where the operation will be monitored. Any problems will bring someone here fast. But I don't expect any problems, do I, Radcliffe?"

"No, sir, of course not. Do our best, thank you, sir."

"I hope so. And may your best be a little bit better than it has been in the past. I'll be back as soon as I am able, to check operation and to see your list of completion. Now—unless there is anything else—I am going to get out of this place."

"No. Nothing, sir."

"Good. See that it stays that way."

Jan waved the manager out as he unclipped his terminal and computer and stowed them in his case. Eagerly, for the first time it seemed, he pulled on the fleece-lined coat and driving gloves. One stop at the hotel to pack his bag and that was that! He whistled between his teeth as he slammed out of the door into the late afternoon gloom. The ground was frozen hard as rock and there was the smell of snow in the air. His car, red and shining, was the only touch of color in the drab landscape. Blighted fields stretched away on all sides in the flat landscape, silent under the drab gray sky. The fuel cell fired as soon as he turned the key; the heater warmed the interior with a rush of air. He drove slowly over the frozen ruts of the yard and out onto the paved road.

This was former fen country, now drained and plowed. But some of the old canals were still there; Wisbech was still an inland port. He would be glad to see the last of it. Packing took ten minutes—he believed in traveling light—and the manager held the front door and bowed him out and wished him a safe journey.

Just outside of town the motorway began. The police at the entrance saluted and he returned them an airy wave. Once on the automated road network he switched over to automatic, giving LONDON EXIT 74 as his destination. This information flashed from the transmitter under his car to the cable buried beneath the surface, to the network computer which routed him and sent back the command to the car computer in microseconds. There was a slow surge of acceleration by the electric wheel motors up to the standard 240 K.P.H., until the landscape became a blur in the gathering dusk. Jan had no desire to look out at it. He unlocked his seat and swiveled it about to face the rear. There was whiskey ready in the bar compartment and water at the touch of a button. The television came on to a colorful and loud production of Peter Grimes. Jan enjoyed it for a minute, admiring the soprano not only for her voice—and tried to think whom she reminded him of.

"Aileen Pettit—of course!" He had a warm glow of memory; if she were only free now. She had little enough to do since her divorce. She should jump at the chance to see him. To think was to act. He punched for phone, then tapped her number quickly into the keys. It rang only twice before she answered.

"Jan. How nice of you to call."

"How nice of you to answer. Do you have camera trouble?" He pointed at his own dark screen.

"No, just blanked for privacy. You caught me in the sauna."

The screen came to life as she said this and she laughed at his expression. "Never saw a nude woman before?"

"If I have I've forgotten. They don't have women where I've been. At least none glowing and wet like you. Honestly, Aileen, I could almost weep for joy. You're the most beautiful sight in the world."

"Flattery will get you everywhere."

"And you're coming with me. Are you free now?"

"Always free, my love, but it depends on what you have in mind."

"Some sunshine. Some hot sun and warm ocean and good food, a case of champagne and you. What do you say?"

"I say it sounds unspeakably lovely. My bank account or yours?"

"My treat. I deserve something after this winter in the wilderness. I know this little hotel, right out in the desert on the shore of the Red Sea. If we leave in the morning we can get there . . ."

"No details, please, my sweet. I'm going to sink back into my sauna and wait there for you. Don't be too long."

She broke the connection with the last word and Jan laughed out loud. Yes, life was going to be a lot better. He drained the glass of scotch and poured another one.

The frozen fen country was already gone from his mind.

He did not know that the man he had fired, Simmons, never would go back on the dole. He committed suicide just about the time Jan reached London.

Two

The circular shadow of the great flying ship drifted slowly over the blue surface of the Mediterranean far below, across the beach and onto the desert beyond. The electric motors were silent, the only sound the whir of the propellers. They were tiny, almost lost from sight under the thick, saucerlike form of the *Beachy Head*, for their only work was to propel her through the air. Lift was supplied by the helium bags concealed beneath the taut outer skin. The dirigible was a superior form of transportation with very low fuel consumption.

Her cargo consisted of great bundles of heavy black pipes slung beneath the body. Tons of them. But the *Beachy Head* carried passengers as well, in cabins in the bow.

"The view is incredible," Aileen said, sitting before the angled window that made up the entire front wall of their cabin, watching the desert move by below. Jan, stretched out on the bed, nodded in silent agreement—but was looking at her. She was combing her shoulder-length coppery-red hair, her raised arms lifting her bare breasts, her back arched and lovely.

"Incredible," he said, and she laughed and put down the comb to come and sit beside him and kiss him.

"Marry me?" Jan asked.

"Thank you, no. My divorce isn't a month old. I want to enjoy my freedom for a while yet."

"I'll ask you next month."

"Do that . . ." The chiming bell cut her off and the steward's voice broke the silence of the cabin.

"All passengers. We will be landing in Suez in thirty minutes' time. Please have your bags ready for the porters. Thirty minutes' time. It has been our pleasure to have you aboard the *Beachy Head* and in the name of Captain Wetherby and the crew I want to thank you for flying British Airways."

"A half an hour and look at my hair! And I haven't started packing yet . . ."

"There's no hurry. And no one will throw you out of the cabin. This is a holiday, remember? I'm going to get dressed and see about the luggage. I'll meet you on the ground."

"Can't you wait for me?"

"I'll be waiting—but outside. I want to see what kind of drilling gear they are unloading."

"You care more about all those filthy pipes than you do about me."

"Absolutely correct——how did you find out? But this is a momentous occasion. If the thermal extraction techniques work, we may be pumping oil again. For the first time in over two-hundred years."

"Oil? From where?" Aileen's voice was distant; she was more interested in getting the thin blouse over her head.

"The ground. It used to be there, a lot of it, petroleum. Pumped dry by the Wreckers, oxidized and wasted just like everything else. A really beautiful source of chemical hydrocarbons that they just burned up."

"I haven't the slightest idea of what you are talking about. I always failed history."

"See you on the ground."

When Jan stepped out of the lift at the foot of the mooring tower, he felt as though he had walked through the open door of an oven. Even in the middle of winter the sun had a bite unknown in the north. After his exile in the frozen fens it felt good.

Bundles of pipes were being lowered now by the cable hoists. Drifting down slowly, bobbing slightly under the buoyant airship, dropping again to clang onto the waiting flatbed truck. For a moment Jan thought of applying for permission to visit the well site —then changed his mind. No. Holiday first. Perhaps on the way back. For the time being he must cleanse his mind of the glories of science and technology, and instead explore the more fascinating glories of Aileen Pettit.

When she appeared from the lift they strolled to the customs

building hand in hand, enjoying the feel of the sun on their skin. A solemn, dark-skinned policeman stood guard at the customs counter and watched while Jan inserted his ID card in the slot.

"Welcome to Egypt," the machine said in a contralto female voice. "We hope that your visit will be an enjoyable one . . . Mr. Kulozik. Would you be so kind as to press your thumb to the plate. Thank you. You may remove your card now. There is a message for you. Will you please proceed to exit four where you will be met. Next please."

The computer dealt with Aileen just as swiftly. While the ritual welcome was being spoken it checked her identity, verifying with her thumb print that she was the person referred to on the ID card. Then making sure that the trip was an approved one.

They were met at the exit by a perspiring, sunburnt man in a tight blue uniform. "Mr. Kulozik and party? I'm from the Magna Palace, your honor. I have your bags aboard and we can leave when you are ready." His English was good, but he had an accent that Jan could not place.

"We'll go now."

The airport had been built at the water's edge and the small hovercraft sat on its pad at the end of the slipway. The driver opened the door for them and they climbed into the air-conditioned interior. There were a dozen seats, but they were the only passengers. In a moment the craft rose up on the blast of air, then drifted down to the water and out onto it, picking up speed.

"We are now going south in the Gulf of Suez," the driver said. "On your left you will see the Sinai Peninsula. Ahead, on your right, you will soon be able to see the peak of Mount Gharib which is one-thousand, seven-hundred and twenty-three meters high . . ."

"I've been here before," Jan said. "You can save the guided tour."

"Thank you, your honor."

"Jan, I wanted to hear it. I don't even know where we are."

"Did you fail geography as well as history?"

"Don't be cruel."

"Sorry. We'll be coming out into the Red Sea soon and making a sharp left turn into the Gulf of Aqaba where the sun always shines and it is always hot, except in the summer when it is even hotter. And right in the middle of all that lovely sun and water is

the Magna Palace where we are going. You aren't British, are you, driver?"

"No, your honor, South African."

"You're a long way from home."

"A continent away, sir."

"I'm thirsty," Aileen said.

"I'll get some drinks from the bar."

"I'll do that, your honor," the driver said, flicking onto automatic and jumping to his feet. "What will be your pleasure?"

"Whatever you suggest . . . I don't know your name."

"Piet, sir. There is cold beer and—"

"Just the thing. You too, Aileen?"

"Yes, thank you."

Jan drained half of the foaming glass and sighed. He was getting into the holiday mood at last. "Have one yourself, Piet."

"I will. Very kind of you, sir."

Aileen looked closely at the driver, the blond hair and reddened skin, and sensed a mystery. Though the man was polite his manners were not the rough ones of a prole. "I hate to admit it, Piet," she said, "but I have never heard of South Africa."

"Few have," he admitted. "The city of South Africa isn't very big, just a few thousand whites in a sea of blacks. We're a fortress built over the diamond mines, nothing else. I didn't like working in the mines and there is nothing else one can do—so I got out. I like the job here and the way I can move around." A shrill bleeping sounded and he put down his glass and hurried to the controls.

It was late afternoon when Magna appeared on the horizon, just a blur where the desert sand met the ocean. The shining glass towers of the holiday complex were soon visible; bright-sailed boats dotted the sea before them.

"I know I'm going to like this," Aileen said, laughing.

The hovercraft slid up onto the beach well clear of the boats and swimmers, at the very edge of the crumbled mud huts that made up the native town. A few burnoosed Arabs were visible, but vanished from sight before the door of the craft was unlocked. There was an open carriage waiting for them—drawn by a donkey. Aileen clapped with joy at the sight, widened her eyes at the dark-skinned, turbaned driver, and enjoyed every moment of the short ride to the hotel. The manager hurried up to hold the door for them and greet them; porters made off with their bags. Their room was spacious with a wide balcony facing the sea. A basket of fruit was waiting on the table and the manager himself opened the bottle of champagne and poured the first glassful.

"Welcome again," he said, managing to bow and pass them the glasses at the same time.

"I love it," Aileen said, kissing Jan soundly as soon as they were alone. "And I'm dying to get into that ocean out there."

"So why don't we?"

It was as good as it looked. Despite the season the water was comfortable, the sun hot on their shoulders. England and winter were a bad dream, very far away. They swam until they were tired, then went and sat beneath the tall palm trees and had a drink in the red glow of sunset. Dinner was served on the terrace and they did not bother to change. To make the evening complete a brightly glowing full moon rose above the desert.

"I just can't believe it," Aileen said. "You must have arranged the whole thing."

"I did. The moon was due to rise two hours from now but I speeded it up for you."

"Very kind of you. Jan, look, what are they doing?"

Dark shapes were moving out from the shore, changing and growing while they watched.

"Night yachting. Getting up their sails."

"Could we do it? Do you know how?"

"Of course I do!" he said with authority, trying to remember the little he had learned about sailing on his first visit here. "Come on, I'll show you."

It was a mess, of course, and they laughed as they stumbled over the tangled ropes, and finally had to shout to the shore for aid. One of the Arab boat handlers came out in a skiff and soon put the lines to right. A light breeze had sprung up, so that with the mainsail set they were soon moving smoothly over the calm sea. Moonlight showed the way clearly; the stars burned from horizon to horizon. Jan held the tiller with one hand, the other about Aileen who leaned against him, kissed him, her skin warm against his in her brief bathing costume.

"Almost too much," she whispered.

"Never enough."

They did not tack and the wind carried them further from shore, until none of the other boats were in sight and the land had vanished in the darkness of the water.

"Aren't we too far out?" Aileen asked.

"Not really. I just thought it would be nice to be alone. I can navigate by the moon, and we can always drop sail and use the auxiliary to get back if we have to."

"I haven't the slightest idea of what you are talking about but I trust you."

A half an hour later, with the air getting cooler, Jan decided to turn around. He managed to go all aback when he tacked, but eventually the sail filled again and they could see the lights of the hotel on the horizon ahead. It was very quiet, the only sound the slight rush of water under the bow and the crackling of the sail, so that they heard the rumble of motors when they were still far away. The sound grew, quickly.

"Someone's in a hurry," Jan said, squinting into the darkness toward the growing whine of straining engines.

"What's out there?"

"I haven't the foggiest. But we'll know soon, they seem to be coming this way. Two engines it sounds like. Funny time of night to go racing."

It happened quickly. The hammering exhausts grew louder and the first ship appeared. A dark form over a froth of white sea. Growing monstrously—aiming right at them. Aileen screamed as it loomed above them, went by them. The wake caught the boat and washed over the coaming, sending them rocking wildly.

"By God that was close," Jan gasped, holding to the cockpit edge with one hand, clasping Aileen with the other.

They had turned, looking after the first ship, so they never even saw the second one until it was too late. Jan had only a glimpse of the bow tearing down on them, crashing into their bowsprit, crushing it, capsizing them. He had only time to grab hard onto Aileen when the boat capsized.

As the water closed over his head something struck him on the leg, numbing it. The sea pulled at Aileen but he held fast, both arms about her until they surfaced again. She was sobbing and coughing as her head came above the surface and he held her up as best he could.

They were in the midst of floating debris. The yacht was gone. So were the two ships, the sound of their engines dying and vanishing.

In the middle of the dark night, in the black ocean, they were alone.

Three

At first Jan did not appreciate the complete danger of their position. Aileen was crying and coughing and it was hard enough to keep his own head above the surface as well as hers. The floating debris was black in the water around them and he pushed away from a mass of ropes, then struck a cushion with his flailing hand. It was floating high in the water and had obviously been designed for flotation use. He guided Aileen to it, pulled it under her arms. Only when he saw that she was holding fast and her head was well out of the water did he let go and look for another cushion.

"Come back!" she called out in panic.

"It's all right. I want another float for myself."

He found it easily enough and kicked his way back toward her anxious voice.

"I'm here now. It's all right."

"What's all right? We're going to die out here, drown, I know it!"

He had no easy answer because he had the terrible sensation that she was right. "They'll find us," he finally said. "The ships will come back or radio in for aid. You'll see. Meanwhile, let's kick toward shore. It's not too far."

"Which way do we go?"

That was a very good question and he was far from sure of the answer. The moon was overhead now and veiled by high clouds. And from their position, low in the water, the hotel lights were no longer visible. "This way," he said, trying to sound reassuring pushing her ahead of him.

The ships did not come back, the shore was miles away—even if they were swimming in the right direction, which he doubted very much—and he was growing cold. And tired. Aileen was only half conscious, he had the feeling that she might have struck her head when they were run down, and soon he had to stop swimming in order to hold her onto the cushion.

Could they last until morning? That was the fact he had to face. He was not going to swim ashore. What time was it? Probably not even midnight yet. And the winter nights were long. The water was not that warm. He kicked out again to get the blood flowing, to warm himself a bit. But Aileen's skin was growing colder and colder in his grasp, her breathing weaker. If she died it would be his fault, he had brought her to this place, put her life at risk. But if she died he would certainly pay for his mistake. He would not last until dawn either. And even if he did—would the searchers find them?

Dark thoughts spiraled around and around in his head and his depression was absolute. Maybe it would be easier to let go now, to drown now, put an end to everything. Yet even as the thought entered his mind he kicked out in anger, pushing them through the wet darkness. Die he might—but not by suicide. However his legs tired quickly and he stopped the futile effort and let them float downward. Holding Aileen's cold shoulders he pressed his face to hers. Was it going to end like this?

Something pushed up against his feet, and he bent his knees in sudden terror. The thought of a creature unseen below him in the dark water was as terrifying as a nightmare. Shark? Were there sharks in this ocean? He didn't know.

It touched him again, hard from below, rising up inexorably. There was no escape. There it was, in all directions, no matter how hard he thrashed to escape.

While behind him something even blacker than the night rose up like a wall, gushing with water.

Jan struck out with his fist in pure fear—bruising his knuckles on hard metal.

Then they were out of the water, on a platform of some kind, the wind blowing coldly on his soaked skin. There was the sudden shock of recognition—then he shouted out loud.

"A submarine!"

The accident had been seen, must have been. Submarines do not rise up beneath one's feet, in the night, by accident. An infrared telescope, or perhaps the new micropulse radar. Gently, he laid Aileen on the wet planking, her head on the pillow.

"Hello there," he called out, knocking with his fist on the conning tower. Perhaps the door was on the other side. He was starting around it when a black opening suddenly appeared and men began to push their way out. One of them leaped on Aileen, stabbing her in the leg with something shining.

"What the hell do you think you're doing?" Jan shouted, jumping at them; relief turned to anger in the instant. The nearest figure turned swiftly, raising his hand with something in it, bringing it down toward Jan.

He fought back, grabbed the arm and pressed hard. The man grunted in surprise as he stabbed himself—his eyes widened with shock. He gave one immense heave, then went limp. Jan pushed him aside, whirled toward the others, fists clenched and ready. They were spread in a circle before him, bent to attack, grunting in guttural voices to one another.

"Oh, hell," one of them said, standing up straight and holding the others back with his hands. "No more fighting. We've botched this thing nicely."

"We can't stop now . . ."

"Yes we can. Get below." He turned to Jan. "You as well."

"What have you done to her?"

"Nothing important. An injection to make her sleep. We had one for you too, but poor Ota got the shot instead . . ."

"You can't force me to go."

"Don't be a fool!" the man shouted in sudden anger. "We could have left you to drown—but we surfaced to save your lives. And every moment we are exposed puts ours in danger. Stay here if you want."

He turned and followed the others through the doorway, helping pass down the unconscious Aileen. Jan hesitated only an instant, then followed. He still was not going to commit suicide.

He blinked in the fierce red glow of the compartment, figures like ruddy devils around him. For the moment he was ignored as the hatch was sealed shut, orders shouted, the deck tilted abruptly. When they were safely below the surface, the man who had spoken to him on deck turned from the periscope and waved Jan toward the door at the end of the compartment.

"Let's go to my cabin. Get some dry clothes for you, something warm to drink. The girl will be taken care of too, don't worry."

Jan sat on the edge of the neatly made bunk, glad of the warmth of the blanket about his shoulders, shivering strongly. He was handed a cup of sweet tea which he sipped at gratefully. His savior—or captor?—sat in the chair opposite lighting his pipe. A man in his fifties, gray hair and tanned skin, dressed in a worn khaki uniform with epaulets of rank on his shoulders.

"I am Captain Tachauer," he said, blowing out a cloud of rank smoke. "Could I have your name?"

"Kulozik. Jan Kulozik. Who are you and what are you doing here? And why the attempt to knock us out?"

"It seemed a good idea at the time. No one wanted to leave you two up there to drown, though it was suggested at least once with a marked lack of enthusiasm. We are not murderers. Yet if we saved you it would reveal our presence and there could be major repercussions. Finally the sleeping shots were suggested and approved. What else could we do? But it's obvious we're not professionals at this sort of thing. Ota got his own needle and is now having a good snore for himself."

"Who are you?" Jan asked again, looking at the unfamiliar uniform, at the books in a rack on the wall printed in an alphabet he had never seen before. Captain Tachauer sighed heavily.

"Israeli Navy," he said. "Welcome aboard."

"Thank you—and thank you as well for saving our lives. I just don't understand why you were worried about us seeing you. If you are involved in security work for the UNO Navy, I'll keep my mouth shut. I have a security clearance."

"Please, Mr. Kulozik, no more." The Captain raised his hand in a stopping motion. "You speak out of ignorance of the political situation here."

"Ignorance! I'm no prole. My education contains two graduate degrees."

The Captain's eyebrows lifted in appreciation of the degrees, but he did not seem too excited by them. "I'm not referring to your technical expertise, which I am sure is considerable, but to certain gaps in your knowledge of world history produced by errors of fact that are firmly implanted in your textbooks."

"I don't know what you are talking about, Captain Tachauer. We have no censorship in our education in Britain. In the Soviet States, perhaps, but not in ours. I have complete freedom of access to any book in our libraries, as well as computer printouts of as many as I wish to consult."

"Very impressive," the Captain said, not looking impressed. "I have no intention of arguing politics with you at this time of night in our present condition. I just want to tell you as an inescapable fact that the nation of Israel is not a UNO conclave of factories and farms as you have been taught in your schools. It is a free and independent nation—almost the only one left on the face of the globe. But we can keep our independence as long as we don't leave this area or make our position known to anyone other than the ruling powers of your world. That is the danger we faced when we rescued you. Your knowledge of our existence, particularly here in this body of water where we are not supposed to be, could cause us immense damage. It might even lead to the nuclear destruction of our country. Your rulers have never been happy with our existence. If they thought they could get away unscathed they would obliterate us tomorrow . . ."

The telephone buzzed and Captain Tachauer picked it up. He listened and muttered an answer.

"I'm needed," he said, standing. "Make yourself comfortable. There's more tea here in the thermos."

What on earth had he been talking about? Jan sipped the strong tea, rubbing unconsciously at the black and blue bruise that was beginning to appear on his leg. The history books can't lie. Yet this submarine was here—and acting very circumspectly—and they were obviously worried about something. He wished that he wasn't so tired, his thoughts so clogged.

"Feeling any better?" the girl said, slipping through the curtains that covered the doorway, then sitting in the Captain's chair. She had blonde hair and green eyes and was very attractive. She wore a khaki blouse and shorts, her legs were tanned and smooth, and Jan drew his eyes away from them with an embarrassed start. She smiled. "My name is Sara and you are Jan Kulozik. Anything more I can get you?"

"No, no thank you. Wait, yes, some information. Do you know what those ships were doing that ran us down? I want to report them."

"I don't know."

But she added nothing else. Just sat and looked at him calmly. The silence grew until he realized that was all she was going to say.

"Aren't you going to tell me?" he asked.

"No. It's for your own good. If you reveal your knowledge at any time you will be put instantly on the security suspect list and watched. For the rest of your life. Your advancement, career, everything will be in jeopardy until the end of your days."

"I'm afraid, Sara, that you know very little about my country. We have Security, yes, in fact my brother-in-law is a rather high officer. But we don't have anything like that. For proles, perhaps, if they are known troublemakers. They must be watched. But not for someone in my position . . ."

"What exactly is your position?"

"I'm an engineer, from a good family. I have the best connections."

"I see. One of the oppressors. A slave master."

"I resent the implications of that . . ."

"I'm not implying anything, Jan. Just stating a fact. You have your kind of society and we have ours. A democracy. Maybe it's a word you don't even know. It doesn't matter since we are probably the last democracy in the world. We rule ourselves and we are all equal. As opposed to your slaveocracy where all are born unequal, live and die that way since nothing can ever change. From your point of view I'm sure it doesn't look too bad. Since you're the one on the top. But don't rock the boat. Your personal position could change very quickly if you were under suspicion. There is vertical mobility in your culture in only one direction. Down."

Jan laughed aloud. "Nonsense."

"Do you really believe that? All right. I'll tell you about the ships. There is a brisk trade in drugs through the Red Sea. The traditional trade from the east. Heroin for the masses. Smuggled in through Egypt or Turkey. Where there is a need—and your proles have a great need for escape—there is always money and men who will supply it. None of these drugs goes through the areas we control, we see to that, which is another reason why we are suffered to exist. This submarine patrol is just one of the ways we make sure. As long as the smugglers stay away from us we ignore them. But your state security forces have patrols as well and one of these was after that smuggler that almost ran you down. It was the coast guard that hit you. We doubt if they saw you in the darkness. In any case, they did take care of the smuggler. We saw the light of the explosion, and we tracked the coast guard returning to port alone."

Jan shook his head. "I've never heard of any of this. The proles have all the bennies and joints they need . . ."

"They need far stronger drugs to numb the existence that they lead. Now, please, stop interrupting every minute to say you have never heard about any of this. I *know* that—and that is why I am trying to tell you what is happening. The world as it really is is *not* the world you have been told about. It shouldn't matter to you, in the ruling minority, fat and rich in a hungry world. But you wanted to know. So I am telling you that Israel is a free and independent country. When all of the Arabian oil ran out the world turned their back on the Near East, happy at last to be free of the burden of the rich sheikhs. But we are here permanently—and the Arabs won't go away. They tried invasion again, but without material from outside, they couldn't win. We stayed alive, just barely, a capacity we have shown before. And we did what we could to help when things got bad. When Arab populations stabilized we taught them the traditional farming crafts of this part of the world, things they had forgotten in their years of financial exuberance. By the time the rest of the world took notice of us we had the area stabilized, viable. There were fruits and vegetables for export. It was a situation they were not happy with —but one that they accepted. Particularly when we demonstrated that our nuclear rockets were as good as theirs and if they wanted to destroy us they would have to accept a good deal of destruction of their own. And that situation has continued to the present day. Perhaps our entire country is a ghetto, but we are used to living in ghettos. And within our walls we are free."

Jan started to protest again, then thought better of it and sipped at his tea. Sara nodded approvingly.

"So now you know. For your own sake don't spread the knowledge around. And for our sake I am going to ask you to do us a favor. The Captain would not ask a favor of you, but I have no such compunction. Don't tell anyone about this submarine. For your own security as well. We are going to put you ashore in a few minutes, on the beach where you could have drifted after the accident. They'll find you there. The girl knows nothing. She was apparently unconscious, concussion, when they gave her the shot. She will be all right, the doctor says that there is no danger. You will be all right too if you keep your mouth shut. Will you?"

"Yes, of course, I won't say anything. You saved our lives. But I think a lot of what you said is lies, it has to be."

"That's very nice." She reached over and patted his arm. "You think whatever you like, *ingileh*, as long as you keep your big goyish mouth shut."

Before he could muster up an answer she was out of the door and gone. The Captain did not return and no one else talked to him until he was ordered on deck. Aileen was brought up as well, with great haste, and they were paddled ashore to an invisible shore in an inflatable dinghy. The moon was behind high clouds but gave enough light to make out the beach and the desert beyond. Aileen was placed gently in the sand and the blanket pulled roughly from his shoulders. The cushion from the yacht was thrown down and then they disappeared. Being as gentle as possible, Jan pulled Aileen above the tide line; the only marks in the sand were of his own making. The dinghy and the submarine were gone, vanished and only a memory. A memory that seemed more and more unreal with every passing minute.

It was soon after sunrise that the search copter spotted them and settled down for a landing on the shore nearby.

Four

"Absolutely sound. Fit as a fiddle," the doctor said. Tapping the readout on the screen. "Look at that blood pressure—wish I had one like it. EKG, EEG, all of it just fine. Here, I'll give you a printout for your own physician, for his records." He touched the controls on the computer diagnostician and a long sheet of typing emerged.

"It's not myself I'm worrying about, it's Mrs. Pettit."

"Please don't concern yourself, my dear young man." The fat doctor patted Jan's knee with more than professional sympathy. Jan moved his leg away and looked coldly at the man. "She has had a mild concussion, swallowed a little sea water, nothing more. You can see her whenever you want to. I would like her to stay in the hospital for a day. To rest mostly, since she needs no medical care. And here is your medical readout."

"I don't want it. Have it transferred to my company's records for the physicians."

"That could be difficult."

"Why? You have a satellite link, the call can be made easily. I can pay for it if you feel it is not within the hospital's budget."

"No such thing! Of course I shall take care of it instantly. Let us just, ha-ha, unplug you first." The doctor's hands moved efficiently, detaching the telltales from Jan's skin, slipping the needle from his vein, then dabbing his skin with alcohol.

Jan was pulling on his trousers when the door burst open and a familiar voice called out to him.

"There you are, alive and well, you had me worried."

"Smitty! What are you doing here?"

Jan took his brother-in-law's hand and pumped it enthusiastically. The great beak of a nose, the lean and hard features, were a touch of home among the rotund softness of the locals. Thurgood-Smythe seemed just as pleased to see him.

"You gave me quite a scare. I was in Italy, at a conference, when word reached me. Pulled some strings, grabbed a military jet, and was just landing when they said you had been found. I must say, you don't look any the worse for the experience."

"You should have seen me last night hanging onto the cushion with one arm and Aileen with the other—and kicking with one leg. Not something I would like to do a second time."

"It sounds quite the experience. Put on your shirt and I'll buy you a drink and you'll tell me all about it. Did you see the ship that ran you down?"

Jan had turned to get his shirt and he pushed his arms into the sleeves. All of the warnings of the night came back in a rush. Had Smitty's voice changed when he had asked that last, not-so-innocent question? He was Security after all—with enough status to commandeer a military jet in the middle of the night. Now was the moment. To tell the whole truth—or to begin to lie. He pulled the shirt over his head, his voice muffled a bit by the fabric.

"Nothing. Night black as pitch, neither ship with a light. First one went past so close we almost capsized—the second sank us." No lies there so far. "I'd like to find out who the bastards were. My fault for being out there without any lights, but still . . ."

"Absolutely right, old son. Plant a rocket and I'll help you to do it. I put a tracer out on them. Two navy ships on maneuvers and well out of the area where they should have been. As soon as they dock they are going to hear a thing or two, you can be sure of that."

"The hell with it, Smitty, it was an accident."

"You're too nice to them—but you're a gentleman. Now let's look in on Aileen, then get that drink."

Aileen kissed them both soundly, then cried a bit, with joy she said, and insisted on telling Thurgood-Smythe every detail of their adventure. Jan waited, trying not to let the tension show. Would she remember the submarine? And someone was lying; there were two completely different stories. Smugglers and an explosion—or two naval vessels? How could he be sure?

". . . and—bang! Just like that we were in the sea. I was chok-

ing and blubbering but the ancient mariner here managed to keep
my head above water. I'm sure I tried to scratch him for his troubles. Panic! I don't think I knew the meaning of the word before.
And my head hurt and things kept getting woozy and going in
and out of focus. Then there was a cushion to hang onto and we
were floating in the water and I remember him trying to cheer me
up and me not believing it at all. And then—nothing."

"Nothing?" Thurgood-Smythe asked.

"A blank. Next thing I knew I was in this bed and they had to
tell me what had happened." She took Jan's hand. "And I'm
never going to be able to thank you. A girl doesn't get her life
saved every day. Now get out of here before I start crying again."

They left the hospital in silence and Thurgood-Smythe pointed
to the nearest café. "In there all right?"

"Of course. Did you talk to Liz?"

"Not last night. I didn't want to wake her up and start her worrying too. There was no point in putting her through a night of
trouble. But I called her this morning as soon as I heard you were
safe and she sends all of her sisterly love. And says to stay out of
small boats after this."

"That's Liz all right. Cheers."

They raised the glasses and drank. The brandy burned, warmed
a spot within Jan that he had not known was chilled. It had been
close. And it wasn't over yet. He had to fight back the desire to
tell his brother-in-law everything about the night before. The submarine, the rescue, the two ships, everything. Wasn't he commit-
ting a crime by not reporting what had happened? Only one thing
stopped him from blurting out the truth. The Israelis had saved
his life—and Sara had said that he would be jeopardizing theirs if
he talked about the submarine. Forget it. He had to forget everything.

"I'll have another one of these," he said.

"And I'll join you. Forget about last night and start enjoying
your holiday."

"My thoughts exactly."

But the memory would not go away and was lurking in the
corner of his mind ready to pounce whenever he relaxed. When
he said good-bye to Thurgood-Smythe at the VTOL pad, there
was guilty satisfaction that he would not have to be alert and
remember his lies all of the time.

The sun, the food, the water, all were good—although they did not go boating again by unspoken agreement. In bed Aileen expressed her thanks for what he had done with a passion that left them both happily exhausted. Yet the other memory was always there. When he awoke at dawn, her red hair against his cheek, he thought of Sara in the sub and what she had said. Was he living a lie? It didn't seem possible.

The two weeks ended and, in a way, they did not mind turning their backs on the warm waters of that sea. Some memories could be left behind there. They had good tans to show their envious friends back in England and they looked forward to it. And some good meat and potatoes after all the rich and unusual food. Good enough, but you wouldn't want to live on it forever. They parted in the air terminal at Victoria, with one last lingering kiss, and Jan went to his apartment. He made a pot of strong tea and took it to his workroom, unconsciously relaxing as he walked through the door and the lights came on. The wall over the bench was racked with instruments, their chrome surfaces polished and gleaming. The workbench was clean, with the rows of tools mounted on it. Held in a frame was the breadboarded apparatus that he had been working on before he had gone away. Jan sat down before it and rotated it—then picked up a jeweler's loupe to examine a soldered connection. It was almost ready to go—if it went at all. It should; the computer simulation had checked out. And the idea was a simple one.

All of the large ocean going vessels used satellites for navigation. There were always at least two of these satellites above the horizon anywhere on the ocean. The shipboard navigating instruments sent out a signal that was bounced back by the satellites. These signals, giving the azimuth, direction and angles of elevation of the satellites, were fed into a shipboard computer. It was simple work then for the computer to work out the ship's position in the ocean accurate within a few meters. These navigation instruments were very efficient, but also bulky and quite expensive— which did not matter at all to a large ship. But what about a small navigation instrument? For a personal yacht. Jan had been working for some time on a simplified design that would accomplish the same thing for any ship, no matter what the size. An instrument small enough and cheap enough for anyone to use. If it worked he might even patent it, make a profit. That was in the future. Meanwhile he had to get it to work—then miniaturize all of the components.

Yet he wasn't relaxing here, as he usually did. Something else was on his mind. He finished the last of the tea and took the tray into the kitchen. Then went into the library on the way back and took down volume thirteen of the Encyclopaedia Britannica and flipped through the pages to the entry he wanted.

ISRAEL. Manufacturing and agricultural enclave on the shores of the Mediterranean. Former site of the Nation of Israel. De-populated during the plague years and resettled by UNO vol-unteers in 2065. Now administers the Arab farmlands to the north and south and is responsible for all shipments of produce from the area.

There it was, in black and white, in a book he could trust. The facts of history shorn of all emotion. Just facts, facts . . .

That was untrue. He *had* been on that submarine, and *had* talked with the Israelis. Or some people who called themselves Is-raelis. Had they been? If not, who were they really? What had he got involved with?

What was it that T.H. Huxley had said? He remembered read-ing it when he first entered university and writing it down and posting it above his desk. It was something about the ". . . great tragedy of science—the slaying of a beautiful hypothesis by an ugly fact." He had adhered to those hard-headed words and stud-ied science in a hard-headed way. Facts, give him facts—then let the hypotheses fall by the way.

What were the facts here? He had been aboard a submarine that could not exist in the world as he understood it. But the *sub* had existed. Therefore his world image was at fault.

Saying it that way made it easier to understand—but made him angry as well. He was being lied to. The hell with the rest of the world, they could take care of themselves, but he, Jan Kulozik, was being lied to on a continuous, full-time basis. He didn't like it. But how could he find out which were the lies, which the truths? With this realization came the accompanying one that Sara was right about the danger he faced. Lies were secrets and se-crets were meant to be kept. And these were state secrets. What-ever he did, whatever he discovered, he could tell no one else about it.

Where did he start? There would be full records somewhere—but he did not know which records to look for or even what he was looking for. That would take some thought, some planning. Yet there was one thing he could do at once. Look closer at the world around him. What had Sara called him? A slave master. He didn't feel like one. It was just that his class was used to taking care of things, taking care of people who couldn't take care of themselves. And the proles certainly couldn't be allowed to be in charge or everything would come to pieces. They just weren't bright enough or responsible enough. That was the natural order of things.

They were there at the bottom, the proles, the millions and millions of unwashed bodies—most of whom were on the dole. Where they had been ever since the Wreckers let the world go to rack and ruin. It was all there in the history books. If they were all alive today it was no thanks to themselves or the Wreckers who had let it happen, but was due to the hard work of the people of his class who had taken up the reins of government. Executives and engineers who had made the most of the world's shrinking resources. The hereditary members of Parliament had less and less to do with the matters of running a technological society. The Queen was just a figurehead. Knowledge was king and knowledge had kept the world alive. It had been touch and go for a while— but mankind had survived. The satellite stations had alleviated the energy crisis when the oil supplies had finally run out, and fusion power had eventually brought security to the world.

But the lesson had been learned; the fragile ecology of a single world could be easily unbalanced. Resources ran out, raw materials were needed. The first step was to the moon, then the asteroid belt where elements were to be had for the taking. Then the stars. Hugo Foscolo made that possible, with his discovery of what had come to be known as the Foscolo Discontinuity. Foscolo had been a theoretical mathematician, an unnoticed genius who earned his living as a school teacher in the state of Sao Paulo, Brazil, in a city with the impossible name of Pindamonhangaba. The discontinuity was in the theory of relativity and when he published, in an obscure mathematical journal, Foscolo had apologized for casting doubt on the accepted theories of a great man and asked humbly that qualified mathematicians and physicists point out the error in his equations.

They could not—and a space drive was born that took men to the stars. It took only a hundred years to search and settle and spread through the nearest star systems. It was a glorious history and it had to be a true history because it existed.

There were no slaves, Jan knew that, and was angry at Sara for saying it. There was peace in the world, and justice, food enough for all, and each man to his station. What was that word she had used? Democracy. A form of government, obviously. He had never heard of it. Back to the encyclopedia—only with a certain reluctance this time. Jan did not enjoy finding an error in those thick tomes. It was like discovering that a treasured painting was in reality a fake. He took the volume down and walked over to the high windows to catch the light.

DEMOCRACY. An archaic historical political science term for that form of government which flourished briefly in the small city-states of Greece. According to Aristotle, democracy is the perverted form of the third form of government . . .

There was more like this and all just about as interesting. Some historical kind of government, like cannibalism, that had come and gone. What had this to do with the Israelis? It was all a little puzzling. Jan looked out of the window at the gray sky and the ice-specked surface of the Thames below. He shivered, still feeling the tropic sun in his bones. Where did he begin?

Not with history. It was not his field; he had no idea where to look. Did he really have to look at all? In truth he didn't want to, and he had the sudden dark sensation that once he started this quest there would be no turning back. Once Pandora's box was opened it could never be closed again. Did he want to find out these things? Yes! She had called him a slave master—and he knew he was not. Even a prole would laugh at the suggestion.

That was it. The proles. He knew enough of them, he worked with them, that was where he would start. He would go back to the Walsoken Plant in the morning—he was expected there in any case to check on the installation and maintenance that he had ordered. Only this time he would talk more to the proles there. Admittedly he had not done this very much in the past, but that was only because he had been busy. As long as he was circumspect he would not get into trouble. There were certain social customs about dealing with proles and he was not going to break them. But he was going to ask some questions and listen closely to the answers.

It did not take him long to discover that this was not an easy thing to do.

"Welcome back, your honor, welcome back," the manager said, hurrying from the works door when Jan pulled up in his car. His breath smoked in the cold air and he moved uneasily from one foot to the other.

"Thank you, Radcliffe. I hope things have been going along well while I have been away?"

Radcliffe's ready smile had an edge of worry to it. "Not bad at all, sir. Not completed, I'm sorry to say, shortage of spares. Perhaps you can help us expedite them. But let me show you the record."

Nothing appeared to have changed. There were still pools of liquid underfoot despite the lethargic actions of a man with a mop. Jan started to snap about this—actually opened his mouth—then closed it again. Radcliffe seemed to be expecting it too because he glanced quickly over his shoulder. Jan smiled back. One for the home team. Perhaps he had been quick to find fault in the past—but he wasn't going to do that now. You do more catching with honey. A few pleasant words and then a conversation. It was working well.

It still took an effort to control his temper when he went through the printouts. He had to say something.

"Really, Radcliffe, I don't mean to be repetitive—but this won't do at all. You've had over two weeks and the list is as long as ever."

"We've had men out sick, sir, a hard winter. And you'll see, this work has been done . . ."

"But you've had breakdowns that more than make up for it . . ."

Jan heard the angry tone in his voice and snapped his mouth shut. He was not going to lose his temper this time. Trying not to stamp he went to the office door and looked out at the main floor of the plant. A movement caught his eye and he saw the tea trolley being pushed down a corridor. Yes, a cup of tea, that was more like it. He went to his case and opened it.

"Blast!"

"Anything wrong, sir?"

"Nothing important. Just that when I left my bag at the hotel this morning I forgot to pick up my thermos of tea."

"I can send a man on a bike, sir. Won't be but a few minutes."

"No, not worth the effort." Then Jan had the tremendous, almost daring idea. "Get the trolley in here. We'll both have a cup of tea."

Radcliffe's eyes opened wide and he was silent for a moment with shock. "Oh, no, your honor. You wouldn't like the stuff we serve here. Right muck. I'll send . . ."

"Nonsense. Get it in here."

It was a trial by embarrassment that Jan never noticed as he went through the printouts again, checking off priorities. The bent tea woman kept rubbing her hands on her skirt and bowing slightly in his direction. Radcliffe slipped out and returned quickly with a clean towel with which she wiped and wiped one of the mugs. When it was finally served it rested alone on the battered tray.

"You too, Radcliffe, that's an order."

The tea was hot and that was about all that could be said for it, the mug thick and chipped where he put it to his lips. "Very good," Jan said.

"Yes, your honor, it is." Agonized eyes above his own cup.

"We'll have to do this again."

The answer was silence and Jan had no idea where to take the conversation from there. The silence lengthened until he had finished his tea and there was nothing to do except go back to work.

There was more than enough calibration to do, as well as some pressing repairs that had been ignored during his absence. Jan became involved in his labors and it was well after six before he yawned and stretched and realized that the day shift had all gone home. He remembered Radcliffe looking in and saying something, but that was all. That was enough for one day. He packed his papers, slipped into the fleece-lined coat, and let himself out. The night was cold and dry, the stars flickering icily above. A long way from the Red Sea. It was a relief to get into the car and turn on the heater.

A good day's work. The control setup was working fine and if he applied pressure the repairs and maintenance might be improved. *Had* to be improved. He pulled hard on the wheel to avoid a bicyclist who suddenly appeared in the beam of his headlights. Dark clothes and a black bike with no reflectors. Wouldn't they ever learn? Empty fields on all sides and not a house in sight. What on earth was the man doing out here in the darkness?

The next turn brought the answer. Glowing windows and a lighted sign beside the road ahead. A public house, of course, he had passed it countless times without even noticing it. No reason to. Jan slowed the car. *The Iron Duke* the board read, with a portrait of the Duke himself, aristocratic nose held high. But not so aristocratic, the clientele; not a car about and bicycles racked along the front wall. No wonder he had never noticed it before.

He hit the brakes. Of course! He would stop here for a drink, talk to people. There could be nothing wrong with this. The customers would surely be pleased to have him. Bring a touch of interest to a cold evening. What a very good idea.

Jan closed and locked the car and stamped across the hard ground to the front door. It swung wide at his touch and he entered a large, brightly lit room, the air thick with the clouds of cheap tobacco and marijuana smoke. A loud, very boring piece of music was pouring from wall speakers and drowned out any sound of conversation from the crowd of men at the bar, or seated at the small tables. No women, he noticed with interest. In a proper pub at least half—or more—of the customers would be women. He found an opening at the bar and rapped for attention when the barman did not notice him.

"Why yes, sir, very pleased to have you here, sir," the man said, hurrying over with a warm smile on his fat lips. "What will be your pleasure?"

"A large whiskey—and something for yourself as well."

"Why thank you, sir. I'll have similar."

Jan didn't notice the brand name; it was rougher than the whiskey he usually drank. But fairly priced. The round was less than a single at his local. These people had no cause for complaint.

There was more space at the bar now—in fact he had it almost to himself. Jan turned about and there, at a nearby table, sat Radcliffe and some of the other workers from the Walsoken Plant. Jan waved and walked over.

"Well, Radcliffe, relaxing a bit?"

"You might say so, your honor." The words were cold and formal; the man seemed embarrassed for some reason.

"Mind if I join you?"

There were some wordless mutters that Jan took to be assent. He pulled an empty stool over from the next table and sat down and looked around. No one met his eyes; they all seemed to be finding things of interest in their liters of beer.

"Cold night, isn't it?" One of them drank noisily, the only answer. "And the winters are going to stay cold for the next few years. It's called a little climatic, a small weather change within the larger cycles of weather. We won't have another ice age, not at once, but we can count on these cold winters lasting awhile."

His audience was not exactly bursting with enthusiasm and Jan had the sudden realization that he was making a fool of himself. Why had he come in here in the first place? What could he learn from these stolid dolts? The whole idea was stupid. He drained his glass and left it on the table.

"Enjoy yourself, Radcliffe. All of you. See you at work in the morning and we'll really get cracking on the maintenance. A lot of work to do."

They muttered something which he didn't stay to hear. The devil with theories and blond-haired girls in submarines. He must be going out of his head to do what he was doing, think what he was thinking. The hell with it. The bite of cold air was sharp and good after the reek of the pub. His car was there with two men bent over the open door.

"Stop there! What do you think you're doing?"

Jan ran toward them, slipping on the icy ground. They looked up quickly, a blur of white faces, then turned and ran into the darkness.

"Stop! Do you hear me—stop!"

Breaking into his car, criminals! They weren't getting away with it. He ran after them around the building and one of them stopped. Good! Turned to him . . .

He never saw the man's fist. Just felt the explosion of agony on his jaw. Falling.

It was a hard, cruel blow, and he must have been unconscious for a moment or two because the next thing he knew he was on his hands and knees, shaking his head with pain. There were shouts around him, more running footsteps, and hands on his shoulders pulling him to his feet. Someone helped him to walk back to the pub, into a small room where he dropped heavily into a deep chair. There was a wet towel then, cool on his forehead, stinging on his jaw. He took it and held it himself and looked up at Radcliffe who was alone in the room with him.

"I know the man, the man that hit me," Jan said.

"I don't think you do, sir. I don't think it was no one who works at the plant. I have someone watching the car, sir. Nothing taken that I can see, you were too quick. Looks like a little damage where the door was jimmied open . . ."

"I said I *know* him. Had a clear view of his face when he hit me. And he did work at the plant!"

The cool cloth helped. "Sampson, something like that. Remember, the man who tried to burn the place down. Simmons—that's the name."

"Couldn't have been him, sir. He's dead."

"Dead? I don't understand. He was in perfect health two weeks ago."

"Killed himself, sir. Couldn't face going back on the dole. Studied for years to get the job. Only had it a few months."

"Well you can't blame me for his incompetence. You agreed with me, as I recall, that firing him was the only thing to do. You remember?"

Radcliffe did not lower his eyes this time and there was an unaccustomed note of hardness in his voice.

"I remember asking you to keep him on. You refused."

"You aren't implying by any chance that I'm responsible for his death, are you?"

Radcliffe did not answer, nor did his empty expression change. Nor did he lower his eyes from Jan's. It was Jan who turned away first.

"Management decisions are hard to make sometimes. But they have to be done. Yet I swear that man was Simmons. Looked just like him."

"Yes, sir. It was his brother. You can find that out easy enough if you want to."

"Well thank you for telling me. The police will deal with this matter easily enough."

"Will they, Engineer Kulozik?" Radcliffe sat up straight and there was a timbre in his voice that Jan had never detected before. "Do you have to tell them? Simmons is dead, isn't that enough? His brother is looking after the wife and kiddies. All on the dole. For all of their lives. Do you wonder he was angry? I'm not excusing him; he had no business doing what he did. If you would forget it there would be some grateful people around here. He hasn't been the same since he found his brother dead."

"I have a duty . . ."

"Do you, sir? To do what? To stay with your own kind and leave us alone. If you hadn't come nosing around here tonight, pushing in where you're not wanted, none of this would have happened. Leave well enough alone, I say. Get in your car and get out of here. Leave things as they are."

"Not wanted . . . ?" Jan tried to accept the thought, that these men could feel that way about him.

"Not wanted here. I've said enough, your honor. Maybe too much. Do whatever you want. What's done is done. Someone will be by the car until you're ready to go."

He left Jan alone. Feeling more alone than he had at any other time in his life.

Five

Jan drove slowly back to his hotel in Wisbech in a poisonous frame of mind. There was a crowd in the bar at the White Lion which he passed by swiftly and on up the creaking stairs to his room. The bruise on the side of his face felt far worse than it looked. He bathed it again in cold water, holding the damp cloth to his face and staring at himself in the mirror. He felt an absolute fool.

After pouring himself a large drink from the room bar, he stared unseeingly out of the window and tried to understand why he had not yet called the police. With every passing minute it was becoming more and more impossible, since they would want to know why he had delayed. Why was he delaying? He had been brutally attacked, his car broken into, damaged. He had every right to report the man.

Had he been responsible for Simmons's death?

He couldn't be, it was not possible. If a man did not do his job well, he did not deserve to have it. When one man in ten had employment he had better be good or he was out. And Simmons had been no good. So he was out. And dead.

"I did not do it," Jan said aloud, firmly. Then went to pack his bag. The hell with the Walsoken Plant and all the people who worked there. His responsibility had ended when the control installation had been completed and come on line. Maintenance was not his job. Someone else could worry about that. He would send in his report in the morning and let engineerconcent worry about what to do next. There was plenty of work waiting for him;

with his seniority he could pick and choose. And he did not choose to stay on at the leaking spirit works among the frozen fields.

His face hurt and he drank more than he should on the trip back. When the car reached the London exit of the highway he switched onto manual control with no result. The computer had been monitoring his blood alcohol level and he was over the legal minimum. It did not relinquish control. The drive was slow, dull, and infuriating since the computer had only a few routes through London and all were out of the way for him. No short cuts. And hesitancy at all crossings, with priority given to any manually operated vehicle no matter how slow. The computer only cut out at the garage door and he exacted a small amount of pleasure from speeding headlong down the ramp and slamming into his space with a fender-scratching crunch. More whiskey followed and he woke at three in the morning to find the light still on and the TV talking to itself in the corner. After that he slept late and was just finishing his first cup of coffee when the door annunciator signaled. He squinted at the screen and pressed the release. It was his brother-in-law.

"You look a little on the ragged side this morning," Thurgood-Smythe said, laying his coat and gloves neatly on the couch.

"Coffee?"

"Please."

"I feel like I look," Jan said, having already fixed on the lie when he awoke. "Slipped on the ice, think I loosened a tooth. Came home and drank too much to numb the pain. Damn car wouldn't even let me drive."

"The curse of automation. Have it looked at yet?"

"No. No need. Just a bruise. I feel the fool."

"Happens to the best of us. Elizabeth wants you over to dinner tonight, can you come?"

"Anytime. Best cook in London. As long as it is not one of her matchmaking sessions." He looked suspiciously at Thurgood-Smythe who pointed a finger and smiled.

"Just what I told her and although she protested that the girl was one in a million, she finally agreed not to have her. Three for dinner."

"Thanks, Smitty. Liz won't face the fact that I'm not the marrying kind."

"I told her that you will probably be sowing wild oats on your deathbed and she thought I was being vulgar."

"I only hope that it will be true. But you didn't come all the way across the city when a call would have done as well."

"Of course not. Got another gadget for you to look at." He took a flat package out of his pocket and passed it over.

"I don't know how well my eyes will focus today. But I'll give it a try."

Jan slipped a metal case out of the envelope and opened it. There were a number of tiny readouts and controls inside. It was beautifully made. Thurgood-Smythe had brought other extra-curricular work to Jan in the past. Electronic instruments that Security was testing, or technical problems that needed expert advice. It was in the family and Jan had always been glad to help. Particularly when there was a cash bonus if he had to devote any time to the work.

"It looks very nice," he said. "But I haven't the slightest idea of what it does."

"Wiretap detection."

"Impossible."

"That's what everyone thinks, but we have some original people in the lab. This device is so sensitive that it analyzes every element of a circuit for basic resistance and loss of strength. Apparently if you eavesdrop on a wired signal the act of detection causes a measurable alteration of the signal which in turn can be detected. Does this make any sense to you?"

"A lot. But there are so many random losses in a transmitted message, through switches, connections and such that I don't see how this thing could possibly operate."

"It's supposed to analyze every loss, find out what it is, see what its true value should be, and if it is correct go on to the next interruption of signal."

"All I can say is *wow*. If they can pack that much circuitry and control into something this big then your boys know what they are doing. What do you want from me?"

"How do we test it outside the lab to see if it works?"

"Simple enough. Put it on a lot of phones, yours and some other people in your shop, and run it for a while. Then put taps on the lines and see if it does its job."

"Sounds simple enough. They said that all you have to do is use it with the microphone input. Any problems?"

"None. Like this." Jan went to his phone and fixed the device over the microphone. The *ready* light came on. "You just talk into the mike it has as you would normally."

"Let's try it. I'll tell Elizabeth you'll be coming tonight."

It was a brief call and they both watched the rapid signals flashing from the VDU. It seemed to be doing its job. Thurgood-Smythe broke the connection and the random flickering stopped. The readout lit up.

TAP ON THIS LINE IN EXCHANGE.

"It seems to be working," Thurgood-Smythe said mildly, looking at Jan.

"Working . . . Do you think it found a tap on my phone? Why on earth . . ." He thought for a moment, then pointed an accusing finger. "Out with it, Smitty. It was no accident you came today and hooked that thing up there. You knew that my line was tapped. But why?"

"Let's say I 'expected' something, Jan. I couldn't be sure." He walked to the window and looked out, tapping his hands together behind his back. "My business is full of uncertainties and suspicions. I had hints that you were under surveillance from a certain department, but I couldn't very well ask or they would have denied everything." He turned about and his face was very cold. "But now I *know* and a head or two will roll. I will not have routine-minded blockheads interfering with my family. This will be all taken care of and I wish you would forget about it."

"I would love to, Smitty. But I'm afraid I can't. I'll have to know what is going on."

"I thought you would." He raised his hand in resignation. "You were just in the wrong spot at the wrong time. That can be enough to cause these low-level bureaucrats to swing into action."

"I haven't been any place unusual—other than the ship accident."

"That's it. I wasn't exactly truthful with you about what you saw. I'll tell you more, but it can't leave this room."

"You know better than to ask."

"Sorry. Been one of those weeks. Those were criminals, smugglers, in the first boat. Running drugs. The second ship was our guard. Caught them and blew them out of the water."

"Illegal drugs? I didn't know there were such things. But if there are and they caught the people—why it sounds a good item for the evening news."

"I agree with you—but others don't. They feel that publicity would only encourage law-breaking. That's policy and we're stuck with it, and you're caught in the middle. But not for long. Just forget the tap and what I have told you and be there for drinks at eight."

Jan reached out and took his brother-in-law's hand.

"If I don't sound grateful it's only because of the hangover. Thanks. It's nice to know you're there. I don't understand half of what you told me and maybe I don't want to."

"That's wisest. See you tonight."

When the door had closed, Jan poured his cup of cold coffee into the sink and went to the bar. Hair of the dog was something he usually avoided, but not today. Had Smitty been acting, or was his story true? Was there more to the story than what he had been told? The only thing he could do was act as though it were. And watch what he said on the phone.

Then came the sudden realization that what Sara had told him on the submarine was true. The world was proving not to be the simple place he had always thought it to be.

It was snowing outside and the city of London had vanished behind a shifting curtain of white. What was to be done? He knew he was at a turning point, a branching in the road of his life. Perhaps the major branch, the one of most importance. There had been a number of shocks administered in the last weeks, more perhaps than he had experienced before in his entire lifetime. Fights in prep school, canings, exams in university, love affairs—all that had really been simple. Life had flowed toward him and he had taken it as it came. All of the decisions had been easy ones to make because they moved with the stream. Yes, this was different; this was the big one.

He could do nothing, of course, ignore everything he had heard and discovered and lead the life he had always led.

No—he couldn't possibly do that. It had all changed. The world he had lived in was not the real one, his view of reality not a true one. Israel, smugglers, submarines, democracy, slaveocracy. They were there and he had not known about them. He had been as misled as the pre-Copernicans who thought that the sun rotated around the Earth. They had believed—no, they had *known* —that it did. And they had been wrong. He had known about his world—and had been just as wrong.

At that moment he had no idea where it would lead, and had

the sudden depressing feeling that it might end in disaster. It might—but the chance had to be taken. He prided himself on the freedom of his thought, the ability for rational and unemotional thinking that led him to the truth, whatever it might be.

Well there was plenty of truth in the world he knew nothing about—and he was going to find it. And he knew just how to go about it. It would be simple, it might leave traces, but if he worked it right he would not be caught.

Smiling, he sat down with a pad and a pen and began to draw a flow chart of a computer program for theft.

Six

"I can't tell you how pleased I am that you have decided to join our program," Sonia Amariglio said. "Almost all of our microcircuits are antiques fit only for museums and I despair daily of ever having anything done about them." She was gray-haired and plump, almost lost behind the big desk. And her Belgian French accent was still pronounced—her "them" sounded more like "zem"—even after her years in London. She looked like a concierge or a tired housewife. She was considered to be the top communications engineer in the entire world.

"It is my pleasure to be here, Madame Amariglio. I must admit that my motives are very selfish for joining your program."

"More selfishness of this order I do need!"

"No, it's the truth. I'm working on a smaller version of the nautical navigator and I'm having problems. I realized, finally, that my biggest problem was I knew very little about the circuitry at the satellite end. When I heard that you were looking for a microcircuit engineer I jumped at the chance."

"You are a most marvelous man and you are doubly welcome. We go to your laboratory now."

"Aren't you going to tell me what my job is first?"

"Your job is everything," she said, moving her hands outward in a quick, all-encompassing gesture. "I want you first to understand our circuitry, ask questions, learn about our satellites. We have difficulties enough that I won't bother you with at the present. When you know your way around I will present you with a stack —so high!—of these problems. You will be sorry you ever came."

"Hardly. I really am looking forward to it."

This was the truth. He needed to work in a very large lab, and the discovery of the opening in the satellite program had been fortuitous. He really could work on the development of his navigator. And he would be of value here if the microcircuitry was as dated as he had been led to understand.

It was worse. The first satellite he examined in any detail was a great two-ton geosynchronous machine that hung in the sky 35,924 kilometers over the Atlantic Ocean. It had been in trouble for years, less than half of its circuits were still in operation, and a replacement was being manufactured. Jan was scanning through the diagrams of the replacement, with an overall schematic displayed on one screen and detailed breakdowns being shown in color on the larger screen before him. Some of the circuitry looked familiar—too familiar. He touched the prod to the screen and signaled for information. A third VDU lit up with a display of specification numbers.

"I can't believe it!" Jan said aloud.

"Did you call, your honor?" A lab assistant pushing an instrument-laden wagon stopped, turning toward him.

"No, nothing. Thank you. Just talking to myself."

The man hurried away. Jan shook his head in wonder. They had had this circuitry in his textbooks when he was in school; it must be fifty years old at least. There had been a dozen advances in the state of the art since its time. If there were more like this he could improve satellite construction easily enough by simply updating existing designs. Boring but easy. Which would give him enough free time for his personal project.

It was coming along well. He had already bypassed most of the seals on the Oxford University computer and was now searching for barred areas in the history sections. His years of computer circuit design were not being wasted.

Computers are completely unintelligent. Just big adding machines that count on their fingers. Except they have an incredible amount of fingers and can count awfully fast. They cannot think for themselves or do anything that they have not been programmed to do. When a computer functions as a memory store it answers any questions asked of it. The memory banks of a public library are open to anyone with access to a terminal. A library computer is very helpful. It will find a book by title, by author's name, or even by subject. It will supply information about a book or books until the customer is satisfied that this is indeed the book he really wants. Upon a signal the library computer will transmit the book—in a few seconds—to the memory bank of the questioning computer terminal. Simple.

But even a library computer has certain restrictions about releasing material. One is the age of the questioner and access to the pornography section. Every customer code contains the date of birth of the customer—as well as other relevant information—and if a boy age ten wants to read *Fanny Hill* he will find his request politely refused. And if he persists he will discover that the computer is programmed to inform his physician of this continuing unhealthy act.

However if the boy uses his father's identification number the computer will supply *Fanny Hill*, in the color-illustrated edition, and no questions asked.

Jan knew just how unthinking computers really were, knew as well how to get around the blocks and warnings built into their programs. After less than a week's work he had gained access to an unused terminal in Balliol College, had assigned it a new priority code, and was using it to gain access to the records he wanted to see. Even if his pryings did tip off alarms the request would only be traced back to Balliol, where things like this were expected to happen. If traced further still the circuit went through the pathology laboratory in Edinburgh before reaching his own terminal. He had installed enough alarms of his own in the program to let him know long before if he were being traced, to give him enough time to break the connection and remove all evidence of his tampering.

Today would be the major test to see if all this work had been worth the effort. He had prepared the program of requests at home and had it with him now. The morning tea break was on and most of the lab workers were away from their positions. Jan had diagrams displayed on four screens. And he was unobserved. He took out a small cigar—part of this ruse involved his taking up smoking again after a gap of almost eight years—then extracted the glow lighter from his pocket to light it with. The element went white hot in an instant and he puffed out a cloud of smoke. And put the lighter on the bench before him. Centered over the apparently accidental ink mark on the surface, that in reality had been very carefully positioned.

He cleared the small screen closest to him and asked it if it was

ready to read information. It was—which meant the lighter was in
the correct position over the wires in the bench. He hit the return
key and the screen said *ready*. The program was now in the computer. The lighter went back into his pocket, along with the 64K
magnetic bubble memory he had built inside it, in the space left
when he had replaced the large battery with the smaller one.

The moment of truth. If he had written the program well it
should extract the information he needed without leaving any
trace of his request. Even if the alarms did go off he was sure they
couldn't track him easily. For as soon as the Edinburgh computer
had the information it would transmit it to Balliol. Then, without
waiting for verification of receipt, it would wipe all of its memories clean of the program, the request, the transmission, and the
address. Balliol would do the same as soon as it had passed on the
information to him in the lab. If the information were not transmitted correctly it would mean laboriously building up the sequence of circuits again. It would be worth the effort. No effort
was too large if it prevented his being traced.

Jan shook the ash from his cigar into the ashtray and saw that
no one was even looking in his direction; no one could possibly
see what he was doing. His actions were completely normal. He
typed the code word ISRAEL onto the screen. Then typed RUN
and hit the return key.

Seconds moved by. Slowly. Five, ten, fifteen. He knew that it
would take time to get through to the memory, to penetrate the
coded blocks, to seek out the right reference, and then to transmit
it. Through tests he had run with nonclassified material from the
same source he had found that eighteen seconds was the maximum time he had ever had to wait. He was allowing twenty seconds this time and no more. Now his finger was poised over the
switch that would break the connection. Eighteen seconds. Nineteen.

He was about to bring it down when the screen cleared and
read PROGRAM COMPLETE.

Perhaps he had something—and perhaps he didn't. But he was
not going to take a chance to find out now. Grinding out the half-
smoked cigar he took a fresh one from the package and lit it. And
placed the lighter on the bench. It was in the right position.

It took only a few seconds to transfer the contents of the computer's memory to the bubble memory in the lighter. Once it was
safely back in his pocket he cleared all traces of what he had done

from the terminal's memory, put a diagram back on the screen, and went to get his tea.

Jan did not want to do anything out of the ordinary this day so he immersed himself in the satellite studies. Once it had captured his attention he forgot all about the contents of the lighter in the intricacy of the circuit design. At the end of the day he was not the first one to leave—nor the last. In the security of his own apartment he threw down his coat and locked the door. And checked the burglar alarms he had installed. The answer was negative and it appeared that no one had been in the apartment since he had left.

The memory dumped from the core in the lighter into his computer. There was something there all right, but there was only one way to find out if his plan had succeeded. He typed RUN and hit return.

It *was* there. Pages and pages of it. The history of the State of Israel from biblical times to the present. With no gaps or fictitious accounts of UN enclaves. And it appeared to be just as Sara had told him, though in greater detail. The point of view was certainly different, but essentially what she had told him was the truth. Which made it fairly certain that everything else she had said was true as well. Was he a slave master? It would take more digging to find out what she meant by that remark and about democracy. Meanwhile he read with growing interest a history that was completely different from the one he had learned in school.

But it was not complete. In fact the record broke off suddenly in mid-line. Could this have been an accident? A glitch somewhere in the complex program that he had set up? It could be—but he did not think so. In fact he had better consider it as deliberate and rethink his whole plan. If he had missed some keying code in his gaining access to the information an alarm could have been sounded. The running program would have been cut in just this way. And traced.

There was a cold chill on the back of his neck, even though the room was warm. Now he was being foolish; the Security forces could not be that efficient. Yet—why shouldn't they be? It was always a strong possibility. He shrugged off the thought for the moment and went and took dinner from the deep freeze and put it into the microwave.

After eating he read through the material again, turning back quickly when he came to the truncated end. After that he scrolled through one more time, stopping to read the more relevant parts, then typed SCR, and cleared it all away, returning intelligence to random electrons at the touch of a button. And the lighter memory as well. He passed the lighter through the strong magnetic field of the eraser—then stopped. Not good enough. It took only a few minutes to remove the bubble memory from the lighter and drop it into his spare parts box. The original battery went back in and all evidence was removed. It might be stupid, but he felt relieved after it was done.

On the way to the lab in the morning he passed the library, usually deserted at this time of day, and a familiar voice called out to him.

"Jan, you're being the early bird."

His brother-in-law waved casually from the doorway.

"Smitty! What on earth are you doing here? Didn't know you cared about satellites."

"I care about everything. Give me a moment, will you. Come in and close the door."

"We're being mysterious this morning. Did you come to hear my discovery that we are still building satellites with circuitry dating back to the last century?"

"Wouldn't surprise me in the slightest."

"But that's not why you are here, is it?"

Thurgood-Smythe shook his head, expression as gloomy as a hound dog. "No. It's more serious than that. There's some hanky-panky going on here and I prefer to have you out of the way while we track it down."

"Hanky-panky? Is that all you're going to tell me?"

"For the moment. Elizabeth has another girl she wants to hurl at your head. This one's an heiress, which she thinks might attract you."

"Poor Liz. She never stops trying. Tell her that I'm really a homosexual and have finally come out of the closet."

"She would start finding you boys."

"You're right, you know. As soon as mother died she began trying to take care of me. I suppose she will never stop."

"Excuse me," Thurgood-Smythe said as his radio buzzed. He took it out of his pocket and listened for a moment before he spoke. "That's good. Bring the tape and the photos here."

A few moments later there was a discreet knock at the door.

Thurgood-Smythe opened it just enough to get his hand through; Jan never saw who was on the other side. He sat down and rummaged through the envelope he had been given.

"Know this man?" he asked, passing over a color photograph. Jan nodded.

"I've seen him around, just to say hello to though. Other end of the lab from me. Don't know his name."

"We do. And we're keeping an eye on him."

"Why?"

"He has just been observed using the laboratory computer for access to the commercial channels. He taped a complete performance of *Tosca*."

"So he likes opera—is that a crime?"

"No. But illicit recording is."

"You can't tell me you're worried about the few pounds fee coming out of the lab's pocket, not his?"

"Hardly. But there is a far more serious matter of unauthorized access to classified material. We have traced the signal to one of the computers in this laboratory, but couldn't pin it down any closer. We have now."

Jan felt suddenly very, very cold. Thurgood-Smythe had his head lowered, his attention on the cigarette case he had taken from his pocket, taking out a cigarette. He would have noticed something if he had been looking.

"We have no real evidence, of course," he said, closing the case. "But this man is now high on our suspect list and will be watched closely. One slip now and we have him. Thanks."

He inhaled deeply as Jan held out his glow lighter and lit the cigarette.

Seven

The pavement along the Embankment had been swept clear, but there were still white mounds up against the wall and snowy circles around the trees. Floes of ice moved swiftly on the black surface of the Thames. Jan walked through the early evening darkness, from pool of light to pool of light, head down and hands jammed into pockets, unaware of the sharp cold and needing the solitude. Ever since that morning he had looked forward to being alone, to ordering his thoughts, to checking the flow of emotions that possessed him.

Time had passed begrudgingly this day. The research had not gone well because, for the very first time, he could not bury himself in his work. The diagrams did not make sense and he went through them time and time again with the same results. Yet the hours had passed and, to his knowledge, he had done nothing suspicious. Not that he had to worry; suspicion of guilt had already been fixed on the wrong man.

Until he had seen Thurgood-Smythe in the library he had not appreciated the force of the Security procedures. He liked his brother-in-law and helped him when he could, all of the time with the knowledge that his work had something to do with Security, but the reality of what Security did was far removed from normal existence. No more. The first lightning bolt had hit very close to home. Despite the cold bite of the north wind Jan could feel a filming of perspiration on his face. Damn, but Security was good! Too good. He had never expected efficiency of this kind.

It had taken skill and knowledge on his part to get through the

blocks that concealed the computer memory he had wanted. But
he realized now that these barriers had been there only to prevent
accidental and casual access to the information. It would take a
determined and resourceful person to get past them—and their
only function was to make sure that this was not done easily.
Once passed, a greater danger lay in wait. National secrets were
meant to be kept secret. The instant he had penetrated to that information the trap had been closed, his signal detected, recorded,
traced. All of his elaborate safeguards had been instantly penetrated. The thought was a frightening one. It meant that *all* of
the communication lines in the country, public and private, were
being monitored and controlled by the Security forces. Their
powers appeared to be limitless. They could hear any conversation, tap any computer memory. Constant monitoring of all
phone calls was of course physically impossible. Or was it? Monitoring programs could be written that would listen for certain
words and phrases and record anything that contained them. The
possible scope of the surveillance was frightening.

Why should they do all this? They had changed history—altered the true story of the world—and could monitor the world's
citizens. Who were *they?* The overall answer appeared obvious
when phrased that way. There were a few people at the top of society and a lot at the bottom. The ones on top wanted to stay
there. And he was one of the ones on top so, unknown to him,
this was all being done to make sure he kept his status unchanged.
So all he had to do to keep his privileged position was absolutely
nothing. Forget what he had heard, what he had uncovered, and
the world would be the same.

For him. And what about the others? He had never thought
about the proles much before this. They were everywhere and nowhere. Always present, always unseen. He had accepted their role
in life as he had always accepted his own; something there and
unchanging. What must it be like to be one? What if *he* were
one?

Jan shivered. The cold, it was getting to him. Just the cold.
There was the laser hologram sign of an all-night store up ahead
and he hurried toward it; the door opened as he approached and
admitted him to the welcoming warmth. There were some things
he needed for the kitchen. He would buy them now and take his
mind away from the morbidity of his thoughts. The next service
number was seventeen, and it changed to eighteen when he

touched the plate. Milk, he was sure he needed some of that. He typed seventeen on the number pad under the display liter of milk, then one. Butter, yes, he was low on that too.

And oranges, firm and ripe. With the word Jaffa bold on each of them, flown in fresh from summer to northern winter. He turned quickly away and hurried to the checkout.

"Seventeen," he said to the girl at the counter and she typed in the number. "Four pounds ten, sir. Do you want them delivered?"

Jan handed over his credit card and nodded. She inserted it into the machine, then returned it to him. His purchases appeared in a basket and she redirected it back inside for delivery.

"Been a cold day," Jan said. "Quite a wind blowing."

She opened her mouth slightly, then turned away when she caught his glance. She had heard his accent, seen his clothes; there could be no casual conversation between them. The girl was aware of that even if Jan wasn't. He pushed out into the night, glad of the cold bite of air on his glowing cheeks.

Back in the apartment he realized that he had no appetite at all. He eyed the whiskey bottle, but that would not be a satisfactory answer. In the end he compromised with a bottle of beer, dialed up a Bach string quartet, and wondered just what the hell he was going to do.

What *could* he do? Through ignorance and good luck he had missed being caught when he had first tried to gain forbidden information. He couldn't try that again, not that way. The work camps in Scotland were waiting if you made trouble for the authorities. For all of his life he had looked on the camps as a stern but necessary measure to weed the troublemakers out of a highly organized society. *Prole* troublemakers of course, the thought of any other kind was unthinkable. Thinkable enough now when he might be one of them. If he did anything at all to draw attention to himself he could be caught. Just like a prole. Perhaps his sector of society was physically better off than theirs—but he was just as much a prisoner of it. What kind of a world *was* he living in? And how did he find out more about it without making that one-way trip to the Highlands?

There was no simple answer to his questions that day or the next, or the next. At the laboratory it was easy enough to get involved in his work, which was still complex and interesting. It was appreciated too.

"I cannot begin to say in words how happy I am with what you have done here," Sonia Amariglio said. "And in such a short time."

"It's been easy so far," Jan told her, spooning sugar into his tea. It was the afternoon break and he was seriously thinking of leaving after it. "Basically what I did was upgrade the old designs. But I see where some original work will be needed very soon, particularly on the comsat twenty-one, and that will not be the easiest job."

"But you can do it. I have infinite faith! Now, to other matters. Social ones. Are you free tomorrow night?"

"I think so."

"Please be sure so. There is a reception at the Italian Embassy then and I think you will enjoy attending. The guest is someone you might enjoy meeting. Giovanni Bruno."

"Bruno? Here!"

"Yes. On the way to America for a seminar."

"I know all of his work. He's a physicist who thinks like an engineer . . ."

"I'm sure you can think of no higher praise."

"Thanks for asking me."

"A pleasure. Nine o'clock then."

Jan had no desire to attend a boring embassy party, but knew that he should not be a recluse. And if he got to talk to Bruno it might be worthwhile. The man was a genius and responsible for the whole new range of memory blocks. Probably wouldn't even be able to get near him in the press of social butterflies. He must check his evening suit to see if it needed pressing.

The crush was just what he had expected. Jan had the cab drop him a street away from the embassy and he walked the rest of the distance. All of the beautiful people were there. The ones with rank and money and no ambition other than social position. They wanted only to be seen with Bruno, to have their faces appear with his in the social columns, to talk about it afterward to acquaintances with equal interests. Jan had grown up with these people, gone to school with them, and they shared a mutual dislike one for the other. They tended to look down their noses at his family because they had a tradition of working in the sciences. There was no point in telling them that this was because of Andrzej Kulozik, a distant and revered ancestor, a physicist who had actually worked on the original and successful development of fusion power. Most of them had no idea of what fusion power was in any case. Now Jan was enveloped by them again and he did not like it. There were many familiar and half-familiar faces among the crowd in the front hall, and when he passed his coat over to the waiting porter, his own face was also fixed in the cold and distant expression he had learned in prep school.

"Jan, that is you, isn't it?" a deep voice said in his ear and he turned to see who was talking to him.

"Ricardo! A sight for sore eyes indeed."

They shook hands warmly. Ricardo de Torres, the Marquis de la Rosa, was a not too distant relation on his mother's side. Tall, elegant, black-bearded, and suave, he was about the only relative that Jan ever saw. They had been in school together and their friendship had even outlived that experience.

"Not here to meet the great man?" Ricardo asked.

"I was until I saw the receiving line for Professor Bruno. I'm not charmed in the slightest by the prospect of queuing for a half hour to press his gloved hand and hear him murmur a few words in my ear."

"How forthright your brash, island-living race has always been. I, product of an older and more leisured culture, will join the queue."

"Social obligation?"

"Right with the first guess."

"Well, while you're doing that, I am going to beat this lionizing crowd to the buffet. I hear the kitchen here is the best."

"It is, and I envy you. For me there will be nothing but cold meats and bare bones."

"I hope not. If you live through the scrum I'll see you in there."

"Let's hope."

It was perfect; Jan had had the display of food almost to himself. A few figures wandered in front of the lengthy linen-covered table, but were far outnumbered by the servers behind it. A swarthy, white-hatted chef sharpened his knife hopefully when Jan looked at the roast; his face fell when Jan went on. He could have roast beef every day of the week. Now he was more interested in the octopus in garlic, the snails, the paté with truffles. Filling his plate with delicacies was an easy matter. The small tables against the wall were still empty and he seated himself at one to get the utmost pleasure from his food without having to juggle it on one knee. Delicious! However, a little wine was very much in order. A servant in a black dress, carrying a tray of glasses, was passing and he waved to her.

"Red. A large one," he said, his attention focused on his plate.

"Bardolino or Corvo, your honor," the waitress said.

"Corvo I believe . . . yes, Corvo."

She handed him the glass and he had to look up to take it. For the first time he saw her face. He almost dropped the glass so she took it from his hand and placed it safely on the table before him.

"*Shalom*," Sara said, speaking very quietly. She gave him a quick wink, then turned and was gone.

Eight

Jan started to rise and go after her—then sank back into his seat. Her presence here could be no accident. And she certainly wasn't Italian. Or was she? If she were the whole story about Israel had been a hoax. For all that he knew the submarine could have been an Italian one. What was going on? His thoughts chased themselves in circles and he slowly ate the plate of delicacies without tasting one of them. By the time he had finished, the room was beginning to fill up and he knew exactly what he had to do.

Nothing too obvious; he knew the dangers of Security surveillance better than she did. His glass was empty, getting another would not be compromising. If she had come here to contact him, he wanted her to know he was aware of that. Then, if she did not get in touch with him or give him some message, her presence was an accident as far as he was concerned. Italian or Israeli she was certainly an enemy agent of some kind. In this country illegally? Did Security know about her and were they watching her even now? Should he identify her for his own protection?

He rejected the idea as soon as it was formed. He couldn't do that; whoever she was, she was also one of the people responsible for saving his life. Not only that—he had no desire to identify anyone to his brother-in-law's branch of the service. Even if he could have done it safely, for if he identified her he would have to say how he knew her and the whole story of the submarine would come out. He was beginning to realize how thin was the layer of ice that supported the world he used to call normal. He had broken through it when he had been rescued, and had been sinking deeper and deeper ever since.

It took a moment to locate her, to push through the crowd and set the empty glass on her tray. "Another Corvo, if you please." His eyes were upon her, yet she would not meet them. She passed the wine over in silence, never looking at him, turning away the instant he had taken it. So what was that supposed to mean? He was angry, feeling rejected. All of these charades just to be ignored! Or was that part of a more devious plan? The entire matter was beginning to disgust him and the noise and light was giving him a headache. Not only that but the unaccustomed spicy food sat like a weight in the pit of his stomach. There was no point in staying on here any longer.

The servant found his coat, bowing deep, holding it up so he could shrug into it. Jan went out, buttoning it, breathing deeply of the icy and refreshing air. A rank of cabs was waiting and he signaled the doorman for one. His hands were getting chilled so he pulled on one glove, then the other—and stopped.

There was something that felt like a piece of paper in the glove, at the tip of his index finger. He knew that it had not been there when he had left his apartment. For an instant he hesitated, then pulled the glove all the way on. This was neither the time nor the place to investigate. The cabby jumped out, held the door open, and saluted.

"Monument Court," he said, dropping into the seat.

The doorman hurried out from under the canopy to open the cab door when they arrived.

"Another cold one, Engineer Kulozik."

Jan nodded; there was no need to answer. He stalked across the lobby and into the elevator, not even noticing the operator who took him to his floor. Natural. He must act naturally at all times.

The alarms had not been tripped; no one had entered the apartment or tampered with anything since he had left that morning. Or if they had it had been done so well it had left no trace, in which case there was no escape. A certain fatalistic acceptance was necessary in this situation. Only when this had been done did he turn the glove inside out and shake the folded bit of paper onto the table.

It opened up to reveal a poorly printed cash register receipt for the sum of ninety-four pence. The time and date were stamped on it as well, one in the morning, some three days earlier. The establishment that had issued it was called SMITHFIELD JOLYON and he had never heard of it.

Was it an accident that this had appeared so suddenly inside his glove? No, no accident, not at the same place, the same evening he had seen Sara. It must be a message—yet a message that would be completely innocuous to anyone who might find it by accident. A register receipt, everyone had them. It would have been puzzling but meaningless to him as well if he hadn't seen her there at the embassy. So it was a message—meaning what?

The phonebook revealed that the Smithfield Jolyon was one of a chain of automated restaurants. He had never heard of them before because they were all located in areas that he never frequented. This one, while not too far away, was in a scruffy dock area. What next?

Why go there of course, at one A.M. Tonight? Of course tonight. It would take a fool not to understand the simple intelligence carried by the slip of paper. It might also take a fool to go there. If he did not go—then what? Another attempt to contact him? Probably not. A wink was as good as a nod in this kind of business.

Jan realized that he had already made up his mind to go when he found himself considering what clothes he should wear. So it was decided. It had to be. He had to find out more. He would put on the rough clothes and boots that he used for field work in the fen district. He wouldn't look like a prole—wasn't even sure that he wanted to do that—but these clothes would be the best compromise.

At a quarter to one he parked his car in a well illuminated area of the Highway and walked the rest of the way. The streets here were not as well lit and were faced with the blank walls of warehouses. The brilliant sign of the restaurant was clearly visible ahead. It was just one o'clock. Showing no hesitancy, Jan walked slowly to the door and pushed it open.

The restaurant was not big. A large, brightly lit room with four rows of tables marching the length of it. Nor was it crowded; solitary individuals were scattered about, with one or two small groups sitting together. The air was hot and smelled strongly of antiseptic and smoke, with an underlying bite of stale food. On the rear wall was a twice-lifesize figure of a cook, constructed of garish and chipped plastic. As Jan walked slowly toward it the arm moved up and down in hesitant greeting and the computer voice spoke to him.

"Good evening . . . madam. What is your pleasure this . . . morning?"

The sex discrimination circuit did not seem to be working very well—but at least it got the time of day right. Then the chef's paunchy stomach lit up with the selection of dishes; not the most appetizing location, Jan thought. He considered the selection— equally unappetizing—and finally touched the illuminated word TEA and the light went out.

"Will that be all . . . sir?" Second time around the computer got it right. He should order something else, even if he didn't eat it, in order to appear normal. He touched the glowing SAUSAGE ROLL.

"May you enjoy your repast. That will be . . . forty pence. Jolyon always happily at your service."

As soon as Jan had inserted the coins into the machine a silver dome on the wall-mounted serving trolley lifted up to display his purchases. Or at least moved halfway where it stopped, humming and vibrating. He pushed it the rest of the way and extracted the tray with cup, plate, and receipt. Only then did he turn around and look closely at the room.

Sara was not there. It took him a moment to discover this because, outside of the small groups, all of the single customers appeared to be women. Young women. And most of them were glancing his way. Quickly lowering his eyes he found the deserted end of one table and slid onto the bench mounted on the floor beside it. There were automatic dispensers fixed to the center of the table which functioned with varying degrees of success. The sugar nozzle, with much grinding, produced only a few grains; the mustard pump enthusiastically sprayed out far too much onto his sausage roll. The food was protective coloration in any case and he had no intention of eating the thing. He sipped at the tea and looked around. Sara came through the door.

He had not recognized her at first glance, not with the garish makeup and absurd coat. It was white, imitation fur, puffing out in all directions. It would not pay to watch her too closely; he put his attention back to his plate and automatically bit into the sausage roll and instantly regretted it. He quickly washed it down with some tea.

"All right if I sit here?"

She was standing across the table from him, holding her tray but not setting it down. He nodded briefly, not knowing what to say in this unusual circumstance. She took this as acceptance and set the tray with her cup of coffee down, then seated herself. Her mouth was thick with lipstick, her eyes surrounded by greenish makeup, her face expressionless under this coating. She took a sip of her coffee, then opened her coat briefly.

Under the coat she wore nothing else. He had a brief glimpse of her firm, tanned breasts before she closed it again.

"Like a good time, wouldn't you, your honor?"

So that was why the rest of the girls were here. He had heard that pickup places like this existed, schoolmates had frequented them. But this was his first encounter and he was slow with the correct response.

"Sure you'll like it," she said. "Not too expensive."

"Yes, good idea," he finally choked out. The idea of the determined woman from the submarine in this highly unusual situation almost caused him to smile. He did not, keeping his face as emotionless as hers. The ruse was a good one and not funny in the slightest. After this she said nothing else; obviously conversation in public was not one of the services being offered. When she picked up her tray and rose he stood up as well.

A light over the table began flashing on and off and a loud buzzer sounded alarmingly. Some faces turned to look in his direction.

"Pick up your tray," Sara whispered sharply.

Jan did; the light and sound stopped. He should have realized that no one would clear up after him in the automated establishment. Following her example he slid his tray into the slot beside the front door and went after her into the cold night.

"It's not too far, your honor," she said, walking quickly along the dark street. He hurried to stay by her side. Nothing else was said until she reached a grimy apartment building not far from the Thames. Sara unlocked the door, waved him through, then led the way to her rooms. When the light came on she touched her finger to her lips signaling silence, then waved him inside. Only after locking the door and examining all of the windows did she relax.

"It is good to see you again, Jan Kulozik."

"And you, Sara. A little different from the first time."

"We do seem to meet under unusual circumstances—but these

are unusual times. Excuse me for a moment. I must get out of this humiliating outfit. It is the only safe way that a woman of my apparent class can meet someone of yours; the police smile on the practice. But it is still disgraceful for a woman, absolutely infuriating."

She was back in a moment wearing a warm robe. "Would you like a real cup of tea? Something better than the muck in that palace of assignation?"

"No, a drink if you have it."

"There is some Italian brandy. Stock. Very sweet but it contains alcohol."

"If you please."

She poured for both of them, then sat on the sagging couch opposite him.

"It wasn't an accident, my seeing you at the party?" he asked.

"Far from it—the entire thing was carefully orchestrated. It took a lot of money and time to set up."

"You aren't Italian, are you? I have no way of telling."

"No, I'm not. But we use them a lot when we need to. Their lower echelons are very inefficient and bribable. They are our best channel outside of our country."

"Why did you go to all this trouble to see me?"

"Because you have been thinking a lot about what you were told that day in the sub. And acting too. You almost got yourself in deep trouble. When you did that it was decided that the time had come to contact you."

"Trouble? What do you mean?"

"The business in the lab. They caught the wrong man, didn't they? It was you who was tampering with the computer files?"

Jan was afraid now. "What are you doing? Having me watched?"

"As best as we can. It's not easy. Just an informed guess that you were the one involved. That's one of the reasons it was decided to contact you now. Before you were caught doing something you shouldn't."

"Your concern across the countless miles from Israel is very touching."

Sara leaned over and took his hand in hers. "I can understand why you are angry—and I don't blame you. This entire situation has come about by accident—and it was your accident that started it."

She sat back and sipped her drink and, for some reason, the brief human contact calmed him.

"When we saw your yacht sunk and the two of you in the water there was some furious debate as to what we should do. When the original plan failed we jury-rigged a second one to compromise you. Giving you enough information so that if you revealed any of it you would be in as much trouble as we would be."

"Then it was no accident that you talked to me as you did?"

"No. I'm sorry if you think we took advantage of you, but it was our own survival as well. I'm a security officer so it was my job to do it . . ."

"Security! Like Thurgood-Smythe?"

"Not quite like your brother-in-law. The opposite if anything. But let me bring you up to date first. We saved you and the girl because you were people in need. That was all. But once saved, we had to keep track of you to see what you would say about the matter. Thank you for doing what you did. It is greatly appreciated."

"So well appreciated that you have been keeping tabs on me ever since?"

"This is a completely different matter. We saved your life, you did not reveal our existence. The two acts cancel out, that matter is over with."

"It will never be over with. That little seed of doubt you planted has been growing well ever since."

Sara shrugged with both hands held wide. An ancient gesture that conveyed resignation, the hand of fate—yet contained also an element of what-is-done-is-done.

"Have some more to drink. At least it is warming," she said, reaching over with the bottle. "While watching you we discovered who you were, what you did. There was enthusiasm in high places. If you had returned to your normal life you would never have heard from us again. But you did not. So I am here this evening."

"Welcome to London. What do you want from me?"

"Your help, technical help that is."

"What do you offer in return?"

"Why the entire world. Nothing less." Her smile was wide and happy, her teeth smooth and white. "We will be pleased to tell you the true history of the world, what really happened in the past and is happening in the present. What lies are being told and what unrest is developing. It makes a fascinating story. Do you want to hear it?"

"I'm not sure. What will happen to me if I do get involved?"

"You will be an important part of an international conspiracy that is hoping to overthrow the ruling governments of the world and restore democracy to those who have been deprived of it for centuries."

"Is that all?"

They both laughed at that and some of the tension went out of the air. "You had better think carefully before you answer," Sara said. "There are very great dangers involved."

"I think I made the decision the moment I lied to Security. I'm in too deep now and I know so little. I must know it all."

"And so you shall. Tonight." She went to the window, opened the curtains, and looked out. Then closed them again and sat down.

"John will be here in a few minutes and will answer all your questions. This meeting was difficult to set up so it was agreed to make the most of it if you went along. I've just let them know that. John is not his real name of course. And you will be called Bill for the same reason. And he will be wearing one of these. Just slip it over your head."

She passed over a soft, masklike object.

"What is it?"

"Face-changer. It has built in thickenings and pressure plates. Your chin will be wider, nose flatter, cheeks hollower, that kind of thing. And dark glasses will hide your eyes. Then, if the worst happens, you can't identify John—he can't accuse you."

"But you know me. What if you are caught?"

Before Sara could answer there was a rapid bleeping from the turned-off radio. Four quick notes and no more. The effect was remarkable.

She was on her feet in an instant, tearing the face-changer from his hand and running swiftly into the other room. "Take your jacket off, open your shirt," she called back over her shoulder. She returned in a few moments wearing a very transparent black gown trimmed with pink lace. There was a knock on the door.

"Who is it?" she asked, calling through the thin paneling.

"Police," was the short, shocking answer.

Nine

When the door was opened the uniformed officer ignored Sara, just pushing past her and crossing to Jan who was still sitting in the chair, glass in hand. The policeman had a riot helmet on with its transparent faceplate lowered. His uniform was thick, padded with layers of woven armor, while his fingers stayed close to the large automatic that swung arrogantly from his hip. He stopped in front of Jan and looked him up and down slowly.

Jan took a sip from the glass and was determined to show no guilt, no matter how bad the situation was.

"What are you doing here?" Jan snapped.

"Sorry, your honor. Routine." The policeman's words were muffled by the faceplate and he swung it open. His expression was blank, professional. "We've had some gentlemen molested by the tarts, sir, and their fancy men. Can't have that in a law-abiding city. Straightened up now, but this one is a new one. Foreigner. Italian, just over here for a while on a temporary. Don't mind her making a bit of extra crumble on the side, novelty for the gentlemen you might say, but we also don't want any trouble. Everything all right, sir?"

"Quite all right—until you came barging in."

"I can understand your feelings, sir. But it is illegal, don't you forget, your honor." There was steel-beneath the calm words; Jan knew better than to force the issue. "Just looking after your best interests. Have you been in the other rooms yet?"

"No."

"Then I'll just have a look-round. Never know what you find under these beds sometimes."

Jan and Sara looked at each other in silence while the policeman stamped heavily through the rooms and finally returned.

"All in order, your honor. Enjoy yourself. Good night."

He let himself out and Jan found himself shaking with rage, flushed and angry. He raised his fist to the closed door as Sara grabbed him around the shoulders and pressed her finger to his lips.

"They do that all the time, your honor. Bust in, boom, looking for trouble. They lie, all of them. Now we have a nice time and you forget."

She held him tightly while she talked and his anger waned as he became aware of the warmth and closeness of her firm body through the thin material of her gown.

"Have another of this good Italian drink," she said, pulling away and crossing to the table. She rattled her glass against the bottle with her left hand while she quickly scribbled a note on a pad with her right. When she came back it was the note she gave him, not the drink.

MAYBE RECORDER OTHER ROOM. YOU ANGRY. LEAVE NOW.

"I'm not sure I want another drink. Do you usually have the police bursting through your door at all hours?"

"It means nothing . . ."

"It means a lot to me. Get my coat. I'm getting out of here."

"But money. You promised."

"Two pounds for the drinks is all you'll get."

When she handed him the coat she had another note ready. YOU'LL BE CONTACTED it read. She squeezed his hand in hers—then kissed him swiftly on the cheek before she let him out.

Almost a week passed before Jan was contacted again. His work in the lab improved when he found that he could now devote his entire attention to it. Though he was still in danger, probably more danger than before since he was consorting with the underground, he was more relaxed. Less lonely. That was the important thing. Until he had talked with Sara, brief as the meeting had been, there had been no one to confide in, no one to talk with about the momentous discoveries and doubts. That solitary existence had ended, would be ended, since he had no doubt that contact would be reestablished soon.

It had been his habit for some weeks now to go into a bar close to the satellite laboratories for a drink or two before going home. The barman, fat, friendly, was a specialist in mixed drinks and devilish concoctions. There seemed to be no end to his repertoire and Jan had settled on a half dozen of the more interesting ones.

"Brian, what was the name of that bittersweet thing I had here a few days ago?"

"A negroni cocktail, your honor, speciality of Italy. Would you like one?"

"Yes. It appears to have great relaxing powers."

Jan was sipping at it, his mind still on orientation circuits for solar cell banks, when someone sat on the stool next to him. Female; he was aware of that when the rich mink coat brushed his arm. The voice was very familiar though the accent wasn't.

"Why Jan! It is Jan Kulozik, isn't it?"

It was Sara, but a very different Sara. Her makeup and clothes were in the same class as her coat—as was her accent. "Why, hello," was the best he could come up with.

"I was sure it was you, though I bet you don't remember little me, Cynthia Barton, we met at that dreadful party a few weeks ago. Whatever you're drinking looks divine; order me up one like a good lad."

"Nice to see you again."

"Nicer to see you, it's been one of those days. Hmmm, this is simply super, just what the doctor ordered. But don't you find it hideously noisy in here, the music and all these people? Let's drink these and go back to your place. I remember you were very insistent about a painting there you wanted me to see. At the time I thought it was just an excuse to get into my knickers, but now I don't know. You're such a serious chap that perhaps you *do* have a painting and I'll risk my honor to find out."

There was more like this, even in the cab, and Jan found that he need not answer but just let himself be washed along on the tide of words. Only after his apartment door was closed did she stop talking and look to him for a lead.

"It's all right," he said. "I've installed a number of alarms, bug detectors and the telltale, that lamp bulb, says all clear. If it were out I would know there had been some tampering. Dare I ask who Cynthia Barton is?"

Sara threw her coat on the chair and looked around the room. "Someone who looks a good deal like me. Not a duplicate by any means, but the same general size and hair color. When she's away —she's at a country house in Yorkshire this week—I use her persona to move in better circles. My ID is pretty good, enough for any casual identification."

"I'm glad she's away. It's nice to see you again."

"The feeling is mutual because there have been some rapid developments since I talked to you last."

"Like what?"

"I'll tell you in a little while, in context. I want you to get a clearer picture of the entire situation first. The man you were supposed to meet last time, code name John, is on his way over here now. I came first to let you know what was happening. You've got a stunning place here," she added, with rapid change of subject.

"I can't take any credit. When I bought it I was going out with a girl who had pretences of being an interior decorator. With my money and her talent this is what we got."

"Why do you say 'pretences'? She seems quite good."

"Well, you know, it's not really a woman's field."

"Male chauvinist pig."

"What does that mean? It doesn't sound nice."

"It isn't. An archaic term of contempt—and I apologize. It's not your fault. You have been raised in a strictly male-oriented society where women are respected, but still second-class citizens . . ." A chime rang and she raised her eyebrows in query.

"That's the entrance. Could it be John?"

"It should be. He was given a key to the garage entrance of this building and told to come to this apartment number. As far as he knows it is just a safe house where we are meeting; he has no way of discovering that you live here. It's not perfect, I know, but it's the best we could do in a hurry. In any case he is not an active man in the organization and there is little contact with him, other than as an information source. Better put this on." Sara took a face-changer from her purse. "And the dark glasses too. I'll let him in."

In the bathroom Jan pulled the flexible disguise over his head and the effect was astonishing. When he looked into the mirror a stranger stared back. If he didn't recognize himself then he would never be able to identify the man called John. If he wore one of these as well.

Sara was talking to a short, stocky man when he returned. Though he had taken off his overcoat he was still wearing his hat and gloves. Hair and hands invisible. Sara was undisguised which meant that her identity was known to them both. "John," she said. "This is Bill. The man who wants to ask you some questions."

"Happy to be of service, Bill." His voice was mellow, educated. "What do you want to know?"

"I don't know where to begin, what to ask. I know some things about Israel that differ from texts I have—and I suppose that is the extent of my knowledge. Other than what I was taught in school."

"Well that's a good beginning. You have doubts and you have seen that the world is not as you always suspected. So I shan't waste time trying to convince you to open your mind. May we sit down?"

John settled into his chair and crossed his legs comfortably. When he talked he tended to lecture, to tick off the points made on his fingers. It was obvious he was an academic of some kind, probably an historian.

"Let us go back to the close of the twentieth century and look closely at events since that date. Let your mind be a *tabula rasa* and try not to interrupt with questions. There'll be time enough later for those. The world of the year 2000 was very much as depicted in the historical texts you have studied, physically that is, although the governments of the world were definitely *not* what you have been told. At that time there were varying degrees of personal freedom throughout the world, with forms of government ranging from the liberal to the most oppressive. All of that has changed in the intervening years. The Wreckers were to blame for it all, just as you have learned. That much at least is true." He coughed. "My dear, might I have a glass of water?"

Sara brought it to him and he went on.

"None of the world leaders or governments, the Wreckers, took any real notice of the depletion of natural resources until it was too late. Populations expanded past the limit of natural resources, while the supplies of fossil fuels quickly ran out. There was much fear of an atomic war that would devastate the world, but apparently the fear was mutually felt among the world powers because the big bang never came. Of course there were some atomic incidents in Africa, using what were quaintly referred to as home-made atomic bombs, but these petered out quickly enough. The world did not end with the bang, as had been feared, but with a whimper. I quote the poet."

He sipped daintily from his glass and went on.

"With no energy, factory after factory closed. With no fuel vehicles could not run and the economies of the world spiraled downward into depression and massive unemployment. The weaker and more unstable nations went by the board, torn apart by starvation and dissent. The stronger nations had enough worries at home without attempting to cope with the troubles of others. The surviving citizens of what used to be called the third world eventually stabilized with small populations and basic agrarian economies.

"A different solution was needed for the developed, industrial economies. I will use Britain to demonstrate this, since you are familiar with what life here has become. You must cast your mind back to an earlier day when the form of government was democratic, regular elections were held, and the Houses of Parliament were not hereditary and powerless as they are now. Democracy, where all individuals are held to be equal, one man one vote to elect the rulers, is a luxury of the very rich. By that I mean very rich countries. Any decline in living standards and the national product can only mean a lessening of democracy. A simple example. An employed man with a regular income has a choice of dwelling, diet, recreation, what might be called lifestyle. An unemployed man on the dole must live where he is told, eat what he is given, and accommodate himself to an unchanging and unvarying, drab existence. Britain survived the disaster years—but paid a terrible price in personal freedom. There was no money to import food, so the country had to be self-sufficient agriculturally. This meant microscopic amounts of meat, only for the very rich, and a vegetarian diet for the rest. A meat-eating nation does not easily take to a change like this so the change had to be enforced. The ruling elite issued the orders and police and troops saw that they were carried out. This was the only alternative to chaos, famine, and death at the time, so it seemed reasonable. And it *was* reasonable given the circumstances. The only trouble was that when the emergency lifted and things were physically much better, the ruling elite liked the authority they had and did not want to relinquish it. A great thinker once wrote that power corrupts and absolute power corrupts absolutely. Once the hobnailed boot is firmly planted on the neck it will not be raised voluntarily."

"What hobnailed boot?" Jan asked, puzzled.

"I do beg your pardon. A simile, very out of date, excuse the excess. I mean to say that recovery was gradual and the governments in power simply stayed in power. Populations gradually reduced and stabilized at a replacement level. The first generating satellites were built and beamed their energy down to Earth. Then came fusion power that assured abundant energy for all needs. Mutated plants supplied the chemicals formerly obtained from petroleum. Satellite colonies processed the raw materials of the moon and their manufactured products were brought to Earth. The discovery of a workable space drive sent ships out to explore and settle on the planets of the nearest stars. So there we have it, what we have today. An earthly paradise, even a heavenly paradise, where no man need fear war or famine. Where all are provided for and none need want.

"However there is one thing wrong with this picture of paradise. Absolute oligarchic rule has clamped down on the countries of Earth, extended to the satellite colonies, and beyond them to the planets. The rulers of each major country are in collusion with all of the other rulers to assure that no hint of personal freedom be allowed the masses. Complete freedom at the top—your class, Bill, from your accent—and economic serfdom, slavery, for all below. With instant imprisonment or death for any bold enough to protest."

"Is it really that bad?" Jan asked.

"It's far worse than you can imagine," Sara said. "And you will have to see for yourself. Until you are absolutely convinced that there is need for a change you will be a danger to yourself and others."

"This orientation program has been carried out at my suggestion," John said, unable to keep the pedantic pride from his voice. "It is one thing to read printed documents and hear spoken words. It is another to experience the realities of the world we live in. Only a brute would be unmoved. I will talk to you again after your descent into the inferno. I will let myself out, if I may."

"He's a funny little man," Jan said after the outside door had closed.

"Funny and endearing and absolutely invaluable to us. A social theoretician with answers rather than questions."

Jan pulled off the face-changer and wiped the perspiration from his face. "Obviously an academic, probably an historian . . ."

"Don't!" Sara said sharply. "Don't theorize about him, even to yourself, or one day you may reveal him to those who shouldn't know. Put the man from your thoughts and remember his words. Can you take off a few days from your work?"

"Any time, of course. I make my own hours. What do you want?"

"Tell them that you need a break and you want to go to the country, to see a friend, something like that, where it won't be too easy to trace you."

"What about skiing? I usually go to Scotland once or twice a winter for cross country."

"I don't know what that is."

"Special kind of skis for going on the flat, not downhill. I carry a pack, camp out a bit, stay in inns and hotels, make my own way."

"That sounds ideally perfect. So tell your people that you are going skiing, starting next Tuesday, for a few days. Don't be specific about how long you will be away. Don't mention any addresses or places in particular. Pack a bag and put it in your car."

"Will I be going to Scotland?"

"No. You will be going even farther away. You are going to descend into that inferno right here in London."

Ten

Jan had been parked at the appointed spot for over a half an hour, well past the time when he was to have been met. Outside only the yellow gleams of the streetlights could be seen through the swirling snow. The pavements were empty. The dark bulk of Primrose Hill vanished into the darkness beyond the road. The only traffic had been a police car that had driven by earlier, slowed a bit, then speeded up and vanished. Perhaps he was being watched for some reason and his contact would not appear.

Even as he thought this the door opened letting in a blast of frigid air. A heavily bundled man slid into the passenger seat, closing the door quickly behind him.

"You wouldn't like to say something, would you, gov?" the man said.

"It's going to get a lot colder before it gets warmer."

"You're right about that." Sara had briefed him with the identification phrase. "What else do you know?"

"Nothing. I was told to park here, wait for someone, identify myself, and wait for instructions."

"Right. Or it's going to be right if you take the instructions and do everything exactly like I say to do it. You're what you are and I'm a prole and you are going to have to take your orders from me. Can you?"

"I don't see why not." Jan inwardly cursed the hesitancy in his voice. This wasn't easy.

"Do you really mean it? Obey a prole—and one that don't smell too good?"

Now that he had mentioned it there was a definite stench in the air from his heavy clothes. Long unwashed fabric and body odor mixed with traces of smoke and cooking.

"I mean it," Jan said, in sudden anger. "I don't think it is going to be easy but I'll do my best. And I'll live with the smell too."

There was a silence and Jan could see the man's eyes, barely visible under his cloth cap, examining him closely. He suddenly shot out a gnarled hand.

"Put it there, gov. I think you're going to be all right." Jan found his hand clamped in a calloused, hard grip. "I was told to call you John, and John it is. I'm called Fryer since I work in a chipper, so we'll leave it at that. If you'll just head east now I'll call out turnings."

There was very little traffic about and the tires cut black marks in the freshly fallen snow. They stayed off the main roads and Jan had very little idea of where they were exactly, just northeast London.

"Almost there," Fryer said. "Another mile to go, but we can't drive. Slow now, it's the second turning on the left."

"Why can't we drive?"

"Security barrier. Nothing to be seen of course, you wouldn't know you were going past it. But circuitry under the road surface would query the transponder in your car and get its identity. Goes in the record. Start people wondering what you're doing here. Walking over is safer, though a lot colder."

"I never knew they did anything like that."

"This is going to be an educational holiday for you, John. Slow —stop. I'll open that lockup garage and you just edge this vehicle in. It'll be safe enough here."

The garage was cold and musty. Jan waited in the darkness while Fryer closed and locked the door, then shuffled by, finding his way with the light from a small flashlight. There was a room beyond, a shed behind the garage, lit by a single unshielded light bulb. Fryer turned on a single-bar electric fire which did little or nothing to relieve the chill of the room.

"Here's where we make the change, gov," Fryer said, taking some rough clothes down from a peg on the wall. "I see you didn't shave today as told, very wise. And your boots will do, after we scuff them up a bit and rub in some ashes. But off with the rest, from the small clothes out."

Jan tried not to shiver, but it proved impossible to control. The thick, stained trousers were like ice on his already cold legs. Rough shirt, waistcoat with buttons missing, ragged sweater, even more ragged greatcoat. However once the chill was off of everything it proved warm enough.

"Didn't know your hat size so I got this," Fryer said, holding up a hand-knitted balaclava. "Best thing for this weather anyway. Sorry to say it, but you'll have to leave behind those fine fur gloves. Not many on the dole have gloves. Just jam your hands into your pockets and you'll be all right. That's it, wonderful. Your own mam would never recognize you in the rig. So here we go."

Once they were moving through the dark streets it was not too bad. The wool of the balaclava covered Jan's mouth and nose, his hands were buried in the deep pockets, his feet warm enough in the old climbing boots he had unearthed in the back of his closet. His mood was good for there was a spirit of adventure in this whole affair.

"You better keep your mouth shut unless I tell you it's OK, gov. One word from you and they'll all know who you are. Time now for a half liter, thirsty work this. Just drink what you're given and say naught."

"What if someone talks to me?"

"They won't. It's not that kind of pub."

A blast of warm, noisome air blew over them when they pushed through the heavy front door. Men, only men, sitting at tables and standing at the bar. Some were eating plates of food served through a hatch in one wall. Stew of some kind, Jan saw when they squeezed past a crowded table, along with chunks of dark bread. There was room at the scarred, damp bar and they stood there while Fryer signaled one of the barmen.

"Two halfs of skrumpy," he said, then confided in Jan, "mild's like swill here, better the cider."

Jan grunted assent and buried his face in the glass when it came. Acid and terrible. What could the beer possibly be like!

Fryer was right; this was not a sociable bar. Men were talking together who had obviously arrived together. Those who were alone stayed alone, seeking communion only with their drink. An air of depression hung over the dark room unchallenged by the stained brewery posters on the walls, the only decoration of any kind. The drinkers were obviously seeking oblivion not relaxation. Jan drank deep when Fryer moved away in the crowd. He returned in a moment with another man, appearing no different from the others in his rumpled dark clothes.

"We'll go now," Fryer said, making no attempt to introduce the man. Once outside they tramped through the snow, now beginning to drift over the curbs, their footsteps silent in its softness.

"My mate here knows a lot of people," Fryer said, nodding his head in the direction of their new acquaintance. "Knows everyone. Knows everything going on here in Islington."

"Been inside too," the man said, his words very liquid and lisping. He appeared to have very few teeth in his head. "Caught using the stuff. Hard work cutting them trees in Scotland. Cured the habit though. The hard way. This old woman now, you'll see how she lives. Not much of a life but she'll be well out of it soon."

They turned in through the gates of a brooding rank of tall council flats, crossing the open area between them. It could have been grassed or paved, impossible to tell now. Spotlights high up on the building lit the area like a prison yard, spilling brightly over the children who were building a giant snowman. An altercation broke out and they fell to shouting and beating one small boy who finally broke from them and ran away crying loudly, leaving a trail of red drops in the snow behind him. Neither of Jan's companions seemed aware of the scene so Jan put it from his mind as well.

"Lift's not working. Usual thing," Fryer said as they followed their guide up the steps. Up five filthy flights, the walls daubed all the way with graffiti. Warm enough though, as it should be with unlimited electric power. The door was locked but the man had a key. They followed him into a single warm, brightly lit room that smelled of death.

"She don't look good, do she?" he said, gesturing toward the woman on the bed.

She was pale as parchment, her skin lighter than the stained covers of the bed. One clawlike hand held them clutched under her chin and her unconscious breathing was slow, scratchy.

"You can talk if you want," Fryer said. "All friends here."

"She's ill?" Jan said.

"Ill to death your honor," the toothless man said. "Saw doctor in the autumn, got some medicine, nothing since."

"She should be in hospital."

"Hospital only for dying on the dole."

"A doctor then."

"Can't go to him. Won't come here without no money."

"But there must be funds available from . . . our people."

"There are," Fryer said. "More than enough to at least help our mates. We don't dare, gov. Go on her record, the Security will want to know where did she get the crumble on the dole, investigation, find out who her friends are. Do more harm than good. So we don't do it."

"So—she just dies?"

"We all die sooner or later. Just sooner on the dole. Let's go get some scoff."

They did not say good-bye to the toothless man who had drawn up a chair and was sitting next to the bed. Jan looked at the box of a room, the decrepit furniture, the sanitary fittings on the wall, barely concealed by a battered screen. A prison cell would be better.

"He'll be with us after a bit," Fryer said. "Wants to sit awhile with his mam."

"The woman—his mother?"

"Indeed. Happens to all of us."

They descended to the basement, to a communal dining room. The dole obviously did not extend to the luxury of private cooking. People of all ages were sitting at the rough tables, eating, or queuing at the steaming counter.

"Put this in the slot when you take your tray," Fryer said, handing Jan a red plastic token.

The tray did not come free in his hand until the token dropped. Jan shuffled behind Fryer, accepting the brimming bowl thrust at him by the perspiring kitchen assistant. Further on there was a great mound of chunks of dark bread and he took one. This was dinner. They seated themselves at a table bare of any condiments or tableware.

"How do I eat it?" Jan asked, looking dubiously at his bowl.

"With a spoon you always carries—but I've an extra knowing you're new at this."

It was a lentil stew with vegetable bits floating in it. Not bad tasting, devoid of any real flavor of anything. There were lumps in it that looked like meat, but certainly didn't taste like it.

"Got some salt in my pocket if you want," Fryer volunteered.

"No thanks. I doubt if it would make any difference." He ate some bread which, though half stale, had a sound, nutty flavor. "No meat in the meal?"

"No. Not ever on the dole. There's chunks of soy immo here, all the protein you need they say. Water at the fountain over there if you want to wash it down."

"Afterward. Is the food always like this?"

"More or less. People earn a bit of money they buy bits of things in the shops. If you've no crumble then this is it. You can live on it."

"I suppose that you could. But I don't really see it as an inspiring regular diet." He shut up as a man came in, shambled over, and sat at their table.

"Bit of trouble, Fryer," he said, looking at Jan while he did.

They stood and moved against the wall to talk. Jan ate another spoonful then pushed the bowl away from him. A lifetime eating this? Nine out of ten workers were on the dole. Not to mention their wives and children. And this had been going on around him for all of his life—and he had not been aware. He had lived his life on an iceberg, unaware of the buried nine-tenths beneath the surface.

"We're going back to the car, gov," Fryer said. "Something's come up."

"Anything to do with me?"

"Don't know. Word just passed for us to get there as soon as we could. No idea of what, except it's trouble. Plenty of it."

They walked hard. Not running, that would draw attention, but solidly and steadily through the clutching snow. Jan had glimpses of lit shops with their displays hidden behind steamy windows. He wondered what they sold, and realized they were as alien to his experience as the shops in the market he had visited on the shore of the Red Sea.

At the rear of the garage once again, Jan held the flashlight so that Fryer could find the right key in its dim light. They went into the shed and on into the garage itself.

"I'll be winged!" Fryer said, flashing the light across the barren floor.

"My car is gone!"

A far brighter torch flashed in their eyes and someone said, "Just stand right there and don't move. Watch where you put your hands."

Eleven

Jan had no thought of moving, could not have moved if he had wanted to. The shock of all this, first his car gone, then the sudden confrontation. The game was up, he was caught, it was all over. He stood, frozen with the dreadful realization.

"Back to the shed, Fryer," the man said again. "Someone here you don't know."

Fryer went out docilely enough and the man with the flashlight followed him; Jan could only make out his outline as he went by. What was happening?

"Jan, I must talk to you," a familiar voice said as soon as the door had closed. The small light was still in his hand and he brought it up and picked Sara's face out of the darkness. "We didn't mean to give you a fright," she said, "but this is an emergency."

"Fright! It was nothing like that. My heart stopped, that was all!"

"I'm sorry," she smiled, but the smile instantly vanished. "Something very bad has happened and we may need your help. One of our people has been captured and we cannot let him be identified. Have you heard of Slethill Camp?"

"No."

"It's a work camp in Sunderland, the far north of Scotland in the Highlands. We are fairly sure that we can get him out of the camp, that is easy enough, but we don't know how to get him out of the area. That is when I thought of you and your saying you go up there for cross-country skiing. Could he ski out of there?"

"He could if he knew the area and knew how to ski. Does he?"

"No, I don't think so. But he's young and fit and could learn. Is it difficult?"

"Very easy to learn the basics. Very hard to be very good. Do you have anyone who could show him what to do . . ." Sudden realization struck him and he turned the light back on her face. Her eyes were lowered and she was very pale.

"Yes. I'm going to ask you to help," Sara said. "It bothers me not only for the danger you will be put in, but because we should not even be mentioning this sort of thing to you. If you decide to work with us, yours could be the most important job in the entire resistance. But if this man is not freed it might very well be the end of everything."

"It's that important?"

"It is."

"Then of course I'll help. But I must go home for my equipment—"

"Impossible. Everyone thinks that you are in Scotland. We have even had your car driven up there to cover your movements here."

"So that's where it went."

"We can have it left wherever you want in Scotland. Will that help?"

"Tremendously. How do I get there?"

"By train. There's one leaving for Edinburgh in two hours and we can get you on it. You'll go as you are, you won't be noticed that way, and you can bring your other clothes in a bag. Fryer will go with you."

Jan thought swiftly, frowning into the darkness. "Arrange it then. Also arrange to meet me yourself in Edinburgh in the morning, in your Cynthia Barton role, and bring some money. At least five hundred pounds in cash. Old notes. Can that be done?"

"Of course. I'll take care of it now. Fryer will be informed of everything. Call to him now, tell him the man with him is to leave with me."

It seemed foolish, that people risking their lives together could not even see each other's faces. But it was simple insurance that if one of them were captured he could not identify the others. They stayed in darkness until Fryer and the unknown man returned, then he and Sara left in silence after a quick muttered conversation with Fryer. Fryer waited until they left before he turned the light on.

"Going for a mystery tour are we," he said. "Nice time of year for a trip." He rooted in the boxes at the end of the garage and produced an ancient army duffle bag. "This will do fine. Just put your clothes in here and we'll be off. A brisk walk should get us to King's Cross just on time."

Once more Fryer showed his superior knowledge of the back streets of London. Only twice were they forced to cross any of the brilliantly lit avenues. Each time Fryer scouted ahead first to make sure they would not be observed, before he led Jan to the security of the darkness on the other side. They reached King's Cross station with forty-five minutes to spare. The funny thing was that Jan, who had been here countless times before on the way to Scotland, did not recognize it.

They turned off the street into a long tunnel. Despite the fact that it was well illuminated it still had been used as a latrine and the smell of urine was sharp in the air. Their footsteps echoed as they went through it and up the stairs at the other end, into a large waiting room filled with scuffed benches. Most of the occupants seemed to be stretched out and sound asleep, although there were a few sitting up, waiting for their trains. Fryer went to the battered cigarette machine and dug a metal box from his pocket which he put under the dispenser. When the machine was satisfied that he had inserted enough small change, it rattled briefly and disgorged some cigarettes into the box. He handed it to Jan, along with a glow lighter.

"Here. Smoke a bit. Try to look natural. Don't talk to anyone no matter what they say. I'll get the tickets."

The cigarettes were a brand Jan had never heard of before; WOODBINE was printed in blue letters the length of each of them, and they crackled like smoldering straw when lit, and burned his mouth.

There was a slow movement of people in and out of the waiting room, but no one as much as bothered to glance his way. Every few minutes the tannoy speakers would garble out an incomprehensible announcement. Jan grubbed his third cigarette out, feeling slightly bilious, when Fryer came back.

"Right as rain, gov. Off to the land of the Scots, but let's go to the bog first. Do you have a bandana with you?"

"In my pocket, here in the bag."

"Well dig it out now, we're going to need it. People sit close in these trains, nosy parkers, talk like old women. And we don't want you doing any talking."

In the washroom Jan recoiled as Fryer snicked out an immense blade from his pocket knife. "Minor surgery, gov, for your own good. Keep you alive it will. Now if you'll just peel your lip back I'm going to make a little nick in your gum. You won't feel a thing."

"It hurts like hell," Jan said thickly through the white kerchief he pressed to his mouth. He took it away and saw it stained with blood.

"That's the way. Good and red. If it starts to heal up just open it again with your tongue. And spit a bit of blood once in a while. Be convincing. Now here we go. I'll bring the bag, you keep that kerchief in front of your mouth."

There was a separate entrance to the Flying Scotsman platform that Jan had never known existed, admitting them to the rear of the train. Far ahead Jan could see the lights and scurrying porters at the first-class section behind the engine, where he always traveled. A private compartment, a drink from the recessed bar if he wanted it, then a good night's sleep to wake up in Glasgow. He knew that there was a second-class section because he had seen them boarding, crowding into their multitiered sleeping coaches, waiting patiently in the station in Scotland until the first-class passengers had disembarked. He had never even suspected that there was a third-class section.

The coaches were warm, that was all that could be said for them; there was no bar, no buffet, no services of any kind. The seats were built of wood lathes, constructed for durability only and not for style or comfort. Jan managed to find a window seat so he could lean back in the corner, resting his head on his bundle of clothing. Fryer sat down solidly next to him, lighting a cigarette and blowing the smoke complacently in the direction of the NO SMOKING sign. Others crowded in and were still seating themselves when the train slid gently into motion.

It was a very uncomfortable journey. Jan's handkerchief was well speckled with blood and he had even managed one carmined expectoration following his companion's orders. After that he tried to sleep, difficult under the bright lights that remained on all night. Despite Fryer's fears no one talked to them, or even noticed him after a first interested examination of his bloodstained mouth. The train rumbled on and he did finally fall asleep, waking up with a start at the firm shake on his shoulder.

"Rise and shine, old son," Fryer said. "Half six of a lovely morning and you can't spend the whole day in bed. Let's get some breakfast."

Jan's mouth tasted terrible and he was sore and stiff from sitting on the slatted bench all night. But the long walk down the platform in the cold air woke him up and the sight of the steamed windows of the buffet made him realize that he was hungry, very hungry indeed. Breakfast was simple, but enjoyable and filling. Fryer paid out the coins for their tea and brimming bowls of porridge and Jan wolfed his down. A man, dressed as they were, put a cup of tea on the table and sat down next to Fryer.

"Eat up, lads, and come wi' me. There's no' much time."

They took the lift out of the station and followed him in silence as he walked briskly through the cold of the dawn fog, into an apartment building not too distant from the station, up endless flights of stairs—were the lifts always in need of repair?—and into a grimy flat that, except for having more rooms, could have been a duplicate of the one they had visited in London. Jan stood at the sink and shaved with an ancient razor, trying not to nick himself too badly, then put his own clothes back on. With a feeling of relief, he had to admit. He tried not to consider the thought that if he had been that uncomfortable in these clothes, in these surroundings, for less than a day—how would a lifetime of it feel? He was tired; it didn't bear considering now. The other two men watched with solid indifference. Fryer held up the boots that he had been working on with dark polish.

"Not too bad, gov. You wouldn't want to go to no dances in them, but they'll do for the street. And I have a message that a certain person will be waiting for you in the lobby of the Caledonian Hotel. If you'll follow our friend here he'll lead you right to it."

"And you?"

"Never ask questions, gov. But I'm for home as soon as I can. Too cold up here in the north." His smile showed a number of blackened teeth; he took Jan's hand. "Good luck."

Jan followed his guide into the street and stayed a good twenty meters behind him as they walked. The sun had burned away the fog and the cold air felt good. As they passed the Caledonian Hotel the man shrugged his shoulder, then hurried on. Jan pushed through the revolving door and saw Sara sitting under a potted palm reading a newspaper. Or appearing to, for before he could walk over she stood and crossed in front of him, apparently without noticing him, and exited through the side entrance. He went after her and found her waiting for him around the corner.

"It's all been arranged," she said. "Everything except the skis. You will be boarding a train at eleven this morning."

"That will be enough time for our shopping. You have the money?" She nodded. "Good, then here is what we will do. I have been thinking about it most of the night—plenty of opportunity for that where I was. Were you on the train too?"

"Yes, in second class. It was bearable."

"All right. We have three shops to go to, the only three sporting goods places in Edinburgh that sell ski equipment. We'll make the purchases between us, using cash so there will be no record of credit card use. They know me here, and I'll say I lost my card on the train and it will be an hour before a new one can be issued, in the meantime I want to buy a few things. I know it works this way because it happened to me a few years ago. They'll take the cash."

"It will work for one, but not for two. I have a card for an account that is solvent, though the person named on the card does not exist."

"That's even better. You'll buy the expensive items like the high density battery and two compasses I'll need. Do you want me to write down what you should get?"

"No. I have been trained to remember things."

"Good. You mentioned a train. What will I be doing then?"

"Both of us will be going to Inverness for the night. You are well known at Kingsmills Hotel, aren't you?"

"You people know more about me than I do myself. Yes, they know me there."

"We thought so. A room has been booked for you for the night. By morning everything else will have been arranged."

"You can't tell me yet what is being planned?"

"I don't know myself. This whole thing has been rush and extemporize and pulled together at the last minute. But we do have a solid base in the Highlands, ex-prisoners for the most part who are glad to help escapers. They know by experience what it is like inside."

They stepped into a doorway so she could give him the money.

He told her what would be needed and she nodded her head and repeated the list word-perfect.

When they met again he had his purchases in a backpack, but the skis and everything else she had bought had been sent ahead to the station, to be put into his compartment. They reached the station a half an hour before the train was to leave and Jan made a detailed search of the compartment, as detailed as he could without instruments, for any concealed bugs.

"Nothing that I can find," he said.

"To our knowledge these compartments are rarely bugged, unless for a specific assignment. It is different in second class where bugging and computer monitoring are routine."

Sara had taken off her coat and sat by the window as the train started, looking out as the buildings gave way to countryside. Her green suit appeared to be soft leather, trimmed with fur that matched her fur hat. She turned and caught his eyes on her.

"I was admiring," he said. "You look very attractive in that getup."

"Protective coloration, a beautiful woman of means. But thank you in any case. Though I believe in complete equality of the sexes it does not offend me, as it does some, to be admired for something other than my brain."

"How could it offend?" Jan was still stopped by some of the things she said. "But don't tell me—not just now. I'm going to open the bar and give you a drink of something strong, and myself one as well, then ring for some sandwiches with meat in them." He felt a flash of guilt which he tried to ignore. "Venison, they do it very well on this train. And perhaps some smoked salmon first. And with it—yes, here it is—Glen Morangie, the finest of the straight malt whiskies. Do you know it?"

"I have never even heard of it."

"Lucky girl, to roll in warm luxury through the cold Highland wilderness—sipping your first malt. I'll join you."

It was impossible not to enjoy the trip, despite the danger it represented. This danger was in the past—and the future. For the brief hours they were on the train the world was held in suspension. Outside the window the sun shone brilliantly on a white landscape of mountains and forest, the occasional flatness of a frozen loch. No smoke rose from the chimneys of the crofters' cottages, even the most remote of them was heated by electricity, but other than this the scene had been unchanged for millennia.

There were sheep in protected fields, and a herd of deer bounding away from the swift approach of the electric train.

"I didn't know it could be so beautiful," Sara said. "I've never been this far north before. But it seems so sterile and barren as well."

"It's really the opposite. Come in the summer and you'll find it bursting with life."

"Perhaps. Could I have a little more of that fascinating whiskey? It has my head spinning!"

"Keep it spinning. You'll sober up quickly enough in Inverness."

"I'm sure of that. You'll go directly to the hotel and wait for instructions. What about all this ski equipment?"

"I'll take half of it with me, check the rest in here at the left luggage."

"That sounds right." Sara sipped the malt whiskey and wrinkled her nose. "So strong. I'm still not sure I like it. Inverness is on the edge of the security area, you know. All hotel records are entered automatically into the police files."

"I didn't know. But I've stayed often enough at the Kingsmills so it won't appear out of the ordinary."

"No. You are fine, the perfect cover. But I don't dare appear on any records. And I don't think I'll be able to catch the last train back tonight. I'll have to stay in your room, if that's all right with you?"

"Absolutely delighted."

When she said this Jan experienced a delightful warming experience somewhere in the middle of his body. He remembered her breasts revealed so quickly in the café in London. He smiled unconsciously at the thought—and found her smiling back.

"You're terrible," she said, "just like all the other men." But there was more humor than anger in her words. "Instead of thinking about the dangerous business ahead I suppose that your hormone-drenched brain is thinking only of seducing me?"

"Well, not only that . . ."

They laughed together and Sara reached out and took his hand. "What you men never seem to understand," she said, "is that women can enjoy love and sex just as much as you can. Is it unladylike to admit that I have been thinking about you since that first disastrous night in the submarine?"

"Unladylike or not, I think it's wonderful."

"Very good," she said, all business again. "After you check in, go out for a walk, get some fresh air, or go drink in a pub. You'll pass me on the street and just tell me your room number without stopping. Then go to your room right after dinner. I don't want to hang about the streets too much after dark and I'll join you as soon as I find out what the plans are to be for tomorrow. Agreed?"

"Agreed."

Sara left the train before he did, vanishing in the crowd. Jan waved a porter over and had him bring the skiing gear to left luggage. It was a short walk to the hotel with his almost-empty pack on his back. Packs were more in use than suitcases in the Highlands at this time of year and it elicited no notice, even when he checked into the hotel.

"Welcome back, Engineer Kulozik, always a pleasure to see you. We are short on rooms so we can't give you your usual one. But there is a fine one on the third floor, if you don't mind."

"No problem," Jan said, taking the key. "Would you have the pack put in the room? I want to go out before the shops close."

"Our pleasure."

Everything went as planned. Sara nodded when she heard the room number and continued past him without stopping. He had an early meal in the grill and was in his room by seven. In the bookcase he found a John Buchan novel, almost required reading here, and he sat down with that and a weak whiskey and water. Without his realizing it the lost night's sleep caught up with him and the next thing he knew he was starting awake at the light tapping on the door. Sara slipped in quickly.

"Everything has been arranged," she said. "You will take the local train tomorrow to a station named Forsinard." She consulted a scrap of paper. "This is in the Achentoul Forest. Do you know it?"

"I know of it. And I have all the maps."

"Good. Emerge from the train with the other skiers, but look for a local man, very husky, with a black eyepatch. He is your contact. Follow him and he will take it from there."

"What will you do?"

"I'll be on the seven o'clock train south in the morning. There is nothing more I can do here."

"Oh, no!"

She smiled, with a warmth he had not seen before. "Turn off

the lights and open the curtains. There is a beautiful full moon tonight."

He did, and it drenched the white landscape with an even paler light. Shadows, darkness, and snow. Jan turned at a sound and the moonlight fell on her body as well. The firm, round breasts he had glimpsed so briefly, her taut stomach, full hips, long thighs. Sara held her arms out and he gathered her to him.

Twelve

"We're not going to get much sleep this way," he said, tracing the contour of her arable breast with his finger, her outline still clearly visible in the moonlight from the window.

"I don't need much. And you'll have plenty of time for it after I leave. Your train's not until noon. Did I thank you yet for what you are doing to help rescue Uri?"

"Not in so many words—but there are other ways. Who is Uri that he is so important?"

"He is not important, not in himself anyway. It is what will happen if Security discovers who they have. His cover is an Italian seaman, and it is a good cover. But eventually they will discover that it is false. Then the interrogation will begin in earnest and there is no way to stop them from finding out he is an Israeli."

"Is that bad?"

"It would be disaster. Our country's international policy is one of strictly no contact, none whatsoever except through official channels. Some of us in external security don't see it the same way. We have to know what is happening in the outside world to protect our own nation. And once we discovered what life is like here it was hard to remain neutral. So, despite all orders to not get involved, despite the logical reasoning that any involvement is a threat to our homeland—we *are* involved. It is impossible just to stand by and do nothing."

"I've been standing by, doing nothing all of my life."

"You didn't know," Sara said, putting her finger to his lips to silence him, moving the warm length of her body against his. "And you are doing something now."

"Oh yes, I certainly am!" he whispered, gathering her in his arms. He silenced her laughter with his lips.

Jan was awake later when she dressed and left, but there was nothing for either of them to say. He did not think he would be able to sleep after that, but he did. It was full daylight when he awoke and he was ravenous. The breakfast did justice to the High-land cuisine, the smoked kipper was a thing of joy, and he was feeling remarkably fit, whistling while he dressed. Since arriving in Scotland it had been more like a holiday than a hurried attempt to save a man's life. Perhaps save an entire country. These were just words, the reality had not sunk in yet.

Nor did the trip on the clanking train do anything to change the way he felt. There were a few locals aboard, but the majority of the passengers seemed to be skiers on holiday, filling the coaches with bright clothes and laughter, bottles passing from hand to hand. One thing, he certainly would not be noticed in this crowd. With people getting off and on at each station there would be no trace of where he had actually alighted.

By midafternoon the sky had darkened and a thin snow had begun to fall. This dampened feelings somewhat and, when he lifted the packs and skis down from the guard's van in Forsinard, the bite of the wind drove the last traces of merriment from him. This desperate business was about to begin.

His contact was easy enough to spot, a dark blob among the colourful anoraks and salopettes. Jan dropped his burden into the snow and knelt to fumble with the lace on his boot. When he arose again he went back in the direction of the station, following the stocky form of his contact. Along the road, then off onto a beaten down path through the trees. The man was waiting in a clearing well hidden from sight of the road.

"What do I call you?" he said when Jan came up.

"Bill."

"Well, Bill, I'm Brackley, and that's no code name and I don't care who knows it. I've done my time and left an eye behind to prove it." He pointed to the black patch and Jan noticed the puckered scar that crossed his cheek and went under the patch, continuing up over his forehead and vanishing under the wool cap pulled low on his head. "They've been trying to do old Brackley for years but they haven't done me so far. You cold?"

"Not very."

"Good. Make no difference if you were. Be dark before the track comes. What do you know about the work camps?"

"Little or nothing. Other than the fact that they exist."

Brackley snorted and nodded at the answer, then extracted a plug of tobacco from his pocket and bit off a corner. "That's the way they want it," he said indistinctly around the large cud he was chewing into shape. "What happens, people get out of line, they get sent up here, maybe a ten-year sentence cutting trees. Good for the health unless you cross the screws, then you get this," he jerked his thumb at the eyepatch again, "or worse. Dead too, they don't care. Then when you serve your term you find out that you got to serve the same term again working in the Highlands, no going back to the joys of the Smoke. And there ain't no work here. Except grazing sheep. You people, begging your pardon, your honor, likes their little bit of meat, don't they. Poor buggers up here freezing their arses off to see you get it. So what with ten years inside and ten years with the sheep, most don't get back south, and them what do, they keep their noses clean so they can stay south. It's a good system they got, works fine." He spat a great brown gob into the white snow.

"What about escapes?" Jan asked, stamping his feet as the cold began to seep through.

"Easy enough to get out. Couple of strands of barbed wire. But then what? Wilderness on all sides, a few roads well watched, trains watched as well. Getting out's no problem, staying out is the one that counts. That's where Brackley and his boys come in. All of us done our time, now we're out but can't leave the Highlands. So while we're here we don't make trouble, but anyone goes through the fence and finds us, why we make trouble for the screws. Get them out of here. South. Like an underground railway. Turn them over to your people. Now you want one out in particular, right out of a security cell. Not easy."

"I don't know the details."

"I do. First time you've given us guns. This could stop other things working around here for a long time. Once we have this man out we go back to our crofts and lay low for a long time. Raise our heads we get 'em cut off. This man better be important."

"He is."

"That's the way I hear it. So let's look at the map before it gets too dark. Here's where we are now." He pointed out the spot with a thick, scarred thumb. "We start cross country after dark to about here, doesn't show on the map but that's their detector screen. Go in on foot after that and they can't tell us from elk or deer. Not that they care. Only start looking after someone breaks out. No one up until now has been fool enough to want to break in. We use snowshoes. We want to use these fancy skis of yours?"

"Yes, they're best for me."

"Good enough. We'll bring the man out in a skibasket so we can make time. Back to the track, back to the road, run the track into a lake, and we go home and no one the wiser."

"Aren't you forgetting something?"

"Never!" He slapped Jan on the back, a friendly blow that sent him staggering. "Right along here there are a number of paths where the skiers cross the road. Even if it's not snowing they'll never be able to follow your tracks—they go every which way from here. You and your friend break west then and you'll have at least eight, ten hours of darkness to stay ahead of anyone looking for you. Not that they will, probably won't think of it. They'll look for someone going to ground, or going north or south by train or road. This is a new way out and a smart one too. You'll get through, though there will be mobile patrols around when you get over near Loch Naver."

"We'll look out for them."

"That's the spirit." Brackley squinted up at the darkening sky, then took up the second pack and pair of skis. "Time to go."

Jan was thoroughly chilled through now, standing in the patch of pine trees by the road, as the dark afternoon thickened into night. Invisible snowflakes melted on his face and he moved stiffly when Brackley pulled him forward at the sight of twin headlights coming slowly along the road. A dark vehicle stopped and a door swung open above them, ready hands pulled them inside.

"Lads, this is Bill," Brackley said, and there was a murmur of greeting from the unseen men. His elbow dug Jan painfully in the ribs, to draw his attention. "This is a snowtrack. He nicked it from the foresters. Can't do it too often because they get right annoyed and turn the whole county over. They'll be annoyed again in the spring when they find it sunk in the lake. Had to do it this time. For speed."

There was a heater on in the body of the vehicle and Jan thawed out a bit. Brackley produced a torch and held it while Jan took off his boots, massaging some life back into his icy feet, then put on high socks and the special cross-country shoes. He was still tying the laces when they lurched to a stop.

They seemed to know just what to do without being told, since no orders were issued. The men piled out of the track into waist high snow, quickly strapping their feet into the round bear-paw snowshoes. The first two men were already away, towing the mountain rescue stretcher on its skis. There was white official lettering stenciled on it, also undoubtedly stolen. Jan strapped on his skis and kicked off quickly after them through the trees, wondering how they could find their way in the snow-filled darkness.

"Hold it," Brackley said, stopping so suddenly that Jan almost ran into him. "This is as far as you go. Take this and wait here." He pressed the bulk of an FM transceiver into Jan's hands. "If anyone comes by and sees the cut wire, don't let them see you. Get back into the trees. Press this button and tell us on the radio so we can come back a different way. Then get further back into the woods and we'll use the radio to find you."

There were some sharp metallic clicks as the barbed wire strands were cut, then silence. Jan was alone.

Very much alone. The snow had stopped but the night was still dark, the moon concealed by thick cloud. The posts and barbed wire vanished away into the darkness on both sides; their presence was marked by the cleared strip of land. Jan slid away to the shelter of the trees, moving back and forth there to keep warm, checking the glowing digits on his watch. A half an hour and still nothing. He wondered how far they had to go, how long it would all take.

By the time a slow hour had dragged by his nerves were tightened to the snapping point. At one point he jumped with shock, almost falling as dark shapes moved out of the trees toward him. Deer. Far more frightened than he was once they caught his scent. After almost ninety minutes more dark shapes appeared, and he almost thumbed on his radio, before he recognized the stretcher being towed behind them.

"Went just wonderful," Brackley said hoarsely, panting for air. They had all been running. "Didn't need the guns, used the knives and did away with a half-dozen of the bastards. Got your friend here all right, though they've knocked him about a bit. Here, take the rope and pull the litter, my lads are fair bushed."

Jan grabbed the rope and passed it over his shoulder, tying it to his belt, then leaned his weight into it. The stretcher moved easily on its skis and he broke into a steady, loping run that quickly caught up and passed the others on their snowshoes. He had to slow then to stay behind Brackley who was leading the way. Short minutes later they were back in the snowtrack and passing the stretcher in over the tailgate. The fuel cell fired with a muffled roar and they started forward even as the last of the men were climbing aboard.

"We have a half an hour at least, maybe an hour," Brackley said, drinking deep from the water bottle, then passing it along. "All the guards at the detention cells are dead—the roof will blow off that place when they're discovered."

"But they got other things to think about," one of the men broke in; there were murmurs of agreement at that.

"We set fire to some of the warehouses," Brackley said. "That will keep the bastards distracted for a bit."

"Would someone be so kind as to unstrap me?" the man in the stretcher said.

A light flashed on and Jan undid the straps that held Uri secure. He looked young, perhaps still in his twenties, with black hair and deepset dark eyes.

"Can anyone tell me what happens next?" he asked.

"You're going with me," Jan said. "Do you know how to ski?"

"Not on snow, but I water ski."

"That's very good. We won't be doing downhill skiing, but cross country. I have the clothes here that you will need."

"Sounds like fun," Uri said, sitting up, shivering. He was dressed only in a thin gray prison uniform. "I'll sit on the bench if someone will give me a hand."

"Why?" Jan asked, struck by a sudden cold sensation of fear.

"Bunch of bastards back there," Uri said, dropping to the bench. "Thought I wasn't talking fast enough, even when they got an Italian translator in. They used some encouragement to speed me up."

He lifted his foot from the tangled blankets. It was dark with dried blood. Jan leaned close with the light and saw that all of the man's toenails had been ripped out. How was he to walk—much less ski—with feet like this?

"I don't know if it helps," Brackley said. "But the people who did this, they're all dead."

"It doesn't help the feet but it cheers me a great deal. Thank you."

"And we'll take care of the feet too. There was always a chance something like this might happen." Brackley struggled a flat metal container out from under his clothing and opened it. He took out a disposable syringe and broke off the safety tip. "People who gave me this said one shot would kill pain for up to six hours. No side effects but very habit forming." He slapped it against Uri's thigh, the sharp needle penetrating the thin fabric, the drug slowly injected by the pressurized gas capsule. "There are nine more here." He passed them over.

"My thanks to whoever thought of this," Uri said. "The toes are getting numb already."

Jan helped him to dress in the swaying snowtrack. The lunging ride improved when they came to a road and speeded up. They only followed it for a few minutes, then turned off into the deep snow again.

"Security checkpoint ahead," Brackley said. "We have to go around it."

"I had no idea of your shoe size," Jan said. "So I bought three pairs of shoes, different sizes."

"Let me try them. I'll wad some bandages around the toes to soak up blood. I think these are the ones that will do."

"Do they fit well in the heel?"

"Fine." Dressed and warming up, Uri looked around at the circle of watching men, barely seen in the light of the torch. "I don't know how to thank you people . . ."

"You don't. Our pleasure," Brackley said as the vehicle slowed and stopped. Two of the men left in silence and the snowtrack started up again. "You two will be the last. I'll be driving and I'll take care of disposing of this thing. Bill, I'll drop you at the spot I showed you on the map. After that you're on your own."

"I'll take care of it," Jan said.

Jan rearranged the packs, putting over three-quarters of the weight into the one he would carry, then adjusting the lighter one on Uri's shoulders.

"I can carry more than that," Uri said.

"On foot maybe, but if you can just carry yourself on skis I'll be happy. The weight's no problem for me."

The snowtrack was empty when they stopped for the last time. Brackley came around from the cab and opened the rear and they slid down to the icy surface of the road.

"That's the trail," Brackley said, pointing. "Get off the road fast and don't stop until you're under the trees. Good luck."

He was gone before Jan could phrase an answer. The snowtrack roared away, sending back a shower of broken bits of ice, and they were alone. Struggling through the thick snow to the trees. Uri held the small torch while Jan knelt and strapped his shoes into the skis, then put on his own.

"Slip the thong of the ski pole over your wrist like this, see. So the pole hangs from your wrist. Now move your hand straight down and grab. This way you can't lose a pole. Now here is the motion you will have to use, a sliding one. As you slide your right foot forward you push against the pole in your *left* hand. Then shift weight and push the opposite ski with the opposite pole. That's it, keep going."

"It's . . . not easy."

"It will be as soon as you get the rhythm right. Watch me. Push . . . push . . . Now you go ahead, follow those tracks, I'll be right behind you."

Uri struggled ahead and was just getting into the swing of the movements when the path turned off and they faced the soft powder snow of the deep forest. Jan went first then, striking a path through the unbroken surface. The sky was growing light above the black silhouettes of the trees and when they came to a clearing Jan stopped, looking up at the moon riding above the moving clouds. Clearly visible ahead was the grim shape of a mountain.

"Ben Griam Beg," Jan said. "We go around it . . ."

"Thank God! I thought you might want to take me over it." Uri was panting, drenched with sweat.

"No need. We'll hit frozen lakes and streams on the other side, going will be easier and we'll make better time."

"How far do we have to go?"

"About eighty kilometers as the crow flies, but we won't be able to get there directly."

"I don't think I can make it," Uri said, staring with misgivings at the frozen wilderness ahead. "Do you know about me, I mean were you told . . . ?"

"Sara told me everything, Uri."

"Good. I have a gun. If I can't make it you are to shoot me and go on. Do you understand?"

Jan hesitated—then slowly nodded.

Thirteen

They went on. They were stopping far oftener than Jan wanted to because Uri was not able to keep up a steady pace. But he was learning, going faster with less effort. They had only four more hours of darkness. At the next stop, around the shoulder of the mountain, Jan checked their heading with the gyro-compass and tried to mark his course with an identifiable spot in the terrain ahead.

"Going . . . to have to have . . . another shot," Uri said.

"We'll take ten minutes then, something to eat and drink."

"Damn . . . fine idea."

Jan dug two dried fruit bars from his pack and they chewed on them, washed down with water from the insulated bottle.

"Better than the food inside," Uri said, wolfing his portion. "I was there three days, nothing much to eat, less to drink. It's a long way to *eretz* Israel. I didn't know there could be this much snow in the whole world. What's the plan when we finish this little holiday trek?"

"We're making for the Altnacealgach Hotel. It's a hunting lodge, right out in the forest by itself. I imagine you'll be picked up there, or perhaps I'm supposed to drive you someplace. My car will be there. In any case you will hide out in the forest a bit while I go ahead."

"I'm looking forward to your hotel. Shall we go on before I seize up and can't move."

Jan was tired himself well before dawn—and he did not want to think how Uri felt. Yet they had to keep moving, to get as much distance as they could from the camp. There had been some snow flurries during the night, not very heavy, but still thick enough he hoped to obscure their tracks. If Security would be looking for tracks. There was a good chance they wouldn't, not yet. But danger would come with sunrise; they had to be concealed before then.

"Time to stop," Jan called back over his shoulder. "We're going to ground over here, under the trees."

"Those are the most beautiful words I have ever heard."

Jan stamped out depressions in the snow and spread the sleeping bags out in them. "Get into yours," he ordered. "But take your shoes off first. I'll take care of them. And I'll get us some warm food."

He had to help with the shoes, saw the socks and bandages sodden with blood. "Good thing I can't feel anything," Uri said, sliding into the sleeping bag. Jan pushed snow over it until it was completely concealed.

"These bags are made of insulcon, fabric developed for space suits. It has a layer of insulating gas in it, almost as good a nonconductor as a vacuum. You'll find you'll have to leave the top loose or you'll stew in your own juice."

"I'm looking forward to it."

The light was growing now; Jan hurried with the food. The electric element on the high density battery quickly melted a potful of snow, into which he dumped a packet of dehydrated stew. A second potful heated while they wolfed down the first. Then Jan cleaned up, melted water to top up their bottles, then packed everything away again. It was full daylight. Well below the horizon an airplane droned by. The search would be on. He wriggled into his own sleeping bag and pulled snow over it. A long snore issued from Uri's bag. That sounded like a good idea. He set the alarm on his watch and pulled the flap over his face. At first he was afraid he would stay awake, worrying about the search that was going on, but sleep overwhelmed him and the next he knew the piercing warble of the alarm was screeching in his ear.

During the second night, even though the going was easier, they covered less distance than they had the previous one. Uri was losing blood, too much of it, and even with the pain-killing injections he found it harder and harder to go on. They crossed a frozen loch about an hour before dawn and came to a sheltered cove with an overhanging rock ledge. Jan decided to stop. The place was ideal and it wasn't worth the few kilometers more to force Uri any further.

"I'm not doing too well, am I?" Uri asked, sipping at a steaming mug of tea.

"You're turning into a good cross-country skier. Be winning medals soon."

"You know what I'm talking about. I don't think I'm going to get there."

"After a good sleep you'll feel better."

It was sometime in the afternoon when Uri's voice dragged Jan from a deep sleep. "That sound. Can you hear it? What is it?"

Jan lifted his head free of the sleeping bag, then heard it clearly. A distant whine, far down the loch.

"A snowcat," he said. "It sounds like it might be coming this way, along the loch. Keep your head down and he won't see us. Our tracks have filled in so he can't follow them."

"Is it the police?"

"Probably. I can't think of anyone other than the authorities who would be running mechanical equipment out here in the winter. Stay quiet, we'll be safe."

"No. When he gets close, sit up and wave, draw his attention."

"What? You can't mean it . . ."

"I do. I'm not getting out of these woods, not on foot. We both know that. But I can do it with transportation. Let him get as close as possible before you make your move."

"This is crazy."

"It is. This whole mess is crazy. There he comes."

The whining rose in volume as the snowcat came around a headland jutting into the loch. It was bright red, its spinning tread throwing a spume of snow behind it, the goggled rider looking straight ahead. He was paralleling the shore and would pass an easy ten meters from them. Concealed as they were, in the snow under the ledge, there was very little chance of his accidentally seeing them.

"Now!" Uri said, and Jan rose up out of the snow, waving his hands and shouting.

The rider saw him at once and throttled down, turning at the same time, swinging toward them. He reached down and unclipped his microphone and was raising it to his mouth when Uri's shot caught him in the chest. A shot from a rocket pistol. It fired a silent, self-propelling projectile that tore right through the man.

He went over backward, arms wide. The snowcat fell on its side, skidding forward, track churning, until the tumble switch cut the power.

Fast as Jan moved, Uri was faster. Out of his bag, his feet making red prints in the snow, rushing toward the fallen man. There was no need.

"Dead as soon as he was hit," Uri said, opening the officer's jacket and peeling it from him. "Look at the hole that thing punched right through him." Uri wasted no time as he pulled on the man's clothing, stopping only to mop blood from the fabric. Jan walked over slowly and righted the snowcat.

"The radio is still switched off. He never sent a message," he said.

"Best news I have had since my bar mitzvah. Will I have any problem making that thing go?"

Jan shook his head *no*. "Almost a full charge in the battery, two hundred kilometers at least. The right handlebar is switch and throttle. They're fun to drive. The front steering ski will tend to go straight unless you lean your weight into the turn as well. Ever ride a motorcycle?"

"Plenty."

"Then you'll have no problems. Except where do you go?"

"I've been thinking about that." Dressed now in uniform and boots, Uri stamped over to their packs and took out the detailed map. "Can you show me where we are now?"

"Right here," Jan pointed. "At this inlet in Loch Shin."

"This town of Durness, on the north coast. Are there any other places in Scotland with the same name?"

"Not to my knowledge."

"Good. I had to memorize a list of towns with safe contacts in case of trouble. I have one there. Can I make it?"

"You'll make it if you don't run into trouble. Go this way, following the streams. That will keep you well away from these two north-south roads. Take a compass and follow this heading. Stay on it until you hit the coast. Then double back and lay-up in hiding until dark. Put on your own clothes and see if you can't drive the machine off the cliffs into the ocean—along with the uniform. After that—you're on your own."

"No problem then. But what about you?"

"I'll go on. Have a nice cross-crountry trek, something I enjoy. No worry about me."

"I didn't think so. But what about our friend the corpse here?"

Jan looked at the man's pink, bloodstained flesh, obscenely sprawled in the snow. "I'll take care of him. Cover him up back there in the forest. The foxes will find him, and then the crows. By spring there'll only be bones left. It's not very nice . . ."

"His job wasn't very nice. I'll appreciate it if you would take care of it. Then I can move out." He put out his gauntletted hand and Jan took it. "And I'm free thanks only to you and your people. We'll win, you wait and see."

"I hope so. Shalom."

"Thanks. But Shalom later. Let's get rid of the bastards first."

Uri twisted the control and moved off, faster and faster. He gave one last wave over his shoulder then was around the bend in the lake and gone, the sound of the electric motor dying away.

"Good luck," Jan said quietly, then turned back to their campsite.

The body first. He dragged it by its heels, arms sprawled over its head and a trail of blood marking its passage. The scavengers would be there as soon as he was gone. He kicked snow over the blood and went back to break camp. The second sleeping bag and all the extra equipment went into one pack, everything he would need into the other. There was no point in hanging about here, it would be dangerous in fact if the scene of the ambush were discovered. If he went through the forest carefully, he could be a good distance away before dark. Donning his pack, he grabbed up the other pack and the skis and went swiftly away from the site. It was good to move quickly and surely and the kilometers sped by. He buried the skis and pack in the middle of a dense thicket, then pressed on. Once he heard another snowcat passing in the distance and he stopped until it had gone. A plane thrummed over head toward sunset, as invisible to him through the trees as he was to it. He went on two hours more before he made camp.

It snowed, heavily, during the night, and he woke up more than once to clear the drifts away so he could breathe. In the morning the sun burned golden-bright on the freshly fallen powder and he found himself whistling as he boiled the water for tea. It was over, all over, and he was safe. He hoped Uri was as well. Safe or dead, Jan knew that the Israeli would not be taken alive a second time.

When he crossed Benmore Loch it was late afternoon. He

stopped and slid under the shelter of a tree when he heard the sound of a car going by on highway 837 ahead. The hotel would not be far now. But what should he do? There would be no difficulty in spending another night in the snow, then going on in the morning. But would that be wise? If he were under any suspicion at any time the shorter the trip he had made the less chance there would be that he might have gone north to Slethill Camp before doubling back. So the best thing would be an early arrival. A steak dinner, with a bottle of wine, by an open fire was not a bad thing at all to look forward to.

Jan swung forward, moving swiftly, onto the slope behind the great hotel, then snowplowing down into the yard. He unstrapped his skis and stuck them into a drift by the front entrance. Then, kicking the snow from his shoes, he pushed through the double doors and into the lobby. It seemed hot and close after his days in the open.

As he walked across to the registration desk a man came out of the manager's office and turned toward him.

"Well, Jan," Thurgood-Smythe said. "Did you have an enjoyable journey?"

Fourteen

Jan stopped, eyes wide, stunned by the presence of his brother-in-law. "Smitty! What on earth are you doing here?" Only later did he realize that his natural response had been the right one; Thurgood-Smythe was studying his reaction closely.

"A number of reasons," the Security man said. "You're looking fit, clear-eyed, and glowing. How about a drink to put some toxins back into your body?"

"Fine idea. But not in the bar. Air's like treacle down here. We can drink just as well in my room—and I can crack the window a bit while you sit on the radiator."

"All right. I have your key here, save you the trouble. Let's go up."

There were others in the lift so they did not talk. Jan stared straight ahead and struggled to compose his thoughts. What did Thurgood-Smythe suspect? His presence here was no accident. Nor was he pretending that it was—not with Jan's key in his possession and making no secret of the fact. But a search would mean nothing: there was nothing incriminating in his luggage. Attack was the best defense and he knew better than to pretend stupidity to his brother-in-law. As soon as the door closed behind them he spoke.

"What's up, Smitty? And do me the favor of not pretending this is an innocent business—not with my key in your pocket. What's Security's interest in me?"

Thurgood-Smythe stood by the window, staring unseeingly at the white landscape. "I'll have a whiskey if you please, neat. A large one. The problem, my dear Jan, is that I don't believe in co-incidence. My credulity is limited. And you have been too close to too many interesting things just once too often."

"Would you mind explaining that?"

"You know as well as I do. The incident in the Red Sea, the il-legal computer tap in your laboratory."

"Means absolutely nothing. If you think I tried to drown my-self for some reason you're the one in need of an analyst, not me. Which leaves us the laboratory—with how many employees?"

"Point taken," Thurgood-Smythe said. "Thank you." He sipped at the whiskey. Jan opened the window a hand's breadth and inhaled deeply of the cold air.

"Taken alone, these two incidents are meaningless. I only worry about them when I find you in the Highlands at this time. There has been a very serious incident at one of the nearby camps which means your presence here *could* be very suspicious."

"I don't see why." Jan's voice was cold, his face expressionless. "I ski up here two or three times, at least, every winter."

"I know you do, which is the only reason I am talking to you like this. If I were not married to your sister this interview would be entirely different. I would have a biomonitor in my pocket which would give me a readout on your heartbeat, muscle tension, respiration, and brainwaves. With this I would know if you were lying or not."

"Why should I lie? If you have one of these devices pull it out and look at it and see for yourself."

Jan's anger was real; he did not like the way the conversation was progressing.

"I don't. I had one in my hand before I left—but I put it back in the safe. Not because I like you, Jan—which I do. That has nothing to do with it. If you were anyone else I would be interro-gating you now instead of talking to you. If I did that, sooner or later Elizabeth would hear about it and that would be the end of my marriage. Her protective instincts for her little brother go far beyond reason, and I do not wish to put them to the test of choosing between you or me. I have the uneasy sensation that it would probably be you."

"Smitty, for heaven's sake—what is this all about?"

"Let me finish first. Before I tell you what is happening I want to make it absolutely clear what is going to happen. I'm going home to Elizabeth and tell her that you have been put under surveillance by a different department of Security. This is true. I will also tell her that I can do nothing to prevent it—which is also true. What will happen in the future will depend upon what you do in the future. Up until now, until this moment, you are in the clear. Do you understand that?"

Jan nodded slowly. "Thanks, Smitty. You're putting yourself out on a limb for me, aren't you? I imagine your telling me about the surveillance is a dangerous thing for you to do?"

"It is. And I would appreciate the return of the favor by your discovering some aspect of the surveillance, then telephoning me and complaining about it."

"Will do. As soon as I get home. Now if you will tell me what I'm supposed to have done . . ."

"Not done—what you *could* have done." There was no warmth now in Thurgood-Smythe's voice, no give in his manner. This was the professional Security man that Jan had never seen before. "An Italian seaman escaped from a work camp up here. An item normally of little interest. But two things make it important. His escape was aided from the outside—and a number of guards were killed. Soon after this happened we had a report from the Italian authorities. The man does not exist."

"I don't understand . . ."

"Does not exist in *their* records. His documentation was forged, very professionally. Which means he is the citizen of another country, a foreign agent."

"He could be Italian."

"Possibly. But for other reasons I doubt that strongly."

"If not Italian—then what country?"

"I thought you might be able to tell me." His voice was quiet, soft as silk.

"How would I know?"

"You could have helped him escape, guided him through the forest, have him hiding out there right now."

This was so close to what he had planned that Jan felt the short hairs stirring on his neck. "I could—if you say so. But I didn't. I'll get out my map and show you where I've been. Then you tell me if I was near your mysterious escapee."

Thurgood-Smythe dismissed the thought with a wave of his hand. "No maps. If you are lying—or telling me the truth—there will be no evidence there."

"Why on earth should another country spy on us? I thought this was a world at peace."

"There is no such thing as peace—just modified forms of warfare."

"That's a rather cynical statement."

"Mine's a rather cynical profession."

Jan filled both glasses again and sat on the window ledge. Thurgood-Smythe retreated as far from the cold blast as he could.

"I don't think I like the things that you are telling me," Jan said. "All this murder and prisoners and surveillance machines. Does this kind of thing happen often? Why don't we hear about it?"

"You don't hear about it, dear brother, because you are not meant to hear about it. The world is a very nasty place and there is no cause to bother people with the sordid details."

"You're telling me that important events in the world are kept secret from people?"

"I'm telling you just that. And if you have never suspected it, then you are a bigger fool than I took you to be. People of your class *prefer* not to know, to let people like me take care of the dirty work for you. And look down upon us for it."

"That's not true, Smitty . . ."

"Isn't it?" There was a cutting edge to his voice. "What was it you just called me? Smitty? Did you ever call Ricardo de Torres—Ricky?"

Jan started to answer, but could not. It was true. Thurgood-Smythe was descended from generations of drab civil servants; Ricardo de Torres from titled, landed gentry. For long seconds Jan felt impaled on that look of cold hatred; then his brother-in-law turned away.

"How did you find me up here?" Jan asked, trying to change the subject.

"Don't pretend to be simple. The location of your car is in the motorway memories. Do you realize the extent of the computer files and programming?"

"I never thought about it. Big I suppose."

"Far bigger than you realize—and far better organized. There is no such thing as having too much memory. If Security wanted to —and we may—we could monitor every second of your life, have it all on record."

"That's stupid, impossible. You're in my territory now. No matter how much circuitry you have, no matter how much memory, there is no possible way you could run surveillance on everyone in the country all of the time. The data would swamp you."

"Of course it would. But I wasn't talking about the entire country. I was mentioning only one individual. You. Ninety-nine percent of the people in this country are neutral, neuters. Names in a memory bank of no interest to us. Proles who are identical as matchsticks. Society butterflies, who while richer and more exotic, are equally uninteresting. In reality, we have very little to do. Petty thievery and embezzling head our list of crimes. Of no real importance. So when we are asked to take interest in someone we do it with a vengeance. Your screen can be two-way—as can your phone. Your computer is accessible to us, no matter how secure you may think. Your auto, your laboratory, the mirror in your toilet, the light above your bed—are all in our employ . . ."

"You're exaggerating!"

"Perhaps. But not by much, not in reality. If we want to know about you we can easily know *all about you*. Don't ever doubt that. And we want to know about you now. I would say that, for a number of years—until your guilt or innocence is proven—this is the last private conversation that you will ever have."

"Are you trying to scare me?"

"I hope so. If you are involved in anything—get out. We'll never know, and I for one prefer it that way. But if your hands are soiled we are going to get you. Yes we will—as certain as the sun rises in the east."

Thurgood-Smythe crossed over to the door and opened it. He turned as though to add something, then thought better of it. He turned and left and the door closed heavily behind him.

Jan closed the window; he was getting chilled.

Fifteen

The only thing to do now was to appear normal—try to act naturally in every way. Jan unpacked his bag, knowing that Thurgood-Smythe had undoubtedly gone through it, apprehensive lest something incriminating had been slipped in by accident. There was of course nothing; but he still could not displace the niggle of fear. It stayed with him while he bathed and changed, went down to dine, talked with old acquaintances in the bar. The feeling stayed with him all night and he slept little. He checked out early the next morning and began the long drive back to London.

It was snowing again, and he had no leisure to think of anything else as he drove carefully down the winding Highland roads. Luncheon was beer and a pasty in a roadside pub, then on until he came to the motorway. Once the computer took control he could relax—but did not. He felt more uneasy if anything.

Sitting back, blinded by the torrent of snowflakes against the window, yet completely safe under electronic control, Jan finally faced up to what was disturbing him. There, right before him, was the evidence. The circle of tiny holes around the center of the steering wheel. Monitoring his breath. He could not drive and escape them. Inlets to an analyzer that detected the parts per million of alcohol on his breath, that only permitted him to drive the car when he was legally sober. An intelligent idea to prevent accidents: an insinuating, humiliating idea when viewed as part of the bigger picture of continuous observation. This, and his other personal data, were stored in the car's memory, could be transmitted to the highway computer—and from there to the Security memory banks. A record of his breath, his drinking, his reaction time, where he drove, when he drove—whom he drove with. And when he went home the Security cameras in the garage and halls would follow him carefully to his front door—and beyond. While he watched TV the set would be watching back, an invisible police-man gazing out from the screen. His phone monitored, indetecta-ble bugs planted in the wiring. Find and remove them—if possible —and his voice within the room would then be monitored by fo-cusing a laser beam on the glass of his windows. Data and more data would be continuously fed to some hidden secret file—where all of the rest of the facts of his life were already recorded.

He had never thought seriously about it before, but he realized for the first time that he existed as two people. The flesh and blood person, and the duplicate electronic file. His birth had been recorded as well as all pertinent medical information. His educa-tion, his dental record, financial record, and purchases. What books he bought, what presents he gave. Was it all on file some-place? With a sinking feeling he realized that it probably was. There was physically almost no limit to the amount of informa-tion that could be stored in the new molecular memory cores. Molecules flipped one way or another to record bits, bits forming bytes, bytes forming words and numbers. More and more and more. An encyclopedia in a piece of material the size of a pin-head, a man's entire life in a pebble.

And nothing he could do about it. He had tried, done his bit for the resistance, helped in a small way. But now it was over. Raise his head and it would be chopped off. Life wasn't that bad. Be glad he wasn't a prole, condemned to that existence for all the days of his years.

Must he stop? Couldn't it be changed? But even as the rebel-lious thoughts possessed him he realized that his heartbeat had in-creased, the muscles in his arm tensed as he made an inadvertent fist. Physiological changes that could be monitored, observed, considered.

He was a prisoner in an invisible cell. Make one step out of it and it would be the end. For the first time in his life he had the realization what freedom was, what he did not have. What lack of liberty was really about.

The drive home was dull and uneventful. The weather im-proved, when he passed Carlyle the snowstorm had ended and he drove under leaden skies. There was a play on the fifth channel and he turned it on but did not watch it; his head was too filled with the turbulence of his thoughts. Now that he could no longer take part in the resistance he realized how important it had become to him. A way to work for something he had come to believe in, to expiate the guilt he was just learning to feel. All over. By the time he reached home he was in the darkest of moods, scowling at the innocent lift attendant and slamming through his front door. He locked it and turned on the lights—and the bulb in the one important lamp did not come on.

So quickly? Someone had been in the flat while he was away.

He was innocent, he had to keep thinking that, innocent. And they could be watching him right now. Jan looked around slowly; nothing visible of course. He tried the windows, one by one, but all were closed and locked. Then he went to his wall safe and pressed the combination, flipped through the papers and cash inside. Everything looked in order. If Security had been here—it *had* to be them—they would surely have found his simple alarm system. Having it wasn't illegal, in fact it was a precaution most of his friends used. Now, there must be a natural reaction. He went to the phone, looking as angry as he felt, and called Building Management.

"Entered while you were away, sir? We have no record of any maintenance or emergency people going in during your absence."

"Burglars, thieves then. I thought you had security in this building?"

"We do, sir, the best. I'll check the recordings at once. Is anything missing?"

"Nothing that I can see after a quick look around, nothing important." He realized that he was looking at the TV while he talked, noticing the marks on the rug. "There is something, I just noticed. The TV has been moved. Perhaps they tried to steal it."

"There is that possibility. I'll report it to the police—and send up the mechanic to change the combination on your front door lock."

"Do that. Now. I'm not happy about this."

"Nor should you be, sir. A complete investigation will be made."

How subtle they were, Jan thought. Could the TV have been left off the marks on the rug on purpose? Was this a warning, a slight nudge in the ribs? He didn't know. But now that he had seen the moved set, reported it, he had to investigate further. If he were innocent that is what he would do.

He rubbed his jaw as he walked around the set. Then knelt to look at the screws that held the back in place. One of them had a fresh shine where a screwdriver had recently cut the surface. They had been inside it!

Within ten minutes he had the back off, the guts pulled, the circuit boards out—and was looking at the device wired across the power leads on one of them. It was the size of an acorn and shaped very much like one, with a glint of crystal in the rounded end. It had lined up with a tiny hole drilled in the front panel. Bugged! With a sharp movement he pulled it loose and bounced it in his palm angrily, making up his mind what to do next, what he would do if he were as innocent as he pretended to be. He went to the phone and called Thurgood-Smythe at home. His sister answered.

"Jan, darling, it's been ages! If you're free tomorrow . . ."

"Sorry, Liz, all tied up. And it was Smitty I wanted to talk to in any case."

"And not a word for your sister I suppose?" She pushed her hair back with her hand and tried to look martyred, but did not succeed very well.

"I'm a beast, Liz, you've always known that. But I'm in a rush now. We'll get together next week, I promise."

"You better. There's the sweetest girl I want you to meet."

"Lovely." He sighed heavily. "Now would you kindly put me through to your husband."

"Of course. Wednesday at eight." She blew him a kiss and touched the transfer button. An instant later Thurgood-Smythe was on the screen.

"Someone broke into my apartment while I was away," Jan said.

"Petty crime is getting very bad this winter. But not my department, as you must know. I'll transfer this to the police . . ."

"Perhaps it *is* your department. Nothing was stolen but I found this wired to the TV." He held it up. "Very compact, very expensive. I haven't looked inside it but I imagine it has full sound video and broadcasts a signal for at least a kilometer. If it doesn't belong to your people it is certainly something you would want to know about."

"Indeed it is. I'll look into it at once. Are you involved in anything the industrial espionage people might have an interest in?"

"No. Communication satellite work."

"Then it is mysterious. I'll have that gadget picked up and let you know."

Jan had just finished putting the back on the set when the door annunciator chimed. A heavy-built man with a somber expression stood outside and produced a Security identification which he held before the camera when asked.

"That was quick," Jan said, letting him in.

"You have something for me?" the man said, tonelessly.

"Yes, here it is."

The Security man pocketed the bug without looking at it. He was staring at Jan instead, coldly. "Don't mention this to Mr. Thurgood-Smythe again," he said.

"What do you mean? What are you talking about?"

"I mean exactly what I said. The matter is out of your brother-in-law's hands because of the family relationship." He turned to leave and Jan called after him, angrily.

"You can't just walk out after saying that kind of thing. Who are you to order me about? What is the meaning of this bug?"

"You tell me," the man said, turning about sharply. "Are you guilty of anything? Do you have a statement to make?"

Jan felt the color rising in his face. "Get out," he finally said. "Get out and don't bother me again. I don't know what this is about and I don't care. Just go away and stay away."

The door closed and it was the door of a cage. Jan was locked in and they were watching him from the outside.

During the day the circuitry work occupied his mind. He buried himself in the communication satellites—much to the pleasure of Sonia Amariglio—working hard to distract his thoughts. He was usually the last one to leave at night. Tired, and very glad that he was. A few drinks at the bar, sometimes even eating dinner there, staying on until he was tired enough to go home and to bed. It was foolish of him—he knew that surveillance could work as well any place—but he detested the idea that they were watching and listening in his own flat. Nor did he bother to search for any of the devices. That would be a fool's game. Better to imagine that he was being watched at all times and act accordingly.

It was the following Wednesday morning when his brother-in-law phoned him in the laboratory.

"Morning, Jan. Elizabeth asked me to call you."

The silence stretched as Jan waited. Thurgood-Smythe was silent as well, watching. It was obvious that nothing more was going to be said about Security.

"How is Liz?" Jan finally answered. "What's up?"

"Dinner tonight. She was afraid you would forget."

"I didn't forget. But I just won't be able to make it. I was going to call with my apologies . . ."

"Too late. There's someone else coming and it would be impossible to cancel now. Too embarrassing for her."

"Oh, God. She did say something about another of her girls! You couldn't . . ."

"Not easily. Better take your medicine. From the way she talks this one is really something different. From Ireland, Dublin, all the charm of the Gael and the beauty and so forth."

"Stop—I've heard it often enough in the past. See you at eight."

Jan broke the connection first, a feeble gesture that made him feel better. He *had* forgotten the damn dinner. If he had called earlier he could have gotten out of it—but not on the same day. Liz would be too unbearable. In fact it might be a good idea to go. Get a decent meal for a change—the food in the bar was giving him indigestion. And it wouldn't hurt Security to be reminded whom he was related to. And the girl might be presentable, though Liz's choices usually weren't. Social connections were more important to her than grace of form, and she had trotted out some diabolical women.

He left work early in the afternoon and mixed a drink for himself at home, soaking some of the tension out in a hot bath, then changing into a good suit. Liz would be looking daggers through him all night if he wore the shabby jacket he used for the office. She might even burn his food. It was best to stay on Liz's best side for peace of life.

The Thurgood-Smythes had a Georgian house in Barnet and the drive made Jan feel better. The countryside was attractive under the waning moon, silver and black and hard. Though it was already March, the winter showed no sign of loosening its grip. All of the lights in the front of the house appeared to be on, but there was only one car in the drive. Well, he would smile and be polite. And at least the food would be good. And he ought to play a few games of snooker with his brother-in-law, whether he wanted to be with him or not. The past was gone. The present and the future had to be innocent.

There was the sound of female laughter from the drawing room and Thurgood-Smythe rolled his eyes as he took Jan's coat. "Elizabeth has made a mistake this time," he said. "This one is actually bearable to look at."

"Thank God for small blessings. I can hardly wait."

"Is it going to be whiskey?"

"Please. Malt."

He put his gloves inside his fur hat and dropped them onto the table, then gave his hair a quick comb in the mirror. There was more laughter and the clink of glasses and he followed the sound. Thurgood-Smythe was bent over the drinks trolley. Elizabeth waved to him and the other woman on the sofa turned toward him and smiled.

It was Sara.

Sixteen

It took all of Jan's will, all of his years of practice at school in not showing emotion, to stop himself from letting his jaw hang or from popping his eyes. "Hello, Liz," he said, in what was definitely not his normal voice, and walked around the couch to kiss her on the cheek. She hugged him to her.

"Darling, so wonderful to see you. I've even made you a special meal, you'll see."

Thurgood-Smythe passed him a drink in a natural way, then refreshed his own. Didn't they know? Was this a farce—or a trap? He finally let himself look at Sara who was sitting demurely, knees together, sipping a small sherry. Her dress was long and dark green, with an old-fashioned look, a gold brooch at her throat the only jewelry.

"Jan, I want you to meet Orla Mountcharles. From Dublin. We went to the same school, not at the same time of course. Now we belong to the same bridge club and I couldn't resist bringing her home so we could chat some more. I knew you wouldn't mind, isn't that right?"

"My pleasure. You've a treat in store, Miss Mountcharles, if you've never tasted Liz's cooking before."

"Orla, please, we're not too formal at home." There was a touch of Irish accent to her voice. She smiled at him warmly, then sipped delicately at her sherry. He desperately drank half the whiskey in a gulp and started coughing.

"Sorry, not enough water?" Thurgood-Smythe asked, hurrying over with the jug.

"Please," Jan gasped. "Sorry about that."

"You're just out of training. Have another one and I'll show you the new cloth on the snooker table."

"Finally replaced. It would have had value as an antique in a few more years."

"Indeed. But you can roll into the top pocket now, you don't need to pot with force to get over that ripple."

It was easy to chat like that, to turn away and follow to the billiard room. What was she doing here? What was this madness?

Dinner was not the trial he thought it would be. The food—as always—was wonderful, beef Wellington with four kinds of vegetables. Sara was demure and quiet, and talking with her was like playing a role on stage. He hadn't realized how much he had missed her, how empty he had felt when he knew that he would never see her again. Yet here she was—in the heart of Security. There was an explanation, of course, but he did not dare ask it. The talk was light, the food, and brandy after, very good. He even managed to play snooker and beat Thurgood-Smythe two games out of three.

"Too good for me," his brother-in-law said.

"Don't apologize—just pay up the five quid you owe me."

"Did we really agree on a fiver a game? All right, you're correct of course. Better than usual, our little Irish colleen."

"Better! Smashing is the word. Where on earth did Liz ever find one like this?"

"The bridge club, she said. I may take the game up myself if this is what the players look like."

"Well don't let on to Liz or she'll be insufferable and she'll be throwing a new one at my head every night."

"Settle for this one, you could do a lot worse."

"I might very well do that."

There was no hint of duplicity or hidden motives in Thurgood-Smythe's voice. The Security officer seemed far away. Could it be true, Jan kept asking himself. Has she really been accepted as an Irish girl? Then, perhaps she is one. He must know.

"It's starting to snow again," Sara said later, as they were getting their coats. "I do hate to drive in the snow."

Liz impaled Jan with the sternest of looks while her husband, in the background, rolled his eyes heavenward and grinned.

"The roads aren't bad yet," Jan said weakly.

"But they'll only get *worse*," Liz insisted, and went so far as to jab her elbow into his ribs when Sara faced away. "This is no night for a girl to drive alone." Her gaze, when it rested on Jan, would have frozen a pail of water.

"No, of course you're right," he hurried to say. "Orla, perhaps I can drive you?"

"I don't want to take you out of your way . . ."

"Not a problem," Thurgood-Smythe said. "He's no more than five minutes from the West End. And I'll have one of my drivers bring the car around to your club in the morning."

"Then it is all set," Liz said, smiling her warmest. "So you needn't worry about the drive at all."

Jan made his good-byes, kissed his sister affectionately, then went to get the car. While the heater took the chill off the interior he scrawled a quick note and palmed it. Sara was waiting at the front door and he held the door open for her, handing her the note as she came in. She had just enough time to read the two words there before the courtesy light went out. CAR BUGGED. As soon as they were out of sight of the house she nodded agreement.

"Where can I take you, Orla?" he asked.

"I really am sorry to make you go out of your way. It's the Irish Club in Belgravia, a bit of the ould sod abroad as people say. I always stay there when I'm in London. It's not really grand, but very homey. With a friendly little bar. They do a lovely hot whiskey, Irish whiskey of course."

"Of course. I can't say I ever had any."

"Then you must try. You will come in, won't you? Just for a few minutes. It's really not late yet."

This innocent invitation was driven home by a firm nod of her head and a slow and languid wink.

"Well, perhaps for a few minutes. It's nice of you to ask."

The conversation continued in this same light vein as he drove down the nearly empty Finchley Road and into Marble Arch. She gave him instructions; the club was easy enough to find. He parked just in front of the entrance and they entered, brushing melting snow from their coats. Except for one other couple they had the bar to themselves. While the waitress took the drink order Sara wrote on the back of the note he had given her earlier. He looked at it as soon as the girl turned away.

STILL SOUND BUGGED. ACCEPT INVITATION TO

COME TO MY ROOM. LEAVE ALL YOUR CLOTHES IN BATHROOM THERE.

He raised his eyebrows high at the invitation and Sara smiled and stuck her tongue out at him in mock anger. While they talked he shredded the note in his pocket.

The hot whiskies were very good, their play-acting seduction even better. No, he didn't think her bold; yes, people would misunderstand if they went to the room together. Right, he would go first with the key and leave the door unlocked.

In her room the curtains were closed and the bed turned back temptingly. He undressed in the bathroom as he had been instructed and found a heavy terry cloth bathrobe behind the door which he put on. Sara came in and he heard her lock the hall door. She had her fingers to her lips when he came out, and did not talk until she had closed the bathroom door behind him and turned on the radio.

"Sit down here and keep your voice low. You know that you are under Security surveillance?"

"Yes, of course."

"Then your clothes are undoubtedly bugged. But we're safe enough away from them. The Irish are very proud of their independence and this club is swept and debugged daily. Security gave up years ago. They lost so many devices that they were supplying the Irish intelligence services with all they needed."

"Then tell me quickly—what happened to Uri?"

"He's safe, and out of the country. Thanks to you."

She pulled him close and hugged him, giving him a warm and lingering kiss. But when his arms went around her as well she wriggled free and sat on the edge of the bed.

"Take the armchair," she said. "We need to talk. First."

"Well, as long as you say first. Would you start by telling me just who you are and how Orla got into my sister's house."

"It's the best cover we have, so I don't jeopardize it by using it too often. We've done a lot of favors for the Irish government; this is something they've done in return. Absolutely solid identification, birth, school records, the lot. All with my fingerprints and details. It was when we were running your records through the computer to see how to contact you again that the bells began to ring. Orla Mountcharles *did* go to Roedean, some years after your sister. The rest was easy. I boned up on the school, saw some friends of friends of friends, and was invited to join the bridge club. The rest was as natural as the law of gravity."

"I know! Expose Liz to a new girl in town, hopefully with fairly good looks, but preferably with good connections, and the trap is instantly sprung. Home and dinner with little brother. But isn't it damn risky with the keen nose of Thurgood-Smythe sniffing the air?"

"I don't think it sniffs quite as well in the cloister of his own home. This is really the safest way."

"If you say so. But what makes you think my clothes are bugged?"

"Experience. The Irish have a lovely collection of intelligence devices. Security builds them into belt buckles, pens, the metal spines of notebooks, anything. They don't broadcast but record digitally on a molecular level to be played back later. Virtually indetectable without taking to pieces every item you possess. Best to think you are bugged at all times. I only hope your body is still all right."

"Want to find out?"

"That is *not* what I meant. Have you had any surgery or dental work done since you came back from Scotland?"

"No, nothing."

"Then you must still be clean. They have put recording devices inside bridgework, even implanted them in bones. They are very skilled."

"This does very little for my morale." He pointed to the bottle of Malvern water on the nightstand. "You wouldn't have a drop of whiskey to go with that, would you?"

"I would. Irish, of course, Paddy's."

"I'm acquiring the taste."

He poured one for each of them, then dropped back into the deep chair. "I'm worried. As much as I love seeing you—I don't think there is anything more I can do for the resistance."

"It will be difficult, but not insurmountable. You remember I told you that you were the most vital man we had."

"Yes. But you didn't say why."

"Your work on the satellites. That means you have access to the orbiting stations."

"It does. In fact I have been putting off a trip for some time now. I have to examine one of the old comsats in situ, in space and in free fall. Everything will change when we bring it down to Earth, to the lab. Why is this important?"

"Because you can be a contact with the deep spacers. Through them we have opened lines of communication with a number of planets. Not perfect, but improving. And there is a revolt brewing already, the miners on Alpha Aurigae Two. They have a chance of success if we can get in contact with them again. But the government is aware that trouble is starting out there and Security has clamped a lid on everything. There is no way of getting a message to our people on the ships from Earth. You should be able to manage it on the station. We've worked out a way . . ."

"You're frowning," Jan said softly. "When you get all worked up like this you frown. You will get wrinkles if you keep it up."

"But I want to explain . . ."

"Can't it keep, just for a little bit?" he asked, taking her hands in his, bending to put his lips on her forehead.

"Of course it can. You are absolutely right. Come, cure my wrinkles," she said, pulling him down to her.

Seventeen

Sonia Amariglio was ecstatic next day when Jan told her that he felt it was time to examine the satellite in space.

"Marvelous!" she said, clapping her hands. "It just floats up there and no one has the intelligence to poke in the nose at the circuitry and see what has gone wrong. I get so angry I want to go myself."

"You should. A trip into space must be something to remember."

"Memories I would love to have. But this ancient machine does not run so well." She patted her ample bosom somewhere in the region of her heart. "The doctors say the acceleration would not be good for my tick-tock . . ."

"I'm so sorry. I'm being stupid, I didn't know."

"Please, Jan, do not apologize. As long as I stay out of spaceships they say I will live forever. It is enough that you will go— and will make a much better job of it. When can you leave?"

"I must finish the circuit that I'm in the middle of now, the multiresonant repeater. A week, ten days at the outside."

Sonia was sifting through the papers on her desk and extracted a gray UNOSA folder which she flipped through. "Yes, here it is. A shuttle for Satellite Station leaving on March twentieth. I'll book you a place on it now."

"Very good." Very good indeed. This was the shuttle Sara had told him to be sure to be on, so that the schedules would mesh correctly.

Jan was whistling when he went back to work, a bit of "Sheep

May Safely Graze." He became aware of the irony of the title and
his present condition. He wasn't going to graze safely anymore—
and he was glad of it. Ever since the beginning of surveillance he
had been over-careful, walking on eggs. But no more of that. Seeing Sara, loving Sara, had put an end to that period of formless
fear. He would not stop what he was doing just because they were
watching him closely. It would make the work more difficult but
it would not stop it. Not only would he work with the resistance,
but he would do a little resisting on his own. As a specialist in
microcircuits he was very interested in seeing just what sort of devices surveillance had come up with.

So far he had been unsuccessful. He had bought a new note-
book to replace the one he had sawn open, then obtained a replacement ID card for the one inadvertently destroyed. Today it
was the turn of his pen, the gold pen Liz had given him for
Christmas. A good place for a bug since he usually had it with
him. It was up his sleeve now, slipped there when he was pretty
sure no optic pickups were on him. Now he would try a little
skilled dissection.

A quick circuit check showed that the instrumentation on his
bench was still bug free. When he had first started this unap-
proved research problem he had found out that his multimeter
electron microscope and all of his electronic instruments were
tapped and reporting to a small transmitter. After that he used
the optical microscope, and saw to it that a short circuit of 4,000
volts went through the transmitter. It had vanished and not been
replaced.

The pen disassembled easily enough and he examined each part
carefully under the low power microscope. Nothing. And the drawn
metal case looked too thin to hold any components; he put a few
volts through it as well as a quick blast of radiation for the printed
circuitry just in case he was wrong. He was about to reassemble it
when he realized that he had not looked inside the ink refill.

It was messy but rewarding. He rolled the little cylinder about
with the tip of one ink-stained finger. As thick as a grain of rice
and perhaps twice as long. Using the micromanipulators he dis-
sected it and marveled at the circuitry and electronics. Half of the
bug was powerpack, but considering the minimal current drain,
it should run six months at least without recharging. A pressure
microphone that used all of the surface of the ink supply as a
sound pickup, very ingenious. Discrimination circuits to ignore

random noise and put the device in the recording mode only for sounds of the human voice. Molecule-level recorder. Transponder circuit that, when hit with the right frequency and signal, would broadcast the stored memory at high speed. A lot of work had gone into this, just to eavesdrop on him. Misapplied technology, which was the history of so much of technology. Jan wondered if the pen had been bugged before Liz had given it to him. Thurgood-Smythe might have arranged it easily enough. She had given him the same kind of pen for Christmas and he could have exchanged one for the other.

At this point the wonderful idea struck Jan. It might be a bit of bravado, a bit of hitting back—but he was going to do it no matter what. He bent to dissect the bug, carefully excising out the Read Only Memory section of the transponder. This was something he enjoyed doing. When it was finished to his satisfaction he straightened up and rubbed the knots from his back. Then called his sister.

"Liz—I have the greatest news. I'm going to the moon!"

"I rather thought you were calling to thank me for having that lovely little Irish girl to dinner."

"Yes, that too, very kind. I'll tell you all about her when I see you. But weren't you listening? I said the moon."

"I heard you. But, Jan, really, aren't people going there all of the time?"

"Of course. But haven't you ever wanted to go yourself?"

"Not particularly. It would be rather cold, I imagine."

"Yes, it would be. Particularly without a spacesuit. In any case it's not the moon I'm going to, but a satellite. And I think it's important, and so might Smitty, and I want to tell you all about it. I'll take you out for a celebratory dinner tonight."

"How thoughtful! But impossible. We have been invited to a reception."

"Then drinks, at your place. I'll save money. Six all right?"

"If you say so. But I don't understand all the rush . . ."

"Just boyish enthusiasm. See you at six."

Thurgood-Smythe did not return home until close to seven and Elizabeth showed very little interest in either satellites or space flight so, after exhausting the conversational possibilities of Orla, Jan turned his attention to mixing a large pitcher of cocktails. A new one called Death Valley, dry, hot, and deadly the bartender had explained, and leave out most of the Tabasco for the ladies.

Thurgood-Smythe arrived in a rush, puckered his lips over the cocktail, and listened with half an ear to the satellite news. Which was undoubtedly old news to him if he were getting surveillance reports. Jan trailed after him, and had not the slightest trouble in exchanging gold pens when his brother-in-law changed jackets.

It would probably come to nothing, but there was a certain sweet feeling of success to know he had bugged the buggers. When he left they were relieved to see him go.

On his way home he stopped at a twenty-four hour shop and made the purchases as instructed. He would be meeting Sara again later this same evening and the instructions had been detailed and precise.

When he returned to his apartment he went straight to the bathroom and extracted the tester from the holder on his belt. He had done this, every day as a matter of routine, since he had found the optic bug set into the light fixture above the sink. Invasion of privacy was one thing, sheer bad taste was another, he had shouted as he had shorted the thing out. Since that time some sort of unspoken arrangement seemed to have been made. He made no attempt to search for bugs in the rest of the apartment; surveillance, as far as he could tell, kept their cameras out of the toilet. It was still clear.

Running water into the tub should take care of the sound bugs. There were so many ways of picking up voices and sound that he did not even try to look for them. Just mask them when needed. He bathed quickly, with the water still running, toweled himself dry, and dressed from the skin out with his recent purchases. Underclothes, socks, shoes, dark trousers—roughly the color of the ones he had taken off—shirt and sweater. All of his discarded clothing went into the bag that had held the new items. He pulled on his overcoat, buttoning it carefully to his chin, picked up gloves and hat and left with the bundle of clothing. With all of the bugs it might contain whirring and recording like mad.

He looked at the dashboard clock and slowed the car. He was to be at the rendezvous at nine precisely. No earlier and no later. It was a clear night and a few people were still about in the streets. He turned into the Edgeware Road and proceeded leisurely toward Little Venice. The radio was playing, a little louder than he usually liked it, but the music was also part of the arrangements.

It was exactly on the hour when he stopped at the bridge over

Regent's Canal. A man walked out of the darkness and held the car door as he opened it. A scarf around his face concealed his identity. He eased the door shut, trying not to click the latch, then drove away. Jan's identity and bugs drove away too, along with his overcoat, shoes, and clothing. Until he was back in the car surveillance did not know where he was, could not see or hear him. A man waved to him from the towpath along the canal.

Jan followed about ten paces behind him, not trying to catch up. The wind was cold, cutting through the sweater, and he hunched his shoulders, hands jammed into his pockets. Their footsteps were soundless in the snow, the night quiet except for the sound of a television playing in the distance. The frozen canal was an unbroken layer of whiteness. They came to canal boats tied by the path. After looking around the leading man jumped aboard the second one and vanished from sight. Jan did the same, finding the rear door in the darkness and pushing it open. Someone closed it and the lights came on.

"Cold evening," Jan said, looking at the girl seated at the table. Her features were invisible behind the face-changer, but her hair and figure were undoubtedly Sara's. The man he had followed in had a familiar smile and gap-toothed grin.

"Fryer," Jan said, wringing his hand strongly. "It's good to see you again."

"And yourself. Survived your little adventure I see, and did well in the bargain."

"We don't have much time," Sara said sternly. "And there is a lot to be done."

"Yes, m'am," Jan said. "Do you have a name or do I just keep calling you M'am like you were the Queen?"

"You may call me Queeny, my good man." There was mischief in her voice and Fryer caught it.

"Sounds like you two met before. So you, old son, we'll call you Kingy because I'm blowed if I remember what name you used last time. Now I have some good beer down in the bilge and I'll get it and we'll get on with the night's business."

They had just time enough for a warm embrace before Fryer clattered back up the stairs.

"Here you are," Fryer said, setting two heavy bottles on the deck. He dropped a metal box next to them and went to get a towel from the galley to wipe them dry. There were glasses ready on the table; Jan unscrewed one of the tops and poured them full.

"Home brew," Fryer said. "Better than the slops they serve in the pubs." He drained his glass in a single go and began opening the seals on the box while Jan poured him a second one. When the top came off Fryer lifted two small aluminum foil envelopes out of the box and set them on the table.

"To all appearances these are ordinary TV recordings," Sara said. "In fact you could play them on your set at home. One is an organ recital, the other a comedy program. Put them in the bag you will be taking with you—along with some recordings of your own. Make no attempt to hide them. Recordings like these are stock in trade with the spacers and there will be plenty about."

"Why are these so special?" Jan asked.

"Fryer, will you go on deck as a lookout?" Sara asked.

"That's the way, Queeny. What they don't know they can't tell."

He picked up the full bottle of beer and went out. As soon as the door closed Sara pulled off the face-changer and Jan had her in his arms, kissing her with a passion that surprised both of them.

"Not now, please, there is so little time," Sara said, trying to push him away.

"When will there be time? Tell me right now or I won't let you go."

"Jan—tomorrow then. Pick me up at the club and we'll go out for dinner."

"And for afters?"

"You know what you'll have for afters." She laughed and pulled away, sitting on the far side of the table from him.

"Maybe my sister is right," Jan said. "I might be the falling-in-love kind after all . . ."

"Please don't talk like that. Not now—or ever. There is only ten minutes before your car comes back, we must finish this."

He opened his mouth to speak—but did not. He nodded instead and she relaxed. But he noticed that she was wringing her fingers together, unknowingly. They would talk tomorrow. She pushed the recordings over to him.

"This is the important one, the organ recital," she said. "I don't know how it is done, but a computer memory has been worked into the background noise, the static."

"Of course! What an interesting idea. Any computer memory is composed of two signals, a yes and a no, that is all you have in binary. So a memory could be stretched out, modulated, changed in frequency, dropped in as apparently random bits of surface noise. And without the key no one else would be able to read it."

"I'm sure you're right. This is the way we have communicated in the past. But it is clumsy and slow and many of the recordings go astray. A new system has been worked out—and details are on this disk. This one *must* get through. The situation out there is ready to blow, and it will go up as soon as we can establish reliable communication. This will be just the beginning. Other planets will follow."

"All right," Jan said, putting the envelopes into his shirt pocket and buttoning the flap. "But why two of them?"

"Our contact on the deep spacer is sure he has been spotted, that the recording will be intercepted. So you will give the dummy to the first man that contacts you. Save the second for the real agent."

"How will I know what to do?"

"You will be watched. As soon as you are used to working in space you will be on your own. You will be contacted then. Whoever approaches you will use the phrase, 'Have you checked your safety line lately?' Give him the recording."

"The dummy?"

"Correct. The real agent will then come to you for the proper recording."

"It all sounds hideously complicated."

"It has to be. Just follow orders."

The cabin door creaked open slightly and Fryer spoke through the crack.

"Car coming in two minutes," he said. "Let's go."

Eighteen

In the beginning the shuttle trip was very much like a flight by normal jet. Jan had flown often enough for the novelty to have worn off. He had read most of the way across the Atlantic, and the only aerial view he had had of Cape Canaveral was of the tropical cloud bank that covered it. A ramp had sealed the jet to the terminal, and it was through another ramp that he had boarded the shuttle. Except for the lack of windows the interior was just like that of a normal aircraft. The TV screen before each passenger showed a reassuring meadow landscape, with nodding lilies and billowing white clouds, matched by the equally reassuring strains of Beethoven's "Pastoral." Liftoff, with a maximum of one and a half G acceleration was surely greater than a normal takeoff, but not of a surprising order. Even when the shielding had slipped back from the nose camera and a view of space had replaced the lilies, there was no great feeling of difference. It could have been just another TV program. Only when acceleration ceased completely and they were in free fall was the real change apparent. Despite the antinausea drugs the passengers had taken, the psychological effect was strong enough to affect a number of stomachs. The attendant was busy with the barfbags, and a hand-vacuum for the bits that missed the bags.

The reality of the occasion finally penetrated when a star ahead grew brighter, then took form. Satellite Station. A specialized satellite for space vehicles. Here the deep spacers came, ships built in the vacuum of space and destined never to enter a planet's atmosphere. They were served by stocky, winged shuttles like this one, vehicles that could land and take off from the planet below. There were spidery space tugs as well, skeletal ships that serviced the Earth satellites, repairing or replacing them as needed. This was the reason for Jan's presence here. A presence that would, hopefully, serve a dual purpose.

With quick blasts from its maneuvering jets the shuttle drifted toward the great bulk of the station, guided to final contact by computer control from the station itself. There was a slight tremor when they touched the contact pads, but no rebound as the magnetic grapples took hold. Short moments later the green light came on above the door and the steward spun the unlocking wheel. Five more uniformed men came aboard, kicking off easily and floating the length of the cabin, then grabbing the hand rails for graceful stops.

"Now you've seen them do it," the steward said. "But please don't try it yourself if you are not experienced. Most of you gentlemen have technical knowledge so you will know what I mean when I remind you that a body in free fall has no weight—but it still has mass. If you push off and hit the wall headfirst, you will feel as though you have hit the wall headfirst. So please remain seated as instructed, with your belts secured. The assistants will guide you out one at a time. Gently as though you were in your mother's arms."

While the steward was talking, four men in the first rows unbelted and kicked themselves free. Experienced spacers by their movements. Jan knew better than to even try. He unlocked his belt when instructed, felt himself lifted and floated the length of the cabin.

"Grab the cable and don't let go until you reach the far end."

A rubbery endless cable emerged from a hole in the boarding tube's wall and moved steadily toward the station. A silvery panel on the tube must have had a weak magnetic field—there was undoubtedly an iron core to the cable—for the cable clung to the wall, sliding with an irritating squeaking sound. Yet it came away easily enough. Jan grabbed onto it and was towed the length of the tube, to the circular bay at the far end.

"Let go now," the man waiting there called out. "I'll guide you to a stop." He did it easily and swung Jan toward the rail to which his toes were hooked. "Do you think you can pull yourself hand-over-hand to that opening to the transfer room?"

"I can only try," Jan said, attempting the not too easy task. It worked well enough, though his legs did tend to float up over his head—if over were the right word. A ladder went down into the transfer room, leading to an open door. Four men were already in the small room beyond and the attendant closed the door as soon as Jan was in. The room began to move sideways.

"As we accelerate to match the station's rotation your weight will gradually return. The red wall will become the floor. Please orientate toward it so you will be able to stand on it."

As the spin increased so did their apparent weight. By the time the transfer room had matched the rotation speed of the station they stood solidly on a floor and waited for the attendant to open the hatch. Perfectly normal steps led downward into the station. Jan went first. The stairway led to a larger room with a number of exits. A tall, blond man was waiting there, looking at the new arrivals. He walked toward Jan.

"Engineer Kulozik?" he asked.

"That's right."

"I'm Kjell Norrvall." He put his hand out. "In charge of satellite maintenance. A pleasure to have you here."

"My pleasure. Getting into space."

"We're not exactly interstellar here—but we're still a long way from Earth. Look, I don't know if you're hungry or not, but I just came off shift and I'm starving."

"Give me a few minutes and I think I'll be able to eat. This going in and out of gravity isn't the easiest thing on the stomach."

"Neither is coming in on the wee-waw express with all the white bags . . ."

"Kjell, please . . ."

"Sorry. Change the subject. Good to see you here. First engineer from the London lab in over five years."

"It can't be."

"Certainly is. They sit there on their fat *balder*—present company excepted—and tell us what to do up here without the slightest idea of what our problems are. So you are welcome, I mean that. So you'll excuse my bad Norwegian jokes, yes?"

"Yes, of course. As soon as I settle down I'll make some myself."

"Right in here."

There was quiet background music in the dining room which had been decorated with some degree of taste. The flowers along the wall only looked like plastic when one came close. A few men were queuing at the self-service counter, but Jan had no desire to get that close to food quite yet.

"I'll find a table," he said.

"Can I get you anything?"

"Just a cup of tea."

"No problem."

Jan tried not to look too closely at the meal Kjell was wolfing with great enthusiasm; the tea went down very well and he was happy with that.

"When do I get to see the satellite?" Jan asked.

"As soon as we finish here, if you like. Your bag will be in your room waiting for you. Before I forget, here's the key, the number is on it. I'll show you how a spacesuit works and we can go out."

"Is it that easy—going into space?"

"Yes and no. The suits are about as foolproof as they can be made, so that's not a worry. And the only way to learn to work in zero-G in space is to go out and do it. You won't be flying, that takes a long time to learn, so I'll take you out in a powered suit and anchor you. Bring you back the same way. You can work as long as you want, to get the hang of tool using, then shout into the radio when you've had enough. You'll never be out there alone. One of us will get to you within sixty seconds. Nothing to worry about."

Kjell pushed his plate away and started on a large and violently red sweet. Jan turned his eyes away. The fabric paneling on the walls was attractive.

"No windows," Jan said. "I haven't seen one since I arrived."

"You won't either—only one is in the control tower. We're in geosynchronous orbit here, where most of the satellites are. Also right in the middle of a Van Allen belt. Plenty of radiation out there—but plenty of shielding too in these walls. The suits we use have heavy shielding as well, and even with that we don't go out during solar storms."

"What is the situation now?"

"Quiet. And it should stay that way. Ready?"

"Lead the way."

Everything that could be automated in the spacesuits was—with multiple standby and fail-safe circuits. Internal temperature, oxygen demand, humidity controls were all computer controlled. As was the control input.

"You just talk to the suit," Kjell said. "Call it suit control, tell it what you want, then say end suit control when you are finished. Like this." He lifted the bowllike helmet and spoke into it. "Suit control, give me a status report."

"*Unoccupied, all internal controls off, oxygen tank full, batteries fully charged.*" The voice was mechanical, but clear.

"Are there specific commands or phrases?" Jan asked.

"No, just speak clearly and the discrimination circuits will sort out the command words and phrases. It'll query if there is any doubt, and repeat any commands before actuating them."

"Sounds simple enough—I hope it is. Shall we start?"

"Now's the time. Sit down and put your legs in here . . ."

It went easily and Jan had faith in the suit circuitry when it warned him that his right glove wasn't sealed completely. With the helmet in place he lumbered after Kjell into the airlock. His suit unwrinkled as the pressure dropped and when it hit zero the outer door automatically unlocked.

"Here we go," Kjell's voice said on the radio hookup, and pushed them out through the opening.

They were on the dark side of the station. Words had not prepared Jan for the sight of the stars, unmasked by any atmosphere or pictured on a screen. There seemed to be too many of them, filling all of space. Varying in brightness and color. He knew the arctic sky at night—but that had only been a suggestion of the grandeur and beauty that filled space around him. Long minutes passed without his realizing it, until Kjell spoke.

"It always hits you like that. But the first time is special."

"Unbelievable!"

"And it's not going away—so we can get some work done now."

"Sorry."

"Don't be. I feel the same way."

Kjell jetted them to the comsat which was anchored to a spar. The bulk of a deep spacer was not far beyond. Some men were working on her hull and there was the sudden red flare of a laser welder. Seen in space, in its correct environment, the communication satellite was more impressive than it had ever looked in the sterile room on Earth. It was gouged and eroded by years of bombardment of microparticles. They clipped onto it and Jan pointed out the cover plates he wanted removed. He watched closely as Kjell used the counter-rotating powered screwdriver. Then he tried it himself, clumsily at first but with increasing skill. After an hour of this he found the fatigue creeping up so he stopped and they returned. He turned in soon after and slept very well indeed.

When they went out again during the next work period he had the metal recording envelopes in his pocket. It was very easy to slip them into the outer leg pocket of his suit.

By the third day he was working well and Kjell seemed satisfied with his progress.

"I'm going to leave you alone now. Shout if you need some help—I'll be inside that navsat there," he said.

"I hope not. I have these boards out where I can get prods to them so I'm all set for a while. Thanks for the help."

"More thanks to you. This equipment has been waiting years for your master's touch."

Jan must have been under constant observation—or his radio messages were being monitored. Probably both. He was still unshipping his monitor screen when a spacesuited figure moved out from behind the nearby spacer, drifting his way with skillful puffs of gas from his backpack. The man came close, stopped, then touched his helmet to Jan's. Their radios were off but the sound of his voice came clearly through the contacting surfaces.

"Have you checked your safety line lately?"

His features were invisible behind the mirrored helmet. Jan fumbled the recording out of his pocket and passed it through the beam of his work light. It was the correct one. The man took it from his hand and pushed off at the same instant, turning as he drifted away.

A second man appeared out of the darkness, moving fast, faster than Jan had ever seen one of the suits move before. It was on a collision course and he slammed into the first man with a soundless impact, triggering the laser welder he held before him just as they hit.

It was a microsecond burst, a jet of brilliant red light that burned a gaping hole through suit and man in an instant. Oxygen puffed out and froze into a cloud of tiny brilliant crystals. There was no radioed alarm either; the attacker must have placed the beam to destroy the suit computer as well.

Jan was still rigid with shock when the second man let the laser swing from its line and grabbed the dead man, triggering his jets at the same time. They must have had specially fitted high-pressure orifices because the two figures accelerated away swiftly—then separated. The attacker reversed thrust, but no longer held onto the dead man. The corpse went out and out, leaving a comet tail of frozen oxygen, growing smaller, dwindling from sight.

The other man braked to a stop next to Jan and held his hand out. For a long moment Jan, still shocked by the speed and deadliness of the attack, did not realize what was needed. Then he reached into his pocket and extracted the second recording, passing it over. He could not help recoiling when the other helmet moved and pressed against his.

"Well done," the distant voice said.

Then he was gone.

Nineteen

Two days later, in the middle of a sleep period, Jan was woken by the shrill beep-beep of the phone. He blinked at the illuminated time readout; he had only been asleep about three hours. With a muttered grumble he turned on the phone and Sonia Amariglio's features filled the screen.

"Jan, are you there?" she said. "My screen's dark."

Still hoping to get back to sleep, he switched to infrared pickup instead of turning on the light. His image would be black and white, but clear enough for the phone.

"I was afraid you would be sleeping," Sonia said. "I am sorry to awaken you."

"That's all right. I had to get up to answer the phone anyway."

She pursed her lips in concentration—then smiled. "Ohh, a joke. Very good." The smile vanished. "It is important I call because you must return to London at once. This is a necessity."

"I'm not really finished here."

"I am sorry. But you will have to leave the work. It is hard to explain."

Jan had the sudden cold feeling that this was not her doing, that she had been ordered to recall him. He did not want to press her. "All right then. I'll get through to shuttle control and call you back . . ."

"That will not be needed. The flight leaves in about two hours and you have been booked on it. There will be time?"

"Yes, just about. I'll phone you as soon as I get in."

Jan broke the connection and turned on the lights, yawning and rubbing his prickly face. Somebody wanted him out of the station and back to London in a hurry. It had to be Security. But why? The answer seemed obvious enough. Men just don't disappear in space. Yet one had. Could it be that? He had the rather unhappy sensation that it was.

The return flight was an easy one—he was well adjusted to the sensation of free fall by now and he felt strangely heavy when he walked down the ramp on Earth. In a few days he had become used to the reduced gravity of the station. The Atlantic flight was equally uneventful, he slept most of the way. His eyes were gritty but he felt rested when he climbed from the plane in Heathrow. Outside was the world of weather again, and he hurried, shivering, to his waiting car where the attendant had left it. The thaw had finally set in and the snow was turning to slush. It still felt cold to someone acclimatized to a controlled environment. His coat was in the boot and he quickly pulled it on.

When he entered his apartment the first thing he noticed was the MESSAGE WAITING light on the phone. He thumbed the button and read the display on the screen:

I WILL BE WAITING IN MY OFFICE. SEE ME AS SOON AS YOU ARRIVE.

THURGOOD—SMYTHE

It was no less than he expected. But Security, and his brother-in-law, could wait until he had washed and changed and put some decent food inside him. Rations at the station had been frozen, nourishing and boring.

While he was eating, Jan had the sudden thought that there was something else he could do when he saw Smitty. Right in the middle of Security! Dangerous, but hard to resist. When he emptied his pockets and changed clothes he managed to pick up a small device that he had constructed with some labor. Now he would find out how well it worked.

Security Central was a great, gray complex of windowless concrete buildings stretched along the north side of Marylebone. Jan had been there before and the central computer carefully remembered this fact. When he slipped his ID into the slot before the garage door, it returned it instantly to his hand and rolled open the door. He left the car in the visitors' bay and entered the lift which took him, under its own control, to the reception floor.

"Good afternoon, Engineer Kulozik," the girl behind the massive desk said, glancing at her screen. "If you will kindly take lift three."

He nodded and stepped through the security arch. There was a quiet buzzing and the guard looked up from the controls.

"Would you please step over here, your honor," he said.

This had never happened before. Jan felt a sudden coldness that he had to hide from the guard.

"What's wrong with the machine?" he asked. "I'm not carrying a gun."

"Sorry, sir. Something metallic in that pocket there. If you please."

Why had he brought it? What criminal bit of stupidity had led him to this folly? Jan put his hand slowly into his pocket and took out the device he had made and held it out before him.

"Is this what you mean?" he said.

The guard looked at the glow lighter and nodded. "Yes, sir. That's it. Lighters don't usually trip the alarm."

He bent to look carefully at it, reached for it. Jan stopped breathing. Then the man dropped his hand.

"Must be the gold plating. Sorry to bother you, sir."

Jan put his hand and the lighter into his pocket and nodded—he couldn't risk saying a word—and walked on to the open doors of the lift. They closed behind him and he relaxed, letting the lighter drop from his clenched fist. Close, entirely too close. He could not risk detection now by actuating the circuitry he had built into it. Far too dangerous.

Thurgood-Smythe sat behind the desk, unsmiling, and only nodded coldly when Jan entered. Uninvited, Jan dropped into an armchair and crossed his legs as casually as he could. "What's all this about?" he asked.

"I have a feeling you are getting into very deep trouble."

"I have the feeling that I don't know what the hell you are talking about."

Thurgood-Smythe leveled a finger like a gun, grimly angry.

"Don't try to play games with me, Jan. There's been another one of those coincidences. Soon after you arrived at Station Twelve a crewman vanished from one of the spacers."

"So? Do you think I had anything to do with it?"

"Normally I would not know or care. But the man was one of ours."

"Security? I can see why you're concerned."

"Can you? It is not that man but *you* I am concerned about." He counted slowly on his fingers. "You have access to a terminal involved in illegal tapping. Then you happen to be in Scotland during trouble at a camp. And now you are present at the time a man disappears. I don't like it."

"Coincidence. You said so yourself."

"No. I don't believe in coincidence. You are involved in security violations . . ."

"Listen, Smitty—you can't accuse me like that, without any evidence . . ."

"I don't need evidence." Thurgood-Smythe's voice had the coldness of death in it. "If you weren't my wife's brother I would have you arrested on the spot. Taken out of here and sent to interrogation and—if you lived—to a camp. For life. As far as the world would know you would simply disappear. Your name would vanish from the public files, your bank account would cease to exist, your apartment would be empty."

"You could—do this?"

"I have done it," was the flat and overwhelming answer.

"I can't believe it—it's horrible. On your word alone—where is justice . . ."

"Jan. You are stupid. There is only as much justice in the world as those who are in control of the world care to permit, to enable affairs to run smoothly. Inside this building there is no justice. None at all. Do you understand what I am saying?"

"I understand, but I can't believe it could be true. You are saying that life as I know it is not real . . ."

"It isn't. And I don't expect you to take my word for it. Words are just words. Therefore I have arranged a graphic demonstration for you. Something you cannot argue with."

Thurgood-Smythe pressed a button on his desk as he talked and the door opened. A uniformed policeman led in a man in gray prison garb, stopped him by the desk, then exited. The man just stood there, staring unseeing into space, the skin of his face limp and hanging, his eyes empty.

"Condemned to death for drug offences," Thurgood-Smythe said. "A creature like this is useless to society."

"He's a man, not a creature."

"He's a creature now. Cortical erasure before execution. He has no consciousness, no memory, no personality. Just flesh. Now we remove the flesh."

Jan gripped the chair arms, unable to speak, as his brother-in-law removed a metal case from his desk drawer. It had an insulated handle and two metal prods on the front. He walked over and stood in front of the prisoner, pressed the prods to the man's forehead, and thumbed the trigger in the handle.

The man's limbs jerked once in painful sudden convulsion, then he dropped to the floor.

"Thirty thousand volts," Thurgood-Smythe said, turning to face Jan. His voice was toneless, empty of expression as he walked across the room and held the electrical device before Jan. "It might just as well have been you. It could be you—right now. Do you still not understand what I am saying?"

Jan looked with horrified fascination at the metal prods just before his face, their ends blackened and pitted. They moved closer and he recoiled involuntarily. At that moment, for the very first time, he was suddenly very frightened for himself. And for this world that he lived in. Up until now he had only been involved in a complicated game. Others could get hurt, he never would. Now the realization struck him that the rules he had always played by didn't exist. He was no longer playing. Now it was all for real. The games were over.

"Yes," he said, and his voice was hoarse. "Yes, Mr. Thurgood-Smythe, I understand what you are saying." He spoke very quietly, barely above a whisper. "This is not an argument or a discussion." He glanced down at the body sprawled on the floor. "There is something you want to tell me, isn't there? Something that you want me to do—that I am going to do."

"You are correct."

Thurgood-Smythe returned to his desk and put the instrument away. The door opened and the same policeman entered and dragged out the corpse. Horribly, by the legs, bumping the limp head across the floor. Jan turned his eyes away from it, back to his brother-in-law as he spoke.

"For Elizabeth's sake, and for that reason alone, I am not going to ask you how deeply you are involved with the resistance—although I know you are. You ignored my advice, now you will obey my instructions. You will leave here and cease any contact, stop any activity. Forever. If you fall under suspicion again, are involved in any way with illegal activity—from that moment onward

I will do nothing to protect you. You will be arrested on the spot, brought here, interrogated, then imprisoned for life. Is that clear?"

"Clear."

"Louder. I did not hear you."

"*Clear*. Yes, clear, I understand."

As Jan said the words he found a terrible anger driving out the fear. In this moment of absolute humiliation he realized how loathsome the people in power were, how impossible it would be to live with them in peace after this discovery. He did not want to die—but he knew he would never be able to live in a world where the Thurgood-Smythes were in charge. His shoulders slumped, and he lowered his face. Not in surrender, but only so that his brother-in-law would not see the rage, the anger that he felt.

His hands were thrust deep into his jacket pockets.

He depressed the button on the glow lighter.

The command signal radiated from the small but powerful transmitter inside. This activated the device concealed in the pen, clearly visible in the Security man's pocket. Upon receipt of this signal the memory bank was emptied and transmitted to the memory in the lighter. It took only microseconds. Jan let go of the button and stood up.

"Is there anything else—or can I go now?"

"It is for your own good, Jan. I gain nothing by this."

"Smitty, please. Be anything—but don't be a hypocrite." Jan couldn't prevent it; some of the anger leaked through. Thurgood-Smythe must have been expecting it because he only nodded expressionlessly. Jan had a sudden realization.

"And you hate my guts, don't you?" he said. "And you always have."

"That is absolutely true."

"Well—very good. The feeling is absolutely mutual."

Jan left then, not daring to say another word, afraid that he would go too far. He had no trouble leaving the building. Only when he was driving up the ramp did he realize what this meant.

He had gotten away with it. He had a recording in his pocket of all his brother-in-law's top Security conversations of the past weeks.

It was like carrying a bomb that could destroy him. What should he do with it? Wipe it clean, then throw the lighter into the Thames and forget forever what he had done. Automatically he turned the car toward the river. If he did anything other than this, it would be the utmost folly, a self-imposed death sentence.

The thoughts chased themselves through his head one after another and he could not think clearly. He almost ran through a red light that he did not see, would have run it if the car's computer had not caught his dereliction of duty and applied the brakes.

This was the sticking point, he realized. This was the moment when he determined what the rest of his life would be like.

He pulled the car into Savoy Street and braked to a stop, too preoccupied to drive. Nor could he sit still. He climbed out and locked the car, and started for the river. Then stopped. No, he hadn't made his mind up yet, that was the worst part. He still didn't know what he should do. He unlocked the trunk and rummaged in his tool box there until he found a pair of small earphones; he stuffed them into his pocket and turned toward the river.

A raw wind had sprung up and the slush was turning into rutted ice again. Other than a few distant, hurrying figures, he had the Victoria Embankment to himself. He stood at the stone rail, staring unseeingly at the ice floes in the gray water hurrying toward the sea. The lighter was in his hand. All he had to do was pull it out and throw it from him and the indecision would be over. He took it out and looked at it. So small, as tiny as a man's life.

With his other hand he plugged the earphones into the opening in its base.

He could still throw the thing away. But he had to hear what Thurgood-Smythe said in the security of his office, when talking to others of his kind. He had to know at least that much.

The tiny voices sounded in the privacy of his ear. Incomprehensible for the most part, conversations about matters, names he didn't know, complicated affairs discussed in a cold and businesslike way. The experts could have a field day with this, would be able to unravel and make sense of all the references and commands. It made hardly any sense at all to Jan. He jumped to the ending and caught some of their own conversation, then jumped back earlier in the day. Nothing of any real interest. Then he froze as the words sounded clearly:

"Yes, that's right, the Israeli girl. We've had enough trouble from her and we are going to finish it tonight. Wait until the meeting in the canal boat is under way and then . . ."

Sara—in danger!

Jan made the decision—unaware at the moment that he had even decided. He hurried, not running, that would be noticed, back to his car through the growing dusk. This evening—tonight! Could he get there first?

He drove coldly and carefully, making the best time possible. The canal boat. It must be the one on the Regent's Canal where they had met last time. How much did Security know? How did they know it? How long had they been watching their every move, toying with them? It didn't matter. He had to save Sara. Save her even if he did not save himself. She came first. The car lights came on as the sky darkened.

He must plan. Think before he acted. This car was probably sound bugged, so he had to treat it as if it were bugged. If he drove directly to Little Venice the alarm would be given at once. He would have to go part of the way on foot. There was a shopping complex on Maida Vale that would do. He drove in and parked and went into the largest shop. Through it and out the door on the far side, walking fast.

It was dark when he reached the canal. The lights were on along the towpath and a couple were walking toward him. He drew back into the shadowed protection of the trees and let them go by. Only when they had turned out of sight did he hurry to the canal boat. It was tied in the same place, dark and silent. A man stepped out of the shadows when he climbed aboard.

"I wouldn't go in there if I were you."

"Fryer, I have to, it's an emergency."

"No way, old son, a very private meeting going on . . ."

Jan struck Fryer's hand from his shoulder, pushed him away so that he stumbled and fell. Then Jan had the door open and was jumping down into the cabin.

Sara looked up, eyes wide with surprise as he burst in.

So did Sonia Amariglio, the head of the satellite laboratories who was sitting across the table from her.

Twenty

Before Jan could react he was seized from behind so tightly that the air was driven from his lungs as he was dragged down.

"Bring him in, Fryer," Sara said, and he was released, pushed forward. "Close the door, quickly."

"You should not be here," Sonia said. "It is a dangerous mistake . . ."

"Listen, there is no time," Jan broke in. "Thurgood-Smythe knows about you, Sara, and he knows about this meeting. The police are on the way now. You have to get out of here, quickly."

They were stunned. Fryer broke the silence.

"Transportation won't be here for an hour more. But I can take care of this one." He pointed at Sonia. "The ice in the canal is still sound. I know a way out that way. But just for me."

"Get going then," Jan ordered. He looked at Sara. "Come with me. If we can reach my car we can start moving, stay ahead of them."

The light was out and the door open. As Sonia went by she reached out to touch Jan's face lightly. "Now I can tell you how wonderful the work has been that you have done for us all. Thank you, Jan." Then she was gone and they climbed the steps after her. The towpath was still clear and Jan and Sara hurried down it.

"I don't see anyone," she said.

"I only hope that you're right."

They ran as fast as they could on the slippery surface, to the bridge over the canal. As they were about to turn onto it a car tore around the corner of the road, motor racing, and accelerated toward them.

"Under the trees!" Jan said, pulling Sara after him. "They may not have seen us."

Running, crashing through unseen branches, while the car grew louder and louder behind them. It hit the humpback bridge with a loud clashing of springs, was up and over, the headlights sweeping toward them. Jan fell face forward, dragging Sara down beside him.

The lights flashed past them and were gone. There was a metallic crash as the car turned into the towpath, riding down the sign that barred the way.

"Come on," Jan said, pulling Sara to her feet. "They'll start searching as soon as they find the boat is empty."

They ran down the first turning, running for their lives. At the next street there were pedestrians so they had to slow to a fast walk. There were more people about now—no sign of pursuit. They slowed to catch their breath.

"Can you tell me what you found out?" Sara asked.

"I'm probably bugged and whatever we say is being recorded."

"Your clothing will be destroyed. But I must know, now, what has happened."

"I bugged my dear brother-in-law, that's what. The biter bit. I have a recording, right here in my pocket, of all of his recent conversations. I couldn't understand most of it—but the last bit was clear enough. Recorded today. Planning to break up the meeting tonight on the canal boat. Those were his words. And he referred to 'the Israeli girl.'"

Sara gasped; her fingers dug into his arm. "How much can they know?"

"An awful lot."

"Then I must get away from London, out of this country at once. And your recording must reach our people. They must be warned."

"Can you do that?"

"I think so. What about you?"

"Unless they know I have been here tonight I'm safe enough." There was no point in telling her about the deadly warning he had received. Her survival came first. When that had been arranged he would worry about himself. "I've checked my car for optic bugs and it should be clean. Tell me now where you are going and don't talk again after we get in."

"The security barrier for vehicles is at Liverpool Road. Find a quiet street this side of it and let me out. I'm going into Islington."

"All right." They walked in silence for a moment, coming out of the side streets into Maida Vale. "The woman in the boat," Jan said. "What about her?"

"Can you forget you saw Sonia tonight?"

"It will be hard. Is she important?"

"Right at the top level in the London organization. One of the best people we have."

"I'm sure of that. Here we are. No talking now."

Jan unlocked the car and got in. He turned the engine and radio on, then muttered to himself. Getting out again he went and opened the boot and rattled his tool box, waving Sara into the car ahead of him. When she was seated he got in and drove slowly away.

Going down Marylebone would have been the most direct way, but Jan had no desire at all to go past Security Central. He turned instead toward St. John's Wood, through the quiet residential streets, then past Regent's Park. As he did so the music died away and a man's voice spoke loudly from the radio.

"Jan Kulozik, you are under arrest. Do not attempt to leave this vehicle. Wait for the police to arrive."

As the words crashed out of the speaker the engine died and the car coasted to a stop.

Jan's fear was mirrored in Sara's horrified eyes. Security knew where he was, had been tracking him, were coming for him. And they would find her as well.

Jan tore at the door handle but it would not move. Locked. They were trapped.

"It's not that easy, you bastards!" Jan shouted, rooting in the glove compartment for a roadmap, jamming in the cigar lighter at the same time. He pulled the map free and tore off a large square just as the lighter popped out. Holding the glowing element to the edge of the paper, blowing on it. It caught fire and he let it blaze, touching it to the rest of the map.

In a moment it was burning fiercely and he jammed it up behind the facia, in among the instruments and circuits.

The instant he did this the fire alarm began sounding and all of the doors unlocked.

"Run!" he said, and they jumped free of the car.

Once again they fled, not knowing how much time they had before the police arrived, running for their lives. Into the dark side streets, racing to put distance between themselves and the car. Running until Sara could run no more, then going on, walking as fast as she was able. There were no signs of any pursuers. Walking until they were in the safety of the crowded streets of Camden Town.

"I'm coming with you," Jan said. "They know all about me, about my connection with the resistance. I've been warned. Can you get me out?"

"I'm sorry I ever got you involved in this, Jan."

"I'm glad you did."

"Two people will be no harder than one. We are trying for Ireland. But you realize, if you do this thing, you'll be a man without a country. You won't ever be able to come home again."

"I'm that already. If they catch me I'm a dead man. Perhaps this way I can be with you. I'd like that. Because I love you."

"Jan, please . . ."

"What's wrong? I didn't realize it myself until I blurted it out just now. Sorry I can't be more romantic. That's my engineer's love song, I guess. And how about you?"

"We can't discuss this now, it's not the time . . ."

Jan took Sara by the shoulders, stopping her, moving them against a shop window. He looked at her, and lightly held her chin when she tried to turn away.

"There's no better time," he said. "I've just declared my undying love for you. And what do you respond?"

Sara smiled. Ever so slightly, but still she smiled, and kissed his fingers.

"You know that I am very, very fond of you. And that is all I am going to tell you now. We must go on."

As they walked he realized that he would have to settle for that. For the time being. He wondered what perverse streak had forced him to discover his love now, in this place, and declare it out loud like that. Well it was true, even if he had just admitted it to himself. True—and he was glad of it.

They were tired long before they reached their destination, yet they dared not stop. Jan had his arm around her waist, supporting her as well as he could.

"Not much . . . farther," she said.

Oakley Road was a street of once elegant rowhouses, now derelict and boarded up. Sara led the way down the crumbling steps to the basement entrance of one of them and unlocked the door, closing and sealing it carefully behind them. The hallway was pitch black, but uncluttered, and they felt their way along the wall to the furnace room in the rear. Only when this door was closed did Sara turn on the lights. There were lockers along the walls, the welcome warmth of an electric fire, and the disused furnace in the rear. She found blankets and handed him one.

"All of your clothes, shoes, everything, into the furnace. They must be burned at once. Then I'll find you some clothes."

"You better take this first," Jan said, handing her the lighter. "Get it to your electronics people, Thurgood-Smythe is in the memory inside."

"This is very important. Thank you, Jan."

They had little time for rest. There was a knock on the door a few minutes later and she went into the hall to talk with the newcomer. After that they had to hurry.

"We have to get to Hammersmith before the buses stop running. Old clothes for both of us. I have some ID, won't stand up to anything more than casual interest, but we must have something. Is everything burned?"

"Yes, all gone." Jan stirred the red ashes with the poker, turning up the smoldering mass of his wallet. ID, papers, identification, his identity. Himself. The unthinkable had happened. The life he knew was over, the world he knew gone. The future an indecipherable mystery.

"We must go now," Sara said.

"Of course. I'm coming." He buttoned the ragged but heavy coat, fighting down the feeling of despair. He took her hand as they felt their way down the dark hallway, and did not release it again until they were out in the street.

Twenty-one

It was the first time in his life that Jan had been aboard a London omnibus. He had driven past them often enough without giving them a thought. Tall, double-decked, and silent, driven by the energy captured in the large flywheel beneath the floor. During the night thick cables would hook the bus to the electrical mains, using the powerful motor to run up the revolutions of the flywheel. During the day the motor became a flywheel-driven generator to power the electric drive motors. Reliable power, nonpolluting, cheap, practical. He knew that, the theory, but he hadn't known how cold the unheated vehicle could be, how littered with rubbish, thick with the smell of unwashed bodies. He held his bit of ticket and looked out at the cars that passed and vanished down the road ahead. The bus stopped for a traffic light and two Security police got on.

Jan stared straight ahead, just as the other people on the bus did, staring at the rigid face of Sara sitting across from him. One of the men stayed by the rear entrance while the other stamped the length of the bus, looking at everyone there. No one glanced his way or appeared aware of him.

The next time the bus stopped the two of them left. Jan felt relief for a few moments, then the fear returned. Would it ever go away again?

They got down at the last stop, Hammersmith Terminal. Sara went ahead and he followed well behind as he had been instructed. The few other passengers dispersed and they were alone. Above them a car thrummed by on the elevated highway of the

M4. Sara headed for the darkness of the arches that supported it. A small man with bent shoulders stepped out to meet her. She waved Jan to join them.

"Hello, hello, you nice people come with me. Old Jemmy will show you the way." The man's scrawny neck seemed too thin to support the globe of his head. His eyes were round and staring, his fixed smile empty of any teeth. He was a fool—or a very good actor. Sara took Jan's arm as they followed Old Jemmy into the totally dark and empty streets, among the rows of ruined houses.

"Where are we going?" Jan asked.

"For a little walk," Sara said. "Just a few miles they say. We have to get past the London Security barrier before we can get transportation."

"Those friendly police who used to salute me when I drove by?"

"The very same ones."

"What happened to all the houses here? They're in ruins."

"London used to be much bigger, centuries ago, many more people. I don't know the exact figures. But population, over the entire country, was cut back to a smaller replacement level. Partly by disease and starvation, partly government policy."

"Don't tell me how they did it. Not tonight."

They were too tired to talk much after that. Plodding slowly after Old Jemmy who found his way unerringly in the darkness. He went even slower when lights appeared ahead.

"No talking now," he whispered. "Microphones about. Stay in the shadows right behind me. No noise neither or we're dead'uns."

Between two of the ruined buildings they had a brief glimpse of a cleared area ahead, well lit, with a tall wire fence down the center of it. They were very close when their guide led them into one of the buildings, an old warehouse of some kind. Out of sight of the road he produced a small flashlight and turned it on; they stumbled after the gleaming circle of light, deep into the ruins, down into the arched cellars below. He pulled some rubble and rusted sheet metal aside to uncover a door.

"In we goes," he said. "I'm coming last to close up."

It was a tunnel, damp and smelling of raw earth. Jan could not stand up fully and had to walk in a tiring hunched manner. It was long and straight and undoubtedly went under the Security barrier. There was muddy ice underfoot and they skidded across sizeable frozen puddles. Old Jemmy caught them up and passed them, leading the way again with his light. Jan's bent back was burning like fire before they reached the far end.

"Gotta keep quiet for a bit, like the other end," their guide warned as they emerged again into the frigid night. "A bit more walking and we're there."

The bit more was over an hour and Sara did not think she could make it. But Old Jemmy was far stronger than he looked, so he and Jan walked on each side of her, half supporting her. They were paralleling the motorway now and could clearly see the head-lights sweeping by in both directions. An island of light appeared ahead in the darkness and they headed for it.

"Heston services," Old Jemmy said. "End of the line. You got a bit of shelter in this house here and you can spy from the window."

He was gone before they could even thank him. Sara sat with her back to the wall, her head on her knees, while Jan found the window. The service area was no more than a hundred meters away, bright as day under the glaring yellow lights. A few passenger cars were refueling, but most of the vehicles were heavy long distance lorries.

"We are looking for a juggernaut from London Brick," Sara said. "Is it there yet?"

"Not that I can see."

"We can expect it any time now. It will stop at the last hydrogen pump. When it does we get out of here. Past the buildings to the exit ramp, beyond the lights. The driver will stop there and open the door. That's our chance."

"I'll look out for it. You take it easy."

"That's all I can do."

The cold was beginning to bite through their heavy clothing when the long, articulated shape pulled in under the lights.

"It's here," Jan said.

There was more than enough light reflected from the area to show them a path through the rubble. They worked their way around it, then climbed the low fence. After that there was a cold wait behind a dark shack until the truck rumbled to a stop; the door swung open.

"Run," Sara said, stumbling toward it.

As soon as they were in, the door slammed and the great vehicle rumbled to life. It was wonderfully warm in the cab. The driver was a big man, half seen in the darkness.

"Tea in a thermos here," he said. "Sandwiches too. Get some sleep, if you want. No stops until we reach Swansea around five. I'll drop you before the Security check. Do you know the way from there?"

"Yes," Sara said. "And thanks."

"My pleasure."

Jan did not think he would be able to sleep, but the warmth and steady vibration of the cab lulled him. The next thing he was aware of was the hissing of air brakes as the driver drew to a stop. It was still dark out, though the stars were bright and clear here. Sara was sleeping curled against him, and he stroked her hair, reluctant to awaken her.

"This is the place," the driver said.

She was awake on the instant, opening the door when they stopped.

"Good luck," the driver said. Then the door slammed and they were alone, shivering in the cold hour before dawn.

"The walk will warm us up," Sara said, leading the way.

"Where are we?" Jan asked.

"Just outside of Swansea. We head for the port. If the arrangements have been made we will go out on one of the fishing boats. Transfer to an Irish boat at sea. We've used the route before successfully."

"And then?"

"Ireland."

"Of course. I mean the future. What happens to me?"

She was silent as they plodded on, their footsteps loud in the dark silence. "There has been so much to do to get out in a hurry, I just never thought. It might be arranged for you to stay on in Ireland under another name, though you would have to be very inconspicuous. There are a lot of British spies there."

"What about Israel? You will be there, won't you?"

"Of course. Your technical skills would be respected."

Jan smiled into the night. "Enough of this respect. What about love? You, I mean. I asked you earlier."

"This is still not the time for a discussion. When we are out of here, then . . ."

"When we are safe, you mean. Will we ever be? Are you forbidden to fall in love in your work? Or can you at least pretend to be to get some cooperation . . ."

"Jan, please. You're hurting me, and yourself as well, when you talk like that. I have never lied to you. I did not have to make love to you to enlist you in the work. I did it for the same reason that you did. I wanted to. Now, for a little while, let us please not talk like this. The most dangerous part is ahead."

It was a clear, cold dawn when they walked through the city. Other early risers were up, hurrying along, breath steaming. There were no police in sight. Security here was not as tight as in London. They turned a corner and there, at the end of the ice-slick street, was the harbor. The stern of a fishing trawler could be seen.

"Where do we go?" Jan asked.

"That doorway, it's the office. They'll know in there."

As they approached it the door opened and a man stepped out and turned to face them.

It was Thurgood-Smythe.

For a single shocking instant they stood, frozen, staring at each other. Thurgood-Smythe's mouth was twisted in a slight and unhumorous smile.

"End of the line," he said.

Sara pushed Jan hard; he slipped on the ice and fell to his knees. At the same time she drew a pistol from her pocket and fired twice, rapidly, at Thurgood-Smythe. He spun about and dropped. Jan was still climbing to his feet when she turned and ran back up the street.

There were Security Police there now, blocking her way, raising their guns.

Sara fired as she ran, over and over.

They returned the fire and she crumpled and dropped.

Jan ran to her, ignoring the guns pointed at him, lifting her and holding her in his arms. There was a smear of dirt and blood on her cheek and he brushed it away. Her eyes were closed and she was not breathing.

"I'll never know," Jan whispered. "Never know."

He held her still body to him, held her tightly, unaware of his tears. Unaware of the ring of police. Not even noticing Thurgood-Smythe who stood there as well, blood dripping between his fingers that he had clamped hard about his arm.

Twenty-two

The room was white, walls, ceiling, and floor. Unblemished and cheerless. The chair was white too, as was the plain table set before it. Sterile and cold, resembling a hospital in a way, but not like a hospital at all. Not at all.

Jan sat on the chair with his arms resting on the table. His clothing was white; white sandals were on his feet. His skin was very pale, as though it were trying to conform to the all-pervading whiteness. The reddened rings around his eyes were in stark contrast to the whiteness all about him.

Someone had given him a mug of coffee and it rested on the table, still held by his fingers. He had drunk none of it and it had grown cold. His red-rimmed eyes stared unseeing into the distance. There was no distance for the room was windowless. The door opened and a white-garbed attendant came in. He held a blast hypodermic in one hand and Jan did not protest, or even notice, when his arm was lifted and the injection was blown through his skin and into his bloodstream.

The attendant went out, but he left the door open. He was back in a moment with an identical white chair which he placed on the opposite side of the table. This time he closed the door when he left.

A few minutes passed before Jan stirred and looked about, then glanced down at his hand as though aware for the first time that he was holding the cup. He raised it and sipped, then grimaced at the cold liquid. As he was pushing the cup away from him, Thurgood-Smythe entered and sat down in the chair opposite.

"Can you understand me?" he asked.

Jan frowned a second, then nodded.

"Good. You have had a shot that should pick you up a little bit. I'm afraid that you have been out of things for some time."

Jan started to talk, but burst into a fit of coughing instead. His brother-in-law waited patiently. Jan tried again. His voice was hoarse and unsteady.

"What day is it? Can you tell me what day it is?"

"That is not important," Thurgood-Smythe said, dismissing the thought with a wave of his hand. "What day it is, where you are, none of this is of any relevancy. We have other things to discuss."

"I'll not tell you anything. Nothing at all."

Thurgood-Smythe laughed uproariously at this, slapping his knee with gusto.

"That's very funny," he said. "You have been here days, weeks, months, the amount of time is unimportant as I have said. What is important is that you have told us everything that you knew. Do you understand? Every single thing that we wanted to know. This is a very sophisticated operation that we run here and we have had decades of experience. You must have heard rumors of our torture chambers—but those are rumors we start ourselves. The reality is simple efficiency. With drugs, training, electronic techniques, we simply enlisted you on our side. You were eager to tell us everything. And you did."

Anger stirred Jan, stirring him from the lassitude that still gripped him.

"I don't believe you, Smitty. You're a liar. This is part of the softening up process."

"Is it? You must believe me when I tell you that it is all over. You have nothing more to say that I want to hear. You have already told us about Sara and your meeting on the Israeli submarine, your little adventure in the Highlands, at the space station. I said *everything* and I sincerely meant it. The people we wanted to apprehend, including Sonia Amariglio, a repulsive person named Fryer, others, have all been picked up and dealt with. A few more are still at large, thinking that they enjoy freedom. Just as you thought you did. I was very happy when you were recruited, and not only for personal reasons. We have plenty of small fry to watch, but they are not important. You led us into more rarefied circles that we wanted to penetrate. And we did. Our policy is simple: we allow these little groups to form, these plots to be made and carried out, we even allow a few to escape. Sometimes. So our catch will be larger later on. We always know what is happening. We never lose."

"You're sick, Smitty. I just realized that. Sick and rotten and all the others like you. And you lie too much. I don't believe you."

"It is unimportant if you believe or not. Just listen. Your pathetic rebellion will never succeed. The Israeli authorities keep us informed of their young rebels who want to change the world . . ."

"I don't believe you!"

"Please. We follow each plot, help it to flourish, encourage the dissatisfied to join. Then crush it. Here, on the satellites, on the planets as well. They keep trying but they can never succeed. They are too foolish to even notice that they are not self-sufficient. The satellites will die if we cut off supplies. The planets as well. It is more than economics that has one planet mining, another manufacturing, another growing food. Each needs the other to survive. And we control the relationship. Are you beginning to understand at last?"

Jan drew his hands down his face, felt them trembling. When he looked at the back of his hand he saw the skin was pale, that he had lost a good deal of weight. And he believed, finally believed, that Thurgood-Smythe was at last telling him the truth.

"All right, Smitty, you've won," he said with utmost resignation. "You've taken away my memories, loyalties, my world, the woman I loved. And she didn't even have to die to keep her secret. She had already been betrayed by her own people. So you've taken it all away—except for my life. Take that too. Have done."

"No," Thurgood-Smythe said. "I won't. I lied about that as well."

"Don't try to tell me you are keeping me alive for my sister's sake?"

"No. It never mattered for an instant what she thought, had no effect on my decisions. It just helped if you believed that it did. Now I will tell you the truth. You will be kept alive because you have useful skills. We do not waste rare talents in the Scottish camps. You are going to leave Earth and you are going to a distant planet where you will work until one day, in the future, you will die. You must understand, you are just a replaceable bit of machinery to us. You have served your function here. You will be pulled out and plugged in again some other place . . ."

"I can refuse," Jan said angrily.

"I think not. You are not that important a bit of machinery. If you don't work you will be destroyed. Take my advice. Do your work with resignation. Live out a happy and productive life." Thurgood-Smythe rose. Jan looked up at him.

"Can I see Liz, anyone . . . ?"

"You are officially dead. An accident. She cried a great deal at your funeral, as did a great number of your friends. Closed coffin of course. Good-bye, Jan, we won't be meeting again."

He started toward the door and Jan shouted after him.

"You're a bastard, a bastard!" Thurgood-Smythe turned about and looked down his nose at him.

"This petty insult. Is this the best you can do? No other final words?"

"I have them, Mr. Thurgood-Smythe," Jan said in a low voice. "Should I bother telling them to you? Should I let you know how indecent the life is that you lead? You think that it will last forever. It will not. You'll be brought down. I hope I'll see it. And I will keep working for it. So you'd better have me killed because I am not going to change what I feel for you and your kind. And before you go—I want to thank you. For showing me what kind of world this really is, and allowing me to stand against it. You can go now."

Jan turned about, faced away, the prisoner dismissing his jailer.

It penetrated, as nothing else had done that he had said. A flush slowly grew on Thurgood-Smythe's skin and he started to speak. He did not. He spat in anger, slammed the door, and was gone.

In the end, Jan was the one who smiled.

WHEELWORLD

One

The sun had set four years ago and had not risen since.
But the time would be coming soon when it would lift over the
horizon again. Within a few short months it would once more
sear the planet's surface with its blue-white rays. But until that
happened the endless twilight prevailed and, in that half-light, the
great ears of mutated corn grew rich and full. A single crop, a sea
of yellow and green that stretched to the horizon in all directions
—except one. Here the field ended, bounded by a high metal fence,
and beyond the fence was the desert. A wasteland of sand and
gravel, a shadowless and endless plain that vanished into dimness
under the twilight sky. No rain fell here and nothing grew here—
in sharp contrast to the burgeoning farmland beyond. But something lived in the barren plains, a creature that found its every
need in the sterile sands.

The flattened mound of creased gray flesh must have weighed
at least six tonnes. There appeared to be no openings or organs in
its upper surface, although close examination would have revealed
that each of the nodules in the thick skin contained a silicon window that was perfectly adapted to absorb radiation from the sky.
Plant cells beneath the transparent areas, part of the intricate
symbiotic relationships of the lumper, transformed the energy into
sugar. Slowly, sluggishly, by osmotic movement between cells, the
sugar migrated to the lower portion of the creature, where it was
transformed into alcohol and stored in vacuoles until needed. A
number of other chemical processes were also taking place on this
lower surface at the same time.

The lumper was draped over a particularly rich outcropping of copper salts. Specialized cells had secreted acid to dissolve the salts, which had then been absorbed. This process had been going on for a measureless time, for the beast had no brain recognizable as such, or any organs to measure time with. It existed. It was here, eating, cropping the minerals as a cow would grass. Until, as in a grazed field, the available supply of food was gone. The time had come to move on. When the supply of nourishment fell away, chemoreceptors passed on their messages and the thousands of leg muscles in the lumper's ridged lower surface began to retract. Fueled now by the carefully stored alcohol, the muscles were actuated in a single, orgasmic spasm that sent the six tonnes of thick, carpetlike hulk hurtling over thirty meters through the air.

It cleared the fence that ringed the farm, and fell with an immense thudding impact into the two-meter high Gammacorn, crushing it flat, vanishing from sight behind the screen of green leaves and arm-long, golden ears. At its thickest point the lumper was only a meter through, so it was completely hidden from the view of the other creature that rumbled toward it.

Neither of them had a brain. The six-tonne organic beast was controlled completely by the reflex arcs that it had been born with some centuries earlier. The metallic creature weighed twenty-seven tonnes, and was controlled by a programmed computer that had been installed when it was built. Both of them had senses—but were not sentient. Each was totally unaware of the other until they met.

The meeting was very dramatic. The great form of the harvester approached, clanking and whirring industriously. It was cutting a swathe thirty meters wide through the evenly aligned rows of corn that marched away to the horizon. In a single pass it cut the corn, separated the ripe ears from the stalks, chopped the stalks to small bits, then burnt the fragments in a roaring oven. The water vapor from this instant combustion escaped from a high chimney in white trails of vapor, the ash billowed out in a black cloud from between the clanking treads to settle back to the ground. It was a very efficient machine at doing what it was supposed to do. It was not supposed to detect lumpers hidden in the corn field. It ran into the lumper and snapped off a good two hundred kilos of flesh before the alarms brought it to a halt.

As primitive as its nervous system was, the lumper was certainly aware of something as drastic as this. Chemical signals were released to activate the jumping feet and within minutes, incredibly fast for a lumper, the muscles contracted and the beast jumped again. It wasn't a very good leap though, since most of the alcohol had been exhausted. The effort was just enough to raise it a few meters into the air to land on top of the harvester. Metal bent and broke, and many more alarm signals were tripped to add to the ones already activated by the beast's presence.

Wherever the gold plating of the harvester had been torn or scratched away the lumper found toothsome steel. It settled down, firmly draped over the great machine, and began placidly to eat it.

"Don't be stupid!" Lee Ciou shouted, trying to make himself heard above the babble of voices. "Just think about stellar distances before you start talking about radio signals. Sure I could put together a big transmitter, no problem at all. I could blast out a signal that could be even received on Earth—someday. But it would take twenty-seven years to reach the nearest inhabited planet. And maybe they wouldn't even be listening. . . ."

"Order, order, order," Ivan Semenov called out, hitting the table with the gavel in time to the words. "Let us have some order. Let us speak in turn and be recognized. We are getting nowhere acting in this fashion."

"We're getting nowhere in any case!" someone shouted. "This is all a waste of time."

There were loud whistles and boos at this, and more banging of the gavel. The telephone light beside Semenov blinked rapidly and he picked up the handpiece, still banging the gavel. He listened, gave a single word of assent and hung the instrument up. He did not use the gavel again but instead raised his voice and shouted.

"Emergency!"

There was instant silence and he nodded. "Jan Kulozik—are you here?"

Jan was seated near the rear of the dome and had not taken part in the discussion. Wrapped in his own thoughts, he was scarcely aware of the shouting men, or of the silence, and had been roused only when he heard his name spoken. He stood. He was tall and wiry, and would have been thin but for the hard muscles, the result of long years of physical work. There was grease on his coveralls, and more smeared on his skin, yet he was obviously more than just a mechanic. The way he held himself, ready yet restrained, and the way he looked toward the chairman spoke as clearly as did the golden cogwheel symbol on his collar.

"Trouble in the fields at Taekeng-four," Semenov said. "Seems a lumper tangled with a harvester and knocked it out. They want you right away."

"Wait, wait for me," a small man called out, fighting his way through the crowd and hurrying after Jan. It was Chun Taekeng, head of the Taekeng family. He was as ill-tempered as he was old, wrinkled, and bald. He punched one man who did not get out of his way fast enough, and kicked ankles of others to move them aside. Jan did not slow his fast walk, so that Chun had to run, panting, to catch up with him.

The maintenance copter was in front of the machine shop, and Jan had the turbines fired and the blade turning as Chun Taekeng climbed arthritically in.

"Ought to kill the lumpers, wipe out the species," he gasped as he dropped into the seat by Jan. Jan did not answer. Even if there were any need, which there was not, wiping out the native species would be next to impossible. He ignored Chun, who was muttering angrily to himself, and opened the throttle wide as soon as they had altitude. He had to get there as soon as possible. Lumpers could be dangerous if they weren't handled right. Most of the farmers knew little about them—and cared even less.

The countryside drifted by below them like an undulating and yellow specked green blanket. Harvesting was in its final stages so that the fields of corn no longer stretched away smoothly in all directions, but had been cut back in great gaps by the harvesting machines. Rising columns of vapor marked the places where the machines were working. Only the sky was unchanging, a deep bowl of unrelieved gray stretching from horizon to horizon. Four years since he had seen the sun, Jan thought, four endless and unchanging years. People here didn't seem to notice it, but at times the unchanging halflight was more than he could bear and he would reach for the little green jar of pills.

"There, down there," Chun Taekeng called out shrilly, pointing a claw-like finger. "Land right there."

Jan ignored him. The shining gold hulk of the harvester was below them, half covered by the draped mass of the lumper. A big one, six, seven tonnes at least. It was usually only the smaller ones that reached the farms. Trucks and track-trucks were pulled up around it; a cloud of dust showed another one on its way. Jan circled slowly, while he put a call through on the radio for the Big Hook, not heeding Chun's orders to land at once. When he finally did set down, over a hundred meters from the harvester, the little man was beginning to froth. Jan was completely unaffected; it was the members of the Taekeng family who would suffer.

There was a small crowd gathered around the flattened harvester, pointing and talking excitedly. Some of the women had chilled bottles of beer in buckets and were setting out glasses. It was a carnival atmosphere, a welcome break from the monotony and drudgery of their lives. An admiring circle watched while a young man with a welding torch held it close to the draping curtain of brown flesh that hung down the side of the machine. The lumper rippled when the flame touched it; greasy tendrils of foul-smelling smoke rose from the burnt flesh.

"Turn off that torch and get out of here," Jan said.

The man gaped up slackly at Jan, mouth hanging open, but did not turn off the torch or move. There was scarcely any distance between his hairline and his eyebrows and he had a retarded look. The Taekeng family was very small and inbred.

"Chun," Jan called out to the Family Head as he tottered up, wheezing. "Get that torch away before there is trouble."

Chun shrieked with anger and emphasised his remarks with a sharp kick. The young man fled with the torch. Jan had a pair of heavy gloves tucked into his belt and he pulled them on. "I'll need some help," he said. "Get shovels and help me lift the edge of this thing. Don't touch it underneath though. It drips acid that will eat a hole in you."

With an effort a flap was lifted and Jan bent to look under. The flesh was white and hard, wet with acid. He found one of the many jumping legs, the size and roughly the same shape as a human leg. It was folded into a socket in the flesh and it pulled back when he dragged on it. But it could not resist a continuous tension and he drew it out far enough to see the direction of bend of the stocky knee. When he released it it slowly returned to position.

"All right, let it drop." He stepped away and scratched a mark on the ground, then turned and sighted along it. "Get those trucks out of there," he said. "Move them off to left and right, at least as far away as the copter. If this thing jumps again it will land on top of them. After the burning it might just do that."

There was some confusion as to what he meant, but no confusion when Chun repeated the orders at the top of his lungs. They moved quickly. Jan wiped his gloves on the stubble then climbed on top of the harvester. A sound of loud fluttering announced the arrival of the Big Hook. The big copter, the largest on the planet, rumbled up and hovered overhead. Jan took his radio from his belt and issued orders. A square opening appeared in the belly and a lifting bar dropped slowly down at the end of the cable. The downdraft of the rotors beat at Jan as he placed the bar carefully, then set the large hooks, one by one, into the edge of the lumper. If the creature felt the sharp steel in its flesh, it gave no indication. When the hooks were set to his satisfaction, Jan circled his hand over his head and the Big Hook began to slowly lift.

Following his directions, the pilot put tension on the cable, then began carefully to reel it in. The hooks sank deep and the lumper began to shiver with a rippling motion. This was the bad time. If it jumped now it could wreck the copter. But the edge came up, higher and higher, until the moist white underside was two meters in the air. Jan chopped with his hand and the Big Hook moved slowly away, towing the edge of the creature behind it level with the ground. It was like taking a blanket by the edge and turning it back. Smoothly and easily the lumper rolled until it was lying on its back on the ground, its underside a great expanse of glistening white flesh.

In a moment it changed, as the thousands of legs shot suddenly into the air, an instantly grown forest of pale limbs. They stood straight up for long seconds, then slowly dropped back to rest.

"It's harmless now," Jan said. "It can't get off its back."

"Now you will kill it," Chun Taekeng said warmly.

Jan kept the distaste from his voice. "No, we don't want to do that. I don't think you really want seven tonnes of rotting flesh in your field. We'll leave it there for now. The harvester is more important." He radioed the Big Hook to land, then detached the lumper from the lift bar.

There was a bag of soda ash in the copter, kept there for just this kind of emergency. There was always some kind of lumper trouble. He climbed on top of the harvester again and threw handfuls of the soda ash into the pools of acid. There did not seem to be much pitting, but there could be trouble inside if the acid had dripped into the machinery. He would have to start taking the plates off at once. A number of the covers were buckled and some of the bogie wheels torn free, so that it had shed one track. It would be a big job.

With the one track still powered, and four trucks towing the other side, he managed to back the harvester a good two hundred meters away from the lumper. Under the critical eye, and even more critical comments, of Chun Taekeng, he had the Big Hook drag the lumper into position and turn it over.

"Leave the ugly beast here! Kill it, bury it! Now it is right side up again and will jump again and kill us all."

"No it won't," Jan said. "It can only move in one direction, you saw how the legs were aligned. When it jumps again it will be headed back for the wastelands."

"You can't be sure, accurate. . . ."

"Accurate enough. I can't aim it like a gun, if that's what you mean. But when it goes it is going out of here."

Right on cue the lumper jumped. It had no reasoning power and no emotions. But it did have a complex set of chemical triggers. They must all have been activated by the rough handling it had had, the apparent reversal of gravity, burning, and having pieces removed. There was a heavy thud as all the legs kicked out at once. Some of the women screamed and even Chun Taekeng gasped and fell back.

The immense form was hurled into the air, soaring high. It cleared the field and the sensor beams and fell heavily into the sand outside. A heavy cloud of dust roiled out on all sides of it.

Jan took his toolbox from the copter and set to work on the harvester, pleased to lose himself in his work. As soon as he did this, when he was left alone, his thoughts returned instantly to the ships. He was tired of thinking about them and talking about them, but he could not forget them. No one could forget them.

Two

"I don't want to talk about the ships," Alzbeta Mahrova said. "That's all anyone ever talks about now."

She sat on the bench on the public way, very close to Jan with the length of her thigh pressed hard against his. He could feel the warmth of her body through the thin fabric of her dress and the cloth of his coveralls. He wrung his hands tightly together so that the tendons stood out like cables in his wrists. This was as close as he was ever going to get to her, here on this planet. He looked at her out of the corners of his eyes; the smooth tanned skin of her arms, the black hair to her shoulders, her eyes wide and dark too, her breasts . . .

"The ships are important," he said, taking his eyes from her with an effort, looking with disinterest at the thick-walled storage building across the width of the lava road. "They are six weeks late today, and we are four weeks late in leaving. Something must be decided tonight. Have you asked The Hradil again about our getting married?"

"Yes," Alzbeta said, turning toward him and taking his hands in hers, even though people walking by could see them. Her eyes were dark and sorrowful. "She refused to hear me out. I must marry someone from the Semenov Family, or I must not marry. That is the law."

"Law!" He grated the word out like an oath, pulling his hands from hers, moving away from her on the bench, tortured by her touch in a way she did not know. "This is no law, just custom, stupid custom, peasant superstition. On this peasant planet around a blue and white star that can't even be seen from Earth. On Earth I could be married, have a family."

"But you are not on Earth." She spoke so softly he barely heard her.

It drained the anger from him, making him suddenly weary. Yes, he was not on Earth and would never return to Earth. He had to make his life here and find a way of bending the rules. He could not break them. His watch read twenty hours, though the endless twilight still prevailed. Though the twilight was four years long, men still measured time with their watches and clocks, with the rhythms in their bodies of a planet light-years distant.

"They've been in that meeting and going at it for over two hours now, going over the same ground again and again. They should be tired." He rose to his feet.

"What will you do?" she asked.

"What must be done. The decision cannot be put off any longer."

She took his hand briefly in hers, letting go quickly, as though she understood what the touch of her skin did to him. "Good luck."

"It's not me that needs the luck. My luck ran out when I was shipped from Earth on a terminal contract."

She could not go with him, because this was a meeting of the Family Heads and the technical officers only. As Maintenance Captain he had a place here. The inner door to the pressurized dome was locked and he had to knock loudly before the lock rattled and it opened. Proctor Captain Ritterspach looked out at him suspiciously from his narrow little eyes.

"You're late."

"Shut up, Hein, and just open the door." He had very little respect for the Proctor Captain, who bullied those beneath him in rank, toadied to those above.

The meeting was just as demoralized as he had expected. Chun Taekeng, as Senior Elder, had the chair, and his constant hammering and screaming when he was ignored did nothing to help quiet things. There was cross talk and bitter denunciation, but nothing positive was being proposed. They were repeating the same words they had been using for over a month, getting no place. The time had come.

Jan walked forward, holding up his hand for attention, but was ignored by Chun. He walked closer still until he stood before the small man, looming over him. Chun waved him away angrily and tried to peer around him, but Jan did not move.

"Get out of here, back to your seat, that is an order."

"I am going to speak. Shut them up."

The voices were dying down, suddenly aware of him. Chun hammered loudly with the gavel, and this time there was silence. "The Maintenance Captain will speak," he called out, then threw the gavel down with disgust. Jan turned to face them.

"I am going to tell you some facts, facts you cannot argue with. First—the ships are late. Four weeks late. In all the years the ships have been coming, they have never been this late. Only once in all that time have they been more than four days late. The ships are late and we have used up all our time waiting. If we stay we burn. In the morning we must stop work and begin preparations for the trip."

"The last corn in the fields. . . ." someone shouted.

"Will be burned up. We leave it. We are late already. I ask our Trainmaster Ivan Semenov if this is not true."

"What about the corn in the silos?" a voice called out, but Jan ignored that question for the moment. One step at a time.

"Well, Semenov?"

With reluctance the gray head nodded solemnly. "Yes, we must leave. We must leave to keep to our schedule."

"There it is. The ships are late, and if we wait any longer we will die waiting. We must begin the trip south, and hope they will be waiting for us when we get to Southland. It is all we can do. We must leave at once, and we must take the corn with us."

There was stunned silence. Someone laughed briefly, then shut up. This was a new idea, and they were only confused by new ideas.

"It is impossible," The Hradil finally said, and many heads nodded in agreement. Jan looked at the angular face and thin lips of the leader of Alzbeta's family, and kept his voice toneless and flat so his hatred of her would not show.

"It is possible. You are an old woman who knows nothing of these matters. I am a captain in the service of science and I tell you it can be done. I have the figures. If we limit our living space during the trip we can carry almost a fifth of the corn with us. We can then empty the trains and return. If we go fast, this can be done. The empty trains will be able to carry two-fifths of the corn. The rest will burn—but we will have saved almost two-thirds of the crop. When the ships come they *must* have the food. People will be starving. We will have it for them."

They found their voices and shouted questions at him and at each other, derision and anger on all sides, with the gavel banging unnoticed. He turned his back and ignored them. They would have to talk it out, walk around the new idea and spit on it a bit. Then they might begin to understand it. They were reactionary, stubborn peasants, and they hated anything new. When they quieted down he would speak to them, now he kept his back turned and ignored them, looking at the great map of the planet that hung from the dome, the only decoration in the big hall.

Halvmörk, that's what the first discovery team had called it. Twilight, the twilight world. Its name in the catalogues was officially Beta Aurigae III, the third planet out and the only one that was habitable of the six worlds that circled the fiercely hot blue-and-white star. Or barely habitable. For this planet was an anomaly, something very interesting to the astronomers who had studied it and entered the facts into their records, and passed on. It was the great axial tilt of the world that made it so fascinating to the scientists, almost habitable to the people who lived there. The axial tilt of forty-one degrees and the long, flattened ellipse of the orbit created a most singular situation. Earth had an axial tilt of only a few degrees, and that was enough to cause the great change in the seasons. The axis is the line about which a planet revolves; the axial tilt the degree that the axis deviates from the vertical. Forty-one degrees is a very dramatic deviation, and this, combined with the long ellipse of its orbit, produced some very unusual results.

Winter and summer were each four Earth years long. For four long years there was darkness at the winter pole, the planetary pole that faced away from the sun. This ended, suddenly and drastically, when the planet turned the brief curve at one end of the elliptical orbit and summer came to the winter pole. The climatic differences were brutal and dramatic as the winter pole became the summer one, to lie exposed to sun for four years, as it had done to the winter darkness.

While in between the poles, from 40 degrees north to 40 degrees south, there was endless burning summer. The temperature at the equator stayed above 200 degrees most of the time. At the winter pole the temperature remained in the thirties and there was even an occasional frost. In the extremes of temperature of this deadly planet there was only one place where men could live comfortably. The twilight zone. The only habitable place on Halvmörk was this zone around the winter pole. Here the temperature varied only slightly, between 70 degrees and 80 degrees, and men could live and crops could grow. Wonderful, mutated crops, enough to feed a half-dozen crowded planets. Atomic-powered desalination plants supplied the water, turning the chemicals from the rich sea into fertilizer. The terrestrial plants had no enemies, because all the native life on the planet was based on copper compounds, not carbon. Each flesh was poison to the other. Nor could the copper based plant life compete for physical space with the faster growing, more energetic carbon forms. They were squeezed out, eliminated—and the crops grew. Crops adapted to the constant, muted, unending light, and unchanging temperature. They grew and grew and grew.

For four years, until the summer came and the burning sun rose above the horizon and made life impossible again. But when summer arrived at one hemisphere, winter fell in the other and there was another habitable twilight zone at the opposite pole. Then it would be possible to farm the other hemisphere for four years, until the seasons changed again.

The planet was basically very productive once the water and the fertilizer were supplied. The local plant life presented no problems. The Earth's economy was such that getting settlers was no problem either. With the FTL drive, transportation costs were reasonable. When the sums had been carefully done and checked it was clear that food crops could be produced most reasonably, and transported cheaply to the nearest inhabited worlds, while the entire operation was designed to show a handsome profit as well. It could be done. Even the gravity was very close to Earth norm, for while Halvmörk was larger than Earth it was not nearly as dense. Everything was very possible. There were even two large land masses around the poles that contained the needed twilight zones. They could be farmed turn and turn about, for four years each. It could be done.

Except how did you get your farmers and equipment from zone to zone every four years? A distance of nearly twenty-seven thousand kilometers?

Whatever discussions and plans had been proposed were long since buried in forgotten files. But the few options open were fairly obvious. Simplest, and most expensive, would be to provide for two different work forces. While duplicating machinery and buildings would not be excessively expensive, the thought of a work force loafing in air conditioned buildings for five years out of every nine was totally unacceptable. Unthinkable to work managers who wrung every erg of effort from their laborers with lifetime contracts. Transportation by sea must have been considered; Halvmörk was mostly ocean, except for the two polar continents and some island chains. But this would have meant land transportation to the ocean, then large, expensive ships that could weather the violent tropical storms. Ships that had to be maintained and serviced to be used just once every four and a half years. Also unthinkable. Then was there a possible solution?

There was. The terraforming engineers had much experience in making planets habitable to man. They could purify poison atmospheres, melt icecaps and cool tropics, cultivate deserts and eliminate jungles. They could even raise land masses where desired, sink others that were not needed. These latter dramatic changes were brought about by the careful placing of gravitronic bombs. Each of these was the size of a small building, and had to be assembled in a specially dug cavern deep in the ground. The manner of their operation was a secret carefully kept by the corporation that built them—but what they did was far from secret. When activated, a gravitronic bomb brought about a sudden surge of seismic activity. A planet's crust would be riven, the magma below released, which in turn brought about normal seismic activity. Of course this could only be effective where the tectonic plates overlapped, but this usually allowed for a wide enough latitude of choice.

The gravitronic bombs had brought a chain of flaming volcanoes from the ocean deeps of Halvmörk, volcanoes that vomited out lava that cooled and turned to stone to form an island chain. Before the volcanic activity died down, the islands became a land bridge connecting the two continents. After this it was, relatively speaking, a simple matter to lower the tallest mountains with hydrogen bombs. Even simpler still was the final step of leveling the rough-shaped land with fusion guns. These same guns smoothed the surface to make a solid stone highway from continent to continent, reaching almost from pole to pole, a single road 27,000 kilometers in length.

Doing this could not have been cheap. But the corporations were all-powerful, and controlled the Earth's wealth completely. A consortium could have been formed easily enough, was formed, for the returns would be rich and continue forever.

The forced settlers of Halvmörk were migrant farmers with a vengeance. For four years did they labor, raising and storing their crop against the day when the ships came. It was the long awaited, highly exciting, most important event in the cycle of their existence. The work ended when the ships signaled their arrival. The standing corn was left in the field and the party began, for the ships also brought everything that made life possible on this basically inhospitable world. Fresh seed when needed, for the mutated strains were unstable and the farmers were not agricultural scientists who could control this. Clothing and machine parts, new radioactive slugs for the atomic engines, all the thousand and one parts and supplies that maintained a machine-based culture on a non-manufacturing planet. The ships stayed just long enough to offload the supplies and fill their holds with the grain. Then they left and the party ended. All the marriages were consummated, for this was the only time when marriage was allowed, all the celebrations finished, all the liquor drunk.

Then the trip began.

They moved like gypsies. The only permanent structures were the machine storage buildings and the thick-walled grain silos. When the partitions had been taken down and the tall doors levered open, the trucks and copters, the massive harvesters, planters and other farm machinery were wheeled inside. With their vitals cocooned and their machinery sealed in silicon grease, they would wait out the heat of the summer until the farmers returned the following fall.

Everything else went. The assembly hall and the other pressurized dome structures were deflated and packed away. When the jacks were retracted, all the other narrow, long buildings settled onto the springs and wheels beneath them. The women had been canning and storing food for months, the slaughter of the sheep and cows had filled the freezers with meat. Only a few chicks, ewe lambs and cow calves would be taken; fresh herds and flocks would be raised from the sperm bank.

When everything was in place the farm tractors and trucks would haul the units into position to form the long trains, before being mothballed and sealed into the permanent buildings and silos themselves. The engines, the main drive units, would be unjacked after four years of acting as power plants, and would rumble into place at the head of each train. With the couplings and cables connected, the train would come to life. All the windows would be sealed and the air conditioning switched on. It would not be turned off again until they had reached the twilight zone of the southern hemisphere, and the temperatures were bearable again. The thermometer could easily top 200 degrees when they crossed the equator. Though the night temperatures sometimes fell as low as 130 degrees this could not be counted upon. Halvmörk rotates in eighteen hours, and the nights are too short for any real temperature drop.

"Jan Kulozik, there is a question for you. Your attention here, Kulozik, that is an order!" Chun Taekeng's voice was beginning to crack a bit after a good evening of shouting.

Jan turned from the map and faced them. There were a lot of questions but he ignored them all until the noise died down.

"Listen to me," Jan said. "I have worked out in detail what must be done, and I will give you the figures. But before I do you must decide. Do we take the corn or not, it is just that simple. We must leave, you cannot argue about that. And before you decide about the corn, remember two things. If and when the ships come they will need that corn because people will be starving. Thousands, perhaps millions, will die if they do not get it. If we do not have that corn waiting, their lives will be on our heads.

"If the ships do not come, why then we will die too. Our supplies are low, broken parts cannot be replaced, two of the engines already have lowered output and will need refueling after this trip. We can live for a few years, but we are eventually doomed. Think about that, then decide.

"Mr. Chairman, I ask for a vote."

When The Hradil rose and signaled for attention, Jan knew that it would be a long, dragged-out battle. This old woman, leader of the Mahrova Family, represented the strength of reaction, the force against change. She was shrewd, but she had the mind of a peasant. What was old was good, what was new was evil. All change worsened things, life must be immutable. She was listened to with respect by the other leaders, because she voiced best all their unreasoned and repetitious rationalizations. They settled down when she stood, ready for the calming balm of stupidity, the repeating as law of age-old, narrow-minded opinion.

"I have listened to what this young man has said. I value his opinion even though he is not a leader, or even a member of one of our families." Well done, Jan thought. Take away all my credentials with your opening words, sound preparation to destroy the arguments.

"Despite this," she continued, "we must listen to his ideas and weigh them on their own merit. What he has said is right. It is the only way. We must take the corn. It is our ancient trust, the reason for our existence. I ask for a vote by acclamation so no one can complain later if things do not go right. I call upon you all to agree to leave at once, and to take the corn. Anyone who does not agree will now stand."

It would have taken a far stronger individual than any of those present to rise to his feet before that cold eye. And they were confused. First with a new idea, something they thought very little of at any time, much less at a time when the decision was one upon which their lives might depend. Then to have this idea supported by The Hradil, whose will was their will in almost every way. It was very disturbing. It took some thinking about, and by the time they had thought for a while it was too late to stand and face the woman so, with a good deal of irritated muttering, and some dark looks, the measure was carried by acclamation.

Jan did not like it, but he could not protest. Yet he was still suspicious. He was sure The Hradil hated him as intensely as he hated her. Yet she had backed his idea and forced the others into line. He would pay for this some time, in some way he could not understand now. The hell with it. At least they had agreed.

"What do we do next?" The Hradil asked, turning in his direction but not facing him squarely. She would use him but she would not recognize him.

"We put the trains together as we always do. But before this is done the leaders here must make lists of nonessentials that can be left behind. We will go over those lists together. Then these items will be left with the machinery. Some of them will be destroyed by the heat, but we have no alternative. Two cars in every train will be used for living quarters. This will mean crowding, but it must be done. All of the other cars will be filled with corn. I have calculated this weight and the cars will carry it. The engines will go slower but, with proper precautions, they can move the trains."

"The people will not like it," The Hradil said, and many heads nodded.

"I know that, but you are the family leaders and you must

make them obey. You exercise authority in every other matter, such as marriage," he looked pointedly at The Hradil when he said this, but she was just as pointedly looking away. "So be firm with them. It is not as though you are elected officials who can be replaced. Your rule is absolute. Exercise it. This trip will not be the easy, slow affair that it always has been. It will be fast and it will be hard. And living in the silos in Southtown will be uncomfortable until the trains return a second time. Tell the people that. Tell them now so they cannot complain later. Tell them that we will not drive the five hours a day as we have always done before, but will go on for at least eighteen hours a day. We will be going slower and we are late already. And the trains must make a second round trip. We will have very little time as it is. Now there is one other thing."

This was the second decision they would have to make, and the most important to him personally. He hoped that Lee Ciou would do as he had agreed. The Pilot Captain did not really like people, did not like politics, and had been hard to convince that he must take a part in what was to come.

"All of this is new," Jan said. "There must be a coordinator for the changes, then the first trip, and a commander for the second trip. Someone must be in charge. Who do you suggest?"

Another decision. How they hated this. They looked around and murmured. Lee Ciou stood up, stood silently, then forced himself to speak.

"Jan Kulozik must do it. He is the only one who knows what to do." He sat down at once.

The silence lasted long seconds, while they ran the thought around and around in their minds, shocked by the newness, the break from tradition, the unexpectedness of it all.

"No!" Chun Taekeng shrieked, his face red with an anger even greater than normal, banging and banging with the gavel, unaware he was even doing it. "Ivan Semenov will organize the trip. Ivan Semenov always organizes the trip. He is Trainmaster. That is the way it has been done, that is the way it will always be done." Spittle flew from his lips with the violence of his words so that those in the front row leaned away, wiping surreptitiously at their faces —though nodding in agreement at the same time. This was something they could understand, neither going back nor going forward, but staying with the tried and true.

"Stop that banging, Taekeng, before you break the hammer,"

The Hradil said, hissing the words like a snake. The chairman gaped, he gave orders, he did not take orders, this was without precedent. As he hesitated the gavel hung in midair and The Hradil spoke again before he could gather his thoughts.

"Better, much better. We must think of what is right, not what has been done before. This is a new thing we are doing so perhaps we will need a new organizer. I do not say we do. Perhaps. Why don't we ask Ivan Semenov what he thinks. What do you think, Ivan?"

The big man rose slowly to his feet, pulling at his beard, looking around at the technical officers and heads of families, trying to read their reactions on their faces. There was no help there. Anger, yes, and a great deal more confusion—but no decision at all.

"Perhaps Jan should be considered, perhaps to plan if you know what I mean. Changes, they must be planned, and two trips. I really don't know. . . ."

"If you don't know, shut up," Chun Taekeng called out, banging once with the gavel for emphasis. But he had been shouting and banging all night so was ignored. Ivan went on.

"If I don't know about these changes, then I will need some help. Jan Kulozik knows, it is his plan. He knows what to do. I will organize as always, but he can order the changes to be made. I must approve, yes, I insist, approval, but he could arrange the new things."

Jan turned away so they could not see his face and know how he felt. How he tried not to, but how he hated these people. He rubbed the back of his hand across his lips to rub away some of the distaste. No one noticed, they were watching The Hradil as she spoke.

"Good. A fine plan. A Family Head must command the trip. That is the way it should be done. But the technical officer will advise. I think this is a good idea. I am for it. Anyone against it up with your hand, quick. There, all for it."

So he was in command—but not in command. Jan had the urge to stand firm, to insist on undisputed control, but this would accomplish nothing. They had bent, so he must bend a bit too. Moving the corn was a necessity, and that came first.

"All right," he said, "we'll do it that way. But there can be no arguing, we must agree upon that. Harvesting will stop at once. The cars must be stripped of every nonessential. We must cut everything by half since we will have far less than half the space we normally do. You must tell your people they have one day to make all the arrangements. If you say it like that, they may be finished in two days. I want the first cars empty in two days so we can start loading in the corn. Are there any questions?"

Questions? There was only silence. Do you ask a hurricane how fast it is blowing as it hurls you into the air?

Three

"I think we're leaving too early. It's a mistake."

Hein Ritterspach fiddled with the breech of the fusion cannon, unable to look Jan in the eye. Jan slammed shut the inspection port on the reduction gear and bolted it into place. It was crowded and stuffy in the tank's driving compartment, and he was aware of the other's acrid sweat.

"Not early, late if anything, Hein." He spoke wearily, tired of repeating the same things over and over. "The trains won't be that far behind you because we'll be moving faster. We'll catch up a lot faster than you think. That's why you will be double-crewed, so you can work a sixteen hour day. I just hope it is enough. Yours is the important job, Hein. Your maintenance people in these tanks have to get over the Road ahead of us and see that it is fit to drive. You know what you are going to find. It's a job you've done before. You'll just have to work at it a bit harder this time."

"We won't be able to move that fast. The men won't do it."

"You'll make them do it."

"I can't ask. . . ."

"You don't ask, you *tell*." The days of frustrating, endless work were telling on Jan. His eyes were red-rimmed and he was perpetually tired. Tired of cajoling, prodding, pushing, forcing these people to do something different just once in their lives. His temper was rubbed raw as well, and the sight of this whining, pudgy idiot became too much. He spun about and poked the man deep in the blubbery gut with his finger.

"You're a complainer, Hein, do you know that? No one needs a Proctor Captain here, they are too busy and too tired to get into trouble. So you loaf. Only when we move the trains do you do any real work. Now you have got to get out ahead of us and clear the Road, and that is all you have to do. So stop finding excuses and get on with the job."

"You can't talk to me like that!"

"I just did. Your tanks and men are ready to roll. I've checked the equipment myself, and it's all on line. Yet this is the third time I have checked this command tank, and there is *nothing* wrong with it. So move out."

"You, you. . . ."

The big man was wordless with rage, raising a large fist over his head. Jan stepped close to him, closing a hard, scarred mechanic's fist, waiting, smiling.

"Yes, do hit me, why don't you."

He had to speak through his teeth, his jaw was so tightly clamped, and his arm shook with restrained tension. Hein could not face him. The fist dropped, and he turned away and climbed clumsily through the hatch, his boots clattering on the rungs outside.

"That's the end of you, Kulozik!" he shouted, his red face framed by the hatch. "I'm going to Semenov, to Chun Taekeng. You're getting thrown out, you've gone too far. . . ."

Jan took one weary step forward and raised his fist, and the face vanished instantly. Yes, he had gone too far, had shown the bully to be a coward. Hein would never forgive him. Particularly since there had been a witness. Lajos Nagy sat in the co-driver's seat in silence, silent but well aware of what had happened.

"Start the motors," Jan said. "You think I was too hard on him, Lajos?"

"He's all right when you work with him a while."

"I'll bet he's worse the longer he's around."

A deep vibration shook the floor as the gear trains were engaged and Jan cocked his head, listening. The tank was in good shape. "Pass the word to the others, start engines," he said. He dogged the hatch shut as the air conditioner came on, then slid into the driver's seat, his feet on the brakes, his hands resting lightly on the wheel that synchronised track speed and clutches. Twenty tonnes of machinery vibrated gently with anticipation, waiting his command.

"Tell them to stay in line behind me, hundred-meter intervals. We're moving out."

Lajos hesitated for just an instant before he switched on his microphone and relayed the order. He was a good man, one of Jan's mechanics when they weren't on the Road.

Jan eased the wheel forward and tilted it at the same time. The whine of the gearboxes grew in pitch and the tank lurched ahead as the clutches engaged, the heavy tracks slapping down on the solid rock of the Road. When he switched on the rear camera he saw the rest of the tanks rumble to life on the screen and move out behind him. They were on the way. The broad central street of the city slipped past, the looming walls of the warehouses, then the first of the farms beyond. He kept the controls on manual until the last of the buildings was behind him and the Road had narrowed. The tank picked up speed as he switched to automatic and sat back. A wire, imbedded beneath the congealed lava surface of the Road, acted as a guide. The column of tanks roared on past the farms toward the desert beyond.

They were into the sandy wastes, the unreeling ribbon of Road the only sign of mankind's existence, before the expected message came through.

"I'm having radio trouble, I'll call you back," Jan said, switching off the microphone. The other tanks were on FM command frequency, so should not have intercepted the message. Now that he had started this thing he was going to finish it in his own way.

They were over three hundred kilometers from the settlement before they hit the first problem. Sand had drifted across the Road, forming a barrier two meters thick at its highest. Jan halted the column while his tank crawled up the slope. It wasn't too bad.

"Which are the two with the biggest dozer blades?"

"Seventeen and nine," Lajos said.

"Get them up here to clean this stuff away. Get a second driver from the house car, have him stay with you until Hein Ritterspach gets here. He won't be bearable for a couple of days, so try to ignore him. I'll radio for him to come in a copter, if it's not on the way already, and I'll go back with it."

"I hope there won't be trouble."

Jan smiled, tired but happy at having done something. "Of course there will be trouble. That's all there ever is. But this column is moving fine, Ritterspach won't dare turn back now. All he can do is push on."

Jan sent the message, then kicked open the hatch and climbed down onto the sand. Was it warmer here—or just his imagination? And wasn't it lighter on the southern horizon? It might very well be; dawn wasn't that far away. He stood aside while the tanks ground up the slope and churned past him, the last in the column, towing the house car, stopping just long enough for the relief driver to climb down. The dozers were just attacking the sand when the flutter of the helicopter could be heard above the sound of their tracks. It had been on the way well before his message had been received. It circled once, then settled slowly onto the Road. Jan went to meet it.

Three men climbed down, and Jan knew that the trouble was not over, was perhaps just beginning. He spoke first, hoping to keep them off balance.

"Ivan, what the devil are you doing here? Who is taking care of things with both of us out on the Road?"

Ivan Semenov twisted his fingers in his beard and looked miserable, groping for words. Hein Ritterspach, an assistant Proctor close by his side, spoke first.

"I'm taking you back, Kulozik, under official arrest. You are going to be charged with. . . ."

"Semenov, exert your authority," Jan called out loudly, turning his back on the two Proctors, well aware of the sidearms that both men wore, their hands close to the butts. There was a tightness between his shoulder blades that he tried to ignore. "You are Trainmaster. This is an emergency. The tanks are clearing the Road. Hein must be with them, he is in command. We can talk about his little problems when we get to Southtown."

"The tanks can wait; this must be done first! You attacked me!"

Hein was shaking with rage, his gun half drawn. Jan turned sideways enough to watch both Proctors. Semenov finally spoke.

"A serious matter, this. Perhaps we had all better return to town and discuss it quietly."

"There is no time for discussion—or quiet." Jan shouted the words, pretending anger to feed the other's anger as well. "This fat fool is under my command. I never touched him. He's lying. This is mutiny. If he does not *instantly* rejoin the tanks I shall charge him and disarm him and imprison him."

The slash of the words was, of course, too great a burden for Hein to bear. He pawed at his holster, clutched his gun and drew it. As soon as the muzzle was clear, before it could be raised, Jan acted.

He turned and grabbed Hein's wrist with his own right hand, his left hand slapping hard above the other's elbow. Still turning, using speed and weight, he levered the man's arm up behind his back so hard that Hein howled with pain. Uncontrollably the big man's fingers went limp, the gun began to drop—and Jan kept pushing. It was cruel, but he must do it. There was a cracking sound that shuddered Hein's body as the arm broke, and only then did Jan let go. The gun clattered on the stone surface of the Road and Hein slid down slowly after it. Jan turned to the other armed man.

"I am in command here, Proctor. I order you to aid this wounded man and take him into the copter. Trainmaster Semenov concurs with this order."

The young Proctor looked from one to the other of them in an agony of indecision. Semenov, confused, did not speak, and his silence gave the man no guide. Hein groaned loudly with pain and writhed on the unyielding rock. With this reminder the Proctor decided; he let his half-drawn gun drop back into the holster and knelt beside his wounded commander.

"You should not have done that, Jan." Semenov shook his head unhappily. "It makes things difficult."

Jan took him by the arm and drew him aside. "Things were already difficult. You must take my word that I never attacked Hein. I have a witness to back me up if you have any doubts. Yet he built this trouble up so large that one of us had to go. He is expendable. His second in command, Lajos, can take over. Hein will ride in the train, and his arm will knit, and he'll cause more trouble at Southtown. *But not now.* We must move as planned."

There was nothing for Semenov to say. The decision had been taken from him and he did not regret it. He took the medical bag from the copter and attempted to fit an airbag splint onto the broken arm. They could only do this after an injection had put the wailing Hein under. The return trip was made in silence.

Four

Jan lay back on his bunk, his muscles too tired to relax, going over his lists just one more time. They were only hours away from departure. The last of the corn was being loaded now. As the silos were emptied the partitions were removed so that the heavy equipment could be rolled in. Coated with silicon grease and co-cooned with spun plastic, they would sit out the 200 degree heat of the four-year long summer. All of them, trucks, copters, reapers, were duplicated and in storage at Southtown, so need not be carried with them on the trek. They had their stocks of frozen food, the chicks, lambs and calves to start anew the herds and flocks, home furnishings—now painfully reduced—and the corn filling most of all the cars. The water tanks were full; he wrote and underlined. Water. First thing in the morning he must hook into the computer relay and put the Northpoint desalination plant on standby. It had already stopped all secondary functions, chemical and mineral extraction, fertilizer production, and was operating at minimum to keep the 1300-kilometer-long canal and tunnel complex filled with water. He could stop that now; the farming was over for this season. There was a knock on the door, so soft at first that he wasn't sure he had heard it. It was repeated.

"Just a moment."

He pushed the sheets of paper together into a rough heap and dropped them onto the table. His legs were stiff as he shuffled across the plastic floor in his bare feet and opened the door. Lee Ciou, the radio technician, stood outside.

"Am I bothering you, Jan?" He seemed worried.

"Not really. Just rattling papers when I should be sleeping."

"Perhaps another time. . . ."

"Come in, now you're here. Have a cup of tea and then maybe we'll both get some sleep."

Lee bent and picked up a box that had been out of sight beside the door, and brought it in with him. Jan busied himself with boiling water from the kitchen tap, hotting the pot, then adding tea leaves to brew. He waited for Lee to talk first. Lee was a quiet man with a mind like one of his own printed circuits. Thought was processed back and forth, emerging only after a measured period of time, complete and final.

"You are from Earth," he finally said.

"I think that is a pretty well known fact. Milk?"

"Thank you. On Earth, I understand, there are many levels of society, not just a single population as we have here?"

"You might say that. It's a varied society; you've seen a lot of it on the programs from Earth. People have different jobs, live in different countries. Lots of variety."

Lee's forehead had a fine beading of sweat; he was disturbed, uncomfortable. Jan shook his head wearily and wondered just where this was all leading.

"Are there criminals, too?" Lee asked, and Jan was suddenly very much awake.

Careful, Jan thought, *be very careful. Don't say too much; don't commit yourself.*

"There probably must be some. There are police after all. Why do you ask?"

"Have you ever known criminals, or people who have broken the law?"

Jan could not stay quiet. He was too tired, his nerves rubbed too raw.

"Are you a narkman? Is that your job here?" His voice flat and cold. Lee raised his eyebrows but his expression did not change.

"Me? No, of course not. Why should I send reports to offworld police about things that happen on Halvmörk?"

You've given yourself away there, my boy, Jan thought. When he spoke again he was as cool as the other.

"If you're not a narkman—how do you know what the term means? It's an earthy slang term that is not in good repute. It mocks authority. I've never seen it on a 3V tape or read it in a book approved for use on this world."

Lee was uncomfortable now, wringing his hands together slowly, his tea forgotten. He spoke reluctantly, yet when he did it all came out in a rush.

"You could tell, of course, you know about these things. You know what Earth, other places are like. I have long wanted to talk to you about it but thought it would be an affront. You have never talked, yourself, you must have good reasons. That is why I am here tonight. Hear me out, please, do not tell me to leave yet. I mean no insult. But—your presence here—the fact you have stayed all these years means, perhaps, you cannot leave. Yet I know you are an honest man, one of good will. I do not think you are a narkman. It is a thing you would not do. If you are not that, then you are no criminal, no, but, you . . . well, perhaps. . . ."

His voice trailed away; these things were no easier to talk about here than they were back on Earth.

"You mean that even if I am not a criminal I must be on this planet for some reason?" Lee nodded rapidly. "Is there any reason why I should talk to you about it? It is really none of your business."

"I know," Lee said desperately. "I should not ask you, I am sorry. But it is very important to me. . . ."

"Important to me, too. I could get into trouble talking to you—get you into difficulties, too. Don't let anything I tell you go any further. . . ."

"I won't—I promise!"

"Then, yes, I was in trouble with the authorities. I was sent here as punishment of a kind. And I can live here as you see me as long as I don't make any waves. Such as telling you things like this."

"I don't mean to ask—but I must. I had to know. There is something I must tell you. I am taking a chance, but I feel that the odds are right. I must tell you or give up everything—and that is something that I could not bear." Lee straightened up and lifted his face as though waiting for a blow. "I have broken the law."

"Well, good for you. You are probably the only one on this primitive planet with the nerve to do it."

Lee gaped. "This does not bother you?"

"Not in the slightest. If anything, I admire you for it. What have you done that bothers you so?"

Lee lifted the flap of his jacket pocket and took out something small and black, and passed it to Jan. It was thin and rectangular and had a row of tiny studs along one edge. "Press the second one," he said. Jan did, and quiet music poured out.

"I made it myself, my own design, but with parts from supply. Not enough for anyone to ever notice. Instead of tape I use a digital memory store on a molecular level, that is why it can be so small. It will record music, books, anything, with perhaps a thousand hours easily accessible."

"This is very good, but not what I would call a criminal act. Since the first man worked on the first machine, I imagine mechanics have been using bits and pieces for their own ends. The amount of materials you have used will neither be heeded nor missed, and I do admire your design. I don't think you can call this breaking the law."

"This is just the beginning." Lee took the box from the floor and put it on the table. It was made of a pale alloy, machine turned and held together by rows of tiny rivets, the construction a labor of love in itself. He worked the combination and opened the lid, tilting it towards Jan. It was filled with row after row of tape cassettes.

"These are from the men who land with the supply ships," he said. "I have been trading my recorders for these. They are very popular and I get more of them each time. There is one man who gets me all I can use. I think this is illegal."

Jan sat back heavily and nodded. "That is indeed against the law, against how many laws you don't know. You shouldn't mention this to anyone else, and if I am ever asked I have never heard of you. The simplest thing that would happen to you if you were discovered would be instant death."

"That bad?" Lee was paler now, sitting bolt upright.

"That bad. Why are you telling me this?"

"I had an idea. It doesn't matter now." He stood and picked up the box. "I had better be going."

"Wait." As soon as he thought about it Jan knew why the radio technician had come. "You are afraid of losing the tapes, aren't you? If you leave them behind the heat will destroy them. And the Elders are checking all personal luggage, as they have never done before, and they'll want to know what you have in the box. So how do you expect me to help?"

Lee did not answer, because this was obvious as well.

"You were going to ask me to conceal them in my equipment for you? Risk death for blackdirt tapes?"

"I didn't know."

"I guess not. Here, sit down, you're getting me nervous standing there. Pour the tea into the sink and I'll give you something better to drink. Just as illegal as the tapes, though with not the same penalties attached."

Jan unlocked a cabinet and took out a plastic bottle filled with a lethal-looking transparent liquid. He filled two tumblers and passed one to Lee.

"Drink up—you'll like it." He raised his own glass and drained half of it. Lee sniffed suspiciously at the glass, then shrugged and drank a good mouthful. His eyes widened and he managed to swallow it without choking.

"That's . . . that's something I never tasted before. Are you sure that it is drinkable?"

"Very much so. You know those apples I raise behind the shop? The little ones about the size of your thumb? Very sweet they are and the juice ferments easily with the right yeast strain. I get an apple wine that must be about twelve percent alcohol. Then I put it into the deep freeze and throw away the ice."

"Very ingenious."

"I admit it's not an original idea of mine."

"But it's such a simple way of concentrating the alcohol. In fact, after drinking a bit it tastes better and better."

"That's not original either. Here, let me top you up. Then you can show me some of those tapes."

Lee frowned. "But the death penalty?"

"Let us say my first fright has vanished. It was just reflex. With the ships late, and they may never arrive at all, why should I worry about the retribution of Earth, light-years away." He flipped through the tapes, squinting at some of the titles. "All pretty innocuous stuff, red hot by this planet's standards, but nothing political at all."

"What do you mean, political?"

Jan poured their glasses full again and stared into his. "You're a rube," he said. "A hick. And you don't even know what those words mean. Have you ever heard me talk about Earth?"

"No. But I never thought about it. And we know about Earth from the taped shows and . . ."

"You know nothing at all here on Halvmörk. This is a dead-end planet, a concentration-camp world at the end of nowhere, been nowhere, going nowhere. Settled by forced migration, probably, or with politico prisoners. Doesn't matter, it's in the records someplace. Just an agricultural machine filled with dumb farmers designed to churn out food for the other planets for maximum profit at minimum input. Earth. Now that is something else again. With the elite on top, the proles on bottom, and everyone in between fitted into place like plugs into a board. No one really likes it, except those at the top, but they have all of the power so things just go on and on for ever. It is a trap. A morass. With no way out. I am out of it because I had no choice. This planet—or death. And that is all I am going to tell you. So leave the tapes. I'll take care of them for you. And why the hell should we worry ourselves about something as trivial as tapes?" He banged his glass down with sudden anger.

"Something is *happening* out there—and I don't know what it is. The ships always arrive on time. Yet they haven't. They may never come. But if they do, we have the corn and they will need it. . . ."

Fatigue and alcohol dragged him down. He finished the last swallow in his glass and waved Lee toward the door. Lee turned back before opening it.

"You didn't say anything to me tonight," Lee said.

"And I never saw any damn tapes. Good night."

Jan knew that a full three hours had gone by, but it seemed that the light and the buzzer clawed him awake just seconds after his head hit the pillow. He wiped at his encrusted eyelids and was all too aware of the vile taste in his mouth. And it was going to be a very long day. As his tea was brewing he shook two stims out of the bottle, looked at them, then added a third. A very long day.

There was a heavy knocking on the door before he had finished his tea, and it was thrown open before he could reach it. One of the Taekeng, he forgot his name, thrust his head in.

"All the corn loaded. Except this car. Like you said." His face was streaked with grime and sweat and he looked as tired as Jan felt.

"All right. Give me ten minutes. You can start cutting the hatches now."

Lee's illegal tapes were in with the machine tools, sealed and locked. All the clothes and personal items he would need were in a bag. As he washed the tea things and stowed them in their cabinet niches there was a burst of ruddy light from the ceiling. The point turned into a line and began to trace a circle in the metal. As he pushed his bed, table and chairs out through the front door, the circle was complete and the disk of metal clanged down, biting deep into the plastic flooring. Jan threw his bag over his shoulder and left, locking the door behind him.

His machine shop car was the last to go. It seemed that everyone was working at once. A thick tube snaked over from the nearest silo and up the side of the car. The man above called out and waved and the hose writhed as the flow began. It bucked in the man's hand and a golden rain clattered down on Jan before the man leaned his weight against it and sent the corn flowing down into the car through the newly cut hole. Jan picked a kernel from his shoulder. It was as long as his middle finger, wrinkled from vacuum dehydration. A miracle food, product of the laboratories, rich in protein, vitamins, nutrition. It could be made into a child's first meal, a grown man's food, an old man's gruel and it would be all the nutrition he would need in that lifetime. A perfect food. For economic slaves. He put it into his mouth and chewed ruminantly on its hard form. The only thing wrong was that it just did not taste like very much of anything.

Metal creaked as the corner jacks lifted the car above its concrete bed. Men were already in the black pit below, shouting curses as they stumbled in the darkness, lowering the wheels and locking them into position. It was all happening at once. They scrambled up the ramp at the end just as the tugtank was backing into position. While it was being hooked up, the corn loaders on the roof topped off and the pumping stopped. So well coordinated were the activities that the men who sealed plastic sheets over the newly cut ports actually rode the roof, shouting protests, as the car was pulled forward slowly, rising as it rode up the ramp. Once it was on the level the brakes were locked while the mechanics crawled beneath its massive bulk to check the tires, unseen for four years.

While Jan slept, the trains had been formed up. This was only the third time he had seen the great migration, and he was as impressed as he had been at the first. The native Halvmörkers took it for granted, though there was excitement at the change in the daily pace of their lives. The move was just as exciting for Jan, more so perhaps since he had been accustomed to the variety and novelty of travel on Earth. Here any escape from the boredom and repetition of everyday life was a relief. Particularly with this unexpected change, this altering of the physical world he had grown to accept since they had arrived. A few days ago this had been a thriving city, surrounded by farms that stretched to the horizon and beyond. Now it had all changed. All of the bustling transport and machines had been locked away in the massive silos, their doors sealed. The domed pressure buildings had been deflated and sealed away as well. The other buildings, the mobile ones, had changed character completely. No longer earthbound structures, they had risen on rows of sturdy wheels and been formed into regular lines, along with the farm buildings which had been trundled in to join them. Where the city had been there now stood just foundations, as though it had been wiped away in some incredible blast.

On the wide Central Way there now stood a double row of trains. The buildings, which had seemed so different as homes and shops, with their canopies and stairs and flowers, now proved all to be of the same size and shape. Cars in a large train, connected together and uniform. Twelve cars to a train, and each train headed by an engine. An incredible engine.

Big. At times Jan still found it hard to believe that a power plant this size could actually move. And power plants they were for all of the time they were off the Road. Jacked up and stationary, their atomic generators producing all the electricity the city and farms could possibly need, waiting patiently for their transformation back into the engines they really were.

Big. Ten times bigger than the biggest truck Jan had ever seen before coming to this planet. He slapped the tire of one as he passed, solid and hard, the top of the tread so high above his head that he could not reach it. Lug nuts the size of dinner plates. Two steerable wheels before, four driving wheels in back. Behind the front wheels were the rungs up to the driving compartment. Fifteen of them, climbing up the burnished golden metal of the solidly riveted side of the beast. In front the battery of headlights, bright enough to blind a man in an instant, if he were fool enough to stand and look at them. There was a glitter of glass from the drivers' compartment, high above. Out of sight on top were the banked rows of tubes and fins that cooled the atomic engines. Engines large enough to light a small city. He couldn't resist slamming his hand against the hard metal as he passed. It was something to drive one of these.

Ivan Semenov was waiting by the lead train.

"Will you drive engine one?" he asked.

"That's your job, Ivan, the most responsible one. The Trainmaster sits in that seat."

Ivan's grin was a little twisted. "Whatever titles are given, Jan, I think we know who is Trainmaster on this trip. People are talking. Now that the work has been done, they think you were right. They know who is in charge here. And Hein has few friends. He lies in bed and rubs the cast on his arm and will talk to no one. People pass his car and laugh."

"I'm sorry I did that. But I still think it was the only way."

"Perhaps you are right. In any case they all know who is in charge. Take engine one."

He turned on his heel and walked away before Jan could answer.

Engine one. It was a responsibility that he could handle. But there was an excitement there as well. Not only to drive one of these great brutes—but to drive the very first. Jan had to smile at himself as he walked faster and faster down the lengths of the trains, to the first train. To the first engine.

The thick door to the engine compartment was open and he saw the engineer bent over the lubrication controls. "Stow this, will you," he said as he slung his bag in through the doorway. Without waiting for an answer he grabbed the rungs and pulled himself up onto the first. To his left was the empty Road surrounded by the barren farms, more and more of the Road appearing as he climbed higher. Behind him the dual row of trains, solid and waiting. He pulled himself through the hatch into the driving compartment. The co-driver was in his seat leafing through his checklists. In the adjoining compartment the communications officer was at his banked radios.

In front, the expanse of the armored glass window, a bank of TV screens above it. Below this, row after row of instruments and gauges that fed back information on the engine and the train it towed, and the trains behind that.

In front of the controls the single, empty chair, solid steel with padded seat, back and headrest. Before it the wheel and the controls. Jan slid slowly into it, feeling its strength against his back, letting his feet rest lightly on the pedals, reaching out and taking the cool form of the wheel in his hand.

"Start the checklist," he said. "Ready to roll."

Five

Hour after frustrating hour passed. Although the trains appeared to be joined up and ready to begin the trek, there were still hundreds of minor problems that had to be solved before the starting signal could be given. Jan grew hoarse and frustrated shouting into the radiophone, until he finally slammed the headset back into the rack and went to see for himself. Fitted into a niche at the rear of the engine was a knobby-tired motorcycle. He unclamped it and disconnected the power lead to the battery—then found both tires flat. Whoever should have checked it hadn't. There was more delay while the engineer, Eino, filled a compressed air cylinder. When he finally mounted the cycle, Jan had the pleasure of twisting the rheostat on full and hearing the tires shriek as they spun against the road surface and hurled him forward.

As Maintenance Captain, Jan's responsibility had been to keep the machinery repaired and in preparation for this day. Physically, it was impossible for him to do alone, and he had had to rely on others to carry through his orders. Too often they had not. The multiple connectors on the thick cables that connected the cars should all have been sealed with moistureproof lids. Many of them had not. Corrosion had coated them with nonconducting scale in so many places that over half of the circuits were dead. After crawling under car after car himself he issued an order to all the trains that *all* connectors were to be opened and cleaned with the hand sandblasts. This added another hour to their departure.

There were steering problems. The lead wheels of every car

could swivel, turned by geared-down electric motors. These wheels were controlled by the engine computer in each train so that every car followed and turned exactly as the engine had done, moving as precisely as if they were on tracks. Fine in theory, but difficult in practice with worn motor brushes and jammed gear trains. Time trickled away.

There were personal difficulties as well, with everyone jammed into a fraction of the normal living space. Jan heard the complaints with one ear and nodded and referred all problems to the Family Heads. Let them earn their keep for a change. One by one he tracked down the troubles and saw them tackled and solved. The very last thing was a missing child, which he found himself when he saw a movement in the corn field nearby. He plunged in with the bike and restored the happy toddler, riding before him, to its weeping mother.

Tired, yet with a feeling of satisfaction, he rode slowly back between the double row of trains. The doors were sealed now and the only people in sight were the few curious faces peering from the windows. Eino, his engineer, was waiting to stow the cycle while he climbed back up to the driving compartment.

"Pre-drive checklist done," his co-driver said. Otakar was as efficient as the machine he commanded. "Full on-line power available, all systems go."

"All right. Get readiness reports on the other trains."

While Jan threw switches and went through his driver's checklist, he heard the reports from the other trains in his earphones. There was a hold with thirteen, a red on the safety standby circuits, which turned out to be an instrument readout failure which was corrected easily enough. They cleared one by one.

"All trains ready, all drivers ready," Otakar said.

"Good. Communications, give me a circuit to all drivers."

"Through," Hyzo, the communications officer, said.

"All drivers." As he spoke the words Jan had a sensation stronger than anything he had ever felt before. Mountain climbing, sailing—making love—each of them had produced moments of pure pleasure, of emotions both wonderful and indescribable. Only drugs had made him feel this way before, drugs that he had stopped taking because they were an easy shot, something that anyone could buy and share. But they could not share this with him because he was alone. In control of everything. Right at the top. More in control than he had ever been at any time back on

Earth. He had had responsibility, more than enough of it, but never this much. Out in front, the very first, with the population of an entire world waiting for his decision to be made.

He was in charge.

The solid frame of the engine beneath him hummed lightly with the still-restrained power of the engine. Heavy couplings and a web of cables connected it to the car behind and to the others behind that. Then there were the other engines and their trains, filled with the goods of this planet and all of its inhabitants. Every person, other than the maintenance crews, was there, waiting for his order. He felt the sudden dampness of his palms and wrapped his hands tightly about the hard steering wheel before him. The moment passed and he was in control again.

"All drivers." Jan's voice was as calm and businesslike as it always was. His internal feelings were still his own. "We're moving out. Set your proximity radar at one kilometer. No variations permitted above 1100 meters or below 900. Set automatic braking controls for 950. If—for *any* reason—we have an engine less than 900, and I mean 899 and down, from the train ahead, we will have a new driver. No exceptions. Minimum acceleration on starting up and watch the stress gauges on your couplings. We're carrying at least twice our normal loaded weight and we can pull those couplings out like rotten teeth without even trying. Right now we are going to use a new maneuver, and I want it used every time we start. Co-drivers, enter it into your checklists. Ready to copy.

"One. All car brakes off.

"Two. Set brakes on last car.

"Three. Select reverse gear.

"Four. Reverse minimum speed for five seconds."

This was a trick he had learned in his cadet days when he was doing maintenance on the freight monorails under the city. Backing up took out all the play in the joints and couplings. Then, when the train started forward, the entire weight of the train would not have to be set into motion at the same time, but bit by bit as the play was taken up. In this way inertia actually aided the starting up, rather than retarding it, as the weight of the cars already in motion was used to accelerate those still at rest.

With the heel of his hand Jan pushed the gear selector into reverse, then set the speed governor at the first notch. All of the brakes in the train were off except for the red light glowing on car twelve. When he stepped on the throttle with his left foot he felt the acceleration of the gear trains and a heavy shuddering through the metal of the floor. The coupling strain gauges dropped to zero, then reversed. *Skid* blinked on and off on twelve's panel, and he killed the power as the digital readout of the clock read five.

"Prepare to move out," he said and pulled the gear selector into *low range.* "Second file of trains hold position until the last of file one has passed. Then fall into position behind. All controls on manual until you are notified different. First stop in nineteen hours. Final stop in Southtown. See you all there."

He took the wheel firmly in both hands and let his foot rest on the accelerator.

"Move out!"

Jan stepped down slowly and the engine revved up. At speed, the hydraulic clutch engaged and the torque was transmitted to the drive wheels. They turned and the engine moved ahead, car after car being set into motion behind it, until the whole giant train was rolling slowly forward. To his left the lead engine of the second file slid back and out of sight and ahead was only the empty expanse of the Road. The rear scanner mounted on top of the engine showed the train following smoothly after. The screen next to it, hooked to the scanner in the last car, showed engine two dropping behind. Strain gauges were all well into the green. Engine speed and road speed moved up to the top of the low range and he shifted to middle.

"All green," Otakar said. He had been monitoring all the other readouts from the co-driver's seat. Jan nodded and turned the steering wheel to the left, then centered it again to hold the turn. Unlike the smaller ground cars, the powered steering was set by displacement of the wheel and held in position by centering. He then turned the steering wheel right to straighten the wheels again and centered it when they were at zero degrees forward. Then he came right to align the engine in the middle of the Road, centered over the control cable buried under the rock surface. The cars of the train behind each turned at precisely the same spot in the same way, like a monotrain going through switches.

Jan kept the speed at the top of the middle range until all the trains had begun to move, strung out in position one kilometer apart. The city site and even the farms had vanished behind before the last train was moving. Only then did he accelerate into the highest, road speed range. The tires hummed below, the Road rushed toward him, the featureless sand desert moved by on each side. He held the wheel, driving still on manual, guiding the engine, the train, all of the trains down the Road, south, toward the opposite continent and Southtown, still 27,000 kilometers away.

One of the few outstanding features in this stretch of desert appeared as a speck on the horizon and slowly grew as they raced towards it. A black spire of rock pointing a dark finger at the sky. It reared up from a ridge massive enough that the Road took a slow swing out and around it. As it passed Jan signaled for the all-driver circuit.

"Needle Rock coming up on your left. Mark it. As you pass you can go on autopilot."

He set the controls himself as he talked, feeding in maximum and minimum speeds with his left hand, max and min acceleration and braking as well. The gridded scope screen on the autopilot showed that he was centered over the central cable. He flipped the switch to *on* and leaned back, realizing that he was stiff from the strain, kneading his fingers together.

"A good start," Otakar said, still looking at the readouts. "It will project to a good trip."

"I only hope you're right. Take the con while I stretch."

Otakar nodded and slipped into the driver's seat when Jan stood up. His muscles creaked when he flexed his arms and he walked back to the rear compartment to look over the communication officer's shoulder.

"Hyzo," he said, "I want a . . ."

"I have a red here," Otakar called out sharply.

Jan spun about and ran to lean over the co-driver's shoulder. A red light had appeared, flashing among the rows of green, and a brief instant later there was a second, then a third.

"Brake drum heat on cars seven and eight. What the devil can that mean? All brakes are off." Jan muttered savagely to himself, things had been going too good, and leaned forward to press the readout button. Numbers appeared on the screen. "Up over twenty degrees on both those cars—and still rising."

He thought quickly. Should he stop and investigate? No, that would mean halting the entire line of trains, then getting them moving again. There were at least 300 kilometers more of desert road before they hit the foothills, and he wouldn't be needing brakes at all until that time.

"Kill the brake circuits in both those cars and see what happens," he said.

Otakar hit the switches while he was still issuing the order. Now the two cars no longer had operating brakes, but the safety circuits should have gone dead in the off position. They did. The temperature in the brake drums dropped slowly until, one after the other, the red lights went out.

"Keep the con," Jan said, "while I see if I can figure out just what the hell is going on." He went to the rear and threw up the cover of the hatch down to the engine compartment. "Eino," he called through the opening. "Pass me up the diagrams and manuals on the car brake circuits. We have a problem."

Jan had done maintenance on the brake systems, as he had on all of the machinery, but had never needed to break down and repair one of the systems. Like all the Halvmörk machines, these had been designed to, hopefully, last forever. Or as close to that as possible. With replacement supplies light-years away, rugged design was a necessity. All components were simply designed and heavily built. Lubrication was automatic. They were designed not to fail under normal use and, in practice, rarely did.

"These what you want?" Eino asked, popping out of the hatch like an animal out of its den. He had diagrams and service manuals in his hand.

"Spread them out on the desk and we'll take a look," Jan said.

The diagrams were detailed and exact. There were two separate braking systems on the cars, each with its own fail-safe mode. Normal braking was electronically controlled by the computer. When the engine driver hit the brake, the brakes in all the cars were applied at the same time, to the same degree. The brakes themselves were hydraulic, the pressure coming from reservoirs that were supplied by pumps turned by the axles of the car. Strong springs held them in the normally off position. The electronic controls opened the pressure valves to apply the brakes when needed. This was alpha, the active braking system. Beta, the passive one, was for emergencies only. These completely separate brakes were held in on position by their springs until the electric circuits were actuated. When this was done powerful magnets pulled them free. Any break in the electrical circuits, such as an accidental uncoupling of the cars, would apply these brakes for an emergency stop.

"Jan, two other trains calling in for advice," Hyzo said. "Sounds like the same trouble, temperature rise in the brakes."

"Tell them to do what we did. Cut the power to the alpha systems. I'll get back to them after I track down the malfunction." He traced the diagram with his finger. "It *must* be the alpha brake system. The emergencies are either full on or full off—and we would certainly know if that happened."

"Electronics or hydraulics?" the engineer asked.

"I have a feeling that it can't be the electronics. The computer monitors all those circuits. If there were an uncalled for on-brake signal it would negate it, and if it couldn't be cut the computer would certainly report it. Let's try the hydraulics first. We're getting pressure in our brake cylinders here. The only way we can get that is if this valve is opened slightly—"

"Or if something is blocking it so it can't close completely."

"Eino, you're reading my mind. And what could be blocking it is just plain dirt. The filter in the line here is supposed to be cleaned out after every trip. A nasty, dirty job, crawling around under the cars. A job I remember assigning to a certain mechanic named Decio some years ago. A mechanic so bad that I eventually demoted him right back to the farm. When we stop we'll drop one of those filters and look at it."

Eino rubbed his jaw with a calloused hand. "If that's the trouble we are going to have to drain each malfunctioning brake system to get the valves out to clean."

"No need. These emergency valves, here and here, shut tight if the line is broken. We won't lose much fluid. There are spare control valves in stock. What we'll do is replace the first valves with new ones, have the old valves cleaned while we are working and exchange them right down the line. The grades aren't too bad this first day; we'll leave the brakes cut out on the few cars with trouble."

"Jan," the co-driver called out. "Mountains in sight, so the tunnel will be coming up soon. Thought you would want the con."

"Right. Leave the specs here, Eino, and get back to your engine. We'll be hitting the slope soon."

Jan slid into the driver's seat and saw the sharp peaks of the mountains ahead, stretching away, unbroken, on both sides. This was the range that kept the interior of the continent a desert, holding all the storms and rain on the far side. Once through the range they would find weather again. The Road ahead began to

rise as they entered the foothills. Jan kept the autopilot on steer,
but released the other controls. As the slope grew steeper he let up
on the accelerator and dropped into the central gear range. He
could see the Road rising up ahead and there, above, the dark
mouth of a tunnel. He switched on his microphone.

"All drivers. The tunnel is coming up in a few minutes. Headlights on as soon as you spot it."

He switched on his own lights as he said this and the Road
ahead sprang into harsh clarity.

The engineers who had built the Road, centuries earlier, had
had almost unlimited energy at their disposal. They could raise islands from the ocean—or lower them beneath the surface, level
mountains and melt solid rock. To them, the easiest way to pass
the mountain range was by boring straight through it. They were
proud of this, too, for the only decoration or nonfunctioning bit
of the entire Road was above the tunnel entrance. Jan saw it now,
cut into the solid rock, as the dark mouth loomed closer. A
hundred-meter-high shield. The headlights caught it as the Road
straightened for the final approach. A shield with a symbol on it
that must be as ancient as mankind; a hand holding a short and
solid hammer. This was clear, growing larger, until it swept by
above and they were inside the tunnel.

Rough stone wall flashed by gray and empty. Other than the occasional stream of water that crossed the Road, the tunnel was
featureless. Jan watched his tachometer and speedometer and left
the steering to the autopilot. Almost a half an hour passed before
a tiny light appeared ahead, grew to a disk, then a great burning
doorway.

They had gone far enough south, and risen high enough, to
have driven into the dawn.

The massive engine tore out of the tunnel and into searing sunlight. The windshield darkened automatically at the actinic onslaught, opaquing completely before the sun. Beta Aurigae was
blue-white and searingly hot, even at this northern latitude. Then
it was obscured by clouds and a moment later dense rain crashed
down on the train. Jan started the windshield wipers and switched
on his nose radar. The Road was empty ahead. As quickly as it
had begun, the storm was over and, as the Road wound down out
of the mountains, he had his first view of the acid green jungle
with the blue of the ocean beyond.

"That's quite a sight," Jan said, hardly aware he had spoken aloud.

"It means trouble. I prefer the inland driving," the co-driver, Otakar, said.

"You're a machine without a soul, Otakar. Doesn't all that twilight monotony get you down at times?"

"No."

"Message from the forward Road crew," Hyzo called out. "They've got a problem."

Otakar nodded gloomily. "I told you, trouble."

Six

"What's happening," Jan said into the microphone.

"*Lajos here. No big problems clearing the Road until now. Earthquake, at least a couple of years ago. About a hundred meters of Road missing.*"

"Can't you fill it in?"

"*Negative. We can't even see the bottom.*"

"What about going around it?"

"*That's what we're trying to do. But it means blasting a new road out of the cliff. It's going to take at least a half day.*"

Jan cursed silently to himself; this was not going to be an easy trip at all if it continued this way. "Where are you?" he asked.

"*About a six hour drive from the tunnel.*"

"We'll join you. Keep the work going. Out."

Six hours. That would mean a shorter day than planned. But they had work to do on the brakes. And there were sure to be other problems as people settled down. Get the brakes fixed, get around the collapsed bit of Road, and press on in the morning. Everyone could use a night's sleep.

The Road had dropped down from the mountain slopes to the coastal plain, and as it fell the landscape had changed completely. Gone were the rocky slopes and the occasional bush with a precarious roothold in the scree. It was jungle now, high, thick jungle that cut out all sight of the ocean and only permitted a narrow view of the sky. There was plenty of evidence here that the jungle was trying to retake the Road. Burned trees and vegetation were on both sides now, where they had been bulldozed aside by the tanks that had gone on ahead. There was animal life, too, dark forms glimpsed briefly in the shadows beside the Road. At one point a line of green flying creatures had floated slowly out of the jungle and across the Road. Two of them had smashed into the engine's windshield, to slowly slide away leaving blue smears of blood behind. Jan washed away the traces with the touch of a button. The engine was back on autopilot and there was little to do except watch the tunnel of the Road open up ahead.

"Tired, Otakar?" he asked.

"A little. A night's sleep will help."

"But tomorrow will be a long day, and every day after that. Even if we spell each other at the wheel, it's going to be hard because we won't be able to rest, not just changing places between driver and co-driver." Jan had the beginnings of an idea and he worked at it. "What we need are more co-drivers. For this engine and all the others. That way we could have an experienced driver at the wheel all the time and the one off duty can get his eyes shut."

"There aren't any other drivers."

"I know that, but we could train some as we go."

Otakar grunted and shook his head. "No way. Every man with a trace of technical ability is already on a job. Or like your ex-mechanic Decio—who is back on the farm where he belongs. I don't want any farmers in the driving compartment."

"You're right—but only half right. What about training some women as drivers?" Jan smiled as Otakar's jaw dropped.

"But . . . women don't drive. Women are just women."

"Only in this outpost of hell, my boy. Even on Earth the exams are strictly competitive and workers rise as high as their ability allows, irrespective of their sex. It makes sound economic sense. I see no reason why the same thing can't be done here. Find the girls with ability and train them for the job."

"The Hradil is not going to like this, or any of the Family Heads."

"Of course not—and what difference does it make? This is an emergency and we need emergency measures." Mention of The Hradil brought a sweeter name to mind from the same family. He smiled at the thought. "Have you ever noticed the embroidery that Alzbeta Mahrova does?"

"I have a piece, traded it from the family."

"Well that takes patience, skill, concentration—"

"All the traits of a successful driver!" Otakar was smiling now too. "This mad idea may work. It will sure make life a bit brighter during the drive."

"I'm for that," Hyzo's voice called out from the speaker; he had been listening on the intercom to the conversation. "Wouldn't like to have me train a radio operator or two?"

"You might very well. Later. Right now we want to put together a list of the women we know who might have ability in this direction. But don't say a word outside of this compartment. I want to hit the Elders with this later, when they are tired and off-balance."

Night fell before they reached the break in the Road. They were climbing again and the rock wall rose up on their right, while to the left the Road ended only in blackness. Jan slowed the speed of the trains gradually as a blip appeared on the nose radar. When he caught a glimpse of metal ahead on the Road he cut the high beams of his lights and sent out the stop signal.

"Begin braking now."

As his own train slowed he knew that, stretching far back into the night, the long column of trains was also reducing speed continually. As they slowed to a complete stop Otakar entered the time in his log, then began shutting down the engine for standby. Jan rose and stretched. He was tired—but knew the night's work was just beginning.

"Nine hundred and eighty-seven kilometers today," Otakar said, entering the figure in the log.

"That's fine." Jan massaged the tired muscles in his legs. "That leaves us only something like twenty-six thousand more to go."

"The longest journey begins with but a single turn of the wheel," Eino said, popping up from the engine room hatch.

"You can just keep your folk philosophy to yourself. Shut down the engine, put all systems on standby and start pulling that brake valve from car seven. By the time you get it out I'll bring you a replacement. And check the filter as well."

Jan cracked the exit door and a wave of hot, moist air washed over him. The engines and the cars were completely air conditioned, and he had forgotten how much further south they were. He could feel the sweat already dampening his skin as he climbed down the rungs. Very soon now they would have to use the cold-suits when they went outside the trains. He walked the hundred meters toward the ragged cliff that marked the end of the road.

Bright lights illuminated the work area, and the roar and grind of the tanks echoed from the rocky wall, punctuated by the continuous explosions of the fusion guns. The flaming mouths of the tank-mounted units had already carved a niche into the sheer rock wall to span the gap of missing Road. Now they were working to deepen and widen it to permit the trains to pass. Jan didn't interfere, they were doing fine without him. And he had business with the Family Elders.

They met in the lead car of the Taekeng family, the largest available compartment. This family, the most conservative and inbred, still kept many of its customs from distant Earth. There were silk hangings on the walls, scenes of water and birds and other strange animals, as well as sentences in an alphabet none of them could read. They were also the most group-social family, so they did not have their living cars broken up into the many small compartments the others preferred. The normal occupants of the room had been dispossessed for the moment, but they did not seem to mind. They were gathered in the Road outside the car, calling excitedly to each other about the work ahead, the stars overhead, the strange smells from the jungle below. Children ran about and were called back with great excitement when they ventured too near the precipice. A baby wailed in the darkness, then smacked contentedly as it was put to the breast. Jan picked his way through the people and entered the car.

Though he had called the meeting they had started without him. That was obvious. Hein Ritterspach stood before the Family Heads, but he stopped talking as Jan entered. He gave one look of intense hatred before he turned his back, holding the cast on his arm before him like a shield. Jan took one look at the circle of stony faces and knew perfectly well what Hein was trying to do. But it wouldn't work. He went slowly to an empty chair and dropped into it.

"As soon as Ritterspach leaves, this meeting can begin," he said.

"No," Chun Taekeng broke in. "He has some grave charges that must be heard. He has said—"

"I don't care what he said. If you wish to hold a meeting of Family Heads to listen to him, you may do it any time you choose. Tonight if you wish. After our business is finished. I have called this meeting as Trainmaster and we have urgent matters to discuss."

"You can't throw me out!" Hein shouted. "As Proctor Captain I have a right to attend."

Jan sprang to his feet and put his face close to the other's ruddy one. "You have the right to leave, nothing else, that is an order."

"You cannot order *me*, you attacked me, there are charges . . ."

"You drew a gun on me, Hein, and I defended myself. There are witnesses. I will prefer charges when we reach Southtown. If you insist on bothering me now I shall arrest you now, for endangering the safety of the train, and I shall imprison you. Now go."

Hein's eyes swept the room, looking for some evidence of aid. Chun opened his mouth—then shut it. The Hradil sat as unmoving and expressionless as a snake. There was only silence. Hein choked out a sound and stumbled to the door, fumbling at the handle with his left hand, then vanished into the night.

"Justice will be done in Southtown," The Hradil said.

"It will be done," Jan answered, his voice as expressionless as hers. "After the trip. Now, are there any troubles I should know about?"

"There are complaints," Ivan Semenov said.

"I don't want to hear them. Morale, complaints, food, personal problems, all of these will be handled by the Family Heads. I mean mechanical problems; air, power, anything like that?"

He looked from face to face, but there was no response. It had to continue this way. He had to keep them off balance, unable to adjust completely to this new mode of life.

"Good. I knew I could rely upon you all to make things smoother for the technical crew. There are other ways in which you can help. As you know, we shall be driving for twice the normal amount each day. This is only the first day, so fatigue is not showing yet. But it will. The drivers will be working double time, so will soon be twice as tired as normal. We may have accidents which we *cannot* afford. Unless we train more drivers as we go."

"Why do you bother us with this?" Chun Taekeng asked abrasively. "This is a technical matter about which you boast great proficiency. With no farming to be done, there are plenty of men to choose from, so choose who you will."

"Begging your pardon, but I would not trust any of your horny handed field workers near my machinery. Every man with any technical skills or abilities is now working or training."

"If you have them all, why do you come to us?" The Hradil asked.

"I said men. My drivers tell me that they know many women with the skills and reflexes we need. They could be trained. . . ."

"Never!" The Hradil exploded the word, her eyes narrowed to slits buried in a webwork of ancient wrinkles. Jan turned to face her, the closest he had ever been before, and realized that her cap of snowy hair was really a wig. So she had vanity. Perhaps that knowledge could be turned to some good use.

"Why not?" he asked quietly.

"Why? You dare ask? Because a woman's place is in the home. With her children, the family, that is the way it always has been done before."

"Well that's not the way it will be done in the future. The ships always come. They did not come. The ships take the corn. We are carrying the corn south. The ships bring the seed and supplies we need. There is no seed or supplies. Women do not do technical work. They do now. My co-driver tells me that Alzbeta Mahrova, of your family, does skilled and delicate embroidery. He feels a woman with those talents could be trained as a co-driver. Then he could relieve me as driver. You can send her there now."

"No!"

There was silence then. Had he pushed too hard? Maybe, but he had to push to keep them off balance—while he kept his balance. He had to stay in command. The silence went on and on, then was suddenly broken.

"You pick on only one," Bruno Becker said in his slow and solemn manner. "The girls in the Becker family are as good at embroidery as the Mahrovas. Some say even better. My daughter-in-law, Arma, is known for the delicacy of her work."

"I know it," Jan said, turning his back on The Hradil, deliberately, smiling and nodding enthusiastically. "And she is a very smart girl, as well. A moment, yes, isn't her brother driver of nine train? I thought so. I'll have him send for her. Her own brother will be able to tell her worth, and whether she will be able to be trained as a co-driver."

"Her embroidery is like chicken droppings in the sand," The Hradil spluttered.

"I'm sure both girls do fine work," Jan said calmly. "But that is not the question. It is whether they can be trained to do a co-pilot's work. I'm sure Otakar will be able to train Alzbeta as easily as Arma's brother can teach her."

"Impossible. Alone, with only men."

"A problem easily solved. Very sensible of you to remind me. When Alzbeta comes in the morning to the engine, be sure a married woman is with her. You've solved in advance what might be a problem, Hradil, I do thank you. Now let us prepare a list of women who might be suitable for this work."

There seemed to be no trouble. The Family Heads were suggesting names, drawing up lists, with Jan agreeing and writing down the ones they thought best. Only The Hradil was silent. Jan chanced a look at her expressionless face and realized that all her feelings were in her eyes; burning pits of hatred. She knew what he had done and was filled with arctic loathing, frozen by it. If she had disliked him before, she hated him now, with a ferocity beyond belief. Jan turned away and tried to ignore her because he knew there was absolutely nothing he could do about it.

Seven

"Another hour at least," Lajos Nagy said. "We have to blast more headroom or the engines will never get through. And I want to do static tests on the outer lip. I don't like the condition of some of the rock." He had been up an entire day and night, had worked right through the night. His skin was pale and marked by dark patches, like soot, under his eyes.

"How many tanks will it take?" Jan asked.

"Two. The ones with the oversize fusion guns."

"Leave those two and start ahead with the rest of the tanks. You must stay ahead of us."

"I'll follow with these. . . ."

"Oh no you won't. You look like hell, do you know that? I want you asleep when the tanks leave. We've got a long trip ahead and a lot more trouble, I'm sure. Now don't argue, or I'll give your job back to Hein."

"You've talked me into it. Now that you mention it, I do feel like lying down."

Jan walked slowly across the newly-carved Road toward the waiting trains. He looked out at the harsh blue of the sky and winced at the glare. The sun was still behind the mountains, but it would rise soon enough. Beyond the sharp edge of the cliff there were only clouds hiding the jungle below. It was going to be a hot day. And get still hotter. He turned back to his engine to see Eino leaning against the golden flank of metal, sucking on a cold pipe. There was grease on his hands and arms and even on his face.

"All done," he told Jan. "Took most of the night, but worth it.

I'll doze in the engine room. Didn't put the new brake valves in, no need. Old ones just gummed up. Rinsed out and put back. Work fine. Changed the filters in the lines, too. Solid with gunk. I'd like to bend that Decio over my knee. He never touched a one of them."

"Maybe I'll let you do that. After the trip."

The few hours' sleep he had grabbed had restored Jan and he enjoyed the climb up the side of the engine. As he clambered up the sun broke over the hills and shone on the metal so that, even through half-closed eyes, he was in the center of a golden glare. Half-blinded, he went through the hatch and slammed it after him. The air was cool and dry.

"Gear box temperature, tire temperature, brake drum temperature, bearing temperature."

It wasn't Otakar who was speaking, but a far sweeter and familiar voice. To think he had forgotten! Alzbeta sat in the co-driver's seat, with Otakar standing behind her nodding his head happily. Not two feet away sat a pudgy, gray-haired woman, knitting with grim ferocity. The Hradil's own daughter, watchdog and guardian of virgins. Jan smiled to himself as he slipped into his driver's chair. Alzbeta glanced up at the motion and her voice died.

"She's doing absolutely fantastic," Otakar said. "About ten times brighter and ten times smarter than the last dim dirt-scratcher I tried to teach this job to. If the other girls are anywhere as good, our driver problem is solved."

"I'm sure they will be," Jan said, but his eyes were on Alzbeta as he spoke. So close he could almost touch her. Those dark eyes looking deep into his.

"I like this work, too," she said. Very seriously, her back to the others. Only Jan could see her eyes move up and down his body, followed by the slow wink.

"For the good of the train," he said, just as seriously. "I am glad that this plan will work. Isn't that so, aunty?"

The Hradil's daughter returned only a glare of pure malice before bending back to her knitting. She had been well briefed by her mother. Her presence could be suffered. It was small enough price to pay to have Alzbeta nearby. When he spoke it was to Otakar—but his eyes were on the girl.

"How soon before you think she will be ready to spell you as co-driver?"

"Compared to some of the dummies on these trains, I would

say she is ready now. But let her have a day here at least, observing, then perhaps tomorrow she can try a trial run in the seat with me standing by."

"Sounds good to me. What do you think, Alzbeta?"

"I'm . . . not sure. The responsibility."

"The responsibility is not yours, it is the driver's. I or Otakar will be in this seat, making the decisions and driving the train. Your job will be to help, to keep track of things, to watch the instruments, to follow orders. As long as you stay calm, you can do it. Do you think you can?"

Her jaw was clamped tight and, beautiful as she was, there was more than a little of The Hradil in her when she spoke.

"Yes. I can do it. I *know* I can do it."

"Very good. Then it is all arranged."

When the fusion guns had finished cutting the new Road, Jan personally walked every foot of it, the exhausted tank operator plodding at his side. They walked along the lip, just a metre from the sheer fall into the jungle far below. Despite the breeze the cutting was like an oven, the rock still warm under their feet. Jan knelt and tapped the edge of the rock with a heavy ball peen hammer he carried. A chunk of stone broke away and rattled down the slope and vanished over the drop.

"I don't like some of this rock. I don't like it at all," he said. The tank operator nodded.

"Don't like it myself. If we had more time I would widen the cut. I've done what I can with melt compacting. Hope the lava flow on the surface will penetrate and hold it together."

"You're not the only one to hope that. All right, you've done all you can now. Get your tanks through and I'll bring the first train over." He started away, then turned back. "You've dug in the guide wire as we planned?"

"Absolute minimum clearance. If it was one more centimeter to the right you would be taking off the top of the engine."

"Good." Jan had been thinking about this and he knew what had to be done. There would be protests, but they would follow his orders. His own crew were predictably the first.

"You'll need an engineer for this job," Eino said. "I promise not to sleep."

"I will not need one. The engines will be dead slow all the way, so they can do without your attention for a few minutes. Nor will I need a co-driver or a communications officer for that short a time. Clear the driving compartment. Once we're past this you'll learn the job, Alzbeta." He guided her towards the hatch with his hand on her elbow, ignoring the gasps and raised knitting needles of her chaperone. "Don't worry."

There were more protests from the passengers as they were unloaded but, in a few minutes, Jan was alone in the train. If anything happened he would be the only one to suffer. They could not afford to waste more time here; they must press on.

"All clear," Otakar called from the open hatch. "I can still come along."

"See you on the other side. Clear the train, I'm starting."

He touched lightly on the accelerator and, at absolutely minimum speed, the engine crawled forward. As soon as it was moving he set the autopilot and took his hands from the wheel. He was committed. The engine would take itself across in a far more controlled manner than he himself could. As the train crept forward he went to the open hatch and looked at the edge of the Road. If there were trouble, it would be there. Centimeter by centimeter they crawled through the newly-burned section of Road, closer and closer to the far end.

The sound was a grinding rumble, easily heard above the drone of the engine, and as the noise began cracks appeared in the hard surface of the stone. Jan started to turn to the controls, then realized he could do nothing. He stood, his fingers tight-clamped to the edge of the hatch, as a great section of Road broke away and vanished with a roar toward the valley floor, far below. Cracks spread like deadly fingers across the surface, reaching for the train.

Then stopped.

There was a great gap now, a chunk bitten out of the solid rock of the Road. But it ended short of the engine. The powerful machine lumbered past the opening and Jan sprang back to the controls, frantically switching from camera to camera to get a view of the following car. Now the engine was through safely, past the gap.

However, the cars it pulled were almost three times wider.

His foot was a fraction of a centimeter above the brake pedal, his fingers resting on the autopilot, his eyes fixed on the screen.

The wheels of the first car crept toward the gap, the outer, double wheel apparently aimed directly at it. It would never get by. He was about to stamp on the brakes when he looked closer. Just possibly.

The wheel rolled to the edge of the gap and dropped over the lip.

The outer tire of the two. It turned slowly in the air, blue sky showing under it. All of the weight of the overloaded car came onto the inner wheel.

As the tire skirted the very edge of the drop it compressed under the weight, flattening to an oval. Then the other tire hit the far edge of the gap and the car was safe on the other side. The radio bleeped in Jan's ear and he switched it on.

"Did you see *that?*" Otakar asked, in a very weak voice.

"I did. Stay close by and report on the broken area. I'm going to take the rest of the train across. If it stays this way it will be fine. But tell me *instantly* if there are any more falls."

"I'll do that, you can be sure."

At minimum crawling speed the cars followed, one by one, until the entire train was safely across the gap. As soon as the last car was reported safely past Jan killed the engine, jammed on the brakes—and let out a deep sigh. He felt as though every muscle in his body had been worked over with a heavy hammer. To relieve the tension he jogged back to the new section of Road to join Otakar.

"No more falls, none at all," the co-driver reported.

"Then we should be able to get the other trains through." The passengers were crossing on foot now, pressed as close to the inside wall as they could, looking with frightened eyes at the cliff edge and the gaping crevice. "Take the first engine and keep going. Half speed until all the trains are over. It should go well now. When they are through I'll catch up on the cycle. Any questions?"

"Nothing I can put into words. This is your show, Jan. Good luck."

It was hours before the last train was past, but they all made it safely. There were no more rock falls. As Jan sped along beside the slow-moving trains he wondered what the next emergency would be.

Happily, it was a long time coming. The Road crossed the coastal ranges and cut across the alluvial coastal plain that fringed the continent. This was an almost entirely flat and featureless swamp, formerly the coastal banks, shoal water, lifted up by the engineers. The Road was on a raised dike for the most part, cutting straight as a ruled line through the reeds and tree-grown hassocks. All that the maintenance tanks had to do, for the most part, was burn off intruding vegetable life and repair the occasional crack caused by subsidence. They moved faster than the heavy-laden trains and were drawing farther and farther ahead, making up most of the two-day lead they had lost. The nights had been growing shorter until the day when the sun did not set at all. It dropped to the southern horizon, a burning blue ball of fire, then moved into the sky again soon afterwards. After this it was always above their heads, its intensity increasing as they headed south. The temperature outside had been rising steadily and now stood at well past 150 degrees. When there had still been a night, many people had emerged from the cramped, boring quarters to move about on the Road despite the breathless heat. With the sun now in the sky constantly this could not be done, and morale was being strained to the breaking point. And there were still 18,000 kilometers to go.

They were driving a full nineteen hours every day now, and the new co-drivers were proving their worth. There had been some grumbling among the men at first about women out of their natural place, but this had stopped as fatigue had taken over. The extra help was needed. Some of the women had not been able to learn the work, or had not the stamina for it, but there were more than enough new volunteers to take their places.

Jan was happier than he had remembered he had been for years. The fat chaperone had complained about the climb up to the driving compartment and, when the heat had increased, it had been impossible to find a coldsuit big enough for her. A married cousin of Alzbeta's had taken the watchdog role for one day, but said she was bored by it and had her children to take care of and refused to come back the following day. Her absence had not been reported at once to The Hradil and by the time she had learned about it the damage—or lack of damage—had been done. Alzbeta had survived a day alone with three men and was none the worse for the experience. By unspoken agreement the chaperone's role was dropped.

Alzbeta sat in the co-driver's seat while Jan drove. Otakar would sleep on the cot in the engine room, or play cards with Eino. Hyzo found it easy to get permission to join the games—Jan cheerfully stood radio watch for him—and though the hatch behind them was open, Jan and Alzbeta were alone for the first time since they had met.

At the very first it was embarrassing. Not for Jan. It was Alzbeta who would blush and hang her head when he talked and forget her job as co-driver. Her lifetime of training was fighting her intelligence. Jan ignored this for one shift, not even making small talk, thinking she would be over it by the second day. When she was not, he lost his temper.

"I've asked you for that reading twice now. That's too much. You are here to aid me, not make my job more difficult."

"I—I'm sorry. I'll try not to do it again."

She lowered her head and blushed even more, and Jan felt like a swine. Which he was. You don't break the conditioning of years in a moment. The Road was clear ahead and dead straight, nothing on the nose radar. The trains rolled at a steady 110 KPH and the wheel could be left unattended, for perhaps a moment. He rose and went to Alzbeta and stood behind her, his hands resting lightly on her shoulders. Like a frightened animal's, her body quivered beneath his touch.

"I'm the one who should be sorry," he said. "I'll drag Hyzo away from the poker game, it's time for a driver check in any case."

"No, not yet. It is not that I don't like being alone with you, the other way around. I have known that I have loved you for a very long time, but only now am I finding out what that really means."

She put her hands up to her shoulders to cover his, turned her face to look up at him. When he bent his head to kiss her, her mouth came up to meet his. When his hands slid down to cup her full breasts her hands held them tight, pulling him to her. It was he who broke away first, knowing this was neither the time nor the place.

"See, The Hradil was right," he said, trying to make light of it.

"No! She was wrong in every way. She will not keep us apart, and I will marry you. She cannot stop. . . ."

The flashing red light on the radio console and the rapid beeping sent him leaping to the driver's chair, thumbing on the radio. Behind him Hyzo shot up from the engine room as though he had been propelled from a cannon.

"Trainmaster here."

"*Jan, Lajos here with the tanks. We've hit something too big to handle. It looks like we've lost one tank, though no one injured.*"

"What is it?"

"*Water, just water. The Road's gone. I can't describe it, you'll
have to see for yourself.*"

There were complaints, but Jan kept the trains rolling until
they caught up with the maintenance tanks. He was asleep when
they picked up the first blip on the nose radar. He awoke at once
and slid into the driver's seat as Otakar vacated it.

As it had for days, the Road still traversed the coastal swamps.
Continually different, yet always the same, the haze-shrouded
wastes of reed and water had been changing imperceptibly. The
ratio of open water to swamp was growing until, most suddenly,
the swamps were gone and there was only water on both sides of
the causeway. Jan slowed the train, and the others behind automatically followed. First the radar picked out the individual
specks of the vehicles, then he could make them out by sight.

It was frightening. The Road dropped lower and lower below
the surrounding water until, a little past the tanks, it vanished
completely. Beyond them there was just water, no sign of the
Road at all. Just a calm ocean stretching away on all sides.

Jan shouted to Otakar to finish the shutdown procedures since,
the instant the brakes were set, he was at the exit hatch, pulling
on a coldsuit. Lajos was waiting below when he dropped onto the
Road.

"We've no idea how far it goes," he said. "I tried to get across
with a tank; you can see the turret of it about two kilometers out.
It's deeper there, flooded me suddenly. I just had time to hit the
dampers and get out. The next tank threw me a rope, pulled me
free."

"What happened?"

"Just a guess. It looks like there was a general subsidence of the
land here. Since it was all under water once, maybe it's just dropping back where it came from."

"Any idea how wide this thing is?"

"None. Radar won't reach, and the telescopes just show more
haze. It may end in a few kilometers. Or go on until it drops
down to the ocean bottom."

"You're optimistic."

"I was in that water—and it's hot. And I can't swim."

"Sorry. I'll go take a look myself."

"The Road cable is still in place. You can't see anything but
the instruments can track it."

Jan clumped around to the rear of the engine, his movements

hampered by the thick coldsuit. The suit was lined with a network of tubes filled with cold water. A compact refrigeration unit on his belt hummed industriously and expelled the heated exhaust air to the rear. Cooled air was also blown across his face under the transparent helmet. The suit was tiring to wear after a few hours—but it made life possible. The outside air temperature now stood near 180 degrees. Jan thumbed on the built-in intercom at the rear of the engine.

"Otakar, can you hear me?"

"Green."

"Set the interlocks to the cars, then disconnect the engine coupling. I'll disconnect the cables back here."

"Are we going for a ride?"

"You might say that."

There was a whirr and a clatter as the metal jaws of the coupling slowly opened. Jan pushed the heavy tongue aside, then unplugged all the cable connectors. There were loud thuds under the car behind him as the beta safety brakes were actuated. The cables retracted like snakes into a hole, and he climbed back up to the driving compartment.

"I need three volunteers," he told the waiting crew members as he pulled off the coldsuit. "You, you and you. Alzbeta, take this suit and get back into the train. What we have to do may take a while."

She did not protest, but her eyes were on him as she pulled on the suit slowly and left. Otakar dogged the hatch shut after her. Jan studied the glimmering expanse of water ahead. "Eino," he said, "just how waterproof are we?"

The engineer did not answer at once. He scratched at his ear in thought as he looked around slowly, looking through the steel walls and floor with a mechanic's eye, seeing all the joints, seals and hatches.

"Not bad at all," he said, finally. "We're made for a certain amount of water, drive trains and bearings, access ports and hatches, all with gaskets. Higher up, all right too, at least for a while. I really think we could submerge right up to the roof without getting into trouble. Higher than that and we could short out the cooling fins on top. Up that far I would say we're waterproof."

"Then I think we better go before we change our minds." He dropped into the driver's chair. "Get on the engine—I may need a lot of power. Hyzo, keep the radio open and keep a report going back. If there is any trouble I want the others to know what happened. Otakar, stand by if I need you."

"Going for a swim?" the co-driver asked calmly, flipping on switches.

"I hope not. But we have to find out if the Road is still there. We can't turn back and we can't stay here. And this is the only Road. This engine stands more than twice as high as the tank. It all depends on the depth of the water. Power."

"Full."

The tanks scuttled aside as the hulking engine ground forward. Straight toward the water until the front wheels sent out the first ripples. Then straight in.

"It's like being in a ship . . ." Otakar said, almost under his breath. *With the slight difference,* Jan thought, *that this engine doesn't float.* He did not say it aloud.

All about them was water of unknown depth. They knew the Road was still beneath them, for the water had not yet reached the hubs of the great wheels. And the cable blip was high and centered, being followed automatically. But a bow wave was pushed up by the moving engine, and they could have been in a ship for all the apparent connection they had with land—or even with the Road now falling back behind them.

The turret of the tank ahead was a solid reference point that they approached cautiously. As they came close, the water rose steadily. Jan stopped a good twenty meters from the drowned vehicle.

"Water doesn't quite cover our wheels yet, plenty to go," Otakar said, looking out of the side window. He tried to speak calmly but his voice was strained.

"How wide would you say the Road is here?" Jan asked.

"One hundred meters, as always, like most of the rest of the Road."

"Is it? You don't think this water may have undercut it?"

"I hadn't thought. . . ."

"I had. We'll go around the tank, as close as we can. And hope that it is solid enough under the wheels."

He flipped off the autopilot as he spoke and turned the wheel slowly as they moved forward under complete manual. The high white blip of the central cable drifted across the screen until it vanished. It had been their only guide. Higher and still higher the water rose.

"I hope you're staying close to the tank," Hyzo called out. He may have meant it as a joke. It had not sounded like one.

Jan tried to remember just how big the tank was under the water. He wanted to remain as near to it as possible without running into it. Passing as close as he could. Water, nothing but water on all sides, the only sound the rumble of the engines and drive and the hoarse breathing of the men.

"I can't see it any more," Jan called out suddenly. "Cameras are dead. Otakar!"

The co-driver had already jumped to the rear window.

"Easy on, almost past, falling slightly behind, you can turn sharp . . . now!"

Jan obeyed blindly. He could do nothing else. He was in the midst of an ocean, turning a wheel, with no reference marks at all. Not too much, straight, he should be past it now. Or was he going in the wrong direction? He would be off the edge of the Road soon. He was unaware of the sweat standing out on his face and dampening his palms.

The tiniest of blips on the cable screen.

"I have it again!"

He centered the wheel, then turned it gradually as the blip slowly moved across the screen to align itself. When it did so he flipped on the autopilot and leaned back.

"So much for that; now let's see how far this goes on."

He kept the speed controls to himself but allowed the autopilot to track the cable. The Road was still beneath them, impossible as it seemed. They watched as a rainstorm blew towards them and washed over the engine, blanketing vision in all directions. Jan turned on the wipers and the headlights. There was a clatter of relays from the engine room.

"You've lost about half your lights," Eino reported. "Shorted out, circuit breakers kicked out."

"Will it mean trouble? What about the rest of the lights?"

"Should be all right. All the circuits are isolated."

They went on. Rain on all sides and just the spattered surface of the water ahead. Water that rose higher and higher, slowly and surely. There was a sudden ascending whine from the engine room and the engine shuddered, lurching sideways.

"What is it?" Hyzo called out, an edge of panic in his voice.

"Revs up," Jan said, clinging to the wheel, turning it, trying to follow the blip of the cable that was sliding off the screen, killing the autopilot as he did. "But Road speed down. We're moving sideways."

"Sand—or mud on the Road!" Otakar shouted. "We're slipping."

"And we're losing the cable." Jan turned the wheel even more. "This thing is almost afloat; the wheels are not getting the traction they should. But they will."

He stamped hard on the accelerator and the transmission roared deeply from below. The drive wheels spun in the mud, churning it up, digging into it, roiling the surface of the water around them. The sliding still continued—the cable blip was gone from the screen.

"We'll go off the edge!" Hyzo shouted.

"Not yet." Jan's teeth almost met in the flesh of his lip, but he was not aware of it.

There was a lurch, then another one as the wheels touched the surface of the Road. He cut the power as they gripped again, then crept forward. Moment after moment of silence. Until the cable blip appeared again. He centered it, and looked at the compass to make sure they were not going in the opposite direction. The engine crawled ahead. The rain passed and he killed the lights.

"I'm not sure . . . but I think the water is lower," Otakar said in a hoarse voice. "Yes, it is, it must be, that rung was under water a minute ago."

"I'll tell you something even better," Jan said, cutting in the autopilot and dropping back heavily in the chair. "If you look directly ahead I think you'll see where the Road comes out of the water again."

The level of the water sank until the wheels were clear, throwing spray in all directions, then they were up on the solid surface once more and Jan killed the power and set the brakes.

"We're across. The Road is still there."

"But—can the trains make it?" Otakar asked.

"They are going to have to, aren't they?"

There was no answer to that.

Eight

Before there could be any thought of taking the trains across the drowned section of Road there was the barricade of the abandoned tank to be considered. Jan drove the engine back down the Road, with scarcely any trouble passing the mud-coated section on the return trip, and stopped a few meters from the tank.

"Any ideas?" he asked.

"Any chance of starting it up?" Otakar asked.

"Negative. The pile has been damped and all the circuits are wet by now. But there is something we have to find out before we even look for a way to tackle this." He put in a call to Lajos, who had been driving the tank when it went under. The answer was not cheering at all. "The drive is still engaged. About the only thing we can do with that tank is push it aside. And we can't do that unless it will roll free. It will be impossible to skid that amount of dead weight."

"You're the Maintenance Captain," Otakar said. "So you are the one to answer that question best."

"I know the answer. With the power dead the manual disengage lever has to be used. But the trouble is that the thing is clamped to the inside rear wall. It has to be unhooked, fitted into place, then turned about a dozen times. All of this under, what? about three meters of water. Do you swim, Otakar?"

"Where would I learn to do that?"

"A good question. Too much fertilizer in the canal to swim there—and that is the only body of water near the city. You think someone would have planned a swimming pool when the cities were designed. It wouldn't have taken much. I imagine that leaves me as the only swimmer on Halvmork. A reluctant volunteer. But I'll need some help."

There was no easy way to make a face mask, but one of the pressure bottles filled with compressed air was simple enough to arrange. Jan worked with the valve until it released a steady flow of air, smelling of oil and grease, that should supply his needs without blowing his head off. Eino arranged a sling so he could carry it at his waist, with a plastic tube to his mouth. That and a waterproof light were all he needed.

"Bring us as close as you can," he told Otakar as he stripped off his clothes. He kept his boots on. The metal would be hot, and he would need gloves as well. When the two machines were touching, nose to nose, he cracked the top hatch. A wave of burning air rolled in. Without a word he climbed to the hatch and pushed it open.

It was like climbing into a baker's oven. The cool air of the engine was left behind in an instant as he emerged into the blinding, burning sunshine. He covered his eyes with his arm and shuffled the length of the engine's roof, picking his way between the cooling fins. Trying not to gasp in the hot air, forcing himself to suck the cooler air from the tube instead. Though the soles of his shoes were thick the heat of the metal was penetrating already. At the edge he did not hesitate, but eased himself over into the water.

It was a steaming cauldron that drained the energy from his body. One, two, three strokes took him to the open hatch on the tank and he did not permit himself to hesitate, but sank instantly beneath the surface. It was dark, too dark—then he remembered the light. The heat of the water about him was all engulfing, draining both his will and energy. Now the lever, he must get it.

Everything moved as slowly as in a dream, and if his chest hadn't hurt he thought he might go to sleep. He was getting air from the tank, but not enough. The lever. It came free easily enough, but fitting it over the stud seemed immensely difficult. When it finally clicked into place he lost precious seconds trying to remember which way to move it. Then the turns, over and over until it would turn no more.

Time. Time to go. The lever and the torch dropped from his fingers and he tried to rise, but he could not. The light of the open hatch was clear above but he did not have the strength to swim up to it. With a last burst of his waning energy he tore the weight of the air tank away, spitting out the tube, and bent his knees. One last time. Pushing upwards, swimming upwards, hard, harder.

His hands came out of the water and clutched the edge of the hatch. Then his head was above the surface and he sucked in great gasps of the burning air. It hurt, but it cleared his head. When he was able, he dragged himself up and staggered across the top of the tank and threw himself in the direction of the engine.

And knew he could not make it, could not swim another stroke.

The rope splashed into the water beside his head and he clutched it reflexively. He was pulled to the engine, to the side, and Otakar reached down and took him by the wrists and pulled him from the water like an expiring fish. Jan was barely aware of this, his consciousness fading in a red haze, until his leg brushed the metal of the engine's roof, searing the flesh almost to the bone. He shouted aloud at the sudden pain, his eyes wide, aware that Otakar was helping him. Otakar without a coldsuit, gasping with exhaustion.

They leaned one on the other as they made their way carefully across the top of the engine. Jan went down first, helped by the co-driver, who followed behind him. The air inside was arctic. For a long time all they could do was sit where they had dropped on the floor, fighting to recover.

"Let us not do that again if we can avoid it," Jan said, finally. Otakar could only nod weak agreement.

Hyzo put burn cream on Jan's leg, then wrapped it in gauze. It was painful, but a pill took care of that. And his fatigue as well. Dressed again, he sat in the driver's chair and checked his controls.

"Any sign of leaking yet?" he asked the engineer.

"Negative. This beast is tight."

"Good. Give me plenty of power. I'm going to push that tank off the Road. What will I break if I push it nose to nose?"

"Couple of lights, nothing important. We have solid steel there, four centimeters thick. Weight for traction. Just push."

Jan did, easing forward at slowest possible revs until metal ground against metal and the engine shuddered. Keeping in the lowest gear he pressed down steadily on the accelerator. The clutches growled deeply and the entire engine shuddered as it fought against the dead weight of the tank. Something had to give.

The tank moved. Once it had started to roll backwards, Jan kept the speed steady and turned the wheel ever so slightly, centering it again to hold the gradual turn. Bit by bit they turned until they left the cable behind and the tank was pointing at right angles to the Road. Jan centered the wheel and went on. Further and further from the center. Closer and closer to the edge.

Suddenly the tank reared up and Jan hit the brakes. It dropped over the edge instantly and, from the angle, the engine was just at the edge itself. Slowly and carefully he put the engine in reverse and backed away from the danger. Only when they were lined up again in the center of the Road did he let the air out of his lungs with a deep sigh.

"I agree," Otakar said. "I hope this is the last of the trouble here."

It was not easy, but there were no major problems in bringing the trains across the drowned stretch of Road. Just time. Wasted time. The cars, far lighter than the massive engines, had a tendency to float in the water. Two were the most that could be taken through at one time, and this possible only with an engine at either end. The shuttle continued without stop until all of the cars were across. Only when the trains had been assembled on the far side of the drowned section did Jan permit himself to relax, to sleep for more than a few hours at a time. He had ordered an eight hour rest period before they continued. Everyone needed it, the engine crews were exhausted, and he knew better than to press on with the drivers in this condition. They could rest but he could not. During the entire operation of moving the trains across the drowned section of Road he had been worrying away at a problem that refused to be dismissed. An obvious problem that faced him squarely when he drove back over the water-covered Road to the squadron of solitary tanks. He stopped the water-streaming engine next to the tanks, pulled on a coldsuit, and transferred to the lead tank.

"I thought you had forgotten about us," Lajos Nagy said.

"Quite the opposite. I've been thinking of nothing else for days."

"You going to leave the tanks here?"

"No—we need them too much."

"But we can't cross under our own power."

"I don't expect you to. Look at this."

Jan unrolled a blueprint, a side projection of one of the tanks. He had marked it up liberally with a large red pen. He tapped the lines he had added.

"These are our problem areas," he said. "We are going to spray them all with mothball sealant. So they should be watertight long enough to get through the water and out on the other side."

"Wait a bit," Lajos said, pointing to the diagram. "You've got all the exit hatches sealed shut. How can the driver get out if he has to?"

"No drivers. We take the treads out of gear, seal the tanks watertight—then tow them across. A single cable will do for each. I tried it and it works."

"I hope so," Lajos said dubiously. "But I would hate to be in the engine towing one of these things if it went off the edge of the Road. It will pull the engine over with it."

"It might very well. That is why we are going to rig a tow release that can be operated from inside the engine. If the tank starts to go we just cut it loose."

Lajos shook his head. "I suppose there's nothing else for it. Let's try it with number six tank first. The clutches are almost shot and we may have to leave it behind in any case."

There was a unanimous sigh of relief when the plan worked. The towed tank vanished beneath the water and wasn't seen again until it emerged on the other side of the sunken section of Road. The sealant was quickly scraped away and, except for a few puddles from a small leak, the tank was intact. The transfer of all the others began.

When the trek was ready to begin again the relief co-drivers were brought back to the engines. Alzbeta was carrying a sealed bundle that she set down when she took off her coldsuit.

"Something special," she said. "I made it myself. It is a family recipe for special occasions. I think this is a special occasion. Beef stroganoff."

It was delicious. The crew sat down to the first meal they had enjoyed since the trek had begun. There was freshly-baked bread with it, liters of beer and fresh green onions. There was even some cheese to follow, though few, if any, had space for this. But they groaned heroically and made room for it.

"Our thanks," Jan said, taking her hand despite the presence of others. No one complained; apparently no one even noticed. They accepted Alzbeta as part of the crew now; an improved part since no one else could do a thing about meals other than heat frozen concentrates. Jan had a sudden inspiration.

"We'll be rolling in about a half an hour. That's just about time to check you out in the driver's seat, Alzbeta. You don't want to just be a co-driver all your life."

"Good idea," Otakar said.

"Oh, no, I couldn't. It's just not possible. . . ."

"That's an order, see that you obey it." His smile softened the impact of his words, and a moment later they were all laughing. Hyzo went for a rag and polished the chair for her; Otakar led her there and adjusted the seat so she could reach the pedals easily. With the power off she tentatively stepped on the brakes and accelerator and tugged on the steering wheel. She already knew the function of all of the instruments.

"See how simple it is," Jan said. "Now put it in reverse and back a few feet." She went pale.

"That's different. I wouldn't be able to."

"Why not?"

"You understand, it's your work."

"For men only, you mean?"

"Yes, perhaps I do."

"Then try it. You have been doing men-only work for the past week, you and the other girls, and the world hasn't come to an end."

"Yes—I will!"

She said it defiantly—and meant it. Things were changing and she liked the changes. Without a word of instruction she turned on the engine, disconnected the autopilot and did all the other things needed to ready the engine. Then, ever so tentatively, she engaged the reverse gear and backed the engine a bit. Then, when she had shut down the engine again, everyone cheered.

When the trek began again they were all in the best of moods, rested and happy. Which was a good thing, since the worst part of the journey was coming up. The engineers who had built the Road had done their best to avoid all the natural hazards of the planet. As much as possible of the Road stayed behind the coastal mountain barriers of the two continents. The penetration of the mountains themselves was done by tunnel. The coasts were avoided for the most part by putting the Road on the dikes offshore. On the raised chain of islands, the isthmus that connected the two continents, the Road ran high along the spine of the islands, the high mountain ridges.

But there was one hazard that could not be avoided. Eventually the Road would have to cross the tropical jungle barrier. The southernmost part of the continent was eternal burning summer. With the air temperature just a few degrees below the boiling point of water, this was a jungle hell.

The Road turned back inland briefly, plunging through a mountain range. The tanks were thirty hours ahead and working on clearing the Road, so Jan had reports on the conditions. But, as always, the reality was beyond description. The tunnel fell at a steep angle and his headlights glared against rock and Road. There were letters here, etched eternally into the surface of the Road itself, SLOW they read, SLOW, repeated again and again. The tires rumbled as they crossed the pattern of letters. As the glaring mouth of the tunnel appeared ahead the trains were doing a lumbering 50 kilometers an hour.

Trees, vines, plants, leaves, the jungle burst with life on all sides, above, even on the Road itself. The Road was over 200 meters wide here, twice the normal width, and still the jungle had overrun it as the burgeoning plant life fought for the light of the sun. In the four years since they had passed last the trees on either side had sent long branches out, questing for the light. Many times these had grown so large that they had overweighed and toppled the parent trees onto the Road. Some had died and been used as a base for other plants and vines, while others, with their roots still fixed in the jungle, had thrived and grown higher from their new positions. Where trees had not obstructed the Road, creepers and vines, some a meter thick and more, had crawled out onto the sunny surface.

The tanks had joined in battle against the trees; the black remains of their victories lined the Road on both sides. With their flame-exploding snouts, the fusion guns had gone first, burning every obstruction before them. Then dozer blades had cleared a path just wide enough for their treads: the tanks that followed had widened this, pushing back the charred remains. Now the trains moved slowly between two walls of blackened debris, still smoking in places. It was a nightmare sight.

"It's horrible," Alzbeta said. "Horrible to look at."

"I don't mean to make light of it," Jan told her, "but this is just the beginning. The worst part is up ahead. Of course it is dangerous out there, always, even when the trip is made at the usual time. And we are late this year, very late."

"Will that make a difference?" she asked.

"I'm not sure—but if there is going to be any difference it will be for the worse. If only better records had been kept. I can't find anything at all from any early planetary surveys. All the memory tapes have been wiped clean. Of course there are logs of all the trips, but they aren't very helpful. Technical notes and distance for the most part. But no personal journals of any kind. I suppose when everything has to be packed to be moved every couple of years odd items usually get thrown out. So I have no hard facts— just a feeling. It's spring that's bothering me."

"I do not know the word."

"Not in the language. No referent. On more reasonable planets there are four seasons in the temperate zones. Winter is the cold time, summer is the hot. The time in between, when everything is warming up, that's spring."

Alzbeta shook her head and smiled. "It is a little hard to understand."

"There is something a little bit like it on this planet. At the edge of the twilight zone there are life forms that have adapted to the cooler environment. They have their ecological niche there and make out fine until summer returns. When it does, all this burgeoning hot-zone life will probably rush in and make a meal of the cooler-adapted forms. Everything out there is eat and be eaten, so the competition for a new food source must be something fierce."

"But you can't be sure. . . ."

"I'm not sure—and I also hope that I am wrong about it. Just cross your fingers and hope that our luck holds out."

It didn't. At first the change seemed innocent enough, just a little incidental traffic slaughter of no real importance. Only Alzbeta seemed put out by it.

"The animals, they don't seem to know about machines. They just come out onto the Road and are run over, crushed."

"There's nothing we can do about it. Don't look if it bothers you."

"I must look. That is part of my job. But those little greenish things with the orange bands, there seem to be a lot of them, coming out of the jungle."

Jan noticed them now, first individuals, then groups, more and more of them. They were like obscene parodies of terrestrial frogs that had grown big as cats. A ripple of movement seemed to go over them as they advanced with a jerking, hopping motion.

"A migration, maybe," he said. "Or they could be chased by something. It's messy—but they can't hurt us."

Or can they? As he spoke the words Jan felt a sudden disquiet. The edge of a memory. What was it? But any doubts at all called for caution. He switched off the speed control and let off on the accelerator, then turned on the microphone.

"Leader to all trains. Decrease speed by 20 K's *now!*"

"What's wrong?" Alzbeta asked.

The Road was becoming almost invisible, covered by the creatures that thronged across it, oblivious of the deadly wheels rushing towards them.

"Of course!" Jan shouted into the microphone. "All drivers stop, *stop*. But don't use your brakes. Ease off on the power, power down to zero, but watch your coupling pressure gauges or you'll jackknife. Repeat. Slow without braking, watch your coupling pressure, watch your nose radar for the train ahead of you."

"What's happening? What's wrong?" Eino called in from the engine compartment.

"Animals of some kind, covering the Road, thousands of them, we're running them down, crushing them. . . ."

Jan broke off as the engine lurched sideways, then he lashed out his hand to cut off the automatic steering, and clutched at the steering wheel.

"It's like driving on ice . . . no friction . . . the wheels are beginning to slide on the bodies."

And the cars were beginning to go too. In the monitor screens Jan saw that the whole train was beginning to wriggle like a snake as the cars skidded and the steering computer fought to keep them following in a straight line.

"Get the computer out of your steering circuits," Jan ordered the other drivers, throwing the switch himself at the same time. A touch of power pulled ahead on the train and stopped the weaving for the moment. He dropped the speed again, slowly, slowly, plunging on into the solid wall of bodies.

"Jan, look ahead!"

Alzbeta's cry alerted him and he saw that the Road, straight until now, began to curve ahead in a shallow bend. An easy curve

—normally. But what would happen now with the road surface as slick as oil?

The speed was dropping—but not fast enough. They were down to 50 and still dropping. And the curve began.

Jan still had the steering on manual, but he had to switch the computer back on so the cars of the train would track correctly behind him. A touch of the wheel, then center it. The shallowest curve he could make, starting from the inside of the bend and drifting slowly to the outside. Halfway through now, almost to the edge. Speed down to 40 . . . 35. A bit more on wheel. Going all right. If he could hold it there.

A quick look at the screens showed the cars snaking slightly, but following in his course. Almost through. There was a sudden bumping as they ran over the charred tree limbs where the tanks had cleared the surface. Good. This would add some friction. Just beyond the edge of the Road was the jungle, a sharp bank and what looked like water or swamp.

"The creatures on the Road, there seem to be less of them," Alzbeta said. "They're coming in groups now, fewer of them."

"I hope you're right." Jan felt, for the first time, the soreness in his hands where he had grappled the steering wheel. "Doing 10 K's now, cars tracking well."

"*I can't hold it!*"

The words burst from the speaker, a cry of despair.

"Who are you? Identify!" Jan shouted into the mike.

"*Train two . . . jackknifing . . . have full brakes, still sliding . . . the EDGE!*"

Jan eased his own train to a stop, automatically, scarcely aware, listening to the scream of pain. The crashing, breaking sounds. Then silence.

"All trains stop," Jan ordered. "Report only if you are in trouble. Report."

There was the hiss of static, nothing else.

"Train two, can you hear me? Come in two, report." Just silence. Nothing. "Train three, are you stopped?" This time there was an answer.

"*Three here. Stopped okay. No problems. Creatures still crossing the Road. There's a great trail of crushed bodies and blood ahead. . . .*"

"That's enough, three. Start up, minimum speed ahead. Report as soon as you have train two in sight." Jan thumbed the switch to internal. "Hyzo, can you raise train two at all?"

"*I'm trying,*" the communications officer answered. "*No signal from the engine. Chun Taekeng has his own radio on the train but he's not answering.*"

"Keep trying. . . ."

"*Hold it. A signal here, I'll put it on.*"

The voice was gasping, frightened. "*. . . what happened. People hurt when we stopped. Send the doctor. . . .*"

"This is the Trainmaster. Who is speaking?"

"*Jan? Lee Ciou here. We had a panic stop and people are hurt. . . .*"

"More important, Lee. Are you still airtight—and is the air conditioning working?"

"*As far as I know. And I hope we're not holed because the ground outside is covered with creatures of some kind. They're crawling over the cars, the windows.*"

"They can't hurt you as long as they can't get in. Get a report from both cars and get back to me as soon as you can. Over and out."

Jan sat stiffly, locked in concentration, staring unseeingly at the front port, his fist tapping heavily on the steering wheel. The train jackknifed—but power still on. So the engine generator must still be functioning. If so—then why couldn't they contact the crew? What had taken the radio out of circuit? He couldn't imagine what could have happened, but one thing was certain: he would need help to straighten out the mess. And he had already wasted precious minutes not calling for it.

"Hyzo," he shouted into the intercom. "Contact the tanks now. Tell them we've had train trouble and we will probably need some muscle to get out of it. I want the two biggest tanks with plenty of cable. Get them started back this way now at top speed."

"*Done. I've got train three on the circuit.*"

"Put them through."

"*I have train two in sight ahead. Cars all over the Road, some even into the jungle. I've stopped now, just behind the last car.*"

"Can you see the engine?"

"*Negative.*"

"Any chance of your getting by with your train?"

"*Absolutely none. This thing is a mess! I've never seen . . .*"

"Over and out."

Hyzo, the communications officer, came onto the circuit as soon as Jan had killed it.

"*I've got Lee Ciou in train two back on. Here he is.*"

"*Jan, can you hear me? Jan . . .*"

"What did you find out, Lee?"

"*I've talked to the other car. They're shouting a lot and don't make sense, but I don't think anyone's dead. Yet. The car has some broken windows, but Chun Taekeng is taking over evacuation to this car. More important, I've got through to the engineer on the internal phone circuit.*"

"Did he tell you what's wrong?"

"*It's very bad. I've patched you through to him on the radio circuit.*"

"All right. Vilho, are you there? Vilho Heikki, come in."

The radio sputtered and crackled, and a distant voice was audible through the static.

"*Jan . . . there's been a crackup. I was in the engine room when we started sliding all over the Road. I heard Turtu shouting something—then we hit. Something real solid. Then the water, and Arma . . .*"

"Vilho, I'm losing you. Can you talk louder?"

"*Real bad crackup. I started up the ladder when I saw the water. It was coming through the hatch. Maybe I should have got them out. But they didn't answer . . . the water was coming in. So I slammed and sealed the hatch lid. . . .*"

"You did the right thing. You had the rest of the train to think about."

"*Yes, I know . . . but Arma Nevalainen . . . she was co-driver.*"

There was no time for Jan to think about it. That his plan for the women to help drive had just killed one of them. He must think only of the others still in danger aboard the train.

"Are you holding power, Vilho?"

"*So far in the green. The engine is tilted forward at a sharp angle. We must have nose-dived into the swamp. All the driver's controls, the radio, are knocked out. But the generator is still turning over, cooling fins topside must still be out of water, and I can supply train power from here. For a little while more . . .*"

"What do you mean?"

"*Air conditioning is out in here too. Temperature going up pretty fast.*"

"Hold on. I'll get you out as fast as I can."

"What are you doing?" Alzbeta called after Jan.

"The only thing possible. You're in charge until I get back. Any problems, Hyzo will help you. When the tanks arrive direct them to the engine of train two and I'll meet them there."

While Jan climbed into a coldsuit, Eino made a tight bundle of a second suit.

"You should let me go, Jan," he said.

"No. Keep the power up. I have to see what can be done back there."

He exited as fast as he could through the rear door of the engine room and heard it slam shut behind him as Eino shut out the burning air. Without haste—but without any waste motion— Jan unshipped the cycle from its housing, strapped the coldsuit into place, then lowered it onto the Road. Only then did he realize the sickening nature of the surface.

It was a charnel house behind the engine. The alien creatures had been crushed, smeared, destroyed. A few maimed survivors, still driven by some unknown urge, were struggling painfully toward the jungle. The thick blue flesh and blood of the others coated the road. It was bearable just behind the engine, but when he swung aboard the cycle and started back past the row of stationary cars it quickly became worse. The wide wheels had worked appalling destruction. Where the cars had skidded, great smears of crushed bodies coated the surface. Finally he had to steer to the inside of the curve of the Road, skirting the burned areas, to find enough surface to ride upon. It was dangerous here, but there was no other way to get by the carnage. Very slowly he went past the train and back into the bend in the Road.

Something very large, clawed and deadly, lurched out of the jungle toward him.

Jan had only a glimpse as it reared up; he threw full power into the rheostats and the cycle screeched forward, pulling away from the creature, skidding wildly as it bumped over the recent corpses. Jan fought for control, skidding his boots through the slippery muck, risking a quick look back over his shoulder. He slowed. The beast was feasting on the crushed bodies and seemed to have forgotten him.

Train two was ahead; a frightening sight. The cars were jack-knifed over the entire width of the Road and into the jungle on both sides. The engine was over the edge and nose down in the swamp.

The destruction on the Road was forgotten now as Jan threaded his way toward the engine. The cause of the tragedy was instantly apparent. A great tree had been burned, then dozed off the Road. It had stopped the engine from plunging headlong into the water. But in stopping it, a thick, broken branch had punched through the armored glass of the front port. It had been a quick death for the drivers.

It would not be easy to pull that dead weight from the muck of the swamp. That would come later. Vilho had to be taken to safety first. Jan stopped behind the engine, then climbed carefully up the cables with the coldsuit bundled under his arm. He could feel the burn of the metal even through his thick gloves and wondered if the engineer was still alive inside. It was time to find out. He flipped up the lid of the phone next to the rear entrance and shouted into it.

"Vilho, can you hear me? Vilho, come in."

He had to do this twice before a weak voice rustled back.

"Hot . . . burning . . . can't breathe."

"It's going to get a lot hotter if you don't do as I say. I can't open this door so you must have sealed it from the inside. Vilho, you have to unlock it. It's out of water. Let me know when that's done."

There was slow scraping inside and an endless time seemed to pass before the trapped engineer spoke again.

"It's open . . . Jan."

"Then you're almost out of this. Get as far from the door as you can. I'm going to come through fast and close it behind me. I have a coldsuit for you. Once you get into it you'll be okay. I'm going to count five, then I'm coming in."

As he said *five*, Jan kicked the door open and dropped through it, throwing the coldsuit before him. It was much harder to close the heavy metal door because of the angle, but he managed to brace his feet against the engine mount and heave with his shoulders. It thudded shut. Vilho was huddled against the far wall, unmoving. His eyes opened when Jan pulled at him and he made feeble movements to help as Jan slid the thick suit up over his legs. Arms in, helmet on, front sealed, full cooling strength on. As the cool air poured over him the engineer smiled up at Jan through the faceplate and raised a weak thumb.

"Thought I was cooked for sure. Thanks . . ."

"Thanks to you, everyone on the train is still alive. Will the engine keep supplying them with current?"

"No problem there. I checked it out and set it on automatic before the heat got me. It's a rugged beast."

"Then we may get out of this in one piece yet. The tanks are on their way now. Let's find the car with Lee Ciou in it and see what is happening. He's in radio contact with my engine."

"That'll be number six in line."

They walked back down the train, stepping over the rapidly decomposing corpses of the beasts that had caused the trouble. Although the cars were across the Road at all angles the couplings and connections still seemed sound; tribute to the long-dead engineers who had designed them. The people inside waved excitedly when they saw them and they smiled and waved back. The angry face of Chun Taekeng appeared in one of the windows, mouth working with unheard curses. He shook his fist at them and grew even more infuriated when Jan waved back and smiled at him. Vilho switched on the outside phone when they reached the door and they buzzed and shouted into it for a number of minutes before someone inside went to fetch Lee Ciou.

"Jan here. Can you hear me, Lee?"

"Is that Vilho with you? Then the drivers . . . ?"

"Dead. Probably instantly. How are the people in the train?"

"Better than we thought at first. A couple of broken bones the worst that happened. The damaged car has been evacuated and sealed off. Chun Taekeng has some strong complaints to make. . . ."

"I can imagine. He waved to us on the way back here. What about the tanks?"

"Due any minute now, I think."

Then we may still get out of this, get these people out of here alive, Jan thought to himself. Though it wouldn't be easy. Two dead. The drivers would have to be replaced. How could the front port be mended? There was so much to do. And fatigue was grabbing at him again, fighting to pull him down.

Nine

By the time the two tanks came rumbling up, Jan had his salvage plan made and the preparations begun. He waved them to a stop, leaned his almost discharged cycle against the scarred metal treads of the first one, then climbed slowly and wearily up into the cab. For the first time in hours he opened the helmet of his coldsuit and breathed deeply of the cool air.

"A real mess," Lajos said, looking out at the crippled train.

"Cold water, a bucketful," Jan said, and didn't speak again until he had drained over a liter of the lifesaving fluid. "It could have been a lot worse. Two dead, that's all. Now let's see that the living stay that way. Give me that pad and I'll show you what we're going to do."

He quickly sketched out the foundered tank and the first cars of the train, then tapped the car with his stylo.

"We'll have to disconnect all the power here, and that's being taken care of right now. The engine of train three is nosed up to the last car of this train and I have been back there jury-rigging connections. There's more than enough power for both trains. Right now Vilho is down there disconnecting the power and communication lines, but not uncoupling from the train yet. From the angle of the engine, I think that the weight of the train is the only thing keeping it from nose-diving into the swamp. Now I want you to get two 500-tonne breaking-strain cables from this tank to the engine, attach them, here and here. Then back up just enough to get them really taut and lock your treads. When that's done we can uncouple the train, and the other tank can pull the cars far enough away to give us access. We then get two more cables onto the engine, both tanks tighten up, and on the given signal we pull her out of there."

Lajos shook his head with concern. "I sincerely hope that you are right. But there is a lot of dead weight there. Can't the engine help? Get a little reverse drive on the wheels?"

"Negative. There is no way of controlling them from the engine room. But Vilho can cut the brakes on and off when we ask him, he's jury-rigged a control for that, and that's about all we can expect."

"No point in waiting then," Lajos said. "We're ready whenever you are."

"Some more water and we start."

It was awkward, exhausting work, made even more so by the deadly heat. Cables were hard to attach with the thick gloves of the coldsuits. They worked without a break until, bit by bit, it was done. Once the cables were attached the train was disconnected; the cables to the tank creaked when they took up the strain. But they held. The other tank had already lashed onto the front axle of the car to pull it out of the way. Because of the angle the first car had to be dragged sideways until it was clear of the engine. Impossible, normally, yet it could be done now because of the alien corpses that had caused the accident in the first place. Groaning and swaying the car was pulled across the road until it was clear. As soon as there was room enough the tank instantly dropped the cable and ground over to its position on the very edge of the road.

"All cables attached." The signal came at last. Jan was in the cab of the second tank, supervising the ponderous yet delicate operation.

"All right. I'm rolling back to get tension on my cables. There we are. One, are you still taut?"

"*I am now.*"

"Good. Start pulling on the signal of *go*. Am I in touch with Vilho on the brakes?"

"*I can hear you, Jan.*"

"Then keep your hand on the switch. We are going to get your weight on the cables. When the strain gauges read 300 I'll signal you *brakes*, and that's when you take the brakes off. Understand?"

"*No problem. Just pull me out of here. I don't feel like a swim.*"

A swim. If a cable broke or they couldn't hold the engine's weight it would slide forward into the water. Vilho stood no chance of getting clear. It wasn't to be thought about. Jan wiped the sweat from his face with his forearm—how could it be hot in the air conditioned tank?—and gave the order.

"Here it comes, one. The signal is one, two, three—*go!*"

The engine and gear train growled as power surged to the tracks. They moved slowly backward, clanking a single tread as the cable stretched under the load. Jan watched the strain gauge as the numbers flicked over. The instant it changed from 299 he shouted into the microphone.

"*Brakes!* This is it! Keep it coming!"

The engine stirred, shifting sideways—then stopped. The strain went up and up, approaching the breaking point of the cables. There was a safety factor built in, more pull could be applied. Jan did not look at the readout as he applied a touch more power. The cables vibrated, shook with the stress—and the engine stirred. Rolling backward slowly.

"This is it! Keep it coming. Watch the front wheels when it comes over the top and hit your power down. There it comes . . . now!"

It was done. Jan permitted himself one deep breath before he faced the next problem. The drowned cab and the drivers there. More weary than he wanted to admit, he pulled on his coldsuit.

There was a burial. Brief, but still a burial, with the few men in coldsuits the only witnesses. Then right back to work. The cab was drained and Jan examined the damage. Jury controls could be rigged and improved later. He supervised the job himself although he was swaying with exhaustion. A small replacement port was set into the center of a heavy steel plate, and the whole thing crudely but carefully welded over the smashed front port. The driver would not be able to see much—but at least he could see. The air conditioning came back on and the compartment began to cool down and dry out. New controls replaced the damaged ones and were wired into position. As this was being done the tanks had carefully straightened out the jackknifed train and all of the couplings were examined carefully for damage. It seemed all right. It *had* to be all right.

Hours later the trains started forward again. At a much reduced speed until the final repairs could be made—but they were moving. Jan was not aware of it. He had collapsed on the bunk in the engine room, unconscious before his head touched the pillow.

It was dark when he awoke, hours later, and climbed wearily back into the driving compartment. Otakar was at the wheel, his face gray with fatigue.

"Otakar, go below and get some sleep," Jan ordered.

"I'm fine. . . ."

"He is not," Alzbeta said, most emphatically. "He made me rest, and the others, but has had none himself."

"You hear the lady," Jan said. "Move."

Otakar was too tired to argue. He nodded and did as he had been told. Jan slipped into the empty seat and checked the controls and automatic log.

"We're coming to the bad part now," he said, soaked in gloom.

"Coming to it!" Alzbeta was shocked. "What would you call that part we have just finished?"

"Normally it would have been one of the easy stretches. The normal life forms there are usually no trouble. It is the ones we are starting through now that are the worst. Residents of eternal summer. All the energy they need from that white hot sun up there, all the food they can consume from the other life forms around them. It's kill and be killed and it never stops."

Alzbeta looked out at the jungle beyond the burned edges of the Road and shivered. "I've never seen it like this," she said in a hushed voice. "It all looks so terrible from up here in the engine with the unknown always sweeping towards us. When you look out of a car window it's so different."

Jan nodded. "I'm sorry to say it, but there's far worse out there that we can't see. Animal life forms never noticed or catalogued. One time I put out nets, just for a few hours when we were going through here, and I caught at least a thousand different kinds of insects. There must be thousands, perhaps hundreds of thousands more. The animals are harder to see—but they are there as well. They are voracious and will attack anything. That's why we never stop out here until we're out on the islands."

"The insects—why did you want to catch them? Are they good for anything?"

He did not laugh, or even smile, at her simple question. How could she know any better, having been raised on this deadened world? "The answer is yes and no. No, they are good for nothing in the way we usually think of things. We can't eat them, or use them in any other way. But, yes, the search for knowledge is an end in itself. We are here on this planet because of the pure search for knowledge and the discoveries made thereby. Though perhaps that is not the best example I could have used. Think of it this way. . . ."

"Malfunction reports from train eight," Hyzo called through from the communication board. "I'm putting you through."

"Report," Jan said.

"*We seem to have some air intakes that are clogging up.*"

"You know the orders. Seal them and recycle the air."

"*We've done that on one car, but there are complaints that the air is hard to breathe.*"

"There always are. These cars aren't airtight—enough oxygen is getting in. No matter how bad the air smells it's still all right. Do not, repeat do *not*, allow any windows to be opened." Jan closed the connection and called out to Hyzo, "Can you put me through to Lajos with the tanks."

The connection was made quickly enough; Lajos sounded exhausted.

"*Some of these trees have trunks ten meters thick; takes time to burn through.*"

"Narrow the track then. We can't be more than five hours behind you."

"*The regulations say . . .*"

"The hell with regulations. We're in a hurry. We'll be back soon enough and we can widen then."

While he talked, Jan reset the autopilot, adding ten KPH to their speed. Otakar looked at the speedometer, but said nothing.

"I know," Jan said, "we're going faster than we should. But we have people jammed in back there, crowded like they have never been before. It's going to start stinking like a zoo soon. . . ."

The nose radar bleeped a warning as they rounded a turn. Jan flipped off the automatics. Something big was on the Road—but not big enough to slow the engine. The creature reared up to do battle as they hurtled toward it and Alzbeta gasped. A quick vision of a dark green body, bottle green, too many legs, claws, long teeth—and then the engine hit it.

There was a thud as they struck, then a jarring as they crushed the body beneath the wheels, then nothing. Jan flipped the autopilot back on.

"We have at least eighteen more hours of this," he said. "We can't afford to stop. For any reason."

Less than three hours had gone by before the alarm came in. It was train eight again, someone shouting so loud the words were unclear.

"Repeat," Jan said, shouting himself above the other's hoarse voice. "Repeat, slow down, we cannot understand you."

"*. . . bit them . . . unconscious now, all swollen, we're stopping, get the doctor from number fourteen.*"

"You will *not* stop. That is an order. Next stop in the islands."

"*We must, the children . . .*"

"I will personally put any driver off the train if he stops along this Road. What happened to the children?"

"*Some sort of bugs bit them, big; we killed them.*"

"How did they get into the car?"

"*The window . . .*"

"I gave orders—" Jan clutched the wheel so tightly his knuckles turned white. He took a deep breath before he spoke again. "Open circuit. All car commanders. Check at once for open windows. *All* of them must be closed. Train eight. There is antivenom in every car. Administer it at once."

"*We did, but it doesn't seem to be working with the children. We need the doctor.*"

"You're not getting him. We're not stopping. He can't do anything other than administer the antivenom. Hook through to him now and describe the symptoms. He'll give you what advice he can. But we're not stopping."

Jan turned off the radio. "We can't stop," he said to himself. "Don't they understand? We just can't stop."

After dark there was more life on the Road, creatures that stood dazzled by the lights until they vanished under the wide wheels, things that appeared suddenly out of the darkness and were crushed against the windshield. The trains kept moving. It wasn't until dawn that they came to the mountains and the tunnel, diving into its dark mouth as into a refuge. The Road climbed as it penetrated the barrier and when they emerged they were on a high and barren plateau, a rocky plain made by leveling a mountain top. On both sides of the Road the tanks were pulled up, the exhausted drivers sleeping. Jan slowed the trains until the last one had emerged from the tunnel, then signaled the stop. When the brakes were set and the engines off the radio hummed to life.

"*This is train eight. We would like the doctor now.*" There was a cold bitterness in the voice. "*We have seven ill. And three children dead.*"

Jan looked out at the dawn so he would not have to see Alzbeta's face.

Ten

The two of them were eating together at the folding table in the rear of the engine. The Road was straight and flat, and Otakar was alone at the wheel. When they talked quietly he could not hear them. Hyzo was below with Eino; the occasional cry and slap of cards indicated what they were doing. Jan had no appetite but he ate because he knew he had to. Alzbeta ate slowly, as though she wasn't aware of what she was doing.

"I had to," Jan said, his voice almost a whisper. She did not answer. "Don't you understand that? You haven't said a word to me since. Two days now." She looked down at her plate. "You'll answer me or you'll go back to your family car with the others."

"I don't want to talk to you. You killed them."

"I knew it was that. I did not—they killed themselves."

"Just children."

"Stupid children, now dead ones. Why weren't their parents watching them? Where was the supervision? The families here must breed for stupidity. Everyone knows what kind of animal life there is in that jungle. We never stop there. What could the doctor have done?"

"We don't know."

"We *do* know. The children would have died in any case, and perhaps the doctors and others as well. Don't you understand I had no choice? I had to think of all of the others."

Alzbeta looked down at her clasped hands, her fingers wrung tightly together. "It just seems so very wrong."

"I know it does—and it was not easy to do. Do you think I have

slept since they died? It's on my conscience if that makes you feel
any better. But how would I have felt if I had stopped and there
were more casualties? The children would have died in any case
before the doctor reached them. Stopping would only have made
matters worse."

"Perhaps you're right; I'm not sure anymore."

"And perhaps I was wrong. But right or wrong I had to do
what I did. There was no choice."

They let it rest there; there was no simple answer. The trek continued, along the chain of islands, along the planed mountain
peaks. At times they could see the ocean on both sides and, from
this high up, it almost looked attractive. The teeming life could
not be seen, just the white tops and the marching rows of waves.
Very soon a blur on the horizon grew to a long range of mountains. Before they arrived at the southern continent Jan ordered a
full eight hour stop. All running gear, tires, brakes, wheels, were
inspected and all of the air filters cleaned again, though they did
not need it. Another jungle was ahead and there would be no
stopping. It was not as wide as the one north of the island chain,
but was just as virulent.

This was the last barrier, the last trial. They went through it in
three days, without stopping, and into the tunnel beyond. When
the last train was well inside the tunnel they halted to rest, then
drove on short hours later. This was the longest of the tunnels, for
it penetrated the entire range. When they emerged into sunlight
again they were surrounded by desert, sand and rock glinting in
the lights of their headlights. Jan checked the outside air temperature.

"Ninety-five degrees. We've done it. We're through. Hyzo, contact all drivers. We're going to stop for one hour. They can open
the doors. Anyone who wants to go out can. Just warn them about
touching metal; it might still be hot."

It was holiday, release from captivity, excitement. All down the
rows of the trains doors crashed open and the exodus began. The
ladders rattled to the hard surface of the Road and people called
to each other as they climbed down. It was hot and uncomfortable—but it was freedom after the cramped discomfort of the cars.
They were all there, men, women and children, walking up and
down in the light from the windows and the headlights of the
trucks. Some of the children ran to the edge of the Road to dig in
the sand and Jan had to issue orders to discipline them. Other

than the lumpers there was little of danger in the barren desert, but he could risk no more accidents. He gave them an hour and by that time most of them, tired and sweat-drenched, were back in the air conditioned cars. After a night's rest they pressed on.

The brief autumn of the Halvmörk year was almost over and the further south they went the shorter the days became. Soon the sun would not rise at all and the southern hemisphere winter would begin, four Earth years of twilight. The growing season.

As the desert swept past the windows of the cars, the passengers forgot all their discomforts and even suggested longer driving days. They would be home soon and that would be the end of their troubles.

Jan, driving the lead engine, saw the posts first. The sun sat on the horizon and the shadows were long. For days now there had only been the unchanging sand and rock of the desert. The change was abrupt. A row of fence posts flashed by marking the limits of a baked and cracked field. First one, then another came into view, the outlying farms. There was cheering down the lengths of all the trains.

"That's a relief," Otakar said. "Here at last. I was beginning to get tired."

Jan was not cheering, or even smiling. "You are going to be a lot more tired before this is all over. We have to unload the corn and turn the trains around."

"Don't remind me. You're going to hear a lot of grumbling."

"Let them. If this planet is to have any future at all it will be because we have the corn here when the ships arrive."

"If," Alzbeta said.

"Yes, there's always the if. But we have to act as though it will happen. Because it will be the end of everything if the ships don't come at all. But we can worry about that later. I don't mean to be the skeleton at the feast. Let's stop these trains on the Central Way, set the brakes and see if we can't have a party tonight. I think everyone is in the mood for one. We can begin unloading the corn after a good night's sleep."

The party was very much in the order of things, there were no complaints about that. With the air temperature now down in the 80s it could be held outside, with elbow room and freedom for everyone. When the trains halted for the last time between the rows of barren foundations the doors burst open. Jan watched them swarming out into the twilight, then climbed slowly down the rungs from the driving compartment.

He still had work to do. The first chairs were being taken out and the trestle tables set up as he went to the rear of the main silo building. After four years of torrid summer the thick walls still radiated heat as he passed. Dust was banked high against the heavy metal door in the rear and he kicked it away with his boot. There were two sets of mechanical locks on the door, and an electronic one. He used his keys to open them, one by one, then pushed against the door. It opened easily and the cool air rushed out around him. Once inside he locked the door behind him and looked around at the familiar scene. This water Central Control was identical with the one he had shut down in Northtown before leaving on the trek. These two control rooms were the only buildings that were permanently air conditioned and climate controlled. They made human life on the planet possible.

Before starting the program Jan sat in the seat before the console and activated the scanners one by one at the water station, over 1500 kilometers away in the mountains above the coast. The first was mounted in thick steel and concrete on top of the station, and when it turned it gave a panoramic view. Everything was as it should be, he knew that from the printout which would have informed him, long before this if there had been any kind of trouble. But he always felt he could not be sure until he looked for himself. Irrational of course, but all good mechanics have a touch of irrationality. You have to like machines to work well with them.

Solid and powerful, a fortress of technology. A featureless blank exterior of weathered concrete, over three meters thick. Some flying lizardoids were on a ledge of the building; they flapped slowly away when the eye of the camera moved towards them. Far below was the sea where waves battered against the solid rock. As the point of view changed the bins came into view, half filled with wealth extracted from the sea, a byproduct of the desalination process. There was at least a ton of gold in one of them. Worth a fortune on Earth, but valuable on Halvmörk only for its untarnishing qualities, for plating on the engines and field machines. The last thing in the slow circuit was the deep canal, stretching down the mountain to the black mouth of the first tunnel, two kilometers below.

Internal cameras revealed the starkness and strength of this giant complex of machines, built for durability and work. So well had it been designed that Jan had gone there in person just once in all his years on the planet. Inspection and maintenance were continuous and automatic. It was an echoing cathedral of science, visited rarely, functioning continually. For four years it had idled, the fusion generator muttering just enough to provide standby electricity for maintenance. Now it would come to life again. The program of startup was long and complex, self-regulating at every step, designed by the builders now centuries dead. They had built well. Jan switched on the computer terminal, received recognition, and keyed in the order to initiate startup.

There would be nothing visible for some time, since internal checks of all components were the first step in the series. When the machine was satisfied that all was in order it would slowly raise the output of the fusion generator. Then the force pumps, buried in the solid rock beneath sea level, would go into operation. Silent, with no moving parts, they would begin lifting the sea water up the large pipes to the station on the crest above. They used a variation of the same magnetic bottle that contained the fusion reaction, modified to seize the water and push it away. Higher and higher the water would be pumped until it spilled over into the flash distillation section. Here it was vaporized instantly, with most of the water vapor drawn off to the condenser. Gravity took over then.

Jan had seen enough people, talked to enough people, and he relished the privacy now. He sat and watched the screens and readouts for hours, until the first splashes of water fell from the outlets, turning into a roaring river just seconds later. Down it rushed, carrying sand and airborne debris before it, until it vanished into the tunnel. It would be days before the first dirty trickle worked through the tunnels and canals to reach the city.

A separate stream of thick brine splashed down a channel cut away in the side of the mountain to fall back into the sea below. He would wait at least a week before starting up the extractors that took all the elements and chemicals from the sea water. In the beginning all that was needed was volume flow to fill and scour clean the channels. All was as it should be and he was tired. The party, he had forgotten about it. It should be well under way by now. Good, perhaps he could avoid it. He was tired and needed sleep. He took a repeater from the shelf—it would monitor the water machinery at all times—and hooked it to his belt.

Outside the night was warm, but a slight breeze kept it comfortable enough. From the sounds, the party was well under way, with the food finished and the drink flowing freely. Let them enjoy it. Even without the rigors of the trek their lives were monotonous enough. When the farming began again there would be no more festivities for years.

"Jan, I was just coming to get you," Otakar said, coming around the corner of the building. "Meeting of the Family Heads and they want you."

"Couldn't they wait until we have all had some sleep?"

"Apparently urgent. They pulled me away from a very cold pitcher of beer which I am going back to. They've put up the dome and are meeting there. See you in the morning."

"Good night."

Jan could not walk slowly enough, and the dome wasn't far away. Now that they had finished this first journey they would be back at their complaints and bickering again. He had to talk to them, like it or not. Let them get it out of their systems so in the morning they could all get to work unloading the corn. A Proctor at the door, complete with sidearm, knocked when he came up, then let him in.

They were all there, the Family Heads and the technical officers. Waiting in silence until he sat down. It was The Hradil who spoke. It would have to be her.

"There have been grave charges, Jan Kulozik."

"Who's in trouble now? And couldn't it have waited for the morning?"

"No. This is an emergency. There must be justice. You are accused of assaulting Proctor Captain Hein Ritterspach and of causing the deaths of three children. These are grave charges. You will be held in confinement until your trial."

He jumped to his feet, fatigue gone. "You can't. . . ."

Strong hands seized him, and pulled him about. Two Proctors held him and there was Hein grinning, gun pointed.

"No tricks, Kulozik, or I shoot. You're a dangerous criminal and you'll be locked up."

"What are you fools trying to do? We have no time for this sort of petty nonsense. We have to turn the trains around and go back for the rest of the corn. After that we can play your games if you insist."

"No," The Hradil said, and smiled, a cold smile of victory empty of any human warmth. "We have also decided that we have enough corn. Another trip would be too dangerous.

"Things will go on here, as they always have. Without you to cause trouble."

Eleven

The Hradil had planned it this way from the very beginning. The thought was bitter as bile and Jan could taste the hatred that welled up inside of him when he thought about it. Planned and carried through by the brain behind those serpent eyes. Had she been a man he might have killed her, there before the others, even if they killed him in return.

Underneath him the stone floor was hot, still burning with the heat of summer. He had his shirt off and under his head as a pillow, yet he still dripped with sweat. It must be a 100 or over in the small storeroom. They must have prepared this even before holding the meeting to accuse him; he could see the marks where the stored parts had rested before being dragged away. There was no window. The light, high above, burned continually. The metal door locked from the outside. There was a gap between the door and the stone and a flow of cooler air came through it. He lay with his face pressed close to it and wondered how long he had been here and if they would ever bring him some water.

Someone had to care about him—but no one had appeared. It seemed incredible that he could be Trainmaster one day, in charge of all the people and all of the resources of the planet, and a forgotten prisoner the next.

The Hradil. They did what she wanted. Her cooperation to have him bring the trains south had been a temporary expediency. She knew he could do the job. She also knew that she had to bring him low and humble him when the trip was over. He stood for too much change and too much freedom of choice and she would not have that. Nor would the others. They would take no convincing to connive in his downfall.

No!

Too much had changed, too much was changing to let her win. If she had her way they would plant the seed corn they had brought, hold the rest of the corn to turn over to the ships when they arrived. With an abject knuckling of the forehead no doubt, a happy sinking back to the old ways, the ways they had always known.

No! Jan pulled himself slowly to his feet. That was not the way it was going to be at all. If the ships never came they would all be dead and nothing else would matter. But if they did come then they would not go back to the old ways. He kicked and kicked at the metal door until it rattled in its frame.

"Shut up in there," a voice finally called out.

"No. I want some water. Open this at once."

He kicked, again and again until his head began to swim with the strain, until there was finally a rattling of bolts. When the door opened Hein stood there with a drawn gun, the other Proctor at his side. He still wore the cast and he held that arm towards Jan, waving it before him.

"You did that and you thought you could get away with it. Well, it's not going to happen that way. You've been condemned . . ."

"Without a trial?"

"You had a trial; it was all very fair. I was there." He giggled. "The evidence was conclusive. You have been condemned to die for your crimes. So why should we waste good water on you?"

"You cannot." Jan swayed, dizzy, and leaned against the door frame.

"It's all over for you, Kulozik. Why don't you crawl, beg me to help you? I might consider that."

He waggled the gun in Jan's face. Jan shuddered back, too weak to stand, sliding toward the floor. . . .

Seizing Hein's ankles and pulling them out from under the big man, sending him crashing back against the other Proctor. Jan had learned about dirty infighting from his karate teacher who had made a hobby of it; these men knew nothing about the nastier kinds of personal combat.

The gun was clumsy in Hein's left hand and Jan pushed it aside as Hein pulled the trigger. There was just the single shot and then

Hein screamed as Jan's knee came up full into his groin. The other Proctor fared no better. The fist in his ribs drove the air from his lungs. His gun was still in its holster when he was battered into unconsciousness by the savage chops to his neck.

Hein was not unconscious, but glassy-eyed, rolling in agony, clutching himself, his mouth a round O of pain. Jan took his gun as well—then kicked him solidly in the side of the head.

"I want you both to be quiet for a while," he said. He dragged the still forms into the storeroom and locked them in.

What came next? He was free for the moment—but there was no place to flee to. And he wanted more than freedom. They needed that corn and the trains would have to make the return trip. But the Family Heads had decided against this. He could appear before them, but knew that would accomplish nothing. They had condemned him to death in absentia, they certainly would not listen to him now. If The Hradil were not there he might convince them—no, he knew that would make no difference. Killing her would accomplish nothing.

The only thing that would make any difference, save his life and possibly the lives and futures of everyone on this planet, would be some major changes. But what changes—and how could they be brought about? He could think of no easy answers. First things first—a drink of water. There was a bucket in the corner filled with water where the Proctors had been cooling beer. Jan took out the few remaining bottles and raised the bucket to his lips, drinking and drinking until he could drink no more. He poured the rest over his head, gasping with pleasure at the cooling shock. Only then did he click open the ceramic stopper on a beer bottle and sip from it. The rudiments of a plan were beginning to form. Yet he could do nothing alone. But who would help him? Doing anything at all would necessitate going against the will of the Family Heads. Or had they overreached themselves this time? If his trial and verdict had been reached in secret he might very well get some cooperation. He needed information before he could do anything else.

The guns that he had taken from the Proctors were pushed inside an empty seed sack, the butt of one of them close enough to reach in a hurry. There was only silence from the cell: it would be some time before there was trouble from that flank. Now—what was happening outside?

Jan eased the outside door open a crack and looked through.

Nothing. An empty street, dusty and drab under the twilight sky. He opened the door wide and stepped through, then strode steadily toward the silent trains.

And stopped. Had there been a massacre? Bodies everywhere. Then he smiled at his black thoughts. They were sleeping, of course. Free of the trains, safely arrived, rest after the storm; they had all eaten and drunk themselves into near extinction. Then, instead of getting back into the jammed and noisome cars, they had sprawled and slept where they dropped. This was wonderful; it could not have been better if it had been planned. The Family Heads must be asleep as well and they were the only ones he had to worry about at the moment. Moving quickly and quietly, he walked down the lengths of the trains until he came to the Ciou family. As always, things were still neatly organized here, the sleeping mats laid out in neat rows, women and children together to one side. He went past them to the still forms of the men, stepping lightly, until he found Lee Ciou. His face was calm in sleep, the worried crease always present between his eyes now erased for the first time to Jan's knowledge. He knelt and shook Lee lightly by the shoulder. Dark eyes slowly opened and the crease between them reappeared instantly as soon as Jan put a silencing finger to his lips. Lee obeyed the pantomime signals to rise silently and follow. He followed Jan up the ladder of the nearest engine and watched as he closed the door.

"What is it? What do you want?"

"I have your tapes, Lee. Your illegal ones."

"I should have destroyed them—I knew it!" The words were a cry of pain.

"Don't concern yourself with them. I came to you because you are the only person I know of on this planet with the guts to break the law. I need your help."

"I don't want to get involved. I never should have . . ."

"Listen to me. You don't even know what I want yet. Do you know anything about my trial?"

"Trial . . . ?"

"Or that I was condemned to death?"

"What are you talking about, Jan? Are you tired? All that has happened since we arrived is that we ate and drank too much and all fell asleep. It was wonderful."

"Do you know about a meeting of the Family Heads?"

"I guess so. They're always meeting. I know they had the pressure dome erected before they would release the beer. I guess they were all in there. It was a better party without them. Could I have a drink of water?"

"There's a dispenser right inside that door."

So the trial had been a secret! Jan smiled at the thought. This was the lever he needed. Their mistake. If they had killed him at once there might have been some grumbling, nothing more. Well it was too late for them to do that. Lee came back in looking slightly more awake.

"Here is a list of names," Jan said, writing quickly on an order form. "The men from my own engine crew, all good men. And Lajos, he learned to think for himself when he took over command of the tanks from Hein. That should be enough." He handed the list to Lee. "I don't want to take a chance of being seen. Would you take this list, find these men and tell them to meet me here? They are to come quietly and quickly on a matter of the utmost importance. . . ."

"What?"

"Trust me for a bit longer, Lee. Please. I'll tell you all together what has happened. And it is important. But it is urgent that they all get here as soon as possible."

Lee took a deep breath as though to protest—then let it out slowly. "Only for you, Jan. Only for you," he said and turned and left.

They arrived, one by one, and Jan controlled his impatience and their curiosity until Lee was back and the door closed again.

"Is anyone stirring yet?" he asked.

"Not really," Otakar said. "Maybe a few stumbling about to take a leak, but they're going back to sleep. That was quite a boozeup. Now—what is this all about?"

"I'll tell you, but I want some facts straight first. Before this drive started I had some heated words with Hein Ritterspach. He claims I struck him at that time. He is lying. There was a witness to all that. Lajos Nagy."

Lajos tried to move away from their eyes as they all turned towards him. There was no escape.

"Well, Lajos?" Jan asked.

"Yes . . . I was there. I didn't hear everything said. . . ."

"I'm not asking that. Did I hit Hein, just tell us that."

Lajos did not want to get involved—but he was. In the end he had to shake his head. "No, you did not strike him. For a while I thought someone would be struck, you were both very angry. But you did not hit him."

"Thank you. Now there is one more thing that is not quite that simple. Some children died, of insect bites, when we were passing through the jungle. You all know about it. I had a difficult decision to make. I did not stop the trains so the doctor could attend to them. Perhaps I was wrong. Stopping might have saved them. But I put the safety of all ahead of the few. It is on my conscience. If we had stopped the doctor might have been able to do something . . ."

"No!" Otakar said loudly. "He could do nothing. I heard him. Old Becker had him in and was shouting at him. But he is a Rosbagh and they only get pigheaded when shouted at. He was shouting back saying that he could have done nothing to save the children, other than administer the anti-toxin, which already had been done. He blamed the people who permitted the windows to be open, even Becker himself."

"Wish I could have listened to that!" Eino said.

"You and me both," Hyzo agreed warmly.

"Thank you. I appreciate hearing that," Jan said. "For a number of reasons. You've now heard the details of the two charges against me. I think they are false accusations. But if the Family Heads want me to stand trial on them, I will."

"Why trial?" Otakar asked. "An investigation perhaps, but a trial only after the charges have been substantiated. That is the only fair thing."

The others nodded agreement and Jan waited until the murmured comments had died away. "I'm glad we agree about that," he said. "So now I can tell you what has happened. While you were all enjoying yourselves, the Family Heads held a meeting in secret. They had me seized and imprisoned. Then had a trial on these charges—without *me* being there—and found me guilty. If I had not escaped I would be dead by now because that was their verdict."

They heard his words with utter disbelief. Their shock was replaced with anger as the truth of the situation sank in.

"Don't take my word for this," Jan said. "It is too important. Hein and the other Proctor are locked in and they'll tell you . . ."

"I don't want to hear what Hein has to say," Otakar shouted. "He lies too much. I believe you, Jan, we all believe you." The others nodded agreement. "Just tell us what we have to do. People must be told. They can't get away with this."

"They will," Jan said. "Unless we stop them. Just telling people won't be enough. Can you see any of the Taekeng standing up to the old man? No, I didn't think so. I am willing to go on trial, I *want* to do it. But by the Book of the Law. In public, with all evidence heard. I want this whole thing out in the open. But the Family Heads will try to stop that. We are going to have to force them to do it."

"How?"

There was silence now for they were waiting, eager to help. But would they go far enough? Jan knew instinctively that if they thought about what they were going to do they would not do it. But if they acted in unison and in anger they might do it. And once done, they would not be able to turn back. They were thinking revolutionary thoughts—now they must consider revolutionary deeds. He weighed his words.

"Without power nothing moves. Eino, what's the easiest way to take the engines out of service temporarily? Remove the computer programming units?"

"Too big a job," the engineer said, immersed in the technical problem, not considering the enormity of the crime they were discussing. "I would say pull the multiple connector plug to the controls. In fact pull the plug at both ends and take the whole cable out. Done in a couple of seconds."

"Fine. Then we'll do just that. Pull them from the tanks too. Bring them to number six tank, the big one. Then we'll wake everyone up and tell them what has happened. Make them have the trial right now. When it's over we put the cables back and go back to work. What do you say?"

He put no emphasis on the last question, though this was the most important decision of all. The point of no return, beyond which there was no turning back. If they realized they were taking all of the power of decision, the real power of the world, into their own hands, they might have second thoughts. A moment's wavering and he was lost.

They were technicians, mechanics—and never thought of it in that manner. They just wanted to right an obvious wrong.

There were shouts of agreement, then they were busy in assigning the various tasks, getting the operation into motion. Only Hyzo Santos did not join in the excitement but sat with wide, in-

telligent eyes watching Jan all the while. Jan gave him no assignment, and soon he was alone with the silent communications
officer. He spoke only when the others had left.

"Do you know what you are doing, Jan?"

"Yes. And you do too. I'm breaking all the rules and making
new ones."

"It is more than that. Once broken, the rules will never be the
same again. The Family Heads will not want to do this . . ."

"They will be made to do it."

"I know. And I can put a word to this even if you will not. It is
revolution, isn't it?"

After a long moment's silence Jan spoke, looking at the other
man's grim face. "Yes, it is. Do you find the idea distasteful?"

Hyzo's face broke slowly into a wide grin. "Distasteful? I think
it's wonderful. It is just what should happen, what is written in
Class and Labor, the Eternal Struggle."

"I never heard of it."

"I don't think many people have. I got it from one of the ship's
crew. He said it was an invisible book, listed nowhere, but some
reference copies did exist and duplicates had been made of them."

"You're on dangerous ground. . . ."

"I know. He said he would bring more—but I never saw him
again."

"Easy enough to guess what happened to him. Then you are in
with me on this? It will be bigger than you can possibly imagine."

Hyzo clasped Jan's hand in both of his own. "All the way!
Every step of the way."

"Good. Then you can help me with one thing. I want you to
come with me to the warehouse where Hein and the other Proctor
are locked up. They were ready to carry out the death sentence so
they both know about the secret trial. They are our witnesses to
what happened."

A few early risers were already stirring as they walked back to
the warehouse. The street door was still ajar as Jan had left it.

But the storeroom door was open as well and the two Proctors
were gone.

Twelve

Jan took a quick look around; the rest of the warehouse was as empty as the storeroom.

"Where are they?" Hyzo asked.

"It doesn't matter. This means trouble so we had better start it before they do. Get them off balance if we can. Come on."

They ran now, ignoring the startled looks, pounding heavily through the dust to the row of silent tanks. They were undisturbed. Jan slowed to a panting walk.

"Still ahead of them," he said. "We'll go on as planned."

They climbed into tank six and started the engines. This would be the only piece of moving apparatus not incapacitated. Jan trundled it slowly down the Central Way and drew it up before the pressure dome.

People were beginning to stir now, but the preparations to immobilize the tanks and engine still went ahead smoothly. At first the conspirators had moved guiltily, trying to avoid being noticed, until they had realized that no one paid them the slightest heed. They were just technicians going about their usual inexplicable tasks. Once they had realized this they carried the cables openly, calling out to one another with secret glee. It was all very exciting.

Not for Jan. He sat at the tank controls staring at the screens, watching the first of the men stroll up with a set of cables; his fist, unnoticed, pounded slowly on the panel beside him. Then another technician, then a third appeared. Hyzo sat in the open hatch above and passed down the cables to Jan as they arrived.

"That's the lot," he said. "What do you want us to do now?"

"You and the others can just stay in the crowd. I think that's best. I don't want a confrontation or charges of conspiracy at this early stage."

"That's all right for them. But you want someone to stand up there with you."

"You don't have to, Hyzo. . . ."

"I know. I'm volunteering. What happens next?"

"Simple. We get the people together."

As he said this he punched the siren button and held it down. The banshee wail screamed out, warbled up and down piercingly. It could not be ignored. People asleep were suddenly awake; those already at work stopped what they were doing and ran toward the sound. As the Central Way began to fill, Jan turned off the siren and unclipped the bullhorn from the bulkhead. Hyzo was waiting for him on top of the tank, leaning relaxedly against the fusion gun.

"There's your crowd," he said. "They're all yours."

"Over here," Jan said into the bullhorn microphone, his amplified words echoing back at him. "Over here, everyone. This is an important announcement." He saw Taekeng appear in the door of his car and shake his fist. "Family Heads as well. Everyone. Over here." Taekeng shook his fist again, then turned as a man hurried up and said something to him. He looked back and threw a single shocked glance at Jan, then followed the messenger towards the pressure dome.

"Over here, everyone, up close," Jan said, then switched off the microphone. "Not one Family Head here," he said to Hyzo. "They're planning something. What do we do?"

"Nothing. That is nothing to start any trouble. Start issuing orders for unloading the corn for the return trip."

"But they've changed that plan. They won't let us go back."

"All the better—they've told no one about this either. Let *them* start trouble—here in front of everyone."

"You're right." Jan turned the bullhorn back on and spoke into it. "Sorry to disturb your rest, but the party is over and we have to get back to work. We must return to get the rest of the corn."

There were groans from the audience at this, and a few people in the back started to shuffle away. Over their heads Jan saw Hein come out of the pressure dome and begin to push forward through the crowd. He was shouting something, his face red with the effort. There was a new gun in his holster. He could not be ignored.

"What do you want, Hein?" Jan said.

"You . . . come here . . . dome. At once . . . meeting."

Most of his words were lost in the crowd noises. He pushed forward angrily, waving his gun now to reinforce his authority. Jan had a sudden idea; he bent and spoke to Hyzo.

"I want that pig up here, talking. Let everyone hear what he has to say. Get the others to help you."

"It's dangerous. . . ."

Jan laughed. "And this whole thing is madness. Get going." Hyzo nodded and slipped away: Jan turned back to the bullhorn. "That is the Proctor Captain there. Let him through, please, he has something to say."

Hein was helped, perhaps more than he wished. He tried to stop below and shout up at Jan, but was jostled forward and before he realized it he was standing next to Jan, still holding his gun. He tried to speak quietly to Jan—who pushed the bullhorn before his lips.

"You are to come with me. Get that thing away!" He slapped at it but Jan kept it close so that their voices boomed out over the crowd.

"Why should I come with you?"

"You know why!" Hein was spluttering with rage. Jan smiled back warmly—and winked at the angry man.

"But I don't know," he said innocently.

"You know. You have been tried and found guilty. Now come with me." He brought up the gun; Jan tried to ignore the whiteness of the man's tight knuckles.

"What trial are you talking about?" He deliberately turned his back on Hein and spoke to the crowd. "Does anyone here know anything about a trial?"

Some of them shook their heads *no*; all of them were listening attentively now. Jan swung about and pushed the bullhorn close to Hein's mouth, watching the gun and ready to strike if the man attempted to pull the trigger, hoping he would condemn himself and the Family Heads before he did. Hein began to shout—but another voice drowned his out.

"That will be enough, Hein. Put your gun away and get down from that machine."

It was The Hradil, standing in the doorway of the dome and

using the PA system. It had to be her, the only one of the Family Heads with the sense to see that Hein was giving their game away for them—and the only one with the intelligence to react so quickly.

Hein deflated like a burst balloon, the color draining from his face. He fumbled the gun back into its holster and Jan let him leave, knowing there would be no more inadvertent help from this quarter. He would have to face The Hradil and that was never an easy thing.

"What trial was he talking about, Hradil? What did he mean I had been tried and found guilty?"

His amplified words reached out to her over the crowd, which was silent and intent now. Her voice answered the same way.

"He meant nothing. He is sick, a fever from his arm. The doctor is on his way."

"That is good. Poor man. Then there has been no trial—I am guilty of nothing?"

The silence lengthened and he could see, even at this distance, that she wanted his death as she had wanted nothing else in her entire life. He did not move but waited like stone for her answer. It came at last.

"No . . . no trial . . ." The words were wrung from her lips.

"That's very good. You are right, Hein is sick. Since there has been no trial and I am guilty of no crimes." He had her now, she was committed in public. He must push the advantage. "All right, everyone, you have heard The Hradil. Now let's get to work, the return trip starts as soon as possible."

"NO!" Her amplified voice rang out over his. "I warn you, Jan Kulozik, you have gone too far. You will be silent and obey. There will be no trip for the corn, that has been decided. You will . . ."

"I will *not*, old woman. For the good of us all it was decided that we must go for the corn. And we will."

"I have ordered you."

She was raging now, as angry as he was, their booming voices godlike over the gaping crowd. Any appeal to law or logic was gone, any attempt to involve the spectators useless. They could not be cajoled, not now, only told. Jan reached into the turret of the tank and pulled out a length of cable and shook it in her direction.

"I do not take your orders. All of the tanks and engines are inoperable—and will not run again until *I* permit it. We are going for the corn and you cannot stop us."

"Seize him, he is mad, kill him. I order it!"

A few people swayed forward, reluctantly, then back as Jan reached into the hatch and fed power to the fusion gun controls. The pitted bell mouth of the gun tilted up—then burst into roaring life sending a column of flame high into the air; there were screams and shouts.

The heat of fusion spoke louder than Jan ever could. The Hradil, her fingers raised like claws, leaned forward—then turned about. Hein was in her way and she pushed him aside and vanished through the door of the dome. The fiery roar died as Jan turned off the gun.

"You've won this one," Hyzo said, but there was no victory in his voice. "But you must watch that one every moment now. In the end it will have to be you or her."

"I don't want to fight her, just change. . . ."

"Change is defeat for her, you must never forget that. You cannot go back now, only ahead."

Jan was suddenly weary, exhausted. "Let's get the corn unloaded. Keep people working, so they have no time to think."

"Hyzo," a voice called out. "Hyzo, it's me." A thin, teen-aged boy climbed halfway up the tread of the tank, calling out. "Old Ledon wants to see you. Said to come at once, no waiting, very important he said."

"My Family Head," Hyzo said.

"It's beginning." Jan thought of the possible consequences. "See what he wants. But whatever he asks you to do come back here at once and let me know. He knows you're with me, it must have to do with that."

Hyzo jumped down and followed the boy—but the engineer Eino took his place. "I've come for the cables," he said. "We'll have to unhook the family cars first. . . ."

"No," Jan said, almost unthinkingly, reacting by reflex. The cables, the immobilized vehicles, they were his only weapon. He had the feeling that great forces were already at work against him and he could not surrender that weapon now. "Wait a bit. Just pass the word to the others that we will meet here in . . . say, three hours. To go over unloading plans."

"If you say so."

It was a long wait and Jan felt very much alone. Through the front port he could see the people moving about; ordinary enough. But not ordinary for him. He had shaken the Family Heads up, caught them off balance, won a victory. For the moment. But could he hold onto what he had gained? There was no use in speculating. He could only work to control his impatience; sit quiet and wait to find out what their next move was going to be.

"It's not good," Hyzo said, climbing down through the hatch.

"What do you mean?"

"Old Ledon has forbidden me to go with the trains on the second trip. Just like that."

"He can't stop you."

"That's right, *me*, but I'm just one person. I know why I'm in this and what it means. I didn't answer him, just walked out. But how many others are going to do that? Right now the Elders are calling in every one of the technicians and mechanics. They will be told what to do—and they will obey. Which leaves us with a two-man revolution and no place to go."

"We're not dead yet. Stay here, sit on those cables, lock the hatch and don't open it until I get back. Without them we're lost."

"And if anyone should try to get them? One of our own men?"

"Don't let them have the cables. Even if . . ."

"If I have to fight? Kill them?"

"No, we're not going that far."

"Why not?" Hyzo was deadly serious now. "The ends justify the means."

"No they don't. Just do your best—without hurting anyone."

The hatch clanged shut behind Jan and he heard the dogs being driven home in the catch. He jumped down from the treads and walked steadily in the direction of the dome. The crowd had dispersed for the most part but there were still a number of people about. They looked at him with curiosity—but turned away when he caught their eyes. They were passive, trained to accept orders, they would be no problem. It was the Elders he would have to deal with.

There were no Proctors at the entrance, which was a help; he wanted no trouble with them. Jan pushed the door open quietly and stood just inside it. They were there, all the Family Heads, too busy shouting at each other to notice him yet. He listened.

"Kill them all, that's the only answer!" Taekeng's voice was cracking; he must have screamed himself hoarse.

"You're a fool," The Hradil said. "We must have the trained men to run the machinery. We must order them to obey us and they will do it. That is enough for now. Later when he is dead, they will be punished, one by one, we will not forget."

"No one will be punished," Jan said, striding forward, as calm as they were angry. "You stupid people just will not realize the kind of trouble we are in. If the ships don't arrive we don't get replacement parts or fuel. Our tanks and engines will be knocked out one by one and then we will all be dead. *If* the ships come they will need all the corn we can possibly get together. They will need it for starving people—and we need it as the only weapon . . ."

The Hradil spat in his face, the spittle striking him on the cheek, running down across his mouth. He wiped it away with the back of his hand and fought to control his anger.

"You will do as we say," she ordered him. "There will be no more talk from you about do this do that. We are the Family Heads and we will be obeyed. There will not be another trip. You will . . ."

"You stupid old woman, can you not understand me? Are you so ignorant that you do not know that nothing will move until I permit it? I have parts of all the machines and they will not run until the parts are replaced. I will destroy these parts now and we will all die the quicker. I will do this at once if you do not permit the return trip for the corn. You do this and I promise to ask no more of you. When we return you are in charge as always. You issue the orders and everyone obeys. Is that agreeable?"

"No! You cannot tell us what to do." The Hradil would accept no compromises.

"I'm telling you nothing. I'm asking you first."

"It is not too bad a plan," Ivan Semenov said. "We lose nothing if they go back for the corn. And we did promise . . ."

"Ask for a vote, Ivan," Jan said. "Or does this cow frighten you all?"

Then she was calm, just that suddenly. The unabated hatred was still there in her eyes, but not in her voice. "All right, we will argue no more. The trains will leave as soon as possible. I am sure you all agree."

They were confused, not understanding her sudden change. But

Jan knew. She was not ready for a showdown now. And she did not really care if the trains went or not. What she wanted was his death, preferably a long and painful one. From now on he walked with that danger and accepted it.

"I know you will all agree with Ivan and The Hradil," Jan said. "We leave as soon as the corn is emptied. We will need all the new drivers. . . ."

"No," The Hradil said. "There will be only men. It is not permitted for young girls to be alone with so many. None of the girls will be allowed to go. Alzbeta will not go."

She threw this last out as a challenge and for a moment he almost accepted it. Then realized he could lose everything if he insisted. He matched her cold calmness with his own.

"All right then, just male drivers. Get out of here and issue the orders to cooperate with me. Make it clear to everyone what is happening. No more lies."

"You should not say that . . ." Ivan complained.

"Why not? It's true, isn't it? Secret meetings, secret trials, secret execution plans, more lying so that fool Ritterspach takes the blame. I do not trust one of you out of my sight. Leave and go to your families and tell them what is to be done. Only when everyone is sure what is happening will the machines be made operable again . . ."

"Seize him now and kill him," Taekeng screamed.

"You can—but someone else will destroy the cables."

"It is Hyzo," Ledon said. "He defied me like this one."

"We will issue the orders," The Hradil said. "Go at once and do it."

Thirteen

The trains were ready to go, had been for almost two hours, standing quiet in the darkness. The drivers were in their seats waiting for orders. Food and supplies for the trip were in the house car, along with an unhappy doctor-in-training, Savas Tsiturides. Doctor Rosbagh said that his assistant was not completely trained, not able to be on his own. Tsiturides had fervently agreed. He had come anyway. Jan could not risk his men on this trip without some kind of medical aid. The last details had been seen to, the off-duty drivers were already asleep, and he could not make excuses much longer.

"Back in five minutes," he said, ignoring the questioning looks of his crew. He climbed down from tank six, he would lead the tanks himself on the return trip, and walked back along the trains. This was the spot—but no one was here. It had been a risk to send the first message, madness to follow it up with a second. But he had had to do it. The Central Way was silent, it was the middle of the sleep period.

"Jan. Are you there?"

He spun about and there she was, by the warehouse. He ran to her.

"I didn't know if you were coming."

"I had the message, but I couldn't leave until now, when they were all asleep. She has them watching me."

"Come with me."

He had meant to build his argument logically and rationally, explaining how important it was she keep the bit of independence gained. To perfect her technical skills. It was a good argument. He wasn't going to mention how he loved her and needed her. Yet at the sight of her he had forgotten it all and just blurted out the words. Alzbeta recoiled, shocked.

"I couldn't do that. There are only men."

"We're not animals. You won't be hurt, touched. It is important for you, for both of us."

"The Hradil would never permit it."

"Of course. That is why you must leave without permission. Everything is changing and we must make it change faster. If the ships don't come all of us have only a few more years to live. When summer comes and we can't make the trip—we burn. I want those years with you, I can't bear losing one day of them."

"Of course, I know."

She was in his arms, and he was holding her tightly, hard to his body, and she was not resisting or pulling away. Over her shoulder he saw Ritterspach and two Proctors running towards them. All the men carried clubs.

A trap, that's why Alzbeta had been late. They had intercepted his message, planned to catch them together. The Hradil must have arranged it all, was gloating now at her success.

"No!" Jan shouted, pushing Alzbeta away from him, crouching in defense, hands extended. The clubs were to beat him with, not kill him, bring him back for her justice. "No!" shouted even louder still as he dived under the swing of the first Proctor's club.

The swing missed and he hit the Proctor hard, hearing the air rush from his chest, slapping his forearm hard against the man's throat as he whirled to face the others.

A club caught him on the side of his head, slammed down onto his shoulder. Jan shouted aloud with pain and grabbed the man, caught his neck in an armlock, pulled him about as a shield between himself and Ritterspach. Luckily the big man was still coward enough to hesitate, to let the other two take the punishment. Now he could wait no longer. He swung wildly, afraid to close, striking the Proctor Jan held so that the man cried out, swung again.

"Don't, please stop," Alzbeta cried, trying to separate the struggling men. The first Proctor shoved her aside rudely and circled to take Jan from the rear. Alzbeta, crying, came forward again, just in time to step in front of Ritterspach's wildly swinging club.

Jan could hear the sharp, mallet-like crack as it caught her full on the side of her head. She dropped without a sound.

He wanted to help her, but this must be finished first. In his anger he could not be stopped, tightening his arm hard so that the man he held tore at the pain in his throat, then went limp. Jan seized his club and spun the man's body about, ignorant of the club that struck him once, twice. Throwing the limp attacker into the moving one, following up with his own club, battering until both were still, turning about and going for Ritterspach.

"Don't . . ." Ritterspach said, striking out wildly in defense. Jan did not answer, his club speaking for him, thudding into the other's arm so the fingers went limp and the club fell. Hitting again, catching the back of the Proctor Captain's head when he turned to flee.

"What is it?" a voice shouted. One of the mechanics running down the train.

"They attacked me, hit her, get the doctor, Assistant Tsiturides. Quickly."

Jan bent and picked up Alzbeta gently, bending his face to hers, afraid of what he would find. More afraid not to know. There was blood, dark on her pale skin. Her breath slow, but regular.

He carried her carefully to the nearest car and took her inside, putting her down gently on the filthy rug.

"Where are you?" a voice called out. "What has happened?"

It was Tsiturides, bent over the men on the ground. He straightened up from Ritterspach, his face shocked. "That other one is unconscious. This one—dead."

"All right then, there's nothing you can do for him. Alzbeta is in here, struck by that pig. Take care of her."

The doctor pushed by and Jan watched while he opened his bag at her side. There were more running footsteps. Jan closed the door and looked at it, then took the keys from his belt and locked it.

"The fun's over," he said, turning to the men as they came up. "They jumped me and I took care of them. Now let us roll these trains before there are any more difficulties."

It was a stupid, impulsive thing to do. But it was done. He had tried to do it by law, by asking The Hradil, by suffering the indignities of her rejection. Now he would do it his own way. There would be no going back from this either.

Buffers clanked together, the cars moved slowly at first, then faster and faster. Jan turned and ran toward his tank, waiting impatiently until the train had rumbled by, then hurrying over almost under the wheels of the next engine.

"Let's go," he said, closing the hatch behind him. "Move out ahead of the trains."

"And about time," Otakar said, gunning the engine.

Jan did not relax until the Central Way changed into the rock surface of the Road, until the warehouses had grown small and vanished behind the last car of the train. Then the fence posts were gone as well and the last of the farms and he still kept watching the monitor screen. They could not be followed—so what was he watching for? The one engine left behind was immobilized as a power station. Who was he running from?

Fourteen

Jan decided that they would have to travel for at least four hours before they could make a stop. But he could not force himself to wait that long. Even three hours was too much; he had to know how Alzbeta was. It hadn't seemed too hard a blow, but she had been unconscious when he left. She might still be unconscious—or dead. The thought was unbearable; he had to find out. At the end of the second hour of driving he admitted defeat.

"All units," he ordered. "A short rest stop. Change drivers if you want to. Begin your slowdown now."

Even as he issued the command he pulled the tank out of line, spun it 180 degrees on its treads and went thundering back along the line of still moving trains. He found the car in which he had left Alzbeta and the doctor, reversed, and swung alongside it, slowing when it slowed, jumping down the instant they had stopped. The right key was ready in his hand and he unlocked the door and threw it open to face an angry Doctor Tsiturides.

"This is an insult, locking me in the way you did. . . ."

"How is she?"

"This car is dusty, uncleaned, with no proper facilities."

"I said—*how is she?*"

The cold anger in his voice penetrated the doctor's complaints and he took a step backwards. "She is doing well, as well as can be expected under the conditions. She is asleep now. Mild concussion, no more than that I am sure. It is safe to leave her alone and that is what I am doing."

He picked up his bag and hurried away. Jan wanted to look in, but was afraid to waken her. It was then that Alzbeta spoke.

"Jan? Are you there?"

"Yes, here I come."

She was propped up on a nest of blankets the doctor had put together, a white bandage around her head. Enough light came through the uncurtained window to show her face almost as pale as the cloth.

"Jan, what happened? I remember we talked, then little else."

"The Hradil set a trap for me—with you as bait. Ritterspach and some of his men. Capture me or kill me, I don't know. Whatever they had planned misfired when you got in the way. I'm afraid I . . . lost my temper."

"Is that a bad thing to do?"

"Yes, for me it is. I didn't mean it to end that way—but Ritterspach is dead."

She gasped at this, a stranger to violence of any kind, and he felt her hand withdraw from his.

"I'm sorry," he said. "Sorry that anyone had to die."

"You didn't mean to do it." She said it, but she did not sound convinced.

"No, I didn't mean to. But I would do it all over again if I had to. Exactly the same way. I'm not trying to excuse myself, just explain. He hit you and you dropped, dead for all I knew. They had the clubs, three against one, and I defended myself. It ended like that."

"I do understand, but death by violence, it is . . . strange to me."

"May it stay that way. I can't force you to understand, or feel the way I do. Do you want me to go?"

"No!" The word burst out of her. "I said that I found it hard to understand. But that doesn't mean that I feel any different about you. I love you, Jan, and I will always love you."

"I hope so. I have acted irrationally, perhaps stupidly. That I did it because I love you is little excuse." Her hands were cold in his. "I can understand if you blame me for what I did next. Putting you in this train and taking you away. We were talking about it when they attacked me. I never heard your answer."

"Didn't you?" She smiled for the first time. "There can be only one answer. I will obey The Hradil always. But now that she is no longer here to give orders it is not a matter of obeying or disobeying. I can love you as I have always wanted to, be with you always."

"Jan," the voice called from outside, then twice again before he heard it. He felt he was smiling like a fool and held her gently for a long moment, beyond words, then pulled away and stood up.

"I have to go. I can't tell you how I feel. . . ."

"I know. I'm going to sleep now. I am much better."

"Do you want some food, something to drink?"

"Nothing. Just you. Come back as soon as you can."

The co-driver of the tank was leaning out of the hatch. "Jan, got a message," he said. "Semenov wants to know why the stop and when we can go on?"

"Just the man I want to see. Tell him we move on as soon as I join him in his engine. Let's go."

Ivan Semenov was still Trainmaster. With the families and all their problems left behind, Jan had relinquished the lead engine to him. Any problems that came up now would probably be with the Road and he could handle them better from the lead tank. Jan climbed the ladder to the driver's compartment and Ivan started the trains forward as soon as he had closed the door.

"What is the delay about?" Semenov asked. "Every hour is important now, as you keep saying."

"Come into the engine room and I'll tell you." Jan was silent until the engineer had left and the hatch was shut. "I would like to get married."

"I know, but that is between you and The Hradil. I can speak to her if you like, the law isn't that exact as to which families the girl cannot marry into. A decision could be made. But it is up to The Hradil."

"You misunderstand. You are a Family Head which means you can perform marriages. I'm asking you to do just that. Alzbeta is here, aboard a train."

"It cannot be!"

"It certainly is. So what are you going to do?"

"The Hradil would never permit it."

"The Hradil is not here to stop it. So think for yourself, just once. Make your own mind up. Once it is done there can be no going back. And there is nothing that evil old woman can do to you."

"It is not that. There is the law. . . ."

Jan spat disgustedly on the floor then rubbed the spittle into the steel plating with the sole of his boot. "That for your law. It is an invention, don't you know that? There are no such things as Families and Family Heads on Earth, or taboos about marriage between chosen groups. Your so-called laws are works for fiction written by hireling anthropologists. Societies to order. They scratch around in the textbooks and put together bits and pieces of vanished societies and brew up one that will keep a population docile and obliging and hardworking—and stupid."

Semenov did not know whether to be shocked or angry; he shook his head unbelievingly, a physicist with the basic laws of energy threatened.

"Why do you say these things? You can't mean them, you've never said anything before."

"Of course not. It would have been suicide. Ritterspach was a police spy—among his other endearing traits. He would have reported anything I said when the ships came, and I would be dead as soon as they found out. But with the ships not coming it doesn't matter now. Everything's changed. I can tell you about dear old Earth. . . ."

"I'll hear no more lies."

"Truths, Semenov, for the first time in your life. Let me tell about cultures. Mankind created them. They are an artifact, invented the same way the wheel was invented. Many different ones, all working one way or another if they were to survive. But that is all a matter of history now, with just two classes left on Earth—the rulers and the ruled. And quick death for anyone who tries to change things. And this final and monolithic society has even been transported to the stars. To all the fat and wealthy worlds that mankind has discovered. But not to all of the planets —just the comfortable ones. When there is a need to occupy a really uncomfortable planet, like this one, then the tame professors are called in and given their assignment. Supply us with a stable and docile culture, because any problems would slow food production, and plenty of nourishing and cheap food is needed. A nice ignorant culture, because farmers can still be stupid and get their work done. But technical skills will be needed as well, so allowance must be made for that. So a bit here, a bit there, choose and select and balance and stir them all together and you have Beta Aurigae III. This planet. Patient factory farmers, slaving their lives away in dim stupidity—"

"Stop this, I won't hear any more of your lies." Semenov was shocked, numbed.

"Why should I bother to lie now? If the ships don't come we're all dead in any case. But until they do I intend to live like a man again, not a silent slave like the rest of you. At least you have a good excuse, you're enslaved by stupidity, lack of knowledge. I have been enslaved by fear. My actions are being watched, I'm sure of that. As long as I stay in line, cause no trouble, I'll be all right. I've been all right for years. The watchers like me here. A planet for a prison—and at the same time they can get value out of me from my skills. But they don't *need* me. If I cause trouble I'm dead. Meanwhile, all of the years and money invested in my education are not going to waste. They sent me here to use those talents. With the strict instructions that I could live here in peace through the days of my years and I would not be bothered. But if I spoke one word about what life is really like off this planet, why then I would be dead. So I'm dead, Semenov, do you realize that? If the ships don't come, I'm dead. If they come and are manned by the same people, why then you speak a word—and I am just as dead. So I deliver myself into your hands and do it for the oldest reason of all. Love. Marry us, Semenov, that's all you have to do."

Semenov was wringing his hands together, not knowing what to think. "These are most disturbing things you say, Jan. To myself, when I am alone, I have had certain questions, but there has never been anyone to ask. Though the history books are most explicit. . . ."

"The history books are dull works of fiction."

"*Jan,*" the voice broke from the engine room speaker. "*Call for you.*"

"Patch it through." There was a burst of static then Lee Ciou's voice spoke.

"*Jan. A little bit of trouble. One of the tanks threw a tread. They pulled to the edge of the Road and are working on it now. You should be up to it in a few minutes.*"

"Thanks. I'll take care of it."

Semenov sat in introverted silence when Jan went out, was unaware that he was gone. The engine slowed when the two stopped tanks came into sight. Jan gauged the distance.

"Slow to 10 K's as you pass, I'll hop off."

He opened the door to a blast of torrid air. Next time out it would probably have to be in a coldsuit. He swung down to the bottom rung and hung there, then dropped off in a run, waving back at the engine, which picked up speed again. Lee Ciou and two mechanics had the broken tread spread out on the rock surface of the Road and were hammering the retaining pin from the damaged section.

"Cracked link," Lee Ciou said. "No way to repair it. Metal's crystallized, you can see here at the break."

"Wonderful," Jan said, scratching the brittle metal with his fingernail. "Put on one of your spares."

"Don't have any. Used them all up. But we can take one from the other tank—"

"No. We won't do that." He looked up at the sky. It's beginning to happen, he thought. The ships don't come and things wear out and they can't be replaced. This is the way it is going to end. "Leave the tank here and let's join the others."

"But we just can't leave it."

"Why not? If we cannibalize spares now what will we use when the next breakdown happens? We leave it and we move on. Lock it up and when the ships come we can put it right."

It took only a few minutes to get out the few personal belongings and to close the hatch. In silence they boarded the other tank and put on speed to catch up with trains that had gone by. It was then that Semenov called on the radio.

"*I have been thinking a lot since we talked.*"

"I hope you have, Ivan."

"*I want to talk to—you know who—before I decide. You understand?*"

"I wouldn't have it any other way."

"*Then I want to talk to you—I have some questions. I don't say I agree with you, not about everything. But I think I will be willing to do what you ask.*"

The tank driver jumped, his hands twitching on the speed controls, so that the tank lurched abruptly at Jan's loud cry of victory.

Fifteen

The engineers who had built the Road must have exacted great pleasure from conquering nature in the most dramatic manner possible. This great range of mountains, labeled simply Range 32-BL on the Road map, could have been penetrated in a number of ways. A simple long tunnel could have done it, slicing through to the lower coastal ranges, where the Road would have been easy to construct. The designers had taken no such simple solution. Instead the Road rose up through long and easy loops almost to the summit of the range; in fact it did cross the leveled peaks of some of the lesser mountains. And here it stayed, piercing peak after high peak with straight-bored tunnels. The rubble from the tunnels had been used as fill to bridge the valleys between, then compacted again to solid rock with molten lava. The energy used to do this had been prodigal but not wasteful. The Road was there, a monument to their skill and craft.

At the entrance to the tunnel that pierced the largest mountain, there was an immense leveled area. The builders had undoubtedly used this as a park for their great machines. Some idea of their size could be gained by the fact that all of the trains, every engine and car, could be pulled up here at the same time. It was a favorite stopping place for the families, where repairs or servicing of the trains could be made, offering a chance to socialize after endless days in the same cars.

A big advantage was the height—and the fact that Flat Spot was on the shadow side of the mountain. This made the temperature, while still hot, bearable enough to go about without coldsuits. The men walked slowly, stretching and laughing, glad of the break from routine, though they did not know the reason. Meeting, 2130 hours, by the lead engine. It made a pleasant change.

Ivan Semenov waited until they were all assembled, then climbed up on the makeshift platform of lubrication drums supporting a thick sheet of plastic. He spoke into the microphone and his amplified voice rolled over them, calling to them for silence.

"I have come to consult with you," he said, and there was a quickly hushed murmur from the men before him. Family Heads never consulted, they issued orders. "That may sound unusual to you but we are now living in unusual times. The pattern to our life and existence has been broken and, perhaps, may never be mended. The ships did not come when they should—and they may never come. If that happens we are dead, and no more need be said. Because they did not come we have brought the corn, all that we could, to Southland and are now returning to get as much more as we can. To accomplish this, the rule of the Family Heads was defied by you men. Don't deny it—face the truth. You defied us and won. If you care to know, I was the only one of the Heads who agreed with you. Perhaps because, like you, I work with machines and am different. I do not know. But I do know that change has begun and cannot be halted. Therefore I am going to tell you about another change. You have all heard the rumors, so I will now tell you the fact. This is not an all-male expedition. We have a woman with us."

This time the buzz of voices drowned him out, and the men moved about trying to get a better view of the platform to see who was there. The silence returned, gradually, when Semenov raised his hands.

"She is Alzbeta Mahrova, whom you all know. She is here by her own choice. Her other choice is that she wishes to marry Jan Kulozik, and he does choose to marry her as well."

After this he had to shout to be heard, begging for silence, turning up the volume until his voice boomed and echoed from the rock wall behind him. When he could at last be heard he went on.

"Quiet, please, hear me out. I said I have come to consult you and I am. As a Family Head I have power vested in me to marry this couple. But the Head of Alzbeta's family has forbidden the union. I feel I know what I should do, but what do you men think the decision should be? . . ."

There was never any doubt. The roar of approval shook the rock with greater sound than the amplifiers had used. If there were any dissenting voices, they were drowned in the sound of the vast majority. When Jan and Alzbeta appeared from the train, they shouted even louder, picking him up and carrying him laughing on their shoulders, yet still too bound by the laws they were breaking to touch her.

The ceremony was brief but affectionate, different from any other they had witnessed because of the all-male audience. The questions were asked and the answers given, their hands joined together, their lives joined as well when the rings were brought forward. A toast was drunk by all present and the deed was done. But it was a single toast since time was pressing. Their honeymoon would be on the rolling trains.

Through the mountain range and into the eternal blasting heat of the tropical sun. They made better time than they had on the outward trip, for the Road was clear and they were lightly loaded. The tank crews stayed far ahead and the only difficulty was crossing the drowned section of Road. The empty cars had a tendency to float and had to be brought over one by one with an engine at each end. The only ones who did not mind the delay were Jan and Alzbeta, who were forbidden to help in the operation and were ordered to remain inside their car. It was the only wedding present that the hard-working men could give them and was appreciated all the more.

Once the water was passed the Road was clear again—though never empty of danger. The never-setting sun now had a brassy color to it and there was an ominous haze in the air.

"What is it?" Alzbeta asked. "What is wrong?"

"I don't know. I've never seen anything like it," Jan said.

They were driving again, driver and co-driver of one of the engines. This way they were together all of the time, work periods and sleep periods. They did not mind; in fact they reveled in the pleasure of their companionship. To Alzbeta it was the final satisfaction of her existence as a woman. For Jan, the end of loneliness. But this was not a world to allow unlimited peace and happiness.

"Dust," Jan said, squinting out at the sky. "And I can think of only one place it could come from. I think, but I can't be sure."

"Where?"

"Volcanic action. When volcanoes erupt they hurl dust high into the atmosphere where the winds bring it right around the planet. I only hope this eruption was nowhere near the Road."

It was closer than they liked. Within twenty hours the tanks sent back word of an active volcano on the horizon. The jungle here was burnt and dead, while the Road was thick with great chunks of scoria and heavy with dust. They were working to clear a way through. The trains soon caught up with them.

"It's . . . horrible," Alzbeta said, looking out on the blackened landscape and the drifting clouds of smoke and dust.

"If this is the worst we hit, we are all right," Jan told her.

They crawled at minimum speed when they passed the volcano, for the Road could not be kept completely clear, and they crept through the constantly falling debris. The volcano was no more than ten kilometers from the Road, still active, wreathed in clouds of smoke and steam which were lit by red flashes and gouts of lava.

"In a way I'm a little surprised that we have not had this kind of trouble before," Jan said. "It must have taken an awful lot of artificial earthquakes to build the Road. That's a matter of record. And the energy it takes to start an eruption is only the tiniest part of the energy that is released. The builders knew their business and did not leave until the seismic processes were reduced. But there can be no guarantee that they are all ended. As we can see out there." He looked out gloomily at the volcano, now dropping behind them.

"But it's over," she said. "We're through."

Jan did not want to erase her happy smile by reminding her that there would have to be a return trip. Better the happiness of the hour.

Then they came to the scorched farmlands and the immense silos baking under the relentless sun. Loading the corn began, a slow process because of the limited number of coldsuits. Nevertheless the work was continuous, one man taking over when the other ended his shift, putting a newly charged powerpack into the coldsuit, careful not to touch the burning metal of the external fittings. Out into the heat to swing the discharge hose over the opening in a car roof, to fill it to overflowing. The car was moved on, the hole sealed, another appeared below. The Road was knee-deep in corn for they made no attempt to be careful; speed was more important than neatness. More corn would be left to burn than they could carry away. When the last train was being filled, Jan consulted with Semenov.

"I'm taking the tanks out now. But I'm worried about the section of Road that passes the volcano."

"You'll clear it easily enough."

"I'm not concerned about that. The volcanic activity seems to have died down. But we did have that big quake some days ago. If we could feel it here, how must it be that much closer? The Road itself may be damaged. I want a good lead time."

Semenov nodded reluctant agreement. "I just hope that you are wrong."

"So do I. I'll report back as soon as I get there."

They ran at top speed and made the journey without a stop. Jan was asleep when they came to the volcanic area, and Otakar, who was co-driving the lead tank with him, came down to shake him awake.

"Big drifts across the road, but otherwise it doesn't look bad."

"I'll come right up."

They left the other tanks with dozer blades to clear the Road, then ground ahead over the mountainous drifts. The air was clear and the volcano itself soon came into sight, silent at last, with just a plume of smoke drifting from its conical summit.

"That's a relief," Otakar said.

"I couldn't agree more."

They went on until the tank was stopped by an immense drift of dust and rock that completely blocked the Road. All they could do was back to one side and wait for the tanks with blades. They caught up quickly because all they were doing on the first pass was making a cut big enough to let them through. They would return and widen it for the trains.

The driver of the dozer tank waved as he tackled the mountainous mass, and was soon out of sight behind it. "*It's getting shallow again,*" he reported by radio. "*Not deep at all on this side . . .*" His voice ended in a gasp.

"What is it?" Jan asked. "Come in. Can you hear me?"

"*Better see for yourself,*" the driver reported. "*But come through slowly.*"

Jan ground his tank forward through the gap, saw the tread marks of the other tank, saw that it had backed to one side so he could see the Road ahead.

It was clear now why the driver had gasped. There was no Road ahead. It ended at the brink of a fissure, a small valley that must have been a kilometer wide at least.

The ground had opened up and swallowed the Road, leaving an unspannable chasm in its place.

Sixteen

"It's gone—the Road's gone," Otakar said, gasping out the words.

"Nonsense!" Jan was angry. He was not going to be stopped. "This fissure can't go on forever. We'll follow it away from the volcano, away from the area of seismic activity."

"I only hope that you're right."

"Well we don't have much choice—do we?" There was no warmth at all in the smile that went with the words.

It was slow and dangerous work once they were away from the hard surface of the Road. The burnt jungle was a barrier of stumps, with ash and dust filled pits between that could trap a tank. They were caught this way time and again, one tank after another. Each time it happened a weary driver would go out in a coldsuit to attach cables to drag the trapped vehicle clear. The dust and ash clung to their suits and was carried back into the tanks, until everything was coated and filthy. After relentless hours of labor the men were close to exhaustion. Jan realized this and called a halt.

"We'll take a break. Clean up a bit, get something to eat and drink."

"I have a feeling I'll never be clean again," Otakar said, grimacing as the grit in the food ground between his teeth. The radio light signaled for attention and Jan flicked it on.

"Semenov here. How is it coming?"

"Slowly. I'm taking a wide swing in the hope we will be able to bypass the fissure. I don't want to have to make a second cut. Is the loading done?"

"Last train filled and sealed. I've pulled the trains two kilometers down the Road. The spilled corn is beginning to catch fire, and I wanted us clear of any danger."

"Yes, keep them well away. The silos will go next—will probably explode from the internal pressure. I'll keep you informed of our progress."

They went through two more sleep periods, locked in the filthy tanks, before they reached the volcanic fissure again. Jan saw it appear suddenly as the burnt tree he was pushing aside disappeared over the edge. He jammed on both brakes, then wiped the inside of the front port as the clouds of ash settled outside.

"It's still there," Otakar said, unable to keep the despair from his voice.

"Yes—but it's no more than a hundred meters wide. If it's no deeper, we'll just start filling it and we won't have to go any further."

It was just possible. As the tanks widened and leveled the new track they had cut, the debris was pushed over the edge. Fusion guns burned and compacted it while more and more rubble was added to the growing mound. Eventually it reached the top and the first tank clanked gingerly forward onto the new surface. It held.

"I want more fill in there," Jan ordered. "Keep the fusion guns on it too. Those engines and trains are a lot heavier than these tanks. We'll split into two groups. One to compact the fill, the other to cut a track back to the Road on the other side. I'll get the trains up behind us, ready to cross as soon as we're done."

It was a rough and ready job, the best they could do. They labored for more than a hundred hours before Jan was satisfied with the result.

"I'm going to bring the first train over. The rest of you stand by."

He had not been out of his clothes since they had started the job; his skin was smeared and black, his eyes red-rimmed and sore. Alzbeta gasped when she saw him—when he looked in the mirror and saw why, he had to smile, himself.

"If you make some coffee I'll wash up and change. That was not a job I would like to do again."

"It's all finished then?"

"All except getting the trains over. I've emptied everyone out of the first one and as soon as I finish this I'll take it through."

"Couldn't someone else drive it? Why does it have to be you?"

Jan drank his coffee in silence, then put down the empty cup and stood. "You know why. Ride in the second train and I'll see you on the other side."

There was fear in her tight-clamped arms, but she said nothing more as she kissed him, then watched him leave. She wanted to ride with him, but knew what his answer would be without asking. He would do this alone.

With the automatic guidance disconnected the train turned away from the center of the Road toward the raw gash that had been slashed through the burnt jungle. The engine left the smooth Road surface and rose and fell as it ground along. Obediently, one by one, the cars tracked behind it, following in its deep-cut wheel tracks.

"So far no problems," Jan said into the microphone. "Bumpy but not bad at all. I'm holding at five K's all the way. I want the other drivers to do the same."

He didn't stop when he came to the filled-in fissure but ground steadily forward out onto its surface. Under the pressure of the engine's weight, stones and gravel cracked free from the sides of the embankment and rattled into the depths. On both sides the tank drivers watched in tense silence. Jan looked down from the height of the engine and could see the far edge approaching slowly; on either side there was only emptiness. He kept his eyes fixed on the edge and the engine centered in the very middle of the dike.

"He's over!" Otakar shouted into his radio. "All cars tracking well. No subsidence visible."

Reaching the Road again was an easy task, once the tension of the crossing was behind. He pulled the train to the far side and ran forward until all of the cars were in the clear. Only then did he pull on his coldsuit and change over to the tank that had followed him.

"Let's get back to the gap," he ordered, then turned to the radio. "We're going to bring the trains over one at a time, slowly. I want only one train at a time on the new sections so we can reach it easily in case of difficulties. All right—start the second one now."

He was waiting at the edge of the chasm when the train appeared, clouds of dust and smoke billowing out from under its

wheels. The driver kept his engine centered on the wheel marks of
Jan's train on the embankment and crossed without difficulty and
went on. The next train and the next crossed, and they came in a
steady stream after that.

It was the thirteenth train that ran into trouble.

"Lucky thirteen," Jan said to himself as it appeared on the far
edge. He rubbed his sore eyes and yawned.

The engine came on and was halfway over when it started to
tilt. Jan grabbed for the microphone, but before he could say anything there was a subsidence, and the engine tilted more and
more in massive slow motion.

Then it was gone, suddenly. Over the edge and down, with the
cars hurtling after it one after another in a string of death, crashing to the bottom in an immense bursting cloud of debris with
car after car folded one after the other in a crushed mass of destruction.

No one came out of the wreck alive. Jan was one of the first
who was lowered down at the end of a cable to search among the
horribly twisted metal. Others joined him, and they searched in silence under the unending glare of the sun, but found nothing. In
the end they abandoned the search, leaving the dead men en-
tombed in the ruins. The embankment was repaired,
strengthened, compacted. The other trains crossed without trouble and, once they were assembled on the Road, the return trek
began.

No one spoke the thought aloud, but they all felt it. It had to
be worth it, the corn, bringing it from pole to pole of the planet.
The men's deaths had to mean something. The ships had to
come. They were late—but they *had* to come.

They were familiar with the Road now, weary of it. The water
crossing was made, the kilometers rolled by steadily, the sun shone
through unending heat, and the trip went on. There were delays,
breakdowns, and two cars were cannibalized for parts and left
behind. And one more tank. The output of all the engines was
dropping steadily so that they had to run at slower speed than
usual.

It was not joy that possessed them when they came out of sunshine into the twilight, but rather more the end of a great weariness and the desire to rest at last. They were no more than ten
hours away from their destination when Jan called a halt.

"Food and drinks," he said. "We need some kind of celebration."

They agreed on that, but it was a subdued party at best. Alzbeta sat next to Jan and, while no one there envied them, the men looked forward to the next day, and wives of their own who were waiting. They had been in touch with Southtown by radio, so the seven dead men in their metal tomb were known to those who were waiting.

"This is a party, not a wake," Otakar said. "Drink up your beer and I'll pour you another."

Jan drained his glass as instructed and held it out for a refill. "I'm thinking about the arrival," he said.

"We all are, but more so you and I," Alzbeta said, moving closer at the thought of separation. "She can't take you from me."

She did not have to be named. The Hradil, absent so long, was close again, ready to affect their lives.

"We are all with you," Otakar told them. "We were all witnesses at your wedding and were part of it. The Family Heads may protest but there is nothing they can do. We've made them see reason before—we can do it again. Semenov will back us up."

"This is my fight," Jan said.

"Ours. It has been since we took over the engines and made them knuckle under for the second trip. We can do that again if we have to."

"No, Otakar, I don't think so." Jan looked down the smooth length of the Road that vanished at the horizon. "We had something to fight for then. Something physical that affected all of us. The Hradil will try to cause trouble but Alzbeta and I will handle it."

"And me," Semenov said. "I will have to explain my actions, account for them. It is against the law . . ."

"The law as written here," Jan said. "A little work of fiction to keep the natives subdued and quiet."

"Will you tell them that, all the things you told me?"

"I certainly will. I'll tell the Heads and I'll tell everyone else. The truth has to come out sometime. They probably won't believe it, but they'll be told."

After they slept they went on. Jan and Alzbeta had little rest, nor did they want it. They felt closer than they had ever been and their lovemaking had a frantic passion to it. Neither spoke of it, but they feared for the future.

They had good cause. There was no reception, no crowds to welcome them. The men understood that. They talked a bit, said goodbye to one another, then went to find their families. Jan and Alzbeta stayed on the train, watching the door. They did not have long to wait for the expected knock. There were four armed Proctors there.

"Jan Kulozik, you are under arrest. . . ."

"Under whose authority? For what reason?"

"You have been accused of murdering Proctor Captain Ritterspach."

"That can be explained, witnesses—"

"You will come with us to detention. Those are our orders. This woman is to be returned to her family at once."

"*No!*"

It was Alzbeta's cry of terror that roused Jan. He tried to go to her, protect her, but was shot at once. A weak charge, minimum setting for the energy gun, enough to stop him but not kill him.

He lay on the floor, conscious but unable to move, able only to watch as they dragged her out.

Seventeen

It was obvious to Jan that his homecoming reception had been planned with infinite care and sadistic precision. The Hradil, of course. Once before she had had him arrested, but the job had been bungled. Not this time. She had not revealed herself, but her careful touch was everywhere. No reception for their return, no crowds. No chance to unite his men and the others behind him. Divide and rule, most skillfully done. A murder charge, that was good, a man had been killed so the charge was certainly in order. And he had resisted arrest just to make her job easier, just as she had undoubtedly assumed he would. She had out-thought him and she had won. She was out there drawing the web tight around him, while he sat in the carefully prepared cell. No rude storeroom this time, that might arouse sympathy, but proper quarters in one of the thick-walled permanent buildings. A barred, narrow slit of a window on the outside wall, sink and sanitary facilities, a comfortable bunk, reading matter, television—and a solid steel door with a lock on the other side. Jan lay on the bunk staring unseeingly at the ceiling, looking for a way out. He felt the eyes of the Proctor on him, staring in through the plasteel observation window in the wall, and he rolled to face away.

There would be a trial. If it were at all fair his plea of self-defense would have to be accepted. Five Family Heads would be the judges, that was the law, and all would have to agree on a sentence of guilty. Semenov, one of the oldest Heads, would sit on the bench. There was a chance.

"You have a visitor," the guard said, his voice rasping from the speaker just below the window. He moved aside and Alzbeta stood in his place.

Happy as he was to see her it was torture to press his hands to the cold plasteel surface, to see her fingers a close centimeter beyond his, yet to be unable to touch them.

"I asked to see you," she said. "I thought they would say no, but there was no trouble."

"Of course. No lynch parties this time. She learns by her mistakes. This time by the book, by the rule of law and order. Visitors allowed, why of course. Final verdict, guilty, of course."

"There has to be a chance. You will fight?"

"Don't I always?" He forced himself to smile, for her sake, and was answered by the slightest smile in return. "There is really no case. You witnessed the attack, were struck yourself, the other Proctors will have to agree with that under oath. They had all the clubs, I fought back when you were struck down. Ritterspach's death was accidental—they'll have to admit that. I'll defend myself, but there is one thing you can do to help me."

"Anything!"

"Get me a copy of the legal tapes that I can play on the TV here. I want to bone up on the niceties of the Book of the Law. Build a strong case."

"I'll bring them as soon as I can. They said I could bring you food; I'll cook something special. And another thing," she looked sideways out of the corners of her eyes, then lowered her voice. "You have friends. They want to help you. If you were out of here . . ."

"*No!* Tell them no as emphatically as you can. I don't want to escape. I'm enjoying the rest. Not only is there no place to hide on this planet, but I want to do this the right way. Defeat that woman by law. It is the only way."

He did not tell Alzbeta that undoubtedly every word they spoke through the communicator was being recorded. He did not want anyone getting into trouble on his account. And basically what he said was true. This had to be done the legal way now. If he had to communicate, there were ways. The cell was clear, there were no visual bugs. She could read a note if he held it up to the observation window. He would save that for any emergencies.

They talked more but there was little to say. The ache of being close to her without touching her was becoming unbearable and he was relieved when the guard told her it was time to go.

His second visitor was Hyzo Santos. The communications officer was undoubtedly well aware that their talk would be listened to and kept their conversation on neutral grounds.

"Alzbeta tells me you are enjoying your rest, Jan."

"I have little choice, do I?"

"Make the most of the quiet, you'll be back in action soon enough. I brought that copy of the Book of the Law that you asked about. I guess the guard will give it to you."

"My thanks. I'll want to study it closely."

"Very closely, if I were you." Hyzo's scowl deepened. "There have been some meetings of Family Heads. Only rumors of course, but there was an announcement this morning, and the rumors are true. Ivan Semenov is no longer Head of his family."

"They can't do that!"

"They can, and they did. You'll find the process described in your copy of the Book of the Law. He broke the law when he officiated at Alzbeta's marriage without The Hradil's permission. Poor Semenov is stripped of all rank and title. He's working as a cook's helper."

"The marriage is still valid, isn't it?" Jan asked worriedly.

"Absolutely. Nothing can touch that. A marriage bond is a marriage bond and completely unbreakable as you know. But, the judges have been chosen for the trial. . . ."

Sudden realization shook Jan. "Of course. He's no longer a Family Head so Semenov won't be there. It will be The Hradil and four more of her kind."

"I'm afraid so. But justice will be seen to be done. No matter how prejudiced they are they can't go against the law in open court. You have a lot of people on your side."

"And a lot more who are looking forward to me getting it in the neck, too."

"You've said it yourself. You can't change people overnight. Even though there are changes going on, the people don't like it. This is a conservative world and people, for the most part, are troubled by change. That's on your side now. This trial will be a legal one and you will have to get off."

"I wish I shared your enthusiasm."

"You will as soon as you have eaten some of the chicken and dumpling stew Alzbeta sent with the tape. That is if the jailers leave you any of it after it is searched for weapons."

All according to law. No doubts about it. Then why was he so worried? There were less than seven days left to the trial and Jan busied himself with a study of the Book of the Law which, admittedly, he had never looked at very closely before. It proved to be a simplified version of Earth Commonwealth law. A great deal had been pruned away—there was certainly no need to go into the details of illegal counterfeiting on a world without money. Or space barratry. But ironclad additions had been written into it that gave the Family Heads the power of absolute rule. What little bits of personal freedom had been in the original were totally missing here.

On the day of the trial Jan shaved carefully, then pulled on the clean clothes that had been brought for him. He carefully pinned on his badge of rank. He was Maintenance Captain and he wanted everyone to remember it. When the guards came he was ready to go, almost eager. But he drew back when they produced the wristcuffs.

"No need for those," he said. "I'm not going to attempt to escape."

"Orders," the Proctor said, Scheer, the same one Jan had felled with the club. He stood out of range with his gun raised. There was no point in resisting. Jan shrugged and held out his arms.

It was more like a feast day than a trial. The law said that anyone could attend a public trial—and it looked like the entire population had decided to do just that. There was little work to be done since the seed corn had not been planted. So they came, all of them, filling the Central Way from side to side. Family groups, with food and drink, prepared for a long siege. But there were no children there: under the age of sixteen they were forbidden to attend trials because of the banned things that might be said. So the older children were watching the younger ones and hating it.

No building could have held this crowd so the trial would take place outdoors, under the changeless twilight sky. A platform had been erected with seats for judges and defendant. A speaker system had been hooked up so that everyone could hear. There was a carnival feeling in the air, some free entertainment so they could all forget their troubles. And the ships that never came.

Jan climbed the flight of steps and sat down in the box, then examined the judges. The Hradil, of course. Her presence there had been as assured as the law of gravity. And Chun Taekeng, Senior Elder, his place guaranteed as well. An unexpected face, old Krelshev. Of course—he would have taken over as Elder when

Semenov was unseated. A man of no intelligence and lesser nerve. A tool like the other two sitting next to him. The Hradil was the only one that counted today. She was leaning toward them, instructing them no doubt, then straightened up and turned to face Jan. The wrinkled face cold as ever, the eyes unemotional icy pits. But she smiled when she looked at him, ever so slightly, but undoubtedly there, though vanished in an instant. A victory smile; she was so sure of herself. Jan forced himself not to react, to sit in stony and expressionless silence. Any emotion he displayed during this trial could only do him harm. But he still wondered what she was smiling at. It was not long before he found out.

"Silence, silence in the court," The Hradil called out, and her amplified voice spread down the Central Way, bouncing from the buildings on each side. She said it just once and the response was instant. This was a most serious moment.

"We are here today to judge one of our number," she said. "Jan Kulozik, the Maintenance Captain. Grave charges have been leveled and this court has been assembled. I ask the technician, is the recorder operating?"

"It is."

"Then proper records will be kept. Let the record show that Kulozik was accused by Proctor Scheer of murdering Proctor Captain Ritterspach. This is a grave charge and the Elders in conference investigated the matter. It was discovered that witnesses to the so-called murder differed with Proctor Scheer. It appears that Ritterspach died when Kulozik was defending himself from an unprovoked attack. Self-defense is not a crime. Therefore it was deduced that the death was accidental, and charges of murder have been dropped. Proctor Scheer has been admonished for his enthusiasm."

What did it mean? The crowd was just as much at a loss as Jan was and a murmur swept through the watchers, silenced when The Hradil lifted her hand. Jan did not like it. All he knew was that with the charges dismissed he was still cuffed. And that oaf Scheer had the nerve to be grinning at him. Admonished and now smiling? More was going on here than was apparent and Jan was determined to strike first. He stood and leaned close to the microphone.

"I am pleased that the truth has come out. Therefore please free my wrists—"

"Prisoner will be seated," The Hradil said. The two Proctors slammed Jan back into the chair. It was not over yet.

"Far graver charges have been leveled against the prisoner. He is charged with inciting to riot, with disloyalty, with disloyal actions, with disloyal propaganda, and with the most serious of all. Treason.

"All of these crimes are most grave, the final one the most grave of all. It carries with it the death penalty. Jan Kulozik is guilty of all of these crimes and will be proven so today. His execution will take place within a day of the trial, for that is the law."

Eighteen

There was shouting from the immense crowd, questions. Angry
men pushed forward, Jan's friends, but stopped when all twelve of
the Proctors drew up in a line in front of the platform, weapons
ready.

"Keep your distance," Proctor Scheer called out. "Everyone stay
back. These guns are set on maximum discharge."

The men called out, but did not draw too close to the ready
weapons. The Hradil's amplified voice washed over them.

"There will be no disturbances. Proctor Captain Scheer has orders to shoot if he must. There may be dissident elements in the
crowd who will attempt to help the prisoner. They must not be allowed to."

Jan sat still in the box, realizing now what was happening. Admonished one minute, Proctor Captain the next; Scheer was
doing all right. The Hradil had him firmly in her hand. Had Jan
as well. He had relaxed his defenses, thought about the crime of
murder, never realizing that this charge was just a front for the
real charges. There was no way out now; the trial would have to
continue. As soon as The Hradil stopped talking he spoke loudly
into the microphone.

"I demand that this farce be ended and that I be freed. If there
is any treason here, it is on the part of that old woman who wants
to see us all dead. . . ."

He stopped talking when his microphone was cut off. There
was no escaping the situation; he only hoped that he could make
The Hradil lose her temper. She was possessed with anger—he

could tell that by the hiss in her voice when she spoke—but she still kept it under control.

"Yes, we will do as the prisoner suggests. I have consulted with my fellow judges and they agree with me. We will drop all the charges, all except the important one. Treason. We have had enough of this man and his flouting of legitimate authority. We have been lenient because these are dangerous times and some leniency must be allowed to get things done. Perhaps we were in error by allowing the prisoner too much freedom to act against the established ways. This error must be erased. I ask the technical recorder to read from the Book of the Law. The third entry, labeled 'treason', under the laws of rule."

The technician ran his fingers over the keys of his computer, finding the proper section and displaying it on the screen before him. As soon as he had the entry correct he pressed the audio output. In commanding tones the law boomed forth.

"Treason. Whomsoever shall reveal the secrets of the state to others shall be guilty of treason. Whomsoever shall reveal the details of the operations of the authorities shall be guilty of treason. Whomsoever shall flaunt the majesty of the authorities and induce others to go against the authority of the state shall be guilty of treason. The penalty for treason is death and the penalty shall be exacted twenty-four hours, after sentencing."

There was shocked silence as the voice faded away. Then The Hradil spoke.

"You have heard the nature of the crime and its punishment. You will now hear the evidence. I will supply the evidence myself. Before the Families and before the Heads of Families the prisoner mocked the authority of the Heads of Families, the duly constituted authorities here. When he was ordered to cease in his disloyalty and obey orders, he defied them. He ordered that the machines be stopped by some mechanical means known to him, unless a second trip was made to get corn. This trip was made and many died because of him. By acting in this manner and causing others to defy authority in this manner he became guilty of treason. This is the evidence, the judges will now decide."

"I demand to be heard," Jan shouted. "How can you try me without my being permitted to speak?"

Although the microphone before him was disconnected, those closest to the platform could hear what he said. There were shouts from his friends, from others, that he be allowed to speak. Not surprisingly there were other cries that he be silenced. The Hradil listened to this in silence, then conferred with the other judges. It was Chun Taekeng, as Senior Elder, who made the announcement.

"We are merciful, and things must be done by the rule of law. The prisoner will be permitted to speak before judgement is passed on him. But I warn him that if he speaks treason again he will be silenced at once."

Jan looked over at the judges, then rose and turned to the massed crowd. What could he say that would not be called treasonous? If he said one word about the other planets or the Earth he would be cut off. He had to play this by their rules now. There seemed little hope—but he had to try.

"People of Halvmörk. I am being tried today because I did everything in my power to save your lives and save the corn which is sure to be badly needed by the ships when they come. That is all I have done. Some have opposed me and they were in error and it will be proved that they were in error. My only crime, and it is not a crime, was to point out the new and dangerous situation and outline ways to handle it. Things we did have never been done before—but that doesn't mean that they were wrong. Just new. The old rules did not apply to the new situations. I had to act as strongly as possible or the new things would not have been done. What I did was not treason, but just common sense. I cannot be condemned for that. . . ."

"That is enough," The Hradil said, breaking in. His microphone went dead. "The prisoner's arguments will be considered. The judges will now confer."

She was arrogant in her power. There was no conferring. She simply wrote on a piece of paper and passed it to the next judge. He wrote and passed it along. They all wrote quickly; it was obvious what the word was. The paper was passed in the end to Chun Taekeng who barely glanced at it before he spoke.

"Guilty. The prisoner is found guilty. He will die by garroting in twenty-four hours. Garroting is the punishment for treason."

There had never been an execution on this planet before, not in the lifetime of any of those present. They had never even heard of the means of punishment. They shouted to each other, calling out questions to the judges. Hyzo Santos pushed through the crowd, to the edge, and his voice could be heard over the others.

"That's not treason, what Jan did. He's the only sane man here.

If what he did was treason then the rest of us are guilty of treason as well—"

Proctor Captain Scheer raised his gun, at point blank range, and fired. The flame wrapped Hyzo's body, charring him in an instant, turning the shocked horror on his face to a black mask. He was dead before he fell.

There were screams as those nearby pushed back, moans of pain from those burnt by the edges of the blast. The Hradil spoke.

"A man has been executed. He shouted aloud that he was guilty of treason. Are there any more who wish to cry out they are guilty of treason? Come forward, speak plainly, you will be heard."

She purred the words, hoping for a response. Those closest pushed back, on the verge of panic. None came forward. Jan looked at the body of his friend and felt a strange numbness. Dead. Killed because of him. Perhaps the charges were right and he did bring chaos and death. He stirred when Scheer stepped behind him and grabbed him by the arms so he could not move. Jan understood why when he saw The Hradil coming slowly towards him.

"Do you see where your folly has led you, Kulozik?" she said. "I warned you not to defy me, but you would not listen. You had to preach treason. Men have died because of you, the last but moments ago. But that is at an end now because you are at an end. We will soon be finished with you. Alzbeta will be finished with you. . . ."

"Don't soil her name by speaking it with your putrid lips!"

Jan had not meant to speak, but she goaded him to it.

"Alzbeta will no longer be married to you when you are dead, will she? That is the only way to terminate a marriage, and this one will be terminated. And your child will be raised by another man, will call another man father."

"What are you talking about, hag?"

"Oh, didn't she tell you? Perhaps she forgot. Perhaps she thought you might find the idea of her married to another repugnant. She will have a child, your child—"

She stopped, gaping, when Jan burst into loud laughter, shaking in Scheer's hard grip.

"Do not laugh, it is true," she cried.

"Take me from her, take me to my cell," Jan called out, turning away, still laughing. Her news had had the opposite effect from that she had wished for. This was such good news. He said that to

Alzbeta when she came to see him in his cell after he had been locked away.

"You should have told me," he said. "You must have known better than that scruffy old bitch how I would react."

"I wasn't sure. It was such wonderful news, just a short while ago. The doctor must have told her, I didn't know she knew. I just didn't want to bother you."

"Bother? A little good news goes a long way in these bitter times. The baby itself is what counts. I could be killed at any time —but you will still have our child. To me, that is the important thing. You should have seen that monster's face when I started to laugh. It wasn't until later that I realized it was the best thing I could have done. She is so evil she can't appreciate that others can have any wholesome or decent thoughts."

Alzbeta nodded. "I used to be hurt when you talked like that about her, it bothered me so. After all, she is The Hradil. But you are right. She is all those things and more. . . ."

"Don't talk like that, not here."

"Because of the recordings being made? I know about that now, one of your friends told me. But I want her to hear, I want to tell her these things myself. She worked so hard to keep us apart."

And in the end she is going to succeed, Jan thought, blackly. She has won. The sight of Alzbeta so near yet so untouchable was too much at the moment.

"Go now, please," he told her. "But come back later, do you promise?"

"Of course."

He fell onto the bed, his back to the window, not wishing to see her leave. Then it was all over. Hyzo was the only one who might have done something to help him. But Hyzo was dead, angered by her as she must have planned. Killed by her as she had carefully planned as well. No one else could organize any help in the short time left. He had friends, many of them, but they were helpless. And enemies as well, everyone who hated change and blamed him for everything. Probably the majority of people on this world. Well he had done what he could for them. Not very much. Though if the ships came now they would have the corn waiting. Not that the people here would avail themselves of the advantage. They would bow like the peasants they were and go back to the fields and servitude, and slave their lives away for no reward, no future. Nothing. He had had the brief time with Alzbeta; that was worth a lot to him. Better to have had something than nothing. And she would have their son, hopefully a son. Or better, a daughter. A son of his might have too many of his father's characteristics. A daughter would be better. The meek did not inherit the earth here, but perhaps they lived a bit longer with a little more happiness. All of which would be academic if the ships never came. They might be able to get most of the people through to the north just one more time with the decaying equipment. Probably not even that, if he were not there to put things back together.

And he was not going to be there, because in a few short hours more he would be dead. He hung heavily from the bars of the tiny window and looked out at the perpetual gray of the sky. The garrote. No one here had ever heard of it. Revived by the rulers of Earth for the worst offenders. He had been forced to witness an execution of this kind once. The prisoner seated on the specially built chair with the high back. The hole behind his neck. The loop of thick cord passed around his neck with the ends through the hole. The handle attached to the cord that turned and tightened and shortened it until the prisoner was throttled, painfully, and dead. There had to be a sadist to tighten the cord. No shortage of them. Surely Scheer would volunteer for the job.

"Someone to see you," the guard called in.

"No visitors. I want to see no one else other than Alzbeta. Respect a man's last wishes. And get me some food and beer. Plenty of beer."

He drank, but he had no appetite for the food. Alzbeta came once again and they talked quietly, closely, as close as they could get. She was there when the Proctors came for him and they ordered her away.

"No surprise to see you, Scheer," Jan said. "Are they going to be nice and let you turn the handle on the machine?"

Jan could tell by the man's sudden pallor and silence that his guess had been right. "But maybe I'll kill you first," he said and raised his fist.

Scheer lurched back, scrambling for his gun, a coward. Jan did not smile at the spectacle. He was tired of them, tired of them all, tired of this stupid peasant world, almost ready to welcome oblivion.

Nineteen

It was the same platform that had been used for the trial; the same public address system still set up. Nothing was wasted; everything was carefully planned. But the chairs and tables placed there for the trial had been removed and a single item put in their place. The high-backed chair of the garrote. Carefully made, Jan noticed in a cold and distant way, not done in a day. All well prepared. He had stopped, unconsciously, at the sight of it, his guard of Proctors stopping too.

This was a moment suspended in time, as though no one was sure just what to do next. The five judges, mute witnesses to their decision, stood on the platform. The crowd watched. Men, women, children, every inhabitant of the planet well enough to walk must have stood there, jammed in the Central Way. Silent as death itself, waiting for death. The perpetually overcast sky pressed down like a mourning blanket against the silence.

Broken suddenly by Chun Taekeng, never patient, always angry, immune to the emotions that gripped the others.

"Bring him over, don't just stand there. Let us get on with this."

The momentary spell ended. The Proctors pushed Jan forward suddenly so that he stumbled against the lowest step and almost fell. It angered him; he did not want to be thought a coward at this moment. He pushed back hard against them, shrugging their hands from his arms. Free for the instant, he started up the steps by himself so that they had to hurry after him. The crowd saw this and responded with a gentle murmur, almost a sigh.

"Come forward. Sit there," Chun Taekeng ordered.

"Don't I get to speak any last words?"

"What? Of course not! It is not ordered that way. Sit!"

Jan strode towards the chair of the garrote, arms firmly gripped again by the Proctors. He saw only Chun Taekeng, The Hradil, the other judges, and an immense loathing welled up within him, forcing out the words.

"How I hate you all, with your stupid little criminal minds. How you destroy people's lives, waste them, subjugate them. You should be dying, not me. . . ."

"Kill him!" The Hradil ordered, raw hatred in her face for the first time. "Kill him now, I want to see him die."

The Proctors pulled at Jan, forcing him towards the garrote, while he pulled back, trying to get to the judges, to somehow break free and wreak vengeance upon them. Every eye was upon this silent struggle.

No one noticed the man in the dark uniform who pushed through the crowd. They made way for him, closed ranks behind him, staring at the platform. He struggled through the jammed front ranks and climbed the steps, until he was standing on the platform itself.

"Release that man," he said. "This affair is now concluded."

He walked slowly across the platform and took the microphone from Chun Taekeng's limp fingers and repeated the words so that everyone could hear them.

No one moved. There was absolute silence.

The man was a stranger. They had never seen him before.

The fact was an impossibility. On a planet where no one arrived, where no one left, every person was known by sight, if not by name. There could be no strangers. Yet this man was a stranger.

Whether he meant to fire or not, Proctor Captain Scheer started to raise his gun. The newcomer saw the motion and turned toward him, a small and sinister weapon ready in his hand.

"If you don't drop that gun I will kill you instantly," he said. There was cold resolve in his voice and Scheer's fingers opened and the gun dropped. "You others as well. Put your weapons down." They did as ordered. Only when the guns were safely out of their reach did he raise the microphone and speak into it again.

"You other Proctors out there. I want you to know that there are men on all sides aiming weapons at you. If you attempt to resist you will be killed at once. Turn and see."

They did, everyone in the crowd, as well as the Proctors, noticing for the first time the armed men who silently appeared on the tops of the buildings along the Central Way. They held long and deadly weapons equipped with telescopic sights, aimed downward. There was no doubt that they would use them efficiently and quickly.

"Proctors, bring your weapons up here," the echoing voice ordered.

Jan stepped forward and looked at the man, at the two other armed strangers who joined him on the platform, and felt an immense relief surge through him. Just for an instant. His execution might only have been postponed.

"You're from the ships," he said.

The stranger put the microphone down and turned toward him, a grayhaired man with dark skin and burning blue eyes.

"Yes, we're from the ships. My name is Debhu. Release Kulozik at once," he snapped at the Proctors who hurried to obey. "We landed out on the Road about twenty hours ago. I'm sorry we had to wait until now to show up but we wanted everyone in one place at the same time. You would have been killed if they knew we were coming. There could have been fighting, more deaths. I'm sorry you had to go through this, with the death sentence hanging over you."

"You're with the ships—but you're not Earth Commonwealth men!"

The words were torn from Jan in an explosion of hope. Something tremendous, incredible had happened. Debhu nodded slow agreement.

"You are correct. There have been . . . changes. . . ."

"What are you doing here? Clear this platform!" Chun Taekeng's anger cut through the paralysis that had gripped them all. "Give me that microphone and leave! This is not to be tolerated—"

"Guards. Move the judges back. Watch them closely."

Burly men with ready guns moved swiftly at Debhu's order, pushing the shocked Elders into a group, facing them with weapons ready. Debhu nodded approval and spoke through the microphone again.

"People of Halvmörk, I would like your attention. The ships

are late because of a change in a number of planetary governments. We will tell you more about this later. For now it is
enough to know that the absolute power of the Earth authorities
known as the Earth Commonwealth has been broken. You are
free people. What that means will be explained to you. For now it
is enough to know that a war is still being fought and there has
been much starvation. Every grain of corn you have grown is
needed and we are grateful for it. Now go to your homes and wait
to be informed. Thank you."

Their voices rose in a loud babble as they turned, walking away,
calling out to each other. Some men tried to stay, technicians,
friends of Jan's, but were moved on their way by the men with
guns, more and more of them appearing down the Central Way.
Jan waited in silence; he had to know more before he spoke.

"You knew about my trial and the verdict?" Jan said. Debhu
nodded. "How?"

"There is an agent on this planet."

"I know. Ritterspach. But he's dead now."

"Ritterspach was only a tool. He just took orders. No, the real
agent is well-trained and has been working here for years. Reporting on the Security network scramble frequency. We seized some
of their equipment and heard the messages when we came out of
jumpspace. That's why we didn't announce our arrival."

Jan was still stunned by the rush of events and found it difficult
to assimilate all the new information so quickly. "An active agent
here? But who . . . ?" Even as he phrased the question the answer was obvious. He turned about and stabbed his finger at the
judges. "There's your undercover agent, right there!"

"Yes, that's the one," Debhu agreed.

The Hradil screamed shrilly and lurched forward at him, her
hands raised, her nails like animals' claws ready to scratch and
rend. Jan waited for her, stepping forward to receive her, seizing
her wrists and prisoning them, staring into her hate-torn face just
inches from his own.

"Of course. My enemy. The shrewdest and most vicious person
on this planet. Too intelligent to be from the low stock of the
others. A creature of Earth. Willing to live a life in exile on this
miserable planet in exchange for the power, the absolute power to
rule as she wished, destroy whom she wished. Who reported se-
cretly to the ships when they arrived so her masters on Earth

would know how well she was doing here. Who would see that anyone died who stood in her way. . . ."

"No problems until you arrived," she shrieked, spittle flying. "They warned me you were a suspected Disrupter, I was to watch you closely. Get evidence."

She swayed as he shook her, slowly and carefully in order not to hurt her ancient bones. His voice was low and triumphant.

"They lied to you, don't you realize that? They know all about me, convicted me and sent me here. It was a death sentence for me—or this prison world. You were just my keeper, sending reports to them. But no more. Do you hear that, agent? We've won and you have lost. Doesn't that make you feel good?"

Jan felt terrible. The touch of her revolted him. He released her, pushed her away to the guards who caught her before she could fall. Turned his back on her, sickened by the corpse-touch of her skin.

"Not quite won everywhere," Debhu said. "But at least we can win here. When we leave I'm taking this woman with me. And that Proctor, the one who murdered your friend. This kind of rule by violence has to end. We are going to have trials, public trials that will be broadcast on every occupied planet. Justice will be done—unlike the sideshow this creature arranged. We hope that the trials, with punishment where due for those found guilty, will bring peace. Get rid of the old hatreds. There are going to be a lot of pieces to pick up when this thing is over. But the end is in sight. We're winning on all fronts except one. The planets are ours, that was the easiest part. No one ever enjoyed being ruled from Earth. The space fleet was spread thin and could be attacked on a planet-by-planet basis. Our surprise was sudden. Deprived of their bases and support the Earth fleet could only withdraw—but they were relatively unharmed in the battles. Hurt but not destroyed. Now they have returned to Earth, to guard the home world. Too tough a nut for us to crack."

"Yet they in turn can't attack the planets—no spacer can hope to succeed in capturing a well-defended planetary base."

"Agreed—but we have the same problem as Earth. So right now we have a stalemate. Earth has reserves of food and minerals, but in the long run their economy, as it stands now, cannot exist without the planets."

"Nor can we exist without them as well."

"Quite true. Their material reserves are high—but not their

food supplies. I doubt if they can produce enough food for their population, even with synthetics. The future is still in doubt. We've won the first battles but not the war. And our need for food is even more desperate than Earth's. We have no reserves. That was Earth policy. Starvation is very close—which is why we need the corn. At once. The cargo ships are in landing orbit now; they started down as soon as I sent the signal that the position was secure. We thank you for getting the corn here despite all of the problems. We'll start loading at once."

"No," Jan said grimly. "That's not the way it is going to be at all. The corn will not be loaded until I say so."

Debhu stepped back, startled, his gun swinging up by reflex.

"Kill me if you like. Kill us all. But the corn is ours."

Twenty

Debhu's eyes were angry slits in his dark face. "What are you getting at, Kulozik? We're fighting a war and we need that food—we must *have* that food. No one is going to stand in our way. I can take your life as easily as I saved it."

"Don't threaten me—or brag about your war. We have been fighting a war too, against this alien world. And we brought this corn for you. It didn't get here by accident. If we had left it behind it would be ashes by now. These people are poor enough, but they lost what little they had for your sake. Their clothing, furniture, personal possessions, all left behind to make room for the corn you want to grab as though you had a right to it. It is *ours*—do you understand that? Good men died when we went back on the second trip, and I don't want to find out that they died in vain. You'll get the corn all right, but we have certain conditions attached to it. You are going to listen to our terms or you are going to have to shoot us. You'll get the corn all right, but it will be the last. The decision is up to you."

Debhu stared at Jan closely, at the tight muscles and half-closed fists. For a long moment they stood that way, facing each other in silence. Until the anger faded from Debhu's face to be replaced by a half smile. He grunted and the gun slipped from sight.

"You're a hard man, Kulozik, I can see that," he said. "I'll just have to talk to you. You have a point. It's been a busy morning. I guess you have as much of a right to the fruits of the rebellion as anyone. Not that we have very much. Let's go find your wife, who will probably want to see you, and have something to drink and talk it over."

"Agreed!"

Alzbeta was beyond words, still not believing what had happened. She buried her face in his shoulder, holding him to her, crying and not realizing why.

"It's all right," Jan said. "All over. Things are not going to be the way they used to be—they are going to be far better. Now make some tea for our guest and I'll tell you why."

He dug out a bottle of his alcohol distillate and poured some into the cups, hoping the tea would ameliorate the taste. Debhu's eyes widened when he sipped some.

"It takes getting used to," Jan said. "Shall we drink then? To sanity and a peaceful future."

"Yes, I'll drink to that. But I would also like to know what your rebellion means."

"No rebellion," Jan said, draining his cup and setting it down. "Just give and take. Equality. The people here are now no longer economic slaves and that will have to end. They will have to work for their freedom—and they have started already. They'll keep supplying all the food you need. But they want something in return."

"We haven't much to give. There has been a lot of destruction, more than I wanted to admit in public. Chaos. We'll be centuries rebuilding."

"All we need is simple equality and what goes with it. The Elders' rule will have to be ended. Not at once; it is the only system they know and nothing would work without it. But it will break down of its own accord. We want full contact with the rest of the Commonwealth—the rest of the planets. I want these people to see democracy at work and compare it to economic slavery. I want the children educated offworld. Not all of them, just the best. They'll bring back intelligence and ideas, then everything will have to change for the better. The Elders will not be able to resist forever."

"You're asking a lot. . . ."

"I'm asking very little. But it must begin at once. Just a few children to begin with, this trip. We'll probably have to tear them away from their parents. But they'll learn, like it or not, and will eventually understand why this had to be done. It will be hard for them, for all of us, because I am sure that education and information is as restricted on the outer planets as it is on Earth. But the facts are there. They will just have to be uncovered and understood. All of us must have free access to the heritage of Earth from which we have been deprived. On this world it will eventually mean the end of the stultifying culture that has forced upon these people. The food we have been supplying has economic power, so we should have some return for our labors. The future must be different. The people here have played their lives out like puppets. Real enough to them perhaps, but just things on strings to the puppet-masters on Earth. The Hradil was the tool they used to make sure that there was no deviation from the empty roles everyone had been selected to play. We were nothing to them, less than machines, unimportant and replaceable parts of a great organic machine built to supply cheap and tasteless food for poor men's dinners. But no more. We'll supply the food, but we want human status in return."

Debhu sipped at his fortified tea, then nodded.

"Well why not. You're not asking for much in the material way now, and that is what counts. Since we have very little to offer. But we'll take the children, find schools for them . . ."

"No. I'll take care of that. I'm going with you."

"You can't!" Alzbeta shouted, a cry of pain. He took her hands.

"It will only be for a little while. I'll return, I promise you. But out there now, in the turmoil, no one really cares about us. I'll have to fight for everything we receive. I know what this planet needs and I'll get it. Though I'm sure not one person out of a hundred here will appreciate it. I'll take their children away for education, introduce change, supply treasonous thoughts, and they are not going to love me for it."

"You'll go away and never come back," she said, so quietly he could barely hear her.

"Don't believe that for a second," Jan said. "My life is here with you. On this strange twilight-and-fire world. Earth is part of my past. I love you, and I have my friends here, and—with some changes life could be most enjoyable. I'm only going now because there is no one else for the job. I'll try to be back before our son is born. But I can't promise that. But I *will* be back before the trains leave again, because I'll be bringing the supplies and replacements that will make that possible." He looked over at Debhu. "I don't imagine you brought pile rods or anything else we have to have?"

"Not really. There was chaos, you know. And the need for food was desperate. Most of the things on the manifests for this planet are of Earth manufacture."

"See what I mean, Alzbeta? We are going to have to take care of ourselves now and I am going to have to start it all by myself. But it will work. People will always have to eat."

There was a rising rumble of braking jets from above. The ships had arrived. Alzbeta stood and put the teapot on the tray.

"I'll make some more tea. I'm sorry if I doubted you, acted foolishly. I know that you will come back. You always wanted things to change here, everything. And maybe they will. No, I'm sure they will. But after the changes—will we be happy?"

"Very," he said, and her smile answered his.

The teacups rattled in their saucers as the roaring rose and rose until conversation was impossible.

The ships had come at last.

STARWORLD

One

The battered freighter had been on fusion drive ever since it had passed the orbit of Mars. It was pointed at Earth—or rather at the place where the Earth would be in a few hours time. All of its electronic apparatus had been either shut down or was operating at the absolute minimum output—behind heavy shielding. The closer they came to Earth the greater their chance of detection. And their instant destruction.

"We're taking the war to them," the political commander said. Before the revolution he had been a professor of economics at a small university on a distant planet; the emergency had changed everything.

"You don't have to convince me," Blakeney said. "I was on the committee that ordered this attack. And I'm not happy with the discrimination target program."

"I'm not trying to convince. I'm just enjoying the thought. I had family on Teoranta . . ."

"They're gone," Blakeney said. "The planet's gone. You have to forget them."

"No. I want to remember them. As far as I am concerned this attack is being launched in their memory. And in memory of all the others savaged and destroyed by Earth down through the centuries. We're fighting back at last. Taking the war to them."

"I'm still concerned about the software."

"You worry too much. One single bomb has to be dropped on Australia. How can you miss an island that big, an entire continent?"

"I'll tell you exactly how. When we release the scoutship it will have our velocity and will accelerate from that basic speed. The computer cannot make a mistake because there will be time for only a single pass. Do you realize what the closing velocity will be? Tremendous!" He took out his calculator and began punching in figures. The ship's commander raised his hand.

"Enough. I have no head for mathematics. I know only that our best people modified the scoutship for this attack. The DNA-constructed virus will eat and destroy any food crop. You yourself prepared the program to pilot the ship, to locate the target, to drop the bomb. They'll know it's war then."

"It's because I worked on the program that I am unsure. Too many variables. I'm going down for another test run."

"Do that. I'm perfectly secure, but please yourself. But watch the time. Only a few hours more. Once we penetrate their detection net it will have to be hit and run with no staying around to watch the results."

"It won't take long," Blakeney said, turning and leaving the bridge.

Everything has been jury-rigged, he thought as he went down the empty corridors of the ship. Even the crew. An unarmed freighter daring to attack the heart of the Earth Commonwealth. But the plan was wild enough to work. They had been building up speed ever since they had shut down the space drive, well outside the orbit of Mars. The ship should hurtle past Earth and be safely away before the defenders could launch a counterattack. But as they passed the planet the small scoutship they carried, secured to the outer hull, would be launched under computer control. This was what worried him. All the circuitry was breadboarded, lashed together, a complicated one-shot. If it failed the entire mission failed. He would have to go through all of the tests just one last time.

The tiny spacecraft, smaller even than a normal lifeboat, was secured to the outer hull by steel braces equipped with explosive bolts. A crawl tube had been fixed in place so that the scoutship shared the larger ship's atmosphere, making installation and servicing that much easier. Blakeney slipped in through the tube, then frowned at the circuits and apparatus bolted onto the walls of the tiny cabin. He turned on the screen, punched up the inspection menu and began running through the tests.

On the bridge an alarm sounded hoarsely and a series of numbers began marching across the watch operator's screen. The political commander came and looked over his shoulder.

"What does it mean?" he asked.

"We've crossed their detection web, probably the outermost one from Earth."

"Then they know that we're here?"

"Not necessarily. We're on the plane of the ecliptic. . . ."

"Translation?"

"The imaginary plane, the level on which all of the planets in the solar system ride. Also all of the meteoric debris. We're too far out for them to have caught any radiation from the ship so we're just another hunk of space junk, a ferrous meteor. Now. The web's alerted to us and more apparatus will be trained in our direction. Laser, radar, whatever they have. At least it should work like that. We'll find out soon. We're recording all their signals. When we get back we'll have a record of everything. When it's analyzed we'll know a good deal more about how their setup works."

When, the political commander thought, not *if*. Nothing wrong with the morale. But there was another half to this mission. The virus strike. He looked at the time readout and called through to the scoutship.

"We're entering the red zone now. Less than half an hour to separation. How are you doing?"

"Just finishing up. As soon as I clear this program I'll join you."

"Good. I want you to . . ."

"Pulsed radar locked onto us!" the watch operator called out. "They know we're here." An auxiliary screen lit up near his elbow and he pointed to the readout. "Our reflectors have been launched. So where they had one blip on their screens before they now have a half dozen all the same, but separating at different speeds on different courses."

"They won't know which one is the real ship?"

"Not at the moment. But they know what we've done and they'll start analyzing course predictions, forward and back in time. They'll spot the real one. But by the time their computers have worked that out, ours will have initiated other defenses. It's a good program. Written by the best physicists and comptechs."

The political commander was less than reassured by the operator's reasoning. He did not like to think that his life depended on the non-random dispersal of magnetic charges and electrons that made up the program. Playing an intellectual game with the enemy computers. He looked out at the tiny sparks of the stars, the growing disk of the Earth, and tried to imagine the web of light beams and radio waves surging around them. He could not. He had to take it on faith that they were there and working at speeds infinitely beyond his own. A human being could not fight a battle in space. The machines did that. The crew were just captive spectators. His hands were clenched tightly behind his back, though he was not aware of it.

There was a series of small thudding sounds, more felt than heard, followed by an explosion that actually shook the deck beneath his feet.

"We've been hit!" he called out unthinkingly.

"Not yet." The watch operator glanced at his screens. "All of our remaining dupes and reflectors have been launched, then the scoutship. Mission accomplished—but now we have to get out of here. Fusion drive cut . . . space drive circuits now energized. As soon as the gravity fields allow we'll be on our way."

The political commander's eyes widened at a sudden thought; he turned sharply about.

"Where's Blakeney?" he called out. But no one on the bridge had heard him. They were counting the seconds, waiting for the missiles that must have surely been launched in their direction.

The political commander felt a sudden arrow of despair. He knew where Blakeney was.

He had been right, absolutely right! And they called themselves comptechs. They couldn't write a program to win at tic-tac-toe. Orbital mechanics, fine, simple trig and geometry and calculus. Child's play. But comparison plane orientation was apparently well beyond them.

Blakeney watched with satisfaction for less than a second while the cursor on the computer roved all over the highly amplified image of Earth—then froze on the great sweep of a circular storm over Europe. He switched on the override and put his finger on the screen, on the only bit of Australia clear of the cloud cover of a tropical storm. When the glowing blob of the cursor jumped to this spot he typed in POSITIVE IDENTIFICATION and took his finger away. At least the moronic thing could be counted upon to stay there once orientated.

None too early. The engine note changed as the course shifted, just moments later. Good. He followed the program display, then unlocked the launching switch as they hurtled toward the top of the atmosphere, ready to release manually if there were any more difficulties.

There were none. At the same instant that zero appeared on the screen the ejection mechanism thudded heavily. As the ship arced slowly away to avoid the outer traces of atmosphere, the heavy ceramic container was hurtling toward Earth. He knew what would be happening next; this thing at least had been well designed. Layer after layer of ablative material would burn away as it impacted on the thickening air. It would grow hot—and slow down—with the frozen virus locked safely into the cryogenic flask inside. Then a layer of ceramic would fall away to reveal an opening for the air to enter, to impact on a pressure gauge inside.

At exactly 10,769 meters, in the middle of the jet stream, the explosive charge would explode releasing the contents of the flask.

The wind would carry the virus across Australia, perhaps to New Zealand as well—A carefully designed virus that would attack and destroy any and all of the food crops grown on Earth.

Blakeney smiled at the thought as the missile hit.

It had an atomic warhead so that, to the watchers below, there was suddenly a new sun just visible through the clouds.

Two

The TWA jet had left New York a few hours after dark. As soon as it had reached its cruising altitude it had gone supersonic and cut a booming path straight across the United States. About the time it was crossing Kansas the western sky had grown light as the Mach 2.5 craft caught up with the setting sun. The sun was well above the horizon again when they lost altitude over Arizona, and the passengers who had seen one sunset in New York City now witnessed a far more colorful one over the Mojave desert.

Thurgood-Smythe squinted into the glare then opaqued his window. He was going through the notes of the emergency meeting that had been hurriedly called at the UN and had no eyes either for the glories of the sunset or the massed technology of Spaceconcent opening up before him. His attaché case rested on his knees with the flat VDU screen pulled out of its slot. The figures, names, dates marched steadily across the screen, stopping only when he touched the keyboard to correct any transcription errors made by the speech recorder. It had been programmed for his voice, but still substituted *one* for *won* a good deal of the time. He made the corrections automatically, still taken aback by the momentous changes and the immense gravity of the situation. What had happened was unbelievable, impossible. But happened it had.

There was a jar as they touched down, then he was thrust forward against the safety harness as the engines reversed. The screen and keyboard disappeared at the touch of a button; the dark window cleared and he looked out at the white towers of the space center, now washed with glowing ochre by the sun. He was the first passenger off the plane.

Two uniformed guards were waiting for him; he nodded at their snapped salutes. Nothing was said, nor did they ask for his identification. They knew who he was, knew also that this was an unscheduled flight arranged for his benefit. Thurgood-Smythe's beak-like nose and lean, hard features had been made familiar by the news reports. His short-cropped white hair appeared severely military compared to the longer-haired styles currently in fashion. He looked exactly what he was; someone in charge.

Auguste Blanc was standing at the ceiling-high window, his back turned, when Thurgood-Smythe came in. As Director of Spaceconcent his office was naturally on the top floor of the tallest administration building. The view was impressive; the sunset incomparable. The mountains on the horizon were purpleblack, outlined against the red of the sky. All of the buildings and the towering spaceships were washed by the same fiery color. The color of blood; prophetic perhaps. Nonsense! A cough cut through Auguste Blanc's thoughts and he turned to face Thurgood-Smythe.

"A good flight, I sincerely hope," he said, extending his hand. A thin, delicate hand, as finely drawn as his features. He had a title, a very good French one, but he rarely used it. The people he needed to impress, such as Thurgood-Smythe, took no heed of such things. Thurgood-Smythe nodded sharply, impatient for the formalities to be out of the way.

"But tiring nevertheless. A restorative, then? Something to drink, to relax?"

"No thank you, Auguste. No, wait, a Perrier. If you please."

"The dry air of the airship. Not humidified as we of course do in the spacers. Here you are." He passed over the tall glass, then poured an Armagnac for himself. Without turning about, as though ashamed of what he was saying, he spoke into the bottles of the cocktail cabinet. "Is it bad? As bad as I have heard?"

"I don't know what you have heard." Thurgood-Smythe took a long drink from his glass. "But I can tell you this, in all secrecy . . ."

"This room is secure."

". . . it is far worse than any of us thought. A debacle." He dropped into an armchair and stared sightlessly into his glass.

"We've lost. Everywhere. Not a single planet remains within our control—"

"That cannot be!" The sophistication was gone and there was an edge of animal fear in Auguste Blanc's voice. "Our deepspace bases, how could they be taken?"

"I'm not talking about those. They're unimportant. All of them on low-gravity, airless moons. They aren't self-sufficient, they must be supplied regularly. More of a handicap than an asset. They can't be attacked—but they can be starved out. We're evacuating them all."

"You cannot! They are our foothold, the cutting edge of the blade for conquest . . ."

"They are our Achilles heel, if you wish to continue this stupid simile." There was no trace of politeness, no touch of warmth in Thurgood-Smythe's voice now. "We need the transport and we need the men. Here is an order. See that it goes out on the Foscolo net at once." He took a single sheet of paper from his case and passed it over to the trembling director. "The debate is done. Two days of it. This is the combined decision."

Auguste Blanc's hands were shaking in the most craven manner so that he had difficulty reading the paper he grasped. But the director was needed. He was good at his job. For this reason, and none other, Thurgood-Smythe spoke quietly, considerately.

"These decisions are sometimes harder to make than to implement. I'm sorry, Auguste. They left us no choice. The planets are theirs. All of them. They planned well. Our people captured or dead. We have most of our space fleet intact, there was no way they could get at them, though a few were sabotaged, a few deserted. We're pulling back. A strategic withdrawal. A regrouping."

"Retreat." Spoken bitterly. "Then we have lost already."

"No. Not in the slightest. We have the spacers, and among them are the only ships designed for military use. The enemy have freighters, tugs, a handful of deserters. Many of their worlds already face starvation. While they are thinking about survival we shall reinforce our defenses. When they try to attack us they will certainly be defeated. Then, one by one, we will reoccupy. You and I will probably not see the end, not in our time, but this rebellion will eventually be stifled and crushed. That is what will be done."

"What must I do?" Auguste Blanc asked, still insecure.

"Send this command. It is a security order to all commanders to change codes. I am sure that the old one is compromised by now."

Auguste Blanc looked at the incomprehensible series of letters and numbers, then nodded. Encoding and decoding were a computer function and he neither knew nor cared how they operated. He slid the sheet into the reader slot in his desk top and tapped a series of commands on the keyboard. A few seconds after he had done this the response sounded from the computer speakers.

"Command issued to all receivers listed. Response received from all receivers listed. Communication code has been changed."

Thurgood-Smythe nodded when he heard this and put another sheet of paper onto Auguste Blanc's desk.

"You will notice that the orders are issued in very general terms. The fleet to be withdrawn to Earth orbit as soon as possible, all advanced bases to be deactivated, the Lunar bases to be reinforced. As soon as enough transports are available they will be used to ferry troops to the Earth-orbiting colonies. They will be occupied in force. I have positive information that the colonies' sympathies are with the rebels, not with their home world. And the same thing will be done with the orbital satellite stations. Do you have any questions?"

"Will there be a shortage of food? I heard that we are going to go hungry. I had my wife send in a large order for food but it was not filled. What does it mean?"

The man is a coward—and a fool, Thurgood-Smythe thought to himself. Worried about his failure to be a hoarder! I suppose that is a new word to him. And to most people. They'll find out what it means when we shoot a few of them. For hoarding, and spreading defeatist rumors as well.

"I'll tell you the truth," Thurgood-Smythe said aloud, "but I'm going to give you a warning first. We are in a war, and morale is very important in wartime. So people who spread false rumors, who attempt to hoard food depriving others of their share—these people are aiding the enemy and they will be punished. Punishment will be imprisonment and execution. Am I expressing myself clearly enough for you?"

"Yes, I didn't really understand. I really am sorry, had no idea . . ."

The man was trembling again; Thurgood-Smythe tried not to let his distaste show in his expression. "Very good. There will be no starvation on Earth—but there will be shortages and rationing.

We have always imported a certain amount of prole food, but I don't think either of us will worry if their rations are short. More important is the fact that a blight has destroyed all of the Australian food crops for this growing season. . . ."

"Blight? All their crops . . . I don't understand."

"Mutated virus. Spread by bombing from space. Self-eliminating after a few months but it will mean completely replanting all of the food crops with imported seed."

"You must destroy them all! Criminal rebels—they are trying to starve us to death!"

"Not really. They were just delivering a warning. It appears that in enthusiasm for revenge some of our space commanders took individual actions. At least two rebel planets have been effectively destroyed. The rebel reaction was to send this ship to bomb Australia. It could just as easily have decimated the entire world's food crops. It was a message. We of course took out the attacking ship. But we have sent a return message agreeing to their terms. Planetary bombings only of military targets."

"We must wipe them out, every single one of them," Auguste Blanc said, hoarsely.

"We will. Our plan is a simple one. Withdraw all our forces to Earth orbit to secure against any invasion or occupation of the space colonies and satellites. Then selective reconquest of the planets, one by one. All of our spacers are being fitted with weapons. The enemy have only a few ships manned by traitors. They may have won these battles. We will win the war . . ."

"Urgent report," the computer said. A sheet of paper emerged from the desk top. Auguste Blanc looked at it then passed it over.

"It is addressed to you," he said.

Thurgood-Smythe read it quickly, then smiled.

"I ordered all reports of enemy ship movements to be screened and analyzed. They need food more than we do. They have now sent a number of ships to Halvmörk. One of the largest food planets. I want those ships to land and load completely. Then leave . . ."

"So we can capture them!" Auguste Blanc was exuberant, his earlier fears forgotten for the moment. "A genius of a plan, Thurgood-Smythe, may I congratulate you. They brought this war upon themselves and now they will pay. We will take the food and give them starvation in return."

"Exactly what I had in mind, Auguste. Exactly."

They smiled at each other with sadistic pleasure.

"They have only themselves to blame," Thurgood-Smythe said. "We gave them peace and they gave us war. We will now show them the high price that must be paid for that decision. When we are done with them there will be peace in the galaxy forever. They have forgotten that they are the children of Earth, that we built the commonwealth of planets for their sakes. They have forgotten what it cost to terraform all of their planets to make them suitable for occupation by mankind, the cost in lives and money. They have rebelled against our gentle hand of rule. We shall now clench this hand into a fist and they shall be punished. They started this rebellion, this war—but we will finish it."

Three

"You're going now," Alzbeta said. She spoke calmly, almost emotionlessly, but her hands were clenched hard on Jan's. They stood in the shadow of a great bulk grain carrier, one of the shining cylinders of metal that rose up high behind them. He looked down into her gentle features and could find no words to answer with; he simply nodded. The love in her face, the yearning there, they were too much for him and he had to turn away.

It was the irony of life that after all his lonely years on this twilight planet, now, married and a father-to-be, with a measure of peace and happiness at last, now was the time he had to leave. But there were no alternatives. He was the only one here who would fight for the rights of the people of this agricultural world, who might possibly see to it that some day a complete and decent society might grow on this planet. Because he was the only one on Halvmörk who had been born on Earth and who knew the realities of existence there and in the rest of the Earth Commonwealth. Halvmörk was a deadend world now, where the inhabitants were agricultural slaves, working to feed the other planets for no return other than their bare existence. In the present emergency the rebel planets would expect them to keep on working as they always had. Well they would farm still—but only if they could be free of their planetary prison. Free to be part of the Commonwealth culture, free to have their children educated—and finally free to change the stunted and artificial society forced upon them by Earth. Jan knew that he would not be thanked, or even liked, for what he was going to do. He would do it still. He owed it to the generations to come. To his own child among others.

"Yes, we must leave now," he said.

"You are needed here." She did not want to plead with him, but it was in her voice.

"Try to understand. This planet, big as it is to us, it's really only a very small part of the galaxy. A long time ago I lived on Earth, worked there very successfully, and was happy enough until I discovered what life was really like for most of the people. I tried to help them—but that is illegal on Earth. I was arrested for this, stripped of everything, then shipped out here as a common laborer. It was that or death. Not too hard a choice. But while the slow years passed here, the rebellion that I was a part of has succeeded. Everywhere but on Earth. For the moment my work here is done, the corn has been saved and will go out to the hungry planets. But now that we have fed the rebellion I want to make sure that we share in the victory as well. Do you understand? I must go. And it is time. The orbits have been calculated and these ships will have to lift very soon."

Alzbeta looked steadfastedly into Jan Kulozik's face as he spoke, memorizing those thin, taut features. She put her arms about his wiry and hardmuscled body then, pressing tight against it, so that the child within her was between them, in the sheltered warmth of their bodies, clutching hard as though when she released him she might never hold him again. It was a possibility she did not consider, yet it was lurking just out of sight all of the time. There was a war being fought among the alien stars and he was going to it. But he would come back; that was the only thought she would let her brain hold on to.

"Come back to me," she whispered aloud, then pulled away from him, running toward their home. Not wanting to look at him again, afraid that she would break down and make him ashamed.

"Ten minutes," Debhu called out from the foot of the boarding ladder. "Let's get aboard and strap in."

Jan turned and climbed up the ladder. One of the crewmen was waiting in the airlock and he sealed the outer hatch as soon as they had passed through.

"I'm going to the bridge," Debhu said. "Since you've never been in space you'll strap in on deck . . ."

"I've worked in free fall," Jan said.

The question was on Debhu's lips, but he never spoke it. Halvmörk was a prison planet. It no longer mattered any longer why anyone should have been sent here. "Good," he finally said. "I can use you. We have lost a lot of trained men. Most of the crew have never been in space before. Come with me to the bridge."

Jan found the operation a fascinating one. He must have arrived on Halvmörk in a ship very much like this one—but he had no memory of it. All he remembered was a windowless prison cell on a spacer. And drugged food that kept him docile and easily controlled. Then unconsciousness, to waken to find the ships gone and himself a castaway. It had all happened far too many years ago.

But this was very different. The ship they were aboard was identified only by a number, as were all of the other tugs. It was a brute, built for power alone, capable of lifting a thousand times its own mass. Like the other tugs it lived in space, in perpetual orbit. To be used only once every four Earth years when the seasons changed on this twilight planet. Then, before the fields burned in summer and the inhabitants moved to the new winter hemisphere, the ships would come for their crops. Deep spacers, spider-like vessels that were built in space for space, that could never enter a planet's atmosphere. They would emerge from space drive and go into orbit about the planet, only then unlocking from the great tubes of the bulk carriers they had brought. Then it would be the time to use the tugs.

When the crews changed over the dormant, orbiting ships would glow with life, light and warmth as their power would be turned on, their stored air released and warmed. They in their turn would lock to the empty bulk carriers and carefully pull them from orbit, killing their velocity until they dropped into the atmosphere below, easing them gently down to the surface.

The carriers were loaded now, with food to feed the hungry rebel planets. Their blasting ascent was smooth, computer controlled, perfect. Rising up, faster and faster through the atmosphere, out of the atmosphere, into the eternal blinding sunlight of space. The computer program that controlled this operation had been written by comptechs now centuries dead. Their work lived after them. Radar determined proximity. Orbits were matched, gas jets flared, great bulks of metal weighing thousands of tonnes drifted slowly together with micrometric precision. They closed, touched, engaged, sealed one to the other.

"All connections completed," the computer said, while displaying the same information on the screen. "Ready to unlock and transfer crew."

Debhu activated the next phase of the program. One after another the gigantic grapples disengaged, sending shudders of sound through the tug's frame. Once free of its mighty burden the tug drifted away, then jetted toward the deep spacer that was now lashed to the cargo of grain. Gentle contact was made and the airlock of one ship was sealed to the other. As soon as the connection was complete the inner door opened automatically.

"Let's transfer," Debhu said, leading the way. "We usually remain while the tugs put themselves into orbit and power down to standby status. Not this time. When each ship is secure it is cleared to depart. Every one of them has a different destination. This food is vitally needed."

A low buzzer was sounding on the bridge and one of the readouts was flashing red. "Not too serious," Debhu said. "It's a grapple lock, not secured. Could be a monitoring failure or dirt in the jaws. They pick it up when we drop planetside. Do you want to take a look at it?"

"No problem," Jan said. "That's the kind of work I have been doing ever since I came to this planet. Where are the suits?"

The tool kit was an integral part of the suit, as was the computer radio link that would direct him to the malfunctioning unit where the trouble was. The suit rustled and expanded as the air was pumped from the lock; then the outer hatch swung open.

Jan had no time to appreciate the glory of the stars, unshielded now by any planetary atmosphere. Their journey could not begin until he had done his work. He activated the direction finder, then pulled himself along the handbar in the direction indicated by the holographic green arrow that apparently floated in space before him. Then stopped abruptly as a column of ice particles suddenly sprang out of the hull at his side. Other growing pillars came into being all around him; he smiled to himself and pushed on. The ship was venting the air from the cargo. The air and water vapor froze instantly into tiny ice particles as it emerged. The vacuum of space would dehydrate and preserve the corn, lightening the cargo and helping to prevent the interplanetary spread of organisms.

The frozen plumes were dying down and drifting away by the time he came to the grapple. He used the key to open the cover of the control box and activated the manual override. Motors whirred, he could feel their vibration through the palm of his hand, and the massive jaws slowly ground apart. He looked closely at their smooth surfaces, at what appeared to be an ice-crystaled clump of mud flattened on one of them. He brushed it away and pressed the switch in the control box. This time the jaws closed all the way and a satisfactory green light appeared. Not the world's most difficult repair, he thought as he sealed the box again.

"Return at once!" the radio squawked loudly in his ears, then went dead. No explanation given. He unclipped his safety line and began to pull back in the direction of the airlock.

It was closed. Locked. Sealed.

While he was still assimilating this incredible fact, trying to get a response on his radio, he saw the reason.

Another deep spacer came drifting across their bow, reaction jets flaring, magnetic grapples hurling toward them, trailing their cables. Clearly visible on its side in the harsh sunlight was a familiar blue globe on white.

The flag of Earth.

For long seconds Jan just hung there, the sound of his heart pounding heavy in his ears, trying to understand what was happening. It suddenly became obvious when he saw the spacelock on the other ship begin to open.

Of course. The Earth forces weren't going to give up that easily. They were out there, watching. They had observed the food convoy being assembled, had easily guessed the destination. And Earth needed the food in these hulls just as much as the rebel planets did. Needed it to eat—and as a weapon to starve their opponents into submission. They could not have it!

Jan's anger flared just as the first of the suited figures emerged and dropped toward the hull close to him. They must be stopped. He groped through his tool kit, pulled out the largest powered screwdriver there and thumbed it on, full speed. It whined to life, its integral counterweight spinning to neutralize the twisting action on his body. He held this extemporized weapon before him as he launched himself at the approaching spacemen.

Surprise was on his side; he had not been seen in the shadows on the spacer's skin. The man half-turned as Jan came up, but he was too late. Jan pushed the whirling blade against the other's side, clutched onto him so he would not drift away, watched the metal bite into the tough fabric—then saw the plume of frozen air jet out. The man arched, struggled—then went limp. Jan pushed the corpse away, turned, kicked to one side so the man coming toward him floated harmlessly by. He was ready then to jab his weapon at another spaceman coming along behind him.

It was not as easy to do the second time. The man struggled as Jan clutched his arm. They tumbled about, floating and twisting, until someone grabbed Jan by the leg. Then still another.

It was an unequal struggle and he could not win. They were armed, he saw rocket guns ready in their hands, but they holstered them as they held him. Jan stopped struggling. They were not going to kill him—for the moment. They obviously wanted prisoners. He was overwhelmed by a sense of blackest despair as they pulled him to one side as more attackers poured by, then dragged him back into their ship and through the spacelock. Once it was sealed, they stripped the spacesuit from him and hurled him to the floor. One of them stepped forward and kicked him hard against the side of the head, then over and over again in the ribs until the pain blacked out his vision. They wanted their prisoners alive, but not necessarily unbruised. That was the last thing he remembered as the boot caught him in the head again and he roared down into painfilled darkness.

Four

"Some they killed," Debhu said, holding the wet cloth to the side of Jan's head, "but only if they fought too hard and it was dangerous to capture them. They wanted prisoners. The rest of us were outnumbered, clubbed down. Does that feel any better?"

"Feels like my skull is crumbling inside."

"No, it's just bruising. They've sewn up the cuts. No broken ribs, the doctor said. They want us in good shape for public display when we get to Earth. They can't have taken many prisoners before they captured us. It hasn't been that kind of a war." He hesitated a second, then spoke more quietly. "Do you have a record? I mean, is there any reason they would like to know who you were, to identify you?"

"Why do you want to know?"

"I've never been to Earth, or in direct contact with earthies before. They may have records on me, I can't be sure. But they took retinal photographs of us all. You too, while you were unconscious."

Jan nodded, then closed his eyes briefly at the pain that followed the movement.

"I think they will be very happy when they identify me," he said. "I doubt if I will be."

The pattern made by the small blood vessels inside the eye is far more individual than any fingerprint. It can be neither forged nor altered. Everyone on Earth had this pattern recorded at birth and at regular intervals thereafter. Given a retinal print a computer could sort through these billions of photographs in a few moments. They would come up with his. Along with his identity and his criminal record. They would be very glad to discover these interesting facts.

"Not that it's worth worrying about anyway," Debhu said, leaning back against the metal wall of their prison. "We're all for the knackers in any case. Probably a show trial first to entertain the proles. Then—who knows what. Nothing good I'm sure. An easy death is the best we can hope for."

"No it's not," Jan said, ignoring the pain, forcing himself to sit up. "We are going to have to escape."

Debhu smiled sympathetically. "Yes. I suppose we ought to."

"Don't patronize me," Jan said angrily. "I know what I'm saying. I'm from Earth, which is more than anyone else in this room can say. I know how these people think and work. We're dead anyway so we have nothing to lose by trying."

"If we break out of here we have no way of taking over the ship. Not from armed men."

"That's the answer then. We don't do a thing now. We wait until we've landed. There will be guards of course, but the rest of the crew will be at their stations. We won't have to take over the ship. Just get away from it."

"Simple enough." Debhu smiled. "I'm with you so far. Now do you have any suggestions how we get out of this locked cell?"

"Plenty. I want you to move around quietly among the others. I want everything they have. Watches, tools, coins, anything. Whatever they were left with. When I see what they have I'll tell you how we are going to get out of here."

Jan did not want to explain, to give them any false hopes. He rested and drank some water, looking around the bare metal room in which they had been imprisoned. There were some thin mattresses scattered about on the hard plastic floor, a sink and toilet unit secured to one wall. A single, barred door was set into the opposite wall. No spying devices were visible, but that did not necessarily mean that they weren't there. He would take what precautions he could, hoping that their captors' surveillance would be a casual one.

"How do they feed us?" Jan asked as Debhu dropped down beside him.

"They pass the food through that slide in the door. Thin disposable dishes, like that cup you have there. Nothing we can use for weapons."

"I wasn't thinking of that. What's beyond the door?"

"Short length of hall. Then another locked door. Both doors are never opened at the same time."

"Better and better. Is there a guard in that short stretch of hall?"

"Not that I've ever seen. No need for it. We've got some things for you from the men . . ."

"Don't show me yet. Just tell me."

"Junk for the most part. Coins, keys, a nail clipper, a small computer . . ."

"That's the best news yet. Any watches?"

"No. They took them away. The computer was an accident. Built into a pendant the man wore around his neck. Now can you tell me what this is all about?"

"It's about getting out of here. I think we'll have enough to build what I need. Microelectronic circuitry. That's my field—or it was until they arrested me. Do the lights ever go out in here?"

"Not yet they haven't."

"Then we'll do it the hard way. I'll want all of the stuff you have collected. I'll pass back anything I can't use. If they are taking us to Earth—how long will the trip take?"

"About two weeks subjective time. Half again as much in spatial time."

"Good. I'll go slow and get it right."

The lights were never turned off or lowered. Jan doubted if the prisoners were being watched more than casually—he had to believe that or there was no point in his even making an attempt at escape. He had sorted through the items in his pockets by touch and separated out the keys. Then, after he had lain down, he spread them out on the floor in the shelter of his body and that of the man beside him. They were small plastic tubes, in different colors, with a ring at one end. To unlock a door they were simply inserted in the hole in the face of the lock mechanism. They were so commonplace and ubiquitous, people were so used to them that they never stopped to think about the mechanism inside. Surely most people probably never even realized that there was anything contained within the apparently solid plastic.

Jan knew that there was a complex mechanism sealed inside the tubes. A microwave receiver, a microchip processor and a tiny battery. When the key was inserted in the lock a signal was transmitted by the lock circuits that activated the concealed key mechanism. A coded signal was sent by the key in return. If it was the correct one the door was unlocked, while at the same time a brief but intense magnetic field recharged the battery. However if the wrong key was inserted and an incorrect code was returned not only did the lock not open, but the mechanism completely discharged the battery rendering the key useless.

Using the blade of the nail clipper, Jan shaved away carefully at the plastic. He was certain now that the job could be done. He had tools, circuitry and power supply. With patience—and skill— he should be able to build what he needed. Microchip technology was so commonplace that people tended to forget that these infinitesimal microprocessors were built into every single mechanical device that they possessed. Jan was well aware of this, since he had designed many circuits of this kind. He knew equally well how to alter them to his own advantage.

One of the keys was scavenged for its battery alone. The two filament-thin wires from it were used to probe the circuitry of a second key. To short out and alter the connections there. The key's transmitter became a receiver, a probe to divine the secret of the lock on the cell door. When it had been constructed to the best of his ability, Jan spoke to Debhu.

"We're ready for the first step now. I'm going to see if I can read out the lock code on this door. This would be impossible on a really sophisticated lock mechanism, so I'm hoping this one has normal interior door security."

"You think it will work?"

Jan smiled. "Let's say that I hope it will work. The only way I can test it is by actually trying it. But I'll need your help."

"Anything. What do you want?"

"A little distraction for the guards. I'm not sure how closely we are being watched. But I still don't want to draw any attention to myself. I'll be at the wall near the door. I would like a couple of your men to start a fight or something at the far wall. Draw their attention for the vital seconds."

Debhu shook his head. "Does it have to be a fight? My people don't know anything about fighting or killing. It is not a part of our culture."

Jan was startled. "But all those guns you were waving around— they looked realistic enough to me."

"Real, but unloaded. The rest was play-acting. Isn't there something else we could do? Hainault there is a gymnast. He could create a diversion."

"Fine. Anything at all as long as it is showy."

"I'll talk to him. When do you want him to start?"

"Now. As soon as I'm in position. I'll rub my chin, like this, when I'm ready."

"Give me a few minutes," Debhu said, moving slowly away across the room.

Hainault was very good and he made the most of the situation. He started with some warming-up exercises, then quickly went on to handstands and backbends, all of this culminating in a gigantic backspring followed by a complete rotation in midair.

Before the acrobat's feet had touched down again, Jan had slipped the modified key into the hole in the lock and just as quickly withdrawn it. He strolled away from the door, the key clutched tightly in his damp fist, his shoulders hunched unconsciously as he waited for the alarm.

It did not come. After a good five minutes had gone by he knew that the first step had been successful.

The most important find, among the objects collected from the prisoners, was the microcomputer. It was a toy, a gadget, a gift undoubtedly. But for all of that it was still a computer. The guards had missed it because to all outward appearances it was just a piece of personal jewelry. A red stone heart on a golden chain, with a gold initial 'J' set into one side. Yet when the heart was laid on a flat surface and the 'J' depressed, a fullsized hologram of a keyboard was projected to one side. Despite the insubstantiality of the image it was still a fully operational keyboard. When a key was touched a matching magnetic field was altered and the appropriate letter or number appeared in front of the operator, also apparently floating in midair. Despite its size it had the capacity of a normal personal computer since its memory was stored at a molecular, not a gross electronic level.

Jan now knew the code for the lock on their cell door. The next step would be to alter one of the other keys to broadcast this same code. Without the computer he could never have done this. He used it to clear the memory from the key's circuitry and then to implant the new memory. This was mostly a trial and error process, that was speeded up when he wrote a learning program for the computer that was self correcting. It took time—but it worked, and in the end he had a key that he was sure would open the cell door without giving an alarm. Debhu looked down dubiously at the tiny cylinder of plastic.

"And you are sure that it will work?" he asked Jan.

"Fairly sure. Say ninety-nine percent."

"I like the odds. But after we open the inner door—then what?"

"Then we use the same key on the other door at the end of the passageway. Here the odds are greater, perhaps fifty-fifty that both locks are opened by a key with the same combination. If they are the same, why then we are through the doors and away. If not, at least we have the advantage of surprise when the outer door is opened."

"We'll settle for that," Debhu said. "If this works we have you to thank for it. . . ."

"Don't thank me," Jan said roughly. "Don't do that. If we all weren't under death sentence already I would not even have considered this plan. Have you thought about what will happen if we are successful? If we get out of this cell and perhaps even manage to escape from the ship?"

"Why—we'll be free."

Jan sighed. "On some other world, perhaps you would be right. But this is Earth. When you get out of this spacer you'll find yourself right in the middle of a space center. Guarded, complex, sealed. Every single person you encounter will be an enemy. The proles because they will do nothing to help you—though they will surely turn you in if there is a reward being offered. All of the rest will be armed enemies. Unlike your people they know about personal combat and enjoy it. Some of them enjoy killing too. You're leaving one certain destiny for another."

"That's our worry," Debhu said, laying his hand on Jan's. "We're all volunteers. We knew when we began this business of rebellion where it would probably end. Now they have us captured and mean to lead us like sheep to the slaughter. Save us from that, Jan Kulozik, and we are in your debt no matter what happens afterward."

Jan had no words to answer with. Imprisoned, he had thought only of escape. Now, with this possibility close to hand, he was beginning to consider the consequences for the first time. They were very depressing. Yet he had to make some plan no matter how small the chance was of succeeding. He thought about this in the few days remaining before their arrival and worked out one or two possible scenarios. Lying quietly, side by side and speaking in a whisper, he explained what had to be done.

"When we leave the cell we stay close together and move very fast. Surprise is our only weapon. Once out of the cell we will have to find our way out of this ship. We may have to capture one of them, force him to lead us . . ."

"No need. I can take care of that," Debhu said. "That is my work, why I commanded the food ships. I'm a construction architect. I build these things. This craft is a variation of the standard Bravos design."

"You know your way around it?"

"In the dark."

"Then, the important question—how do we avoid the main lock? Is there any other way out of the ship?"

"A number of them. Hatches and airlocks both, since these craft are designed to operate in and out of an atmosphere. There's a large hatch in the engineroom for heavy equipment—no, no good, takes too long to open." He frowned in thought. "But, yes, close by that. An access port for resupply. That's the one that we want. We can get out that way. Then what?"

Jan smiled. "Then we see where we are and figure out what we do next. I don't even know what country we are coming down in. Probably the United States, Spaceconcent in the Mojave Desert. That presents a problem too. Let me think about it. It's a desert location with only a few road and rail connections in and out. Easy to block."

It was after the next meal that the guards entered in force, heavily armed.

"Line up," the officer ordered. "Against that wall, faces to the wall. That's it, arms high, fingers spread so we can see them. First man, get your chunk over here. Kneel down. Get working on him."

They had brought a sonic razor. The prisoners were manhandled forward, one by one, and the operating head run over their faces. The ultrasonic waves gave a perfectly clean shave, severing the facial hairs without affecting the skin. It worked just as well on their heads too, removing every trace of hair from their skulls. They were shorn and humiliated; the guards thought it was very funny. The floor was thick with tufts and hanks of hair before they left. The officer called back to them.

"I want you all lying down when the warning goes. We may

have up to five gees on landing and I don't want you falling around and breaking bones and giving us trouble. If you are foolish enough to get hurt you will not be repaired but will be killed. I promise you that."

The metal door slammed behind them and the prisoners looked at each other in silence.

"Wait until after we're down and they switch from ship's gravity," Debhu said. "That will be when they are busiest in the shutdown routines. No one will be moving around yet and the outer hatches will still be closed."

Jan nodded just as the alarm horn sounded.

There was vibration when the ship entered the atmosphere, then the pressure of deceleration and the rumble of distant engines sounding from the metal walls around them. A sudden tremor and they were down. They lay still, looking at Jan and Debhu.

A sudden twisting sensation pulled at them, followed by a feeling of heaviness as Earth's slightly stronger gravitational field took hold.

"Now!" Debhu said.

Jan had been lying next to the door. He was on his feet instantly and pushing the key into the lock; the door swung open easily in his hand. The short hall beyond was empty. He sprinted the length of it, aware of the others close behind him, slammed his weight against the door at the end—then carefully slid the key into the opening in the lock. Holding his breath.

The door unlocked. No alarms were sounded that they were aware of. He nodded to Debhu who grabbed the door and hurled it open.

"This way!" he called out, sprinting down the empty corridor. A spaceman walked around the bend, saw them and tried to run. He was overwhelmed, crushed down, held, then pounded into unconsciousness by Jan's bare fists.

"We're armed now," Debhu said, tearing the pistol from the man's holster. "Take it, Jan. You know more about its use than we do."

Debhu was up on the instant and they were close behind him. He ignored the lift shaft, too slow, and instead hurled himself down the emergency stairwell, risking a fall with every leap. When he reached the door at the bottom he stopped and let the others catch up.

"This opens into the main engine compartment," he said. "There will be at least four ratings and an officer there. Do we try to take them, knock them down . . ."

"No," Jan said. "Too risky. They may be armed and they could sound the alarm. Where would the officer be?"

"At the ancillary control panel. To your left about four meters away."

"Fine. I'll go first. Fan out behind me but don't get between me and any of the crew if you can prevent it."

"You mean . . ." Debhu said.

"You know exactly what I mean," Jan said, raising the gun. "Open the door."

The officer was very young and his frightened cry, then scream of pain before the second shot silenced him, brought the escaping prisoners to a stumbling halt. Only Jan ran on. The engines were lightly manned. He had to murder only two other men; the second by shooting him in the back.

"Come on!" Jan shouted. "It's clear."

They kept their faces averted from his as they ran by, following Debhu to the hatch. He did not waste time looking for the electrical controls but instead seized the manual emergency wheel and began turning. After two turns he was pushed aside by Hainault who used his athlete's muscles to whirl the wheel, over and over, until the latches clacked free.

"And no alarm yet," Jan said. "Push it open and see if there is any kind of welcome waiting for us outside."

Five

It was dark and quiet in the landing pit, the only sounds the click of contracting metal and the drip of water. The air was warm but not hot, the hull and pit itself had been cooled by the water sprays after landing. Jan led the way, through the open hatch and onto the wide metal gangway that had extended automatically after the landing. They were at least fifty meters above the pit bottom that was still boiling with steam. High above them there were harsh lights and the sound of machinery, engines.

"There should be exit doors near the water jets," Debhu whispered. "If these pits are designed like the ones I'm familiar with."

"Let's hope they are," Jan said. "You had better show us the way."

He stood aside as Debhu led the others past, looking on all sides for any sign of pursuit. Their escape must have been discovered by this time.

The lights flared on, set into the rim of the pit above, bright as the unshielded sun of Halvmörk. An instant later the guns began firing. Rocket-powered slugs ricocheted and screamed off the concrete and steel, sent up explosions of water from the puddles. Tore through the soft flesh of human bodies.

Jan shielded his eyes with his arm as he fired upwards, blindly. Throwing the gun aside and falling backwards when his ammunition was exhausted. By a miracle of chance he was unharmed as yet—hoarse screams brutally informed him that the others weren't that lucky. His shoulder crashed painfully into a metal support and he sought shelter behind it, trying to blink away the floating spots of light before his eyes.

He was only three meters from the hatch they had used to flee from the ship into this bullet-filled trap. Their escape had not gone unnoticed; the guards had taken instant revenge. There was only death in this pit. Trying to ignore the rain of bullets, Jan ran forward and fell through the open hatch.

It was an act of instinct, to escape the sure death outside. He lay on the hard steel for a moment, knowing that he had not escaped but just postponed his destruction. But they could not find him like this, not just lying here waiting to be captured or shot. He scrambled to his feet and stumbled back into the engine room. It was populated only by the dead. But the lift door was opening . . .

Jan dived for the bank of instruments against the bulkhead, jammed himself into the narrow space behind them, pushing back deeper and deeper as the many thudding footsteps came close.

"Hold it right there," a voice ordered. "You'll get blown away by our own men."

The murmur of voices was cut short by the same man again. "Quiet in the ranks." Then more softly. "Lauca here, come in command. Do you read me command . . . Yes, sir. Ready in the engine room. Yes, firing stopping now. Right, we'll mop up. No survivors." Then he shouted aloud as the gunfire ceased in the pit outside.

"Try not to shoot each other in your enthusiasm—but I want those rebels wasted. Understand? No survivors. And leave them where they fall for the media cameras. The Major wants the world to see what happens to rebels and murderers. Go!"

They streamed by shouting angrily, guns ready. Jan could do nothing except wait for one of them to glance aside, to see for just one instant what was behind the instrument board. No one did. Their guns were ready for the vengeance waiting them outside. The officer came last.

He stopped not an arm's distance from Jan, but staring intently after the troops, then spoke into the microphone on his collar.

"Hold all firing from the rim, repeat, hold firing. Mop-up troops are now in the pit."

Jan sidled forward—and his shirt caught on a protruding bolt-head, held an instant, then ripped free. The officer heard the slight sound and turned his head. Jan lunged forward and seized him by the throat with both hands.

It was unscientific and crude. But it worked. The officer thrashed about, trying to kick Jan, to tear his fingers from his throat. They fell and the man's helmet went rolling away. He tore at the throttling hands, his fingernails tearing bleeding welts in Jan's skin, his mouth gasping for air that he could not breathe. But Jan's muscles were strengthened by hard work, his fingers squeezing even tighter now with the desperate fear of failure. One of them would live; one die. His thumbs bit deep into the flesh of the officer's neck and he looked with no compassion into the wide and bulging eyes.

He held on until he was sure that the man was dead, until there was no trace of a pulse under his thumb.

Reason returned—and with it fear. He looked around wildly. There was no one else there. Outside the firing was becoming more spasmodic as the soldiers ran out of targets. They would be back, someone else might enter soon . . . He tore at the officer's clothing, ripping open the magnetic fasteners, pulling the boots from his feet. It took less than a minute to strip the man, to throw off his own clothes and pull on the uniform. The fit was adequate though the boots were tight. The hell with that. He jammed the helmet on his head then stuffed the limp corpse and discarded clothing behind the instrument bank where he had hidden, pushing them as far back as he could. Time, time, there was not enough of it. As he ran toward the lift he fumbled with the chin strap of the helmet. His thumb was raised to the button when he looked at the indicator.

It was on the way down.

The emergency stairs, the way they had entered. He slammed through the door and pushed hard against the mechanism to make it close faster. Now. Up the stairs. Not too quickly, don't want to be out of breath. How far? What deck? Where would there be an exit from the ship? Debhu would know. But Debhu was dead. They were all dead. He tried to blame himself for their deaths as he stumbled on the treads, but he could not. Murdered here or murdered later. It was all the same. But he was still free and he would not be as simple to kill as it had been to slaughter the unarmed men in the pit—who did not even know how to fight. Jan loosened the officer's pistol in the holster. Well he knew how. It would not be that easy with him.

How many decks had he climbed? Four, five. One was as good as any other. He laid his hand on the next door and took a deep breath, then pulled his uniform down. Shoulders back, another breath—then through the door.

The corridor was empty. He walked down it at what he hoped was a brisk military pace. There was a junction ahead and one of the crewmen came around it. He nodded at Jan and started to hurry by. Jan put out his hand and stopped him.

"Just a minute my good man." The accents of his prep school, long forgotten, sprang instantly to his lips. "Where is the nearest exit?"

The crewman started to pull away, eyes widening. Jan spoke again, more firmly.

"Speak up. I came into this ship from the pit. Now how do I get out to report?"

"Oh, sorry your honor. I didn't know. Up one deck, that's the stairwell over there. Then right and first right again."

Jan nodded and walked stiffly away. So far so good. He had fooled the spaceman—but would this bluff work with any others he met? He would find out soon enough. What had the dead officer called himself? He dredged his memory. Loka? No, Lauca, or something very close to that. He glanced at the ring on the uniform cuff. Sub-lieutenant Lauca. Jan pushed open the door and climbed the flight of steps.

It was only when he had turned the corner that he saw the two guards stationed at the exit from the ship. The airlock controls had been overridden and both interior and exterior locks were open. Beyond the outer lock a metal bridge led across the pit to safety.

The guards snapped to attention, slamming their heels down and bringing their weapons to port arms. He could only go forward toward them now, even when they stepped in front of them. Jan walked steadily on to stop before them. And noticed something of utmost importance.

Their unit numbers were different from the ones on the uniform he wore.

"I am Lieutenant Lauca. Mop-up squad. My radio is dead. Where is your commanding officer?"

They snapped to attention as he spoke.

"The major is down there, sir. Command post in the company office."

"Thank you."

Jan returned the salute in the correct manner that had been drilled into him with great precision during his cadet days at school, wheeled smartly about and stamped away.

As soon as he was out of sight of the airlock he turned in the opposite direction, away from the command post, and walked off between the machines and harsh lights and on into the night.

Not that he was free. He knew better than to believe that for an instant. No one was really free on Earth with its ubiquitous webs of surveillance spreading completely about the globe. The lieutenant's body would be found soon, that was certain. The man's uniform would be an asset until that moment—but after it a terrible liability. And he didn't even know where on Earth he was. Probably Spaceconcent at Mojave, though he could not be sure. The military might very well have their own bases kept secret from the public. But that wasn't important, not now. The first order of business was getting off the base. There was a road of some kind off to his left, well lit with occasional vehicles going by, and he went in that direction.

From the shelter of some large crates he looked out at the brightly lit gate. It would need more than bluff to get through this one. Perhaps he ought to try the fence, although he knew that there was no way through this without setting off a number of alarms. Speed. Whatever he did he had to do it fast.

"*Lieutenant Lauca, come in.*"

He started as the voice sounded loudly inside his head. Transmitted by the bone conduction field inside the helmet. The radio, of course. Now where would the switch be? He fumbled at his belt, finding the radio controls, trying to make them out in the dark.

"*Lauca, come in.*"

Was this the right one? It seemed to be. Only one way to find out. He pressed it and spoke.

"Yes, sir."

"*That's enough. We want some remains for the press. Call your men back.*"

The commander's voice died away and the carrier tone vanished. The ruse worked, he had gained a few minutes—but no more. He switched the radio to broadchannel reception and listened with one ear to the commands passing back and forth. He must do something, even something desperate. And fast.

Jan ran forward to the illuminated traffic lane and waited out of sight of the guards at the exit. A car came toward him, there was someone next to the driver though, and Jan faded back out of sight. A motorcycle was close behind the car. Then nothing more. Seconds, then minutes ticked away. There seemed to be a steady stream of traffic into the base but nothing at all going out. The radio murmured in his ear. Routine commands. No emergencies yet. Something, anything!

There! A flatbed truck with a heavy load lashed in back. He couldn't see inside the high cab. It was a chance he had to take.

Jan stepped out in front of the slowly moving truck and raised his hand. Standing, unmoving, as it braked to a stop. The driver leaned out of his window.

"Can I help your honor?"

"Yes. Has this vehicle been searched yet?"

"No, sir."

"Then open the other door. I'm coming up."

Jan climbed the ladder and swung in through the open door. The driver, beefy and middle-aged, roughly dressed and wearing a cloth cap, was all alone. Jan slammed the door shut, turned back to the man and drew the pistol.

"Do you know what this is?"

"Yes your honor, I know, yes I do."

The man was stammering with fear, staring wide-eyed at the muzzle of the pistol. Jan could not afford to feel sorry for him.

"Good. Then do exactly as I say. Drive through the gate as you always do. Say nothing. I shall be on the floor and will kill you if you so much as open your mouth. Do you believe that?"

"Yes, I do! I certainly do . . ."

"Start driving."

The turbine whined under the hood as they started forward. They moved for a while, they must be close, then the driver touched the brakes. Jan pushed the gun up between the driver's legs and hoped that the raw fear in the man's face could not be seen by the guards below. A voice said something indistinct and the driver took a sheaf of papers from the door pocket and passed them down. And waited. Jan could see the sweat streaming down his face to drip from his double chin. He did not move the gun.

The papers were handed back and the driver let them drop from his fingers to the floor as he kicked the truck into gear and rolled it forward. They drove for less than a minute before a loud voice sounded in Jan's ears, overriding the murmurs of all the others.

"*Emergency. An officer has been killed, a sub-lieutenant. His uniform is missing. All patrols, all units, check in with your commanders. All gates sealed at once.*"

They were just that little bit too late.

Six

The truck was out of sight of the gate, but still on the main road, passing now through a dark and deserted warehouse area illuminated only by wide-spaced street lights.

"Turn at the next corner," Jan ordered. There was a good chance that pursuit might be close behind them. "And again at the next corner. Stop."

The air brakes hissed and the truck shuddered to a halt. They were in a back street, a hundred meters from the nearest light. Perfect.

"What time is it?" Jan asked.

The driver hesitated, then glanced at his watch. "Three . . . in the morning . . ." He stammered.

"I'm not going to hurt you. Don't worry." He tried to reassure the frightened man; he also did not lower his gun. "What time is dawn?"

"About six."

Three hours of darkness then. Not very much time. But it was all he had. Another, even more important question. "Where are we?"

"Dinkstown. All warehouses. No one lives here."

"Not that. The base back there. What's its name?"

The driver gaped at Jan as though he had lost his mind, but finally answered. "Mojave, your honor. The space center. In the Mojave desert . . ."

"That's enough." Jan had decided on the next step. It was dangerous, but he needed transportation. And everything was dangerous now. "Take your clothes off."

"Please, no, I don't want to be killed . . . !"

"Stop it! I said you wouldn't be hurt. What's your name?"

"Millard, your honor. Eddie Millard."

"Here's what I'm going to do, Eddie. I'm going to take your clothes and this truck and tie you up. I'm not going to injure you. When they find you, or you get loose, just tell them everything that happened. You won't get in any trouble . . ."

"No? I'm in that trouble now." There was despair as well as anger in the man's voice. "Might as well be dead. I'm out of a job, the least of it. On the welfare. Police will talk to me. Might be better off dead!"

He shouted the last words hysterically and reached over to clutch at Jan in the seat next to him. He was very strong. Jan had no recourse. The gun caught the driver in the forehead, then a second time when he still kept struggling. Eddie Millard sighed deeply and slumped, unconscious. What he had said was true, Jan realized as he struggled to strip off the man's clothes. One more victim. Are we all victims? There wasn't enough time now to think about things like that.

As he pushed the heavy man from the cab, lowering him as best he could to the roadway, Jan began to shake. Too much had happened, too quickly. He had murdered too many men. It was a brutal galaxy and he was turning into another one of the brutes. No! He wouldn't accept that. The means never justified the ends—but he had been fighting solely in self defense. From the time he had sacrificed his comfortable position here on Earth, there had been no turning back. When he had discovered that he had been one of the captors in a police state he had made a decision. Personally, he had lost a lot. But there were others who believed as he did— and the galaxywide rebellion had been the result. It was war now, and he was a soldier. For the moment it had to be just that simple. Recriminations would come after victory. And the revolutionaries would triumph, had to triumph. He dared consider no other outcome.

Eddie Millard's clothes stank of old sweat, were big as a tent wrapped about him. They would just have to do. The cap would conceal his new-shaven head. And there was no thought of possibly jamming the man into the stolen uniform. His stained underwear would have to suffice. There was some insulated wire behind the seat and he used this to secure the unconscious man's hands. That would do well enough. He would have to abandon the truck very soon in any case. Run, that's all he could do, just run.

The engine ground to life when he turned the key and the truck moved slowly down the narrow street. Jan was wearing the stolen officer's helmet, there was no other way of hearing the military radio, but after a few minutes he realized that it was a waste of time. There were a few distant signals, and even these died away. The military knew that he had the stolen radio so the communication computer was changing all of the frequencies to cut him off from their radioed commands. He threw the helmet to the floor and stepped on the accelerator, slowing down only when he saw an intersection ahead with a main road. Computerized traffic control changed the light to green as he approached, letting him merge with the sporadic traffic. Most of it large rigs like his. There were signs for a freeway ahead, 395 to Los Angeles, but he went right by the entrance. He would have no chance at all of getting through the police check at the outskirts of the built up area.

There were brighter lights coming up now, and a heavy semi approaching from the opposite direction cut in front of him so that he had to slow down. Good. A fuel area with parking behind it, an all-night restaurant of some kind. He turned in, going slowly, past the group of vehicles and on towards a darkened building beyond. It was a garage. Locked now, and he could just get his rig behind it. It would do. At least it would be safe there for a while; with a little luck it might be some hours before it was found. What next?

Keep moving. He had Eddie Millard's identification, but that would be good only for the most casual inspection. And a purse with some money in. Bank notes and a handful of change. He stuffed them into his pocket, pulling at the clothes so they didn't look obviously ill-fitting. If the proles here were anything like those back in Britain he doubted if this outfit would even be noticed. Fine. But what about the officer's uniform? Worthless. The alarm would be out for that. But the gun and extra clips of bullets? No, he couldn't part with them. He rooted under the seat and behind it until he found a grimy sack. It would have to do. He stuffed the gun and ammunition into it, then pushed the discarded uniform and helmet out of sight behind the seat. With the gun under his arm he got out, locked the cab, then climbed down. Then threw the keys over the fence. There was little else he could do. Drawing a deep breath he started forward, walking slowly through the warm night air toward the lights of the restaurant.

Jan stood in the concealing darkness, hesitating, unsure of the next step. He was tired and thirsty—no, not tired, completely exhausted now that he thought about it. From the time when he had opened the cell door he had been on the run, in deadly danger most of the time. Adrenalin had kept him going, had masked the growing fatigue. He felt it now, staggering at the release of tension, lurching forward to lean against the wall of the restaurant. His eyes were on a level with the bottom of the window and he could look in. A large room, booths and tables, a counter with two men sitting at it; otherwise empty. Should he take a chance and go in? It was a risk, but everything was a risk. Some food, something to eat, a chance to sit for a few moments and get his thoughts together. He needed it. Fatigue was making him fatalistic. He would be caught in the end—but at least when he was taken he would have a full stomach. Pushing away from the wall he walked to the entrance steps, up them and into the building.

During his other visits to the United States—how many years ago?—he had seen nothing like this place. Of course he had been at the best restaurants in New York City and Detroit, so he had nothing to judge by. The floor was concrete, stained and ancient. The men at the counter did not bother to look up or glance at him when he slipped into the booth nearest the door. The table and seat seemed to be made of aluminium, dented and worn with time. How did one order, by going to the counter? Or was there a selector and delivery mechanism at the table? It had a transparent top, now almost translucent with scratches, with a menu beneath it. Under DRINKS coffee was listed, but no tea. A number of strange items followed the EATS heading. The meaning of the word was obvious, but it seemed an unusual construction. He tried touching the coffee entry but this did not seem to do anything. Looking around he noticed the button on the wall under a TV screen. It read RING FOR SERVICE. He put out a tentative finger and pressed it.

In the silence of the room a buzzer could be heard sounding somewhere behind the counter. Neither of the diners moved. But a moment later a girl came around the counter and walked towards him. She had a slate in one hand. Personal service in a place like this! Her uniform was faded, and as stained as the floor, nor was she as young as she had looked at a distance. Her coarse hair was touched with gray and she apparently was toothless; no recommendation for the quality of the food.

"What'll it be?" she asked, looking at Jan with complete disinterest.

"Coffee."

"Anything to eat?"

He looked back at the menu and stabbed a finger down.

"Hamburger."

"With the works?"

He nodded, having not the slightest idea what she meant, which appeared to satisfy her because she scrawled on the slate then went away. He had never had a hamburger in his life, had not even the slightest idea what it was. But he knew that his accent was English, and decidedly public school English at that. So when he read the menu that word had leaped out at him. Hamburger. An old joke when he was a boy, with his mates, a line from a long-lost American film. "Gimme a hamboygah." They said it a lot. Apparently this bit of regional accent still made sense.

One of the men at the counter put some coins down on it, their clinking drawing Jan's attention. He stood and started for the door, glancing at Jan as he went by. Had his eyes widened slightly at the same time? There was no way of telling because he pushed on out into the night. Could he have recognized Jan? How? Or was Jan just being paranoid? He moved the sack closer to him on the seat and shook the mouth open so he could reach the gun easily. Instead of worrying about every stranger he knew that he should be thinking about ways of escape.

When the food arrived some minutes later he had not even the glimmer of a plan. After the waitress had served him she looked pointedly at his clothes.

"That'll be six bucks even."

Cash on the line, dressed as he was. Jan didn't blame her. He dug out the handful of green notes and put them on the table, extracting a five and a one and passing them over to her. She shoved them into the pocket of her apron and left.

The coffee was hot and delicious, burning a wakeful track down his throat. The hamburger a different matter entirely. It appeared to be a bap of some kind with stuffing. There was no knife or fork and Jan had not the slightest idea of how to go about eating it. In the end, sure that no one was watching him, he seized it up and took a bite. It was very different from anything that he had ever tasted before, but interesting nevertheless. Buried in its heart was a layer of barely cooked mince which had a number of sauces and bits of salad spread over it. But it was immensely satisfying too. He wolfed it down. It took him only a few minutes to eat it and he was finishing the coffee when the two men came in.

Without looking around and without hesitation they slid into the booth across the table from him. Jan put the coffee cup slowly down and seized the butt of the pistol with his other hand.

They weren't looking at him; appeared not to notice him. One of them took a coin from his pocket and reached over to put it into a slot under the table TV screen. The machine came to life with a blare of music. Jan did not look at it; he drew the gun from the bag under the shelter of the table. The thin man who had inserted the coin touched the controls, changing channels until he was satisfied, then sat back. It was a sports broadcast, about a racing match of some kind.

What did it mean? Jan thought. Both men were middle aged, dressed very much the way he was. They appeared to be examining the menu, but did not press the service button. As yet neither of them had caught his eye. The words of the television announcer cut suddenly through his concentration.

". . . further news of the criminal rebels who attempted to seize the *Alpharon*. The fighting has ended and the murderers have met the fate they wished for others. Quick justice at the hands of the comrades of those brave men who gave their lives for their home world . . ."

One glimpse of the torn, twisted and blood-drenched bodies of his friends was enough. Jan looked back at the two men. The announcer's next words froze him motionless.

"One criminal escaped. His name is Jan Kulozik and the public is warned that he is dangerous. He is wanted alive for questioning concerning details of this mutinous plot. There is a reward of twenty-five thousand dollars for anyone supplying information that might lead to his recapture. All citizens of California and Arizona are warned to be on the lookout for this man . . ."

Jan permitted himself one swift look at the screen. There was his face, full front and profile. Taken years ago before he was shipped from Earth, but instantly recognizable. When he looked back he found that the two men were now looking straight at him.

They both had their hands on the table so they were either very sure of themselves—or very stupid.

"Is all that true, what he said?" The thin man spoke for the first time. Jan did not answer so after awhile he added, "Why do they want you, Kulozik?"

Jan's answer was to bring the barrel of the gun up over the edge of the table.

"This is a standard issue 65 calibre, rifleless pistol. It fires rocket slugs that can blow a hole through a cow. I want you to stand up and walk out of here ahead of me. Now."

They obeyed instantly, sliding out of the booth and waiting for him, their backs turned. Then they went out the door with Jan following them. As he walked through after them Jan was barely aware of the figure in the darkness to one side, swinging something. He half turned and was just bringing up the gun when he was struck.

Seven

"I can only repeat what I've told you before," Jan said.

"Then do it."

It was a different voice—but the questions were the same. Jan was bound so tightly to the hard chair that his arms and legs were numb; his eyes were bandaged. It seemed that he had been tied there for eternity.

"My name is Jan Kulozik. I arrived on the *Alpharon*. I didn't know the ship's name until I heard the broadcast. I was with a group of prisoners who escaped. I was the only one that got away. I killed an officer . . ."

"His name?"

"Lauca, Sub-lieutenant Lauca. And it was not murder but self-defense. I've told you all this already. I took his uniform and gun, commandeered a truck driven by a man named Eddie Millard. I left the truck behind the garage before going into the restaurant where you jumped me. Now you tell me something. Who are you? You're Security, aren't you?"

"Shut up. We ask the questions . . ."

The man's voice broke off as someone else entered the room. There were footsteps and muttered voices. They came towards him—and his face burned with pain as the adhesive tape that covered his eyes was torn away. He gasped with shock and kept his eyes shut against the searing light.

"What was the registration number of the last car you owned in England?"

"How the hell do I know? That was a long time ago." He

blinked at the three men standing before him. Two of them were the ones from the restaurant. "If you're Security then you know all about me. So why these games?"

The newcomer, a scrawny man with a head as naturally bald as Jan's shaved one, answered him. "We're not Security. But maybe you are. A plant. To find our people. So you should answer our questions. We can help you—if you are what you say you are. If not, we'll kill you."

Jan looked at their faces, then nodded slowly.

"I feel the same hesitancy on my own part. You could be Security no matter what you say. So I will tell you only what is in my record. I'll not compromise others."

"Agreed." The bald man looked at a sheaf of printout. "What was your phone number in London?"

Jan closed his eyes, tried to think. It was another age, really another life. He visualized his apartment, the doorman, the lift. Going into his flat, picking up the phone . . .

"Oh one . . . two three six . . . treble one two. That's it."

There were more questions like this. He answered them more quickly as memory flooded back. That must be his security file they held—but how had they obtained it? Only Security would have that. Were they just playing with him?

"That's enough," the bald man said, throwing aside the accordion-folded paper. "Cut him loose. We'll just have to take a chance that he's telling the truth."

They had to hold Jan up when the ropes were removed. Until feeling—and pain—returned to his numbed body. He rubbed at his sore legs. "Fine," he said. "You're satisfied. But as far as I know you are still Security."

"For our job, we don't carry ID's," baldy said, smiling for the first time. "So you will just have to act as though we are. If you are a Security plant let me tell you, truthfully, that we know no others in the underground. That's why we were picked for this job. There must be one of the brotherhood in the police—that's where this printout came from. My party name is Shiny." He pointed to his hairless skull and smiled again. This time Jan smiled in return.

"I hope that you're telling the truth, Shiny. If you are Security you can find out everything that I know without all this rigmarole. I know. I've been through it."

"And you've been to the other worlds?" one of the men blurted out, unable to contain himself further. "The rebellion. Tell us about it. All we know is the official propaganda."

"What do they say?"

"Nothing. Hogwash. Misled few . . . rebellion put down. Saboteurs have destroyed food crops, so there will be rationing. All of the rebels captured or destroyed . . ."

"Hogwash—just like you said. They wouldn't dare tell you that we've won! They have been kicked off every world and have fled back here to Earth."

Their stern faces changed while he talked, relaxing, smiling—then shouting with glee.

"You mean it—you actually mean it?"

"I've no cause to lie. They rule here in the solar system—but nowhere else."

It was Christmas, holiday time, all of the pleasures of the world rolled into one. If they are faking this, Jan thought, they are the best actors in the world. He was sure now that he had fallen into the hands of the resistance instead of the police. He told them all that he knew, then finally interrupted the flow of questions.

"It's my turn," he said. "How was it that you got to me ahead of Security?"

"Just luck," Shiny told him. "Or maybe there are more of us. As soon as they began broadcasting that flash about you the word came down to try and find you. We have more sympathizers than members. One of them saw you here and got through to us. The rest you know."

"So—what comes next?"

"You can be very important to the cause, Jan. If you agree to work with us."

There was a wry twist in Jan's answering smile. "That's how I got into this trouble in the first place. I don't see why not. My future will be short with a very unhappy ending if I don't have help from someone."

"Good. Then we're getting you out of here at once. Before they discover that you're being helped. I don't know how it's being done—nor do I want to. We have some clothes here for you. Put them on while I make a call."

Jan pulled on the sleazy cotton slacks and shirt. He was glad to be rid of the military boots which were hurting even more now. The open sandals were a relief. One of the men went out and brought back a peaked cap that had *Dodgers* printed on it in yellow script letters.

"Take this," he said. "Cover that shaven head until your hair grows back in. Got some rotgut bourbon here. Be mighty pleased if you would drink with us."

"My pleasure," Jan said, taking a plastic beaker of the pale fluid. It was very strong. "Here's to freedom. May Earth some day share it with the stars."

"That's something to drink to."

Jan was on his third glass of bourbon—it tasted better and he felt better with each glass—by the time Shiny came back.

"Gotta move fast," he said. "Someone's waiting for you. We'll have to walk. Everything on wheels is being searched."

It wasn't far, and the night air cleared Jan's head. Through dark back streets all the way. Shiny kept looking at his watch and made them run the last few blocks.

"Got to be there at a certain time. I'll leave you in front of a door. As soon as I'm out of sight, you knock on it. You'll be let in. Good luck, Jan. This is the place."

It appeared to be a small side entrance in a very large building. He shook hands quickly and moved away. Jan knocked once, lightly, and the door opened. It was dark inside.

"Come on, quick," a voice whispered. The darkness was even deeper when the door closed behind him.

"Listen carefully," the unseen man said. "You go through that door and you're in a garage. Full of trailers. They're all going out tonight. Every one of them is sealed because they been in bond. They won't be searched. The third one from the door, the back is opened. Go there and get in. We got seals so they'll never know it's been opened. Get in, I'll come and close it. It's important you shouldn't see my face. Someone will get you out the other end, in LA. Look natural now when you go out there. May be others around, but no one will bother you if you look natural. And don't let them see you getting into the thing or you have had it. Stand there while I take a look."

Another door opened a crack and Jan could see the outline of a man's head against the light. He looked for a short time, then moved aside.

"Quick now," the voice said. "And good luck."

The building was gigantic, echoing with the distant hammer of a loud exhaust. Rows of trailers, each with a large shipping container secured to it, stretched into the distance. He walked towards the nearest one, slowly as though he belonged there. The sound of the exhaust died away to be replaced by the clang of metal upon metal. He looked around casually when he reached the third trailer; there was no one in sight. He pulled open the heavy door and climbed in. As he pulled the door shut behind him he had a quick glimpse of stacked boxes filling most of the body of the trailer, leaving an area just big enough for him. A few minutes later the door was slammed all the way shut from the outside and locked into place.

It was dark, warm and slightly musty. He sat down with his back against the wall, but found that this was hard and uncomfortable. Lying down was better and he pillowed his head on his arm. He was asleep without knowing it, nor did he stir when a tractor backed into place and sealed itself to the trailer. The big rig lurched into easy motion and out onto the road; Jan slept on. Waking only when they shuddered to a stop, air brakes hissing. Jan was pulled awake, blinking into the darkness, feeling a cold stab of fear until he remembered what had happened, where he was. He caught his breath as someone outside rattled the bars that sealed the door. When they opened it he would be caught and that would be the end of everything. He crouched there in the darkness, waiting—and relaxed only when the rig lurched into motion again. If that had been the checkpoint, then they were safely through. Tension drained away as they kept rolling, not stopping again. The motion lulled him to sleep and he welcomed it gladly, did not fight against it.

Jan stirred on the hard surface but did not waken completely until the next time the truck stopped. There was a short wait, then they started up again. A police check before entering a city? This was what would have been done in Britain; there was a good chance the same security procedures might be used here. The next time they stopped Jan could hear rattling again at the door seals next to him and he was ready when the door swung open. He shielded his eyes with his hand under the onslaught of tropical light.

"Come on out, Buster, this is the end of the line for you," a hoarse voice said. Jan slid to the ground and squinted through the glare at the uniformed policeman who stood in front of him. Captured! He turned, started to run, and the man's large hand seized him by the arm and swung him about.

"No games! Just get into the back of the black and white and lie on the floor. They made me break my cover for you, Buster, and it had better be worth it." He pulled Jan forward as he talked, then shoved him in the direction of a black and white car that was heavily festooned with lights and sirens, parked behind the tractor trailer in the narrow alleyway. The rear door was open and Jan got in and dropped to the floor as the door was slammed behind him. A moment later the policeman climbed into the front and they reversed out of the alley at high speed, braked to a squealing stop, then shot off down the road. Once they were moving the driver relaxed and looked over his shoulder at Jan.

"Is it true, what you told them, that all of the planets are, like, what do you call it . . ?"

"Free. Yes, they are. It was a rebellion that could not be stopped."

"Well that's good to hear. Maybe it's catching and we'll get a bit of it here on old mother Earth. They could sure use some of it where you're going. I'm turning you over to the spooks. I don't know how comfortable you're going to be there, but you'll be safe enough for a while."

Spooks? Jan thought. Ghosts? What was the man talking about? "I'm afraid that I'm not acquainted with the term."

"You sound like a Limey. Are you? A Brit?"

"Yes, I was born in England. I left there some time ago."

"You sounded like one, you know, the way they talk in the flicks. Well I don't know how things work over where you come from, Mr. Limey, but over here, well, things I guess are different. We're going to New Watts. When you see it you'll know what I'm talking about. Take a look. I'll stop and you just lift your nose up and see for yourself."

They drove on, slowly, then eased to a stop. "All right, now," the policeman said.

Jan rose up carefully to see that they had parked beside a row of small homes. They had been attractive once, but now they were collapsed and tumbledown, windows knocked out and roofs sagging. On the other side of the street was a high wire fence with a wasteland behind it, mounds of burned earth with only the occasional bit of grass or weed growing there. A good hundred meters beyond was another, identical fence. On the other side of this were buildings, homes and office blocks. Jan couldn't see any details clearly but they definitely had a ramshackle look.

"Get back down," the policeman ordered. "That's where you're going. Don't look so bad from here . . ." He laughed, not humorously but more of an ironic comment. "Going through a checkpoint now. But all the guys there know me and they'll just wave. I'll give him a blast so they'll think that it's a call."

The car surged forward and the siren began to wail. They turned, picked up speed, and bumped over something hard in the road, then went on. After a bit the siren was killed and their headlong pace slowed.

"Get ready," the policeman said. "I'm going to go along real easy, but not stop all the way. You bail out when I tell you to. You'll be next to a kind of little back alley between some yards. Walk down it nice and slow and you'll be met."

"Thanks for the help."

"Don't thank me until you see what you got into. Now!"

Jan pulled the handle and pushed the door open. He stepped out and it was torn from his hand as the car accelerated, the sudden motion slamming the door shut. The police car spun around the next corner and vanished from sight. Jan looked at the wooden, rickety fences stretched away on both sides of a packed dirt lane. He followed instructions and walked down it, feeling that he was being watched, but seeing no one. There were doors let into the fencing and as he passed one it swung open.

"Get in here," a rough voice said.

Jan turned to look at the man, at the two others with him. All three carried pistols, pointing at him. All three of them had coal-black skins.

Eight

"Are you the one they say come in the starship?" the nearest man asked. Jan nodded and the man waved the gun. "Then come on in so's you can tell us all about it."

They crowded around him, pushing him into the house and down a dank corridor to an interior room. Behind him he heard bolts rattling shut. The room had sealed windows and was airless, unfurnished except for a round wooden table surrounded by ramshackle chairs. One of the men pulled him by the arm, dragging him to a chair, then waved his long and well-worn pistol in Jan's face.

"You a spy," he said angrily, grating the words through his clamped teeth. "You ofay spy . . ."

"Come away now, nuf of dat," an older man said, pulling gently at the angry man's shoulder. He moved away reluctantly and the older man sat down across from Jan.

"Trouble is the bolly dogs brung you here, he don' like it. Who does? I'm Willy. You called Jan, saw your picture on television."

Jan nodded, straining to understand the other man's words. He was speaking in dialect, as thick and incomprehensible to him as Glaswegian.

"The teevee say you from the stars. If that true, you tell us what happening out there."

Once again Jan told about the success of the rebellion, and while he spoke the man leaned forward, listening intensely, making him repeat things; apparently his accent was equally difficult for them to understand. Fatigue began to catch up with him again and his throat grew dry. When he asked for some water, Willy signaled to one of the men.

"You hungry too?" he asked. Jan nodded and Willy called instructions through the open door.

The food was unfamiliar but filling. Boiled greens of some kind, white beans with black spots on them, and a slab of some sort of highly seasoned meat substitute. The men watched him while he ate and talked excitedly among themselves.

"What they wants to know," Willy said, "is they any brothers in the star people."

"I don't understand."

"Black. Black people like us. Or is this more whitey fightin' an' killin' each one the other."

This was the important question and the room was silent as Jan finished his meal and pushed the dish away.

"Thank you. I was very hungry." He thought for a moment. "First, just one question myself. Is everyone here in, what's the name? New Watts? Are they all black."

"You better believe it!"

"That's not the way on the planets. I mean I have never before seen people separated by their skin color. Here on Earth, yes, there are different skin colors among the indigenous populations of Africa and Asia. That is, there are divisions by racial types on a purely geographical basis. But once people have been transported to the planets these separations break down. They don't matter. There are enough other things to worry about . . ."

"You talkin' a little fast," Willy said. "Do I catch you saying they all color blind out there? All kind of skins mix together?"

"Yes. Of course. Skin color doesn't matter, you see."

"Sure matter here!" Willy said and slapped his knee and all of the men laughed aloud at this. Jan smiled, not quite sure what the joke was.

"Just hope you is tellin' the truth," Willy said, and one of the men shouted "Amen!" very loud. "Jes hard to believe, that's all. I think you better talk to the Preacher. He kinda talk your language. He'll tell us what is what."

Jan was led from the room by the men, still carrying their guns. The weapons were all old and worn, museum pieces. They entered another room in the house, a bedroom where small black children sat on the patched quilts of a bed. They and an old and white-

haired woman followed their passage in staring silence. There was
an exit here, a rough-edged hole that had been chopped through
the wall. It led into a covered passage to another house. When
they had passed through four separate dwellings in this manner
Jan realized that the houses must all be connected like this, making one extended building. They finally came to a closed door on
which Willy knocked lightly.

"Come in," a voice called out. Jan was hustled through the
door into an extensive, book-lined room. The difference from the
other quarters he had seen was striking. This could well have been
his old tutor's study at university, resembling it in more ways than
one. The desk was thick with papers and opened books, there
were framed drawings on the walls, and even a globe of the world.
Soft chairs and there, behind the desk, the tutor himself slumped
back comfortably in his chair. A black man, just like all the
others.

"Thank you, Willy," he said. "I gonna talk to this here Jan by
m'self."

"You be all right . . ."

"Sure will. Jus' leave a man outside so's I can give a shout needs
be."

When the door had closed the man rose to shake hands with
Jan. He was middle-aged with a full beard and long hair, both
shot through with gray. His clothing was dark and conservative,
well suited to the clerical dog collar.

"I'm Reverend Montour, Mr. Kulozik. It is my very great pleasure to welcome you here."

Jan shook his hand and could only nod his thanks. All traces of
patois had vanished and the Reverend spoke with an easy and cultivated voice.

"Sit down, please do. May I offer you a glass of sherry? It's a
local wine and I think that you will find it enjoyable."

Jan sipped the sherry; it was quite good, and looked around the
room.

"You'll pardon me for staring," he said. "But it's been years
since I have been in a room like this. I admire your library."

"Thank you. Most of the volumes are centuries old and quite
rare. Every page has been absorption preserved."

"Wrecker books, really? May I? Thank you." He put his glass
down and stepped up to the shelves. The bindings were worn and
heavily repaired, and many of the titles obliterated. Reaching up,

he took down what looked like the soundest one and opened it carefully to the title page. It was entitled *The Middle Ages 395–1500*. He turned the page carefully and on the back read "Copyright, 1942".

When he spoke he had trouble keeping the reverence out of his voice. "This book . . . it's over five hundred years old. I didn't know anything like this existed."

"They do, I assure you, and there are many more like it. But I can understand your feelings. You are British, I take it?"

Jan nodded.

"I thought so. The accent and that term, the Wreckers. I understand it is in common usage in your country. You must understand that I have these books because of the varying paths that were followed during the period that historians call the Retrocession. At that time the different countries and areas of the world suffered the same declining fate, but they accommodated to it in different ways, usually following the existing social divisions. Great Britain, traditionally a class-orientated society, utilized its historical class system to consolidate the rigid societal structure that still exists today. The ruling elite had never been happy with education for the masses and were only too relieved when physical circumstances did away with that necessity. But restriction of education and information, once begun, has no end. I understand that most British citizens today have no idea of the true nature of history or even of the world they live in. Is that true?"

"Very much so. My accidental discovery of this fact was the beginning of a chain of events that, well, brought me to this room."

"I understand. Conformity must be most intellectually oppressive under a system such as yours. History followed a completely different course here, since there are many roads to tyranny. America, without a class system, has traditionally substituted a system of vertical mobility based for the most part on money. It was always a truism here that it was not your lineage but your bank account that determined your status. With the exception, of course, of the physically visible minorities. Irish, Polish, Jews, traditionally rejected minorities, were assimilated after the first few generations because their racial types permitted them to merge with the general population. Not so the dark-skinned races who, once firmly planted at the bottom of society, were forced to stay there by the repeated cycles of physical and educational deprivation. This was the situation existing when the Retrocession began, and it ended with this country as you see it now."

He reached for the sherry decanter. "Your glass is empty; I'm afraid that I am being a bad host."

"Yes, please, not too much. And do go on. I have been for years on a planet that must be the cultural wasteland of the universe. Your words, conversation like this, you can't understand how I feel . . ."

"I think I do. I know I felt the same way myself when I opened my first book. It was that same thirst for knowledge that led me to this room, to the position that I have today. I wanted to know just why the world was the way it was. I had good reason to hate it—but I also wanted to understand it. As I said, the Retrocession just increased the traditional divisions. Your police state in Britain came about through an excess of kindness, an attempt to see that everyone had at least the minimum needed for existence, the food to stay alive if nothing else. But once the state controls everything, why the men who control the state have absolute power. They do not relinquish it easily as I imagine you have found out. A completely different course was followed here. The American tradition has been to declare that the needy are really slackers and that the unemployed are that way because they are naturally lazy. The Retrocession saw the complete victory of *laissez faire*, which is simply institutionalized selfishness carried to the extreme. It is amazing, the nonsense that people will believe when it is in their own interest. There were actually adherents then of an intellectually bankrupt theory called monetarism, which enabled the rich to get richer, the poor to get poorer, by applying a completely disproven economic theory in place of intelligence."

Montour sighed at the thought, then sipped a little of his sherry.

"So the obvious happened. When the food and energy began to run out the rich first kept most of it, then all of it. After all, this had always been national policy during the years leading up to the collapse when America consumed most of the world's petroleum, caring nothing for other countries' needs. So who can blame individuals for following the same course? Any country that permits its citizens to die for want of medical attention simply because they cannot afford it, becomes a nation in moral trouble. There were riots, killing, and more riots. Guns and weapons were everywhere and they still are. The end product was a nation divided, with the browns and the blacks living as you see them, in ghettos surrounded by barbed wire. Here they grow a certain amount of food on their own, or go out to earn a bit by laboring at the menial jobs that have not been mechanized. They die in infancy or live brutally short lives. The benefits of technological society do not trickle down to them at all. Unlike your country there is no attempt to conceal the history of their physical status from them. The oppressors want the oppressed to know just what happened to them. So they will not be so foolish as to try it all over again some day. So—do you wonder at our interest in this rebellion of the planets? We look forward to it spreading to Earth."

Jan could only nod and agree.

"Please excuse my rudeness for asking, but I don't understand why the ruling powers permitted your education."

Montour smiled. "They didn't. My people originally came to this country as slaves. Completely without education, torn from their roots and culture. What we have achieved since that time was done despite the position our masters had placed us in. When the breakdown began we had no intention of giving up what we had so painfully achieved. We matured as a people even as we were being oppressed as a people. If they took away everything except our intelligence—why then we would have to rely on our intelligence alone. In doing this we had the opportunity to emulate the example of another oppressed minority. The Jews. For millennia they kept their culture and their traditions alive through religion and respect for learning. The religious man, the educated man was the honored man. We had our religion, and we had our professors and educators. Under the pressure of circumstance the two became amalgamated. The brightest boys are now honored by being permitted to enter the ministry when they come of age. My formative years were spent in those streets. I speak the ghetto language that has developed since we were cut off from the mainstream of life. But I have learned the language of the oppressor as well, as part of my education. If salvation does not come in my generation I shall pass on my wisdom to those who follow after me. But I know—I have faith—that it will come some day."

Jan drained the last of the sherry and put the glass down, waving away the offer of more. The rapid passage of events had left him dazed; his mind was almost as tired as his body, his thoughts turning around and around. What crippled lives people were forced to lead. The proles in Britain were at least fed and protected like cattle—as long as they accepted this cattle-like role. While the people here in the black ghettos of America had no such comforts, they did at least know who they were and what they were. But along with this knowledge was the fact that they were forced to live in a state of constant rebellion.

"I really don't know which system is the worse to live under," Jan said. "Yours or mine."

"No system of oppression should be condoned. And there are far worse ones in the world. The great socialist experiment in the Soviet Union was always hampered by the Czarist heritage with its obscene bits of madness like internal passports and labor camps. Whether the state there would have withered away in the end as Marx predicted we will never know. By the time of the Retrocession they still had not industrialized their basically peasant economy. It was an easy slide back to an almost feudal culture. Many died, but many have always died in Russia. The commissars and upper echelon party leaders took the place of the nobility. The titles might be different today, but any of the Czars transported ahead in time would feel right at home there now."

"The rebellion must spread to Earth," Jan said.

"I agree completely. We must work for that day . . ."

The door was suddenly flung open and Willy stood there, gasping for breath, a gun in each hand.

"Trouble," he said. "Bad trouble. Worst I ever seen."

Nine

"What happining?" Montour asked, shifting his speech quickly into the demotic.

"Dey's all around. More of the bolly dogs I never seen. Right around New Watts, shooting at anything moves. Wid big heat guns to burn dere way in . . ."

His words were interrupted by the distant roar of fusion cannon, overlaid with the sharp crackling of gunfire. It was loud, close by. A hard knot of fear formed in Jan's middle and he looked up and saw both men were looking at him.

"It's me they want," he said. Reverend Montour nodded.

"Very possibly. I can't remember the last time they raided in strength like this."

"There's no point in running any longer. Those fusion guns will burn these old buildings flat. I'm going to give myself up."

Montour shook his head. "We have places where you can hide. They put the fires out as they advance. They just use the guns to burn their way in."

"I'm sorry. No. I've seen too many people killed recently. I can't be responsible for any more deaths. I'm going out to them. I will not change my mind."

Montour stood for a moment, then nodded. "You are a brave man. I wish we could have done more for you." He turned to Willy. "Leave dem guns here and show this gen'mum where the bolly dogs at."

The two pistols thudded to the floor. Jan took the scholar's hand. "I'll not forget you," he said.

"Nor I, you." Montour took a spotless white handkerchief from his breast pocket. "Better take this. They tend to fire first."

Willy led the way, muttering angrily to himself, through passageways and connecting buildings. They had to move aside as two gunmen ran by, dragging a third man whose clothes were soaked with blood. No end, Jan thought, no end ever.

"Fuckin' bolly dogs jes out dere," Willy said, pointing to a door, then turned and hurried back the way they had come.

Jan shook out the folds of the handkerchief and stood to one side of the door as he eased it open. A burst of rocket slugs tore through it, screaming away down the hallway behind him.

"Stop shooting!" he called out, waving the white cloth through the gap. "I'm coming out."

A shrill whistle blew and the sound of firing began to die away. An amplified voice called out. "Open the door slowly. Come out, one at a time. Hands on your head. If your hands aren't there, if I see more than one man, I'm going to fire. All right—now."

Jan laced his fingers together on top of his head and eased the door open with his toe, then walked slowly forward to face the ranked police officers. They were impersonal as robots behind their riot masks and shields; every weapon was pointed at him.

"I'm all alone," he said.

"That's him!" somebody called out.

"Silence," the sergeant commanded. He holstered his weapon and waved Jan to him. "Nice and easy, that's the way. Everson, get the car up here."

He seized Jan's right arm with a practiced motion, pulling it down behind his back to lock the handcuffs to his wrist. Then the cuffs on his other wrist. His fingers dug deep into Jan's arm as he pulled him forward.

The blackened ground was still warm as they walked through the gap in the wire to the waiting patrol car. The sergeant held Jan's head down as he pushed him into the back, then climbed in after him. There was the scream of rubber as the driver gunned the vehicle forward.

They rode in silence. Jan was defeated, empty even of words, knowing full well what was in store. Since he came originally from Earth, Security was sure to think him one of the leaders of the rebellion. They would take his mind apart looking for evidence. He knew what men looked like after treatment like that. Death would be a release.

As the car drew up before an official building the door was pulled open; the sergeant pushed Jan through it. A uniformed officer held each arm securely as he was hurried through the entrance and into a waiting elevator. Jan was too emotionally exhausted to notice or care where they were going. There had been too much killing, running. It was over at last. They dragged him into a room, slammed him into the chair. The door opposite him opened slowly and he looked at it with dull and unseeing eyes.

Thurgood-Smythe came in.

All of the fatigue, the despair, everything was washed away by a red surge of hatred.

"You've led us quite a chase, brother-in-law," Thurgood-Smythe said. "Now if you will promise to behave yourself I'll have those handcuffs taken off. You and I must have a serious talk."

Jan had his head down, eyes lowered, shaking with rage, his throat too tight to speak. He nodded. "Good," Thurgood-Smythe said, mistaking the emotion for fear. "I won't hurt you, you can take my word for that."

The cuffs clicked free and Jan rubbed the marks on his wrists, listening as heavy footsteps receded. But he could wait no longer. A harsh sound was torn from his throat as he hurled himself at his tormentor. Their bodies crashed together, Thurgood-Smythe went over and down with Jan straddling him, his arched fingers reaching for his throat. But Thurgood-Smythe had seized his wrists and was holding him at bay. Jan leaned his weight forward, pressing down, his nails clawing into Thurgood-Smythe's face, his thumbs sinking into the sockets of his eyes. Thurgood-Smythe cried out hoarsely—just as hands grabbed at Jan's shoulders, a foot thudded into the side of his neck knocking him away, other hard boots crushing into his body.

"That's enough . . ." Thurgood-Smythe said. "Put him into the chair and get out." He groped behind him for a chair, found it, eased into it. The gun in his hand aimed steadily at Jan. For long seconds the only sound in the room was their hoarse breathing. "I won't have that repeated," Thurgood-Smythe finally said. "I have some important things to tell you, important for all of us, but I still will not hesitate to shoot you the instant you move in this direction. Do you understand?"

"I understand that you killed my friends, murdered Sara before me . . ."

"What is done is done. Your mewling about it or feeling sorry for yourself will not change it . . ."

"Kill me and have it over with. Your cat and mouse game doesn't interest me. When we parted you told me to work or be destroyed. I've ceased work, other than to work for the overthrow of you and people like you. Get it over with."

"Such a rush for annihilation." Thurgood-Smythe smiled slightly and pushed a runnel of blood from the corner of his mouth; his face was torn and bruised, blood welling from the sockets of his eyes. He ignored the pain; the gun did not move at all from its target. "Not quite like you."

"I've changed. You saw to that."

"Indeed you have. And matured as well, I sincerely hope. Enough to sit and listen to what I have to say. I've come a long way since last we met. Now I sit on the United Nations council and act as liaison chief between global security and space defenses. The UNO itself is just a toothless debating society, since there is no shared power in this world—no matter what the propaganda in the papers says. Every country is a law unto itself. However there are committees to handle international trade agreements as well as the space program. Spaceconcent in California is a truly international, and until recently, an interplanetary organization. We both know that it is slightly reduced in size these days. Since there is little feedback between Spaceconcent and the various countries that profit from its enterprises, my position is both a secure and a powerful one. A most responsible position, as your sister keeps telling me. She is very fit, by the way, I thought you would want to know. My work is so responsible that I report to no one at all about security matters. That means I can do exactly what I want with you. Exactly."

"Do you expect me to plead for mercy?"

"You misunderstand, Jan, please hear me out. Everything has changed in the last few months. As you know our forces have been defeated, driven from every planet that Earth settled. These are drastic times and they call for drastic measures. Therefore all charges against you have been dropped. You are a free man, Jan, with all the rights of a free citizen.

Jan laughed. "Do you really expect me to believe that? The next thing will be you asking me to go to work for you."

"You are being prescient. I did have something like that in mind. I have a job that is perfectly suited to your background and experience." He hesitated a moment, enjoying the drama of the occasion.

"It is quite an important job for you to undertake. I want you to contact some resistance people here on Earth. As a liaison man for me."

Jan shook his head slowly. "Do you really think that I would betray them to you? What a sick creature you are."

"My dear Jan, I can understand your attitude, it is a reasonable one under the circumstances. But hear me out, please. I am going to tell you things about myself that you have never known or suspected. Remember, we were friends once. Perhaps we can be so again after you hear what I have to say. Like you, as a young man, I became intrigued about the world and how it was run. Since I had no resources other than my ambition I knew I would have to make my own way. Like you I became disgusted when I discovered the sort of lives we were leading. Unlike you, I joined the forces of oppression rather than attempt to fight them. Sort of burrow from within, you might say . . ."

"Sorry, you dirty son of a bitch, but it won't wash. I've seen you at your work, seen how you enjoy it."

"I am rather good, aren't I? But it is all protective coloration. I saw that Security was the real force in control of the world—so I determined to run Security. To do this I had to outdo all my rivals, to be the best at my chosen task. It was not easy but it was worth it, and I achieved two goals at the same time. I rose to power by being the most reactionary of all. No one has ever doubted me. Nor have they ever understood that by operating in this manner I was increasing oppression and therefore the forces of resistance. I am proud to feel that this policy created the climate that fostered the present rebellion. Since the planets are free my work has succeeded."

Jan shook his head. "No, that is impossible to believe."

"It happens to be true—but true or no it will make no difference to our relationship. From this moment on you are a free man with all the privileges that go with that status. Your criminal record has been expunged from the files and your own record returned to the computer banks. Your absence from Earth for these last years has been explained as a matter of Security. For anyone with first priority identification, the record also shows that you have always been a high Security officer and that all of your other work has been a front for your operations. You are now very rich and your bank account is full. Here is your identification card. Welcome back, Jan. There's a bar here and I have had the foresight to stock it with champagne."

It was all some kind of sadistic trick, Jan knew that. His body, his neck, ached where he had been kicked, but he had no time to consider the pain, he ignored it, fought it away so that he could order his thoughts. He had to use intelligence, not raw emotion. Though he had no regrets over the anger that had hurled him at his brother-in-law; how he had enjoyed the animal pleasure of actually laying his hands on the one person that he hated the most! But what was the man up to now? This had to be a plot of some kind; Thurgood-Smythe was incapable of any straightforward action. But whatever he was planning could not be uncovered at the present moment. Should he play along? Pretend to believe him? Did he have any choice? If the identification were real then there might be a chance to escape from the Security net. So it did not matter what he said if he managed to leave this room alive. He had no compunction about lying to his brother-in-law; it was almost an obligation. Therefore it was of no importance what he promised, but what he did. Promise anything, get away to safety. That was a good deal better than the certain death that awaited him if he refused. Jan watched with unbelief as Thurgood-Smythe carefully levered the cork out of the bottle, then poured two glasses of champagne without spilling a drop. He turned and smiled as he crossed the room and handed one to Jan. Who repressed the desire to smash in that smile now that the gun had been laid aside for the moment.

"That's a good deal better," Thurgood-Smythe said. "Just resist the urge for violence and you will stay alive. You are not the suicidal type."

"All right. I'll work along with you. Do what you ask. But I will betray no one, give you no information."

"Very good. I ask no more. So we can drink to the future and hope that it will be a bright one for mankind." He raised his glass in salute; they drank.

"What must I do?" Jan asked.

"Go on a mission for me. To Israel. Now do you see the trust and faith behind my offer? If you doubt what I say, why you can defect and simply stay there—and none the wiser."

"I can't believe that. You proved to me that you had liaison with the Israeli government, to keep track of their agents."

"Liaison, yes. But I have no say over what happens in that sovereign state. As you will discover, they are a very strong-willed people. And now I will tell you a secret, one that is proof of my sincerity in this matter because it puts my life in your hands. Under the code name Cassius, I have been supplying the Israelis with classified Security information. They are very grateful, since I have asked nothing in return other than the knowledge that I am working for the benefit of the human race. They think very well of Cassius, so will trust you implicitly when you reveal that you are Cassius. I will give you the identification code, also a copy of all the information I have sent them in the past few years. What happens next is up to you. If you reveal this fact in the right quarters here, you will find that there are any number of Security people who would love to topple me and take my place, to destroy me. Or you can go to Israel and pass on what could be the most important message you ever carried in your entire lifetime. The choice is yours, Jan."

Choice? Jan could not believe that there was one. He was sure that any attempt to convey information to another Security officer here would only end in his instant destruction. Thurgood-Smythe was incapable of allowing a thing like that to happen. No. He had to go along with the plan. Take the message to Israel and let them decide what his brother-in-law was up to. The world was turning upside down. A portion of Thurgood-Smythe's story might be true. He might very well be deserting the sinking ship for his own benefit. Jan knew that he was out of his depth.

"All right," he said. "Tell me what I have to do."

"Good man. You'll not be sorry."

Thurgood-Smythe went to the desk and took up a thick plastic envelope. He handed it to Jan.

"I'm going to put you on a plane to New York now. You're not very safe here since everyone in California and Arizona is still on the lookout for you. But I did not let the alarm go out nationwide. A room has been booked for you at the Waldorf-Astoria. Get some rest, buy some clothes, eat a few good meals. Then, when you feel up to it, open this package and memorize the basic material it contains. No need to be word perfect, you just want to be aware of everything here. It contains the security information I passed on to the Israelis. Very incriminating for me, so don't leave it lying about. You'll have about eight hours to read it before the paper disintegrates. Then phone me at the number on the outside of the envelope so I can take the next step. Any questions?"

"So many that I wouldn't know where to begin. This all takes a bit of getting used to."

"I realize. Welcome aboard, Jan. It's nice to have someone to help me, to confide in after all of the years of working alone." He extended his hand.

Jan looked at it and, after a long moment's hesitation, shook his head.

"I can't forget that easily. There is too much blood on that hand for me to touch."

"Aren't you being a little over-dramatic?"

"Perhaps. I'll work with you since I have no choice. But that doesn't mean that I have to like it—or like you. Understood?"

Thurgood-Smythe's eyes narrowed slightly, but when he spoke there was no anger in his voice.

"Whatever you say, Jan. Success is more important than our personal feelings. It's time for you to leave now."

Ten

During the night the thudding of distant explosions had woken Jan, he had clearly heard them here, on the thirtieth floor, despite the soundproofing and the double-glazed windows. He had opened the door and stepped onto the balcony outside. Something was burning brightly across the city. Sirens and warblers wailed as police and fire equipment tore by in the streets below. The fire burned for a long time. It was muggy and hot outside of the air-conditioned room and he did not watch long. He was still tired and fell asleep again as soon as he was back in bed.

Bright sunshine poured through the windows in the morning when he touched the button to open the curtains. An apparently original Rembrandt painting hanging on the far wall became a screen as he switched the television on. Jan scanned the news headlines, punched for LOCAL NEWS, then brought up EXPLOSION AND FIRE. The list vanished and was replaced by a scene centered around a park bench. There were green grass and trees behind the bench, while a few pigeons pecked at the path before it. A man and a woman sat at opposite ends of the bench, both radiant and healthy, good-looking and suntanned. All over, for they were both nude. They smiled at him with glowing white teeth.

"Good morning," the man said. "I'm Kevin O'Donnell."

"And I'm Patti Pierce. Would you like me or Kevin to bring you the news today?"

Then they waited, frozen and unmoving, the pigeons motion-

less as well, even the breeze-tossed leaves were still. The computer
control waited for him to decide.

"Patti, of course," Jan said, and the camera moved in slowly on
the girl who stood and smiled in his direction. Whether she was
real or only a program in the computer was unimportant. She was
both beautiful and desirable and certainly made the news more interesting. Though he could not understand what nude announcers
had to do with the news.

"The Apple was busy last night," Patti said, standing and pointing over her shoulder. The park vanished to be replaced by a burning building, flames billowing high against the black sky. Fire
equipment was drawn up in the street before it and men with
hoses were fighting the blaze. Patti, rotating her behind sweetly,
walked over and climbed into the driver's seat of a hook and
ladder.

"This warehouse caught fire in the early hours and burned like
a house on fire, yes sir! Four companies were called out and it
took until dawn to damp down the blaze and keep it from spreading. Paint and chemicals had been stored in the building which
kept things mighty hot for our helmeted heroes, yes sir! No one as
yet knows how the blaze started, but arson has definitely been
ruled out."

One of the helmeted heroes ran up and unclipped a piece of
equipment from the truck near Patti. He never noticed her. The
computer simulation was perfect; she could really have been at
the fire rather than recording in the studio.

Someone knocked on the door. Jan turned off the TV and
smiled at himself for feeling guilty; everyone else would be watching the nude news announcers as well. "Come in," he called out,
and the door unlocked.

"Good morning, sir, lovely morning," the waiter said, carrying
in Jan's breakfast on a tray. He was young, white, and slightly
adenoidal; a wispy moustache struggled for existence on his upper
lip. He bowed as he put the tray down on the bedside table.

"That was quite a fire last night," Jan said.

"Jigaboos done it," the waiter answered, breathing hard through
his open mouth. "None of them come to work in the kitchen
today, not one. Shows they done it."

"You think they started the fire? The news said the cause was
unknown . . ."

"They always say that. It had to be the spooks. This time they oughta let Harlem burn to the ground."

Jan was uncomfortable in the presence of the raw hatred. He poured some coffee; the waiter bowed again and left. He had never before realized how divided America was by racial barriers. It must always have been there, below the surface. War fever was bringing it out now. There was nothing he could do about it, nothing at all. He turned the news on again and watched Patti prance through the scenes while he gave his attention to the scrambled eggs and bacon.

When he got out of bed, Jan noticed the sealed envelope on the sideboard where he had dropped it. He wasn't ready to open it yet—was not even sure if he should open it. Because when he did so he knew he would have to join Thurgood-Smythe in his mad scheme. He realized suddenly that his head was fuzzy, that he had trouble coming to grips with reality. It was not surprising. The changes had been too abrupt. After the years of dull toil on Halvmörk, everything had been turned upside down. First leaving that planet on the spacer, then being captured, escaping, capture again—and finally his brother-in-law's revelation that everything was all going to turn out right after all. Jan was very suspicious of sudden happy endings. He went into the marble-and-gold luxury of the bathroom and looked at himself in the mirror. Red eyes with dark circles around them, and gray in the stubble on his chin. Whatever he decided to do next would be done in a leisurely fashion. He was not going to rush into anything for some time.

There was a circular bathtub here that was big enough to swim in. He set the temperature to warm and pressed the FILL button. It did, instantly, with a quiet rushing sound. There must be a reservoir, preheated, somewhere close by. He stepped into the tub, aware of just how far he was from New Watts and the Harlem that the waiter had talked about. Aware also how close he was to them at the same time. This world where a few lived in luxury, where most existed at the brink of despair, was a precarious place. The waves of revolution from the stars were touching Earth now. Would they carry the rebellion here as well?

"I hope you like the bath," the girl said, stepping forward to the middle of the room. She was dressed in a short terrycloth robe which she slowly took off; she was gorgeously naked underneath.

When she dropped the robe it vanished—and Jan realized he was looking at a holograph projection.

"The management of the Waldorf-Astoria wants you to enjoy the best in comforts during your stay. If you wish I can massage your back while you are relaxing in the tub, soap you and scrub you as well. Dry you and give you a more exciting massage in the bed. Would you like that, sir?"

Jan shook his head, then realized that the frozen hologram image was waiting for a verbal instruction.

"No. Get thee behind me, Satan." The girl vanished. Jan's wife was light-years away, yet she was very close still in his emotions. He finished soaping and washing and when he stepped out of the tub the water vanished behind him in a single mighty insufflation.

When he had arrived the day before no eyebrows had been raised nor any attention paid to his sleazy clothes or lack of luggage. Not when he was occupying one of the best suites in the hotel. But he would need new clothes; that was the first order of business. He dressed quickly and kicked into the sandals. There was a safe set into the wall of the sitting room and he put Thurgood-Smythe's envelope in it, keying in a new combination so that only he could open it. With his ID card in his shirt pocket he would have everything he needed. He patted the card and went out.

The lobby of the hotel was filled with elegantly dressed guests, mostly women, who were strolling toward the doors leading to a fashion show. Jan felt decidedly scruffy as he pushed through them and out into the soggy heat of the day. When he had arrived the previous evening he had noticed that there were a number of shops along Lexington Avenue. Clothes, shoes, luggage—there was everything here that he might need.

Though some vehicles passed there seemed to be few pedestrians. None at all he realized, just as a policeman stepped out of a doorway and stopped him by pushing his nightstick hard into Jan's chest.

"All right, stupid. You want trouble, you got trouble."

Jan's temper flared; he had seen enough of the police in the last twenty-four hours.

"I'm afraid that you are the one who is in trouble, officer." He took out his ID. "You will look at this and then you will apologize for your brutal manner."

The policeman let the stick drop slowly. Jan's refined accent and manner did not match his clothing. When he saw the Security symbol next to the three-digit number indicating Jan's rank he actually began to tremble. He saluted and Jan felt ashamed of himself for bullying the man with his newly-attained rank and position. His actions, in essence, were really the same as those of the police officers who had raided New Watts.

"I didn't know, I'm sorry, but the things you're wearing . . ."

"I understand," Jan said, putting the card back into his pocket. "It was an emergency. I'm going to buy new clothes now."

"I'll show you, sir, just follow me. I'll wait to take you back. You don't want to be on the streets today."

"Is there an alert?"

"No. But people know. The word goes around. We shot the two guys what burned down the armory. Both white. What the fuck did they think they was doing? In here. Best place on Lexington. I'll be outside." He hammered loudly on the sealed door with his nightstick and it was quickly unlocked. "Take good care of this gentleman," he told the wide-eyed clerk, spinning the stick swiftly on the end of its thong.

It was a gentleman's outfitters, very exclusive, very expensive. Jan took a great deal of pleasure in spending a large amount of his newly-acquired money. Shirts, slacks, undergarments, suits, everything lightweight, easily packed and uncrushable. If it was hot in New York, Israel was sure to be an oven. He did not mind heat, but he liked to be dressed for it. Shoes and a better grade of sandal than he was wearing completed his outfit. His image in the mirror was greatly improved.

"Send the rest to the Waldorf," he said, passing over his card. He pointed to his discarded clothing. "And dispose of these."

"Very good, sir. If you would approve the sales slip . . . ?" Jan waved it away; it wasn't his own money being spent. The clerk slipped Jan's ID into the machine, entered the sum to be debited, then returned the card. The money had been transferred from Jan's account to that of the shop's.

The waiting policeman nodded approvingly at Jan's new clothing. The world was in order again. He led the way to a luggage shop, then found an optician where Jan could get some sunglasses; he was not used to the glare of full daylight after his years on the twilight world. On impulse he bought a second pair and handed them to the policeman when he came out. The man gaped, then slowly put them on, pulling in his stomach as he looked at his image in a shopwindow.

"I ain't gonna forget this, sir. You're a right guy. I never met a Limey before, but I think you're right guys."

There were a few more pedestrians about now and the officer looked closely at each one as they passed. His nightstick spun faster as a black man in ragged clothing came toward them. The man kept his eyes lowered and touched a large plastic badge on his shirt as he went by; identification of some sort. Very suddenly Jan had had enough of the city and was happy to be off the street and in the cool seclusion of the hotel. The keyboy led the way to the elevator, then unlocked the door to the suite for him.

His purchases had been delivered and were waiting in a neat row of boxes on the lounge. He looked from them to the decorated door of the safe. The moment could be put off no longer. It was time to find out what he was getting into. When he pulled the tab on Thurgood-Smythe's envelope there was a brief hiss as the air entered it. Inside was a thin file of papers. He sat down and began to read.

It was a chronicle of evil covering the past two years. Each parcel of information was dated, each statement brief and to the point. People arrested and imprisoned, people killed. Foreign agents detected and their movements chronicled, intelligence supplied by British agents and embassies. There were interesting tidbits of information that surely had never appeared in the news. The Lord Mayor of London, a prominent wholesaler, had apparently been deeply involved in the black market for food. Security knew this but did nothing—until they observed that some German agents had uncovered the fact as well and had used it to blackmail the man. Murder, or rather a fatal accident, had eliminated the problem. There was more like this. Jan scanned quickly through the pages, then went back and memorized the names and dates of the most important events. It was boring but necessary work. After a few hours of it he realized that he was hungry, and phoned down to room service. The menu was extensive and far more interesting than anything he had eaten in the past years. He ordered a broiled lobster and a chilled bottle of Louis Martini sauterne and kept on reading.

Later, when he was turning over a sheet, the corner broke off in his hand. He quickly riffled through the stack to be sure that he could recall as much as he had need of. There were fragments of paper and ink on his hands now and he went into the bathroom to wash them off. When he came out the sheets of paper had turned into a pile of gray dust.

Jan picked up the envelope and looked at the telephone number on it. Thurgood-Smythe's number. Had he any choice?

The answer was still *no*. This entire matter might be some devious plan of his brother-in-law, undoubtedly was. There was still nothing he could do about it. If he did not cooperate he was sure that his new status would be stripped from him as quickly as it had been bestowed. He would go along with the scheme, get out of the country—then reassess it when he was safe.

He punched the number into the phone and sat back. Seconds later Thurgood-Smythe's grim features appeared on the screen. He smiled slightly when he saw who it was.

"Well, Jan, enjoying your stay in New York, I trust?"

"I've read the papers."

"Very good. And your decision . . . ?"

"I'll go along with your plan until I learn different. You knew that all the time."

"Of course. Welcome aboard. If you will send for a taxi in about an hour you will be just on time for a specially chartered flight to Cairo. It is full of technicians and engineers for the reopened oil fields. Since you have been away the thermal extraction technique has succeeded in pumping petroleum from these depleted fields for the first time in four centuries. You will be joining them as a specialist in microelectronic circuitry, which of course you are. Tickets, passport and a new ID card are waiting for you at the porter's desk. Keep your present ID for emergencies. Your new ID has another function as well. Your file number is also Cassius's identification code. When this number is divided by day of the month, all of the digits to the left of the decimal point are the code for that day."

"So I go to Cairo. Then what?"

"You will be contacted. Enjoy your trip. And make a note of this number for later use. With it you can contact me instantly, wherever I am. Good-bye."

Jan had just enough time to pack his bags leisurely before ringing down to the desk. He wondered where it would all end. He had a certain amount of trepidation about setting his foot on this road when he had no idea of where it might lead. Yet he was not sorry to be leaving the United States.

Eleven

For six full days, Jan lost himself in his work. The petroleum wells in the Sinai desert were the first installation to make use of the highly complex thermal extraction technique. But it was like working in the cemetery of a forgotten age, because their camp was in the center of the played-out oil fields. Ancient pumps and drilling towers stretched away on all sides, silent and still, preserved through the past centuries by the arid desert. The modern installation was as new and bright as a freshly minted coin, standing out in stark contrast to the desolation on all sides. The buildings were prefabricated and glossy, as was all of the equipment. Their techniques were new and original as well, but very prone to develop operational bugs. Karaman, the petrologist, sat in the laboratory swirling a dark and tarry liquid about in a glass flask.

"It is good, very good—but pumping has stopped again, the third time in as many days," he said. "Why?"

"Feedback controls," Jan said. "You've been on this project longer than I have so you know the problems. There is a little bit of white-hot hell that we have created down there in the sand. First the nitrogen is pumped down and converted to a plasma by the fusion generator. That in turn heats the sand and rock which evaporates some of the volatiles, which in turn creates pressure which pushes that petroleum to the surface. That's the theory. But in practice there are about a hundred different things that can go wrong with the process . . ."

"I know. Everything from blowing the whole thing up or setting fire to it, or even melting down the reactor, which happened to us once in California. But, honestly Jan, we're years past that stage."

"But you are not years past monitoring inputs. There just aren't enough of them to keep accurate watch on the process. It begins to cycle and the cycles build and get out of control, so you have to shut down and go back to the beginning and start over. But we have some new learning software that is beginning to predict the cycles and stop them before they happen. You have to give it a chance."

Karaman swirled the oil around gloomily, then put the jar down to answer the phone. "It's the director," he said. "Wants you in his office soonest."

"Right."

The director held out a communication to Jan when he came through the door. "Something big coming apart at the central office. They need you, they say, yesterday or earlier. I have no idea what it is about, except the bastards could not have picked a worse time to pull you out. We're finally getting the production leveled and on line. Tell them that, will you. They don't seem to listen to me any more. Make them happy and grab the next plane back here. A pleasure to have you on the site, Kulozik. There's a cab here to pick you up."

"I'll have to pack . . ."

"Don't worry. I took the liberty of having the BOQ servant put all your stuff into your bags. Get moving, so you can get back."

Jan had more than a suspicion that he was not on his way to Suez and Cairo. The Arab cabdriver put Jan's bags into the back then *salaam*ed respectfully as he held the door open for him. It was cool in the air-conditioned interior, after the walk from the buildings. As they pulled away from the installation the driver took a flat metal box from the seat and passed it back to him.

"Lift the lid, sir, and a push-button lock is revealed. If you are not aware of the combination do not experiment in cab, I beg you. Explosions follows error."

"Thanks," Jan said, weighing the package in his hands. "Is there anything else?"

"A meeting. I am taking you to the place of assignation. There is, I regret, a payment of eighty pounds for this service."

Jan was sure that the man had been well paid for this service and that this additional payment was a little bit of free enterprise. He passed the money over in any case. His bank balance was still unbelievable. They drove down the smooth highway for a half an hour—then turned sharply into one of the unmarked tracks that led out into the desert. A short while later they came to the scene of some forgotten battlefield filled with the shells of wrecked tanks and disabled field guns.

"Here please," the driver said, opening the door. Heat pressed in in a savage wave. Jan got out and looked around. There was nothing in sight except the empty desert and the burned wreckage. When he turned back he saw that his bags were on the sand and the driver was climbing back into the cab.

"Hold it!" Jan called out. "What happens next?"

The man did not answer. Instead he gunned the engine to life, spun the vehicle in a tight circle and sped back toward the highway. The dust of his passage swirled over Jan who cursed fluently while he wiped his dripping face with the back of his hand.

When the sound of the cab died away the silence and the loneliness pressed in. It was very peaceful, but a little frightening at the same time. And hot, searingly hot. If he had to walk back to the highway he would have to leave his bags here. He wouldn't want to carry them, not in this temperature. He laid the metal box in the shade of the bags and hoped the explosive it contained was not heat sensitive.

"You are Cassius?" the voice said.

Jan turned about, startled, since he had not heard any footsteps in the muffling sand. The girl stood there, near the ruined tank, and the arrow of memory startled him so that he almost spoke her name aloud. No, Sara was dead, killed years ago. Yet the first glimpse of this suntanned girl in the brief khaki shorts, with her blonde, shoulder-length hair, had startled him. The resemblance was so close. Or was his memory betraying him after all the years? She was an Israeli like Sara, that was all. He realized that he was still staring in silence and had not answered her.

"I'm from Cassius, yes. My name is Jan."

"Dvora," she said stepping forward and taking his hand; her grip was firm, warm. "We have long suspected that Cassius was more than one person. But we can talk about that later, out of this sun. Can I help you with your bags?"

"I think I can manage. There is transportation?"

"Yes, out of sight of the road behind this wreck."

It was the same sort of vehicle they used in the oil camp, a half-track, with wheels at the front and tractor treads behind. Jan threw his bags into the back and climbed up into the high front seat next to Dvora. There were no doors. It was open at the sides for air, but a solid metal roof kept the sun off them. Dvora threw a switch on the steering column and they started forward silently, with only the slightest hum coming from the wheels.

"Electric?" Jan asked.

She nodded and pointed at the floor. "High density batteries under the floor, about four hundred kilos of them. But out here these vehicles are almost self-sufficient. The roof is covered with macroyield solar cells, a new development. If you don't put too many K's on this thing during the day it will stay recharged without being plugged to the mains." She turned her head and frowned slightly when she found him staring at her again.

"Please excuse me," Jan said. "I know I'm being rude looking at you like that. But you remind me of someone I knew, a good many years ago. She was also an Israeli like you."

"Then you have been to our country before?"

"No. This is the first time. We met near here and I saw her again in England."

"You're lucky. Very few of our people get to travel at all."

"She was—how shall I say—a very talented person. Her name was Sara."

"Very common, like all of the biblical names."

"Yes, I'm sure so. I heard her last name just once. Giladi. Sara Giladi."

Dvora reached down and switched off the wheel motors. The halftrack clanked jerkily to a stop. Then she half-turned on the seat to face Jan, her face impassive, her large dark eyes staring into his.

"There are no coincidences in this world, Jan. Now I know why they sent me instead of one of the musclebound field agents. My name is Giladi as well. Sara was my sister."

She was, she had to be. So much of Sara was in the turn of her cheek, her voice, reminding him constantly of the girl he had once known.

"Sara is dead," Dvora said quietly. "Did you know that?"

His smile was twisted, humorless. "I was there when she was killed. We were together. Trying to get out of England. And there was no need for it, stupid, she shouldn't have died. It was a terrible, terrible waste."

Memory flooded back, the guns, the murder. And Thurgood-

Smythe's presence. All done under his command. Jan's jaw was locked tight as he remembered and Dvora saw his fingers clench onto the grab handle.

"They told me nothing, no details," Dvora said. "Just that she had died in the service. You . . . you were in love with her?"

"Is it that obvious?"

"It is to me. I loved her too. Can you tell me what happened?"

"Of course. It's simple enough. We were trying to leave the country, but we never had a chance. We were betrayed from the very beginning. But she didn't know that. Instead of surrendering she fired at them, made them shoot back, willing herself to die so they could not have her knowledge. And that is the most terrible part. They had known everything all of the time."

"I didn't hear anything about that. It is terrible, even more terrible for you because you are alive to remember it."

"It is, yes, but I suppose that it is all past history. We can't bring her back."

That was what he said. But he was silent about the rest of his thoughts as the halftrack started up again. Perhaps Thurgood-Smythe and Security had physically killed her. But she had been betrayed by her own people, by her own organization right here in Israel. At least that is what Thurgood-Smythe had said. Where was the truth? He was going to try and find that out before he had anything more to do with these people.

It was a grueling drive and they had little to say to each other, locked in their own thoughts. The sand gave way to rock, then sand again, then to low hills. Road signs in Hebrew began to appear and he realized that they were out of the Sinai and in Israel.

"Is it much further?"

"A half an hour, no more. We are going to Beersheba. He is waiting for you there."

"Who?"

Her silence was an answer, and they drove on in the same silence after that. On a paved road now, through small, dusty villages and irrigated fields. Suddenly the desert was gone and everything was green. Across a valley a small city appeared ahead, but they turned off before they reached it. Up a narrow winding road to a solitary villa surrounded by jacaranda trees.

"Leave your bags," Dvora said, climbing down and stretching. "They'll be taken care of. But bring the metal box. He's expecting that."

Two young men came out as they entered, waving to Dvora as they passed. Jan followed her through the cool house to a balcony overlooking the valley and the city beyond. An old man, gray-haired and rail thin, easily in his eighties, came forward to meet them.

"Shalom, Jan Kulozik," he said in a strong voice, its richness unexpected in a man his age. "I am Amri Ben-Haim. Please sit down."

"Then sending Dvora to meet me was no coincidence?"

"No, of course not."

"Then some explanations are in order," Jan said. Still standing.

"Yes they are. And I imagine you would like to discuss that part of the affair first."

"I want Dvora to hear it."

"That is understood, the why she is here. Now we sit down?"

Jan relented and dropped into one of the cane chairs. There was cold lemonade in a jug on the table and he gratefully accepted a large glass of it. He drained it quickly and it was refilled for him. He sat tensely, the bomb-protected metal box on his lap. He would turn it over to them, but he wanted to hear what Ben-Haim had to say first.

"Do you know who Thurgood-Smythe is?" Jan asked.

Amri Ben-Haim nodded. "The former head of British Security. He has climbed still higher in the last few years and is now perhaps the top Security officer in the world. His position might even be stronger than that. We know that he is directly involved with military liaison with the United Nations."

"Did you know that he is my brother-in-law? That he is the one who trapped me and Sara—and saw her shot?"

"I am aware of all those things, yes."

And now the important question. Jan carefully set his glass on the table and tried to relax. Nevertheless his next words had a sharp edge to them.

"Thurgood-Smythe was apparently aware of the London resistance movement from the very beginning. He had it penetrated and watched, and arrested its members when it suited him. He also knew that Sara was an Israeli, a secret she died to keep because she was sure this country would suffer if her nationality was known. Her sacrifice was needless because not only did he know about her, but he claimed to be working with your government here. He said that you identified any Israelis who tried to work on their own outside this country. Is that true?"

"Yes and no," Amri Ben-Haim said.

"That's not much of an answer."

"I will attempt to explain. This nation has a dubious relationship with the large power blocs who operate under the name of the United Nations. During the Retrocession they completely forgot the Near East. Once the oil wells ran dry they were happy to turn their backs on this troublesome part of the world. Free of outside interference, Israel finally could make peace here. There was war, of course, as soon as the major countries went away. We died by the thousands, but we survived. The Arab governments very quickly used up their imported weapons and were naturally enough not resupplied. Defeated here, they fell back upon tradition and squabbled and fought among themselves as they had always done. A *jehad*, a holy war, spread from Iran and swept up to our borders. We survived that as well. Hunger finally replaced their consuming interest in religion and people began to starve and die of disease. That is where we helped. Unlike the world powers we have never attempted to impose a western-oriented, machine-intensive and high-consumption society on this part of the world. It does not suit the local conditions. What we have done is to develop and improve on the ancient agricultural techniques, while introducing suitable technological processes, such as desalination of water, that have important applications in the area."

"Aren't you straying from my question?"

"Please indulge me a moment longer, Jan Kulozik. Everything that I say is relevant. We cultivated our back garden you might say. Encouraged food and light manufacturing suitable to this part of the world, cured disease and built hospitals, trained doctors. Nor did we forget our own defense. We made peace on all sides, since peace is the best form of security. I don't think you realize what that means, historically speaking. The oldest written records, including the Old Testament of the Bible, are records of warfare. Unending warfare. It is over now. So when a measure of stability returned and other nations once again became aware of the Near East it was settled and peaceful and ready to supply them with year-round supplies of agricultural products. I won't say that they exactly fell into our arms with happiness, in fact a few overtures were made for more direct control. This was when our atomic missiles, most of them located outside of Israel, became important. We will never start an atomic war, if for no other reason than the inescapable fact that we are small enough to be eliminated by a few well-placed hydrogen bombs. But the others know that even when dead we would fight back. The price for an atomic war then became such a high one that no country in the world was willing to pay it. So an arrangement was worked out, which has continued happily for hundreds of years. We stay in and they stay out. It means that we Jews, at one time the most cosmopolitan people in the world, have become the most insular. Of course in order to maintain this carefully balanced relationship we do have governmental liaison at a high level. We also rely a good deal on intelligence agents."

"Spies?"

"Another word for them. The other countries have theirs too. We know because we capture them regularly. Unfortunately they capture some of ours as well. To return to your question. By the time we discovered that Sara's cover had been penetrated it was effectively too late to do anything to help her . . ."

"Excuse my interrupting again, Mr. Ben-Haim, but I think you are just waffling. That may be taken as an insult to a man of your age and position, but it's true. You have yet to answer my question."

"Patience, young man," Ben-Haim said, raising his hand palm outwards. "I am almost there. Thurgood-Smythe told us he was going to capture Sara and wanted to exchange her for three of his own agents that we had in custody. I of course agreed. So we did know that Sara was in danger of capture, and yes, I was in contact with Thurgood-Smythe."

"He told me that you had informed on Sara and told him as well of the presence of all your younger agents in Britain who were working on their own."

"He lied to you. We never had any such arrangement. None of our agents work on their own, no matter what Thurgood-Smythe or the agents themselves have told you."

Jan sat back, exasperated.

"Then one of you is lying," he said.

"Exactly. Now you see why I forced you to listen to a boring history of our country's problems. So you might be able to judge who is the biggest liar. Myself—or Thurgood-Smythe."

"You both could be. He from the most selfish of motives, you from the most noble. All I know is that Sara is dead."

"She is," Ben-Haim said, and the words were a sigh. "I did not know it was going to happen and I would have done anything to prevent it. Anything else is a lie, a filthy, filthy lie."

"And Thurgood-Smythe is the world's dirtiest liar. We are all stuck in his web. Myself in particular. I have come here as Cassius, the one who provided you with the top-secret information for the past two years."

"Thank you, Cassius. We are most grateful."

"If you like I can tell you all about that information, as proof of my authenticity. I memorized that information about a week ago. Would you like to know who Cassius really is?"

Ben-Haim nodded. "Verification would help. We have been sure from the start that it could only be Thurgood-Smythe. That was why we were so intrigued when you appeared."

"He's playing with us," Jan said with sudden realization. "Playing games with us all."

"Yes," Ben-Haim nodded, "I am sure that is a part of it. Though not all. He could have prepared the Cassius role for a number of reasons. But when you returned to Earth so suddenly, out of the blue so to speak, he seized upon your arrival as an opportunity not to be refused. Now we will just have to find out for ourselves what he is up to. I believe you have a package there?"

Jan put the metal box on the table.

"It has a combination lock," he said. "And explosives that will be detonated by the wrong combination. At least that is what a very slippery cab driver told me."

"I am sure that you are informed correctly. I have a seven-digit number given me by Cassius when this affair began. Could that be the combination?"

"I don't know." Jan stared at the smooth case. "I have no idea what the combination is."

"Then we will have to try mine." Ben-Haim reached for the box, but Dvora leaned over and took it first.

"I don't feel it is wise for all of us to sit here while the lock is tried. We want a volunteer. Me. Could I have the number please, Amri Ben-Haim?"

"Get someone else," Jan said, quickly. "I'll do it."

"There is already a volunteer," Ben-Haim said as he passed a slip of paper over to the girl. She took this and the case and went down the steps into the garden, walking to the far end by the wall. When she reached it she turned to wave to them, then turned back and bent over the sealed metal box.

Twelve

Jan felt the tension drain from him when she straightened up and held the box over her head.

"There was little danger," Ben-Haim said. "Or I wouldn't have sent her—and you wouldn't have let her go."

Dvora ran up the stairs, smiling and breathless, and lay the open case on the table. Ben-Haim reached in and took out a flat rectangle of black plastic.

"A Mark fourteen hard disc memory," Jan said. "Where is your terminal?"

"Inside. I will take you there," Ben-Haim said, leading the way. Dvora stood aside to let Jan by and on sudden impulse he took her hands in his.

"That was a foolish thing to do . . ."

"No it wasn't, and you knew that. And besides, it will look good on my service record."

She was laughing, only half serious, and Jan's laugh echoed hers. Only then did he realize that he was still holding her hands; he tried to pull away but Dvora held them firmly. The same impulse had seized her and before she released her grip she leaned out and kissed him. Her eyes were open, dark, her lips moist and warm. He returned the kiss and this time it was she who dropped his hands. She stepped back, and after a long and expressive look she turned and led the way into the house.

Ben-Haim was standing in front of the computer terminal tapping the buttons.

"No success," he said. "It keeps asking for a code reference before it will run. I have no idea what it means."

Jan leaned over and looked at the letters on the screen.

> ENTER CORRECT ACCESS CODE
> NOW — ENTERING INCORRECT
> CODE WILL WIPE THE MEMORY

"And you have no idea what the code is?" Jan said, mostly to himself. "Then if you don't have it—I must. And I can think of only one thing." He took out his new ID card and looked at the number. "Thurgood-Smythe told me that this number was Cassius's identification code when divided by the day of the month. But you never asked me for an identifying code?"

"We had no reason to—or instructions."

"Then this must be it."

Jan fed the number into his calculator, divided it by 27 then read off the twelve digits to the left of the decimal point. He entered them into the terminal and hit RETURN. The screen came to life with Thurgood-Smythe's nodding image.

"Very glad to see that you have arrived safely, Jan, and are now with my old associate Amri Ben-Haim. As you must realize, this recording is far too important to have risked accidental disclosure. Ben-Haim had half the key to it, you Jan, the other, as you have now discovered. Now please make yourself comfortable while I explain what I have in mind."

Jan touched the STOP button and Thurgood-Smythe's image froze on the screen. "Don't you think we ought to record this?" he asked. "This disc is liable to selfdestruct for all we know, so a copy is very much in order."

"Of course," BH said. "Please do that."

Jan slipped a blank disc into one of the drives then started the recording again.

". . . I want the present war of rebellion to end as soon as possible. Ben-Haim, Jan will tell you my personal reasons behind this decision. I suppose you will not believe them any more than he does, which is a pity. I am most sincere in this matter. But that is beside the point. The arrangements I suggest to end the war will appeal to you on completely pragmatic grounds. I count upon self-interest to secure your aid, not sympathy for any cause I might espouse.

"Firstly I shall outline the grand design of my plan so you will understand it and realize that circumstance will force you to join me in implementing it. I'm sure that we share a mutual goal in believing that the coming conflict must end with victory for the human race.

"Details. My intelligence sources reveal that a large force of ships is on the way towards Earth. This has been hastily assembled and is made up of every deep space ship in serviceable condition. The planets are gambling their future, their very existence on this single try. Of course they have no other choice. Earth policy has always been to keep the manufacturing of all industrial and space drive components safely here on Earth. As key control equipment breaks down it will not be replaced. The same applies to the fuel and basic circuitry for the Foscolo space drive. Now that all of the Earth forces have withdrawn, the only thing the rebel forces can do is attack. It must be done sooner or later—and soonest is best before the attrition of time begins to take its toll of the machinery. I do not know the details of the rebels' plans, but I do know that there is one thing that they must do if they hope to win. They must attack and capture the Mojave base of Spaceconcent. Any other course would be suicidal. All supplies essential for the existence of the space forces go through here. If it is captured or destroyed that is the end of the defensive forces.

"This will be accomplished in the following manner. Firstly attacks must be made in space to divide the strength of the defending fleet. Then the Mojave complex must be captured. This will have to be done from the ground since the missile defenses are too strong to penetrate from space. After capture the victory will be secured by the landing of the attackers. Surrender and final victory will follow.

"Now for details. Jan, I will arrange for you to contact the rebel fleet in order to coordinate the operation. When this is done the Israeli forces will attack and capture Spaceconcent, and will hold it until relieved. Before they make a decision on whether to take part, I wish to remind them of the raid on Entebbe and the rising in the Warsaw ghetto. It is time to leave the ghetto again . . ."

Jan stopped the replay and turned to Ben-Haim. "I think the man's mad. What were those last things he was talking about?"

"Not mad—but criminally sane. He tempts us with salvation knowing that it could mean destruction. And in order to help us decide, he quotes from our own history. His thinking is as convoluted as that of a Talmudic scholar."

"The Warsaw rising was during the Second World War," Dvora said. "Jews were being slaughtered there by the Nazis, were dying of starvation and disease as well. They rose up and fought their attackers, bare hands against guns, until they were all killed. They knew they would die—but they would not submit."

"And equally important," Ben-Haim added. "They fought to break out of the ghetto. And still, today, the Jews are forced to live in a ghetto. It may be an entire country but, comfortable as it is—it is still a ghetto. Thurgood-Smythe knows that we want to leave."

"And Entebbe," Jan asked. "What was that?"

"A commando raid half way around the world that should not have stood a chance of succeeding. But it did. Thurgood-Smythe puts Satan to shame with his temptations!"

"I don't quite understand these temptations," Jan said. "You're not threatened or at war with anyone. You can just sit this one out and see what happens."

"Basically, that is quite true. But in a very real sense our freedom is but an illusion of freedom. We are free to stay in our nation-wide jail. There is also an ironical sense of justice and injustice that appeals to us. We in our little free prison are surrounded by a world of economic and physically enslaved *goyem*. Shouldn't we help them? We who were in bondage for millennia know well what it is. Should we not aid others to achieve what we always prayed for for ourselves? I said, this is a riddle for Talmudic scholars. I'm old so perhaps I doubt too much. I like my security. But hear the voice of young Israel. Dvora—what do you think?"

"I don't think—I know!" she said fiercely. "Fight! There is no other course possible."

"My response is equally simple," Jan said. "If there is any chance at all of this thing succeeding I must go along with it. Thurgood-Smythe says that he will put me in contact with the attacking fleet. Very good, for not only will I tell them about his plan, but I can tell them also about our reservations and what kind of twister Thurgood-Smythe really is. Then the responsibility for a final decision will not rest with me. So my response is clearcut. I do what he says."

"Yes, in your position I would do the same," Ben-Haim said. "You have nothing to lose—but the world to gain. Yet it all sounds too good. I have the feeling that the man must be playing a devious game."

"That doesn't matter," Dvora said. "His personal fate should not concern us. If this is all a trap then the attackers must be warned and turn the knowledge to their advantage. If it is not a trap Israel must fight in this final battle, this war to end all wars."

Ben-Haim sighed deeply and rocked back and forth in his chair. "How many times have those words been spoken? The war to end all wars. Have they ever been true?"

"No. But they could be now," Dvora insisted. "Turn it on again, Jan. Let's hear the end of it."

It made a lot of sense—or nonsense. Jan felt himself as entrapped as the Israelis. Basically the one thing he wanted to do with Thurgood-Smythe was kill him. Instead he found himself working for him. He shook his head in wonderment and reached out and touched the button.

". . . time to leave the ghetto again. So think carefully about what I have said. Weigh your decisions. Take the Knesset into your confidence and ask them for a decision. There are no separate parts to this proposal. You must accept it or reject it. It is all or nothing. This is the only argument from me that you will hear. There is time, but not very much, to reach your decision. The attacking fleet will be here in approximately ten days. Your attack will take place just before dawn on the date that you will be given. You have four days to decide. On next Friday night your radio station will be broadcasting the usual weekly memorial service to honor those who have passed on. If you wish to take part simply list Jan Kulozik's name among the noble dead. He is not a superstitious man so I am sure he will not mind. However, if you decide not to participate in the salvation of mankind simply do nothing—since you will be doing nothing. You will not hear from me again."

"Such guilt he gives us," Ben-Haim said as the screen went dark. "Are you sure he was never trained in theology?"

"I am sure of nothing about my brother-in-law. Though I am sure now that all of his earlier background is his own invention. Perhaps he is the father of lies, just as you said. What will you do next?"

"Just as he commanded. Take the proposal to the Knesset, our parliament. Let a little of the responsibility and guilt slip off onto their shoulders."

Dvora and Jan left the room when Ben-Haim turned to the telephone. They had not noticed, because of the automatic lighting, that darkness had fallen while they had been listening to Thurgood-Smythe. They went out onto the balcony, not speaking, each of them wrapped in private thought. Jan leaned against a pillar and looked out at the ascending lights of the town, where it climbed up the side of the darkened valley across from him. It was a moonless night and the stars burned clear and sharp, filling the sky as far down as the black cutout of the horizon. A world at peace, comfortable and secure. And Thurgood-Smythe wanted them to give it all up, to go to war for an ideal. Jan did not envy them their decision; his had been easy enough to make. Turning around he saw that Dvora was sitting on the couch, quietly, her hands folded in her lap.

"You must be hungry," she said. "Let me fix you something."

"In a moment. What do you think the Knesset will do?"

"Talk. They are very good at that. Just a bunch of old men who prefer talk to action. Thurgood-Smythe should have given them four months to make their minds up instead of four days."

"Then you don't think they will decide?"

"They'll decide all right. Against the idea. Play it safe, they always want to play it safe."

"Perhaps that's how they got to be old men."

"Are you laughing at me? Let me see your face."

Dvora pulled him down next to her on the couch and saw that, indeed, he was smiling. She could not help smiling back.

"All right, so I am getting angry over nothing. It hasn't happened yet. But it will, just as I said it would. Then I'll get angry. But if that happens what will you do? In case they say no."

"I haven't begun to even think about that possibility. Go back and get in touch with Thurgood-Smythe again, I imagine. I just can't stay safely here when the fate of everyone in the world—all of the worlds—is being decided. Perhaps I can still contact the attacking fleet, tell them what I know. There's no point in trying to decide before I have to."

While he was talking Jan realized that they still had their hands clasped together; neither would pull away from the bond. What am I thinking of, Jan worried, then became aware that he wasn't thinking at all. But feeling, reacting physically. And he knew, without asking, that Dvora felt the same way. He wanted to question the sensation but did not, was afraid to. When he turned toward her she was already facing him. Then, without conscious effort, she was in his arms.

An unmeasurable space of time passed before she drew her mouth away from his, but still held him tightly in her arms. Her words were only a whisper.

"Come to my room. This place is far too public."

He stood up when she did but tried hard to express the tiny niggle of doubt that tapped at him.

"I'm married, Dvora. My wife, light-years away . . ."

She touched her finger to his lips.

"Shh. It's chemistry, not matrimony I have in mind. Just follow me."

He did. Quite willingly.

Thirteen

"We never did get anything to eat," Jan said.

"You are a very greedy person," Dvora answered. "For most men this would be enough."

She kicked the covering sheet from her and stretched the brown length of her naked body in the morning sunlight that streamed through the window. Jan ran his fingertips down her side and across the tight rise of her stomach. She shivered at his touch.

"I'm so glad that I'm alive," she said. "Being dead must be very gray and boring. This is so much more fun."

Jan smiled and reached for her, but she pulled away and stood up, a splendid, warm-fleshed sculpture as she arched her back and ran her fingers through her hair. Then reached for a dressing gown.

"You're the one who mentioned food, not me," she said. "But now that you have raised the subject I realize that I'm starving. Come along and I'll fix us some breakfast."

"I better get to my own room first."

She laughed at this, pulling the comb through her knotted hair. "Why? We're not children here. We're adults. We come and go as we please, do as we please. What sort of a world do you come from?"

"Not that kind. Not now at least. Though in London—God, it seems like centuries ago—I suppose I was very much my own person. Until I got in the way of the authorities. Since then I have been living in a social nightmare. I can't begin to tell you the ugliness and restrictions of life on Halvmörk—nor do I intend to try. Breakfast is a far better idea."

The plumbing was functional, instead of ultraluxurious like the Waldorf-Astoria. He approved of it this way he realized, as the pipes gurgled and clanked and finally produced hot water. It worked—and he was sure that everyone in the country had one that was just as good. A concept of democracy he had not considered before. Equality of physical comfort as well as equality of opportunity. A growl of hunger in his midriff drove all philosophical thoughts away; he quickly washed and dressed. Then followed his nose to a large, open kitchen, where a young man and a woman sat at a long trestle table. They nodded as he came in and Dvora handed him a steaming mug of coffee.

"Food first, introductions later," she said. "How do you like your eggs?"

"On a plate."

"Intelligent decision. There's some *matzoh brei* here which will introduce you to good heavy kosher cooking if you have not had that pleasure before."

The young couple waved and slipped away without being introduced. Jan realized then that few names would be exchanged here in the heart of the secret service. Dvora served them both at the same time and sat down across from him. She ate with as good an appetite as he did, while they chatted lightly about totally unimportant things. They were just finishing up when the other girl returned, bursting into the room. Her smile was gone now.

"Ben-Haim wants you both right away. It's trouble, big trouble."

The atmosphere was thick with it. Ben-Haim sat slumped wearily in the same chair where they had left him the night before, might very well have been there the entire time. He was sucking on a pipe long dead and seemed completely unaware of it.

"It appears that Thurgood-Smythe is putting on some pressure. I should have realized that he would not simply ask for a favor from us. That's not his way."

"What happened?" Dvora asked.

"Raids. Right around the world in every country. Reports are still coming in. Protective custody, they say. Because of the emergency. Our people, all of them. Business representatives and trade missions, even secret operatives we thought were still secret. He's got them, all of them, arrested. Two thousand, maybe more."

"Pressure," Jan said. "He's tightening the screw. Have you considered what else he might do?"

"What else can he do? The few thousand of our citizens that he has taken into custody are the only ones who, legally or illegally, are outside Israel and the adjoining countries. He has them all."

"I'm sure that he is up to something. I know Thurgood-Smythe's manner of operation by now, and this is just the first step."

Jan was unhappily proved right within the hour. All of the television programs, on every one of the hundred and twelve channels, were interrupted with news of an important announcement. It would be carried on every channel and would be presented by Doctor Bal Ram Mahant, the President of the United Nations. The position was an honorary one, and the Doctor's activities were usually confined to opening and closing UN sessions. However he did make the occasional important announcement such as this one. A military brass band played patriotic marches while the world watched—and waited. The band's image faded and Doctor Mahant appeared. He nodded his head at the unseen audience and began to speak in his familiar, high-pitched voice.

"Citizens of the world. We are in the midst of a terrible war brought to us by anarchist elements among the body of faithful citizens of the planets of the great Commonwealth of Earth. But I am not here to discuss that now, that great battle that our citizen-soldiers are waging and winning for the freedom of mankind. I am here to tell you of an even greater threat to our security. Certain individuals in the United Nations Conclave of Israel have been holding back vital food supplies for their own benefit. They are war profiteers, making money out of the starvation of others. This will not be permitted to continue. They must be made to understand the error of their ways. Justice must be done before others try to follow their example."

Doctor Mahant sighed; the weight of responsibility for the world was upon his shoulders. But he accepted the burden and went on.

"Even as I talk our soldiers are moving into Egypt, Jordan, Syria and all of the other important food-producing countries in this area. No one of you will go hungry, that I promise you. Food shipments will continue despite the efforts of the selfish minority. Rebellion will be put down and we will march on together to victory."

The President faded from view to the accompaniment of jubilant recorded applause and his image was replaced by the blue and white flag of Earth cracking in the wind. The brass band played enthusiastically. Ben-Haim turned off the set.

"I don't understand," Jan said.

"I do, only too well," Ben-Haim answered. "You are forgetting that the rest of the world does not even know that our nation exists. They will be only too happy to see these countries occupied to make sure their bellies stay full. These are lands of peasant farmers for the most part, shipping out their produce through their cooperatives. But we are the ones who taught them how to irrigate and fertilize the desert to grow these crops, and we are the ones who set up their marketing boards as well. And our country has handled all of the external shipments with our fleet of air transports. Until now. Now do you see what he is doing to us? We are being pushed out, sent back within our own borders. And more attrition will follow. This is all Thurgood-Smythe's doing. No one else cares about the fate of this tiny corner of the world, not at this time. And see what a good student of history he is. With what care he revives those sneering twentieth century terms of approbation, those anti-semitic labels that surely date back to medieval Europe. Profiteers, usurers, getting rich while others starve. His message is very clear."

Jan nodded. "Forcing your hand. If you don't do as he ordered, the country is going to suffer."

"Either way we suffer. We lose—or we lose. As long as the big powers of the world paid no attention to us we survived. Our tiny balance of terror, our few atom bombs in exchange for their myriad atom bombs made us not worth bothering about. As long as we kept peace in the Near East, stayed humbly in this area—and saw that they had continuous supplies of fresh oranges and avocados in the winter time, why then we just weren't worth bothering about. Now Thurgood-Smythe is tightening the clamps and this war gives him a perfect excuse. Their troops will move in slowly, up to our borders. We can't stop them. They'll occupy all of our external missile sites. When that is done they can drop their bombs or send in the tanks. It makes no difference. We lose either way."

"And Thurgood-Smythe will do it," Jan said angrily. "Not out of revenge for your not helping him—that would be a show of emotion, and an emotional person can always be appealed to, possibly convinced to change his mind. But Thurgood-Smythe will proceed calmly to do this, even if all of his plans fail. What he begins he finishes. He wants you to be sure of that."

"You know him very well," Ben-Haim said, looking closely at Jan. "Wheels within wheels. I can see why he sent you as emissary. There was really no need to have you carry his message in person. But he wanted us to be absolutely sure of his resolve, to know exactly what kind of a man he really was. So you are the devil's advocate, God help you, whether you like it or not. We are back once again to the father of lies. Best not to let the rabbis get hold of this theory or they will have us all believing it."

"What are we to do?" Dvora asked, her voice empty and lost.

"The Knesset must be convinced that our only chance now is to proceed along the lines Thurgood-Smythe has laid out. I will have the radio message sent that we will cooperate, whether the Knesset has agreed or not by that time. They'll come around in the end. They have no alternative. And then there will have to be a second Diaspora."

"Why? What do you mean?"

"The Diaspora occurred when the Jews were expelled from the land of Israel, thousands of years ago. This time we will go voluntarily. If the attack on the Mojave base fails their retribution will be instant—and atomic. This entire tiny country will become a radioactive pit. We must therefore plan to reduce the mortality if we can. There will have to be volunteers who will stay behind to keep the services going and conceal our withdrawal. Everyone else will leave, quietly, by filtering out into the surrounding countries where we have our good Arab friends. Hopefully, if the raid is a successful one, they will be able to come home again. If not, well, we have carried our religion and our culture with us before to alien lands. We will survive."

Dvora nodded in grim agreement and Jan knew for the first time what had kept these people going through the millennia, despite the worst kind of persecution. He knew that they would be in the future as they were in the past.

Ben-Haim shook himself, like someone upon whom a chilling wind has blown. He took the cold pipe from his mouth and stared at it as though he had just become aware of its presence. Laying it carefully on the table he rose and went slowly from the room, walking like an old man for the first time. Dvora watched him go, then turned to Jan and held him tightly, her face pressed against his chest, as though finding some security there to ward off the dark future hurrying towards them.

"I wonder where it will end," she said, in a voice so quiet he could barely hear it.

"In peace for all mankind. You're the one who said it. The war to end all wars. I have been in this fight from the beginning. Now, like it or not, it looks like your people are as well. I just wish I knew what Thurgood-Smythe was thinking. Whether this is a plot to destroy us—or to bring lasting peace. I just wish that I knew."

It was late in the afternoon, almost dusk, when the helicopter arrived, dropping out of the sky with a roar of engines and blades. Jan and Dvora were in the garden when he was sent for.

"Look at this," Ben-Haim said, pointing to the sealed suitcase on the floor. "Special delivery for you from the United Nations in Tel-Aviv. They brought it to our supposedly secret office next door to them, the one that monitors their communications. The manner of delivery identifies its sender. It is a message for me that they know more about our operations than we think they do. And for you—you will have to look and see."

"Hasn't it been opened?"

"Sealed shut. With a combination lock. Dare we guess that we know the correct number by now? And no need to send Dvora to the bottom of the garden to open this one. Our friend has bigger goals than blowing up an old man. May I?"

Without waiting for an answer Ben-Haim leaned forward and touched the buttons in quick succession. The lock clicked as it unsealed itself. Jan picked up the case and put it on the table, opened it.

There was a black uniform inside, black boots and a matching cloth cap with a starburst insignia on it. Lying on top of the clothing was a transparent plastic envelope. It contained an ID card in the name of John Halliday and a thick technical manual with a computer disc inside the cover. Tucked into the manual so it projected a bit was a brief note. It was addressed to Jan. He took it up and read it aloud.

"John Halliday is a UNO technician working at the communications center in Cairo. He is also in the Space Forces Reserve where he is a communications technician. You will master this occupation very quickly, Jan, and the enclosed manual should help. You have two full days to learn the job and to get to Cairo. Your friends in Israel will be able to arrange that without your being detected en route. Once in the city I suggest you wear this uniform and go directly to the airport. Your orders will be waiting at the Security desk there. I wish you good luck. We are all depending on you." Jan looked up. "That's all it says. It's unsigned."

It did not have to be. They all knew that Thurgood-Smythe's plans had moved forward one more notch.

Fourteen

"You cut it pretty fine, soldier," the Security man said, looking Jan up and down coldly as though trying to find an open button in his uniform. There were none.

"I got here as soon as I heard," Jan said.

"Just because you're over here enjoying the luxuries of life don't mean you're exempt from your duties."

As he proceeded with the ritual chastisement, the Security officer slipped the ID into his terminal and nodded to Jan, who placed the fingertips of his right hand on the identification plate. Almost as exact as a retinal print and much faster to use for normal identification. The ID was ejected and handed back to Jan, his identity accepted. Thurgood-Smythe must have access to identification files at the topmost level—with no one to monitor his actions.

"Well, sir, it looks like they're giving you first class transportation." The change in the Security man's attitude was very abrupt and Jan knew that his new status was far higher than the man had expected. "There's a military jet on the way for you now. If you would like to wait in the bar I'll have someone come and get you when the plane arrives. Is that all right? I'll look after your bag for you."

Jan nodded and headed for the bar, not as pleased with his new high-ranking status as Security was. He was by himself, completely alone. It is one thing to consider that in theory, another to actually be subjected to it. The shadowy form of Thurgood-Smythe lurked behind him all of the time, but that just made him more insecure. A pawn on a chessboard with Thurgood-Smythe manipulating all of the pieces. Not for the first time did he wonder just what the man was planning.

The beer was tasteless but cold, and he limited himself to one bottle. This was not a day to have a thick head. He was alone with the Egyptian bartender who solemnly polished glass after glass in silence. There was apparently little traffic through Cairo airport. Nor was there any sign of the occupation troops that featured so largely in President Mahant's speech. Had it all been a ruse? There was no way of telling. But his position was real enough and he was not looking forward to the coming encounters with any great enthusiasm. Events were rushing past him, getting ahead of him so that it was growing more and more difficult to keep up with the accelerating changes. The boring years he had spent on Halvmörk seemed almost attractive by comparison. When he returned—if he returned—life would be quiet and satisfactory. He would have a family there, his wife, a child on the way, more children. The future of the planet to worry about. Alzbeta; she had scarcely been in his thoughts at all of late. Too little time. He saw her now in his mind's eye, smiling, her arms out to him. But it was hard to hold this image; it melted away, was overlaid with the far stronger one of Dvora, naked and close, the musky smell of her body in his nostrils . . .

Damn! He drained his glass and signaled for a second one. Life was very complex. As dangerous as it had been since his arrival back on Earth it also had been . . . what? Fun? No, he couldn't call it that. Interesting, it was surely that, and damn exciting once he knew that he was going to live for at least a little bit longer. He shouldn't be thinking about the future now, not until he was sure that he was going to have one. Wait and see, that was all that he could do.

"Technician Halliday," the PA system said. "Technician Halliday to Gate Three."

Jan heard the message twice before it penetrated that it was for him. His new identity. He put down his glass and headed for Gate Three. The same Security officer was waiting for him there.

"If you'll come with me, sir. The plane's been refueled and is ready to go. Your bag's aboard already."

Jan nodded and followed the man out into the heat of the day, the sun reflected and glaring from the white concrete. They came to a supersonic two-place fighter marked with the white star of the

United States Air Force; travel in style indeed. The mechanics held the stairs as Jan climbed aboard, one of them following him up to close and seal the hatch. The pilot turned and waved his hand over his shoulder in greeting.

"Someone sure in a hurry to get your ass out of here. Pulled me out of a poker game, never even let me play my hand. Strap in."

The jets roared and vibrated beneath them and they were airborne almost as soon as they turned into the runway.

"Where are we going?" Jan asked, as soon as the gear was up and they were in a steady climb up to cruising altitude. "Mojave?"

"Shit no. I wish we were. I been out in a desert field here so long I'm beginning to grow a hump like a camel. And hump, real hump, that's what I'd be getting if I were flying into Mojave. No, we're vectored right into Baikonur, soon as I get above the commercial lanes. Them Russkies don't like no one, even themselves. Lock you in a little room, guards with guns everywheres. Sign eight thousand goddamn forms for the fuel. Get crabs from the furniture, I swear I know an old boy lay over there and got crabs. Says they jump further than Texas crabs and they jump fourteen feet . . ."

It took no large effort to tune out the pilot's reminiscences. Apparently his voice worked separately from his mind because he flew the plane with great precision, instrument and navigation checks and all. Without shutting up for a second.

Baikonur. Somewhere in southern Russia, that's all Jan remembered. Not an important base, too small for anything other than orbital lifters. Probably just there to prove that the Soviets were members of the big-nation club. He was undoubtedly going to be put into space from there. With no idea yet of his final destination.

Wartime had intensified the traditional Russian paranoia and the tower at Baikonur was in continual radio contact with the pilot as soon as they had started across the Black Sea.

"This is a security warning, Air Force four three niner, and must be obeyed exactly. Any deviation will cause automatic reprisal. Do you read me?"

"Read you? For Christ's sake, Baikonur, I told you I did, about seventeen goddamned times now! My autopilot's locked on your frequency, I am steady at your specified height of twenty thousand. I'm just a passenger in this plane, so you bring it in and talk to your machinery if you want to issue any more orders."

Unmoved, the deep voice carried on insistently.

"No deviation will be allowed. Do you read me, Air Force four three niner?"

"I read you, I read you," the pilot said wearily, defeated by Slavic stolidity.

It was night when they crossed the Soviet shore and began their approach to the space complex. The lights of towns and cities swept by beneath them, but Baikonur itself was completely blacked out because of the hostilities. It was disconcerting to see that the plane was dropping lower and lower toward the ground while still completely under airport control. It is one thing to know abstractly that radar and electronic communications need no light, that they work just as well in complete darkness; still another to hear the wing flaps grinding into position, the landing gear locking down—when there is nothing visible in any direction. All of this was controlled by the computer on the ground—the ground which was still totally invisible in the darkness ahead. The aircraft's landing lights stayed off, as did the runway lights. Jan found that he was holding his breath as the engine throttled back and they dropped.

To make a perfect landing on the still invisible runway. Only when they had come to a complete stop at the end of the taxiway was control returned to the pilot.

"Feel like a goddamned passenger," he muttered to himself, settling his infrared goggles firmly into place. The FOLLOW ME car finally arrived and they taxied after it into a blacked-out hangar; the lights came on only after the door was closed. Jan blinked in the sudden glare as he unbuckled his straps. An officer, wearing the same black uniform as his, was waiting at the foot of the steps.

"Technician Halliday?"

"Yes, sir."

"Get your bag and come with me. There's a supply shuttle on line now with a window coming up in about twenty minutes. We can make it if we hurry. Let's go."

After this, Jan was just a passenger. The chemical-fueled rocket boosted into a low orbit that was barely outside the atmosphere. A deep space fusion shuttle locked to them and the passengers, all military personnel, transferred to this. Every one of them was at home in null-G. Jan was thankful that he had worked in space before, or his clumsiness would have given him away instantly.

Once in their seats they had to wait while the cargo was transferred as well; in the interval they enjoyed the dubious pleasure of
a Russian squeezepak meal. It had a soapy texture and tasted
vaguely of fish. Afterwards Jan read the instructions on the free
fall toilet very carefully before he used it. There were as many disaster stories about its use as there were about the equivalent bit of
sanitary engineering that was fitted into submarines.

Boredom very quickly replaced tension, since there was little to
do other than look at recordings or catch up on sleep. The space
colony of Lagrange 5 was unluckily almost at its maximum distance from Earth, nearly 200,000 miles, so the trip was a long one.
While pretending to doze, Jan eavesdropped shamelessly on his
fellow spacemen. The colony was being used as a base for the
Space Force and headquarters for the Earth defense fleet, he discovered. Most of the conversation seemed to be a mixture of
rumor and gossip and he memorized the best bits to be used as
part of his cover.

He quickly discovered, when talking with the others, that most
of them were reservists who had never served in the regular Space
Force before. This was encouraging, since it would help to cover
any omissions or slips on his part. As it turned out these precautions were not necessary; Thurgood-Smythe had planned his future quite precisely. When they finally docked and disembarked at
Lagrange 5, Jan never even had the opportunity to see the interior
of the manufacturing colony. A messenger was waiting in the
spacelock chamber as they emerged.

"Technician Halliday," he shouted as the men floated by him.
"Which one of you is Tech Halliday?"

Jan hesitated just an instant before he kicked off in the man's
direction. His cover could not have been discovered; this development had to be part of Thurgood-Smythe's complex planning. It
was.

"Get suited up and leave your gear here, Halliday. It'll be waiting when you get back. We got a scout going out and we're one
tech short. You're the lucky lad who's elected." He looked at the
printout he held. "Commander name of Captain Lastrup. Ship's
the Ida Peter Two Five Six. Let's go."

They used a jaxter, an open skeletal framework with six metal
seats fixed to it. Other than this it was little more than four jets
and a control pedestal. The pilot was familiar with the little craft
and kicked it away from the airlock, flipped it end for end neatly,

and was on a new trajectory even before their turn was complete.

The fleet of Earth made an impressive sight. Grouped around the two kilometer-long colony were scores of deep space vessels of all sizes. They ranged from gigantic bulk carriers down to jaxters like the one they were in, with a spectrum of sizes, shapes and functions in between. Their course took them in an arc up over the fleet toward the shining needle of a scoutship. The crew quarters in the bow was tiny in comparison to the engines and auxiliary fuel tanks to the rear. It bristled with antennas and detection devices of all kinds. In space, beyond the fixed network of early warning stations, it was ships like this that were the eyes and ears of the fleet. The jaxter floated toward it, slowed and stopped with a quick flare of the bow jet. The large characters of identification were painted across the bow, IP-256, just above the open door of the spacelock. Jan unbuckled his safety belt, floated free of the seat, then pushed off toward the ship. He drifted gently into the lock, seized one of the grabirons, and waved back to the jaxter pilot as he pressed the cycle button. The outer port ground slowly shut.

When the pressure in the airlock equaled that in the ship, the inner lock opened automatically. Jan cracked his helmet and floated inside. The circular chamber, obviously the living quarters, couldn't have been more than three meters across and just about as high. Around nine cubic meters of living space for two men, Jan estimated. Wonderful. No expenses spared to make our boys in space comfortable.

A man's head appeared through a circular opening in the bow end of the room, upside-down to Jan's orientation. A red face with slightly bulging eyes.

"Not accomplishing very much, are you, Tech, just floating around and sightseeing." This undoubtedly was Captain Lastrup. A fine spray of saliva exploded in Jan's direction with every angry word. "Just peel out of that suit and get up here on the double."

"Yes, sir," Jan said, obeying instructions.

Within two hours, after they had unlocked from their moorings and got under way, Jan was beginning to dislike the Captain. By the time he was permitted to retire, more than twenty hours after his arrival, he loathed the man. It was painful, after only three hours' sleep, to be dragged back to blurry consciousness and summoned to the control room.

"I'm going to close my eyes for a bit, Tech Halliday, which means that you are on watch. Don't touch anything or do anything because you are just a totally incompetent reservist amateur. The machines will do all the things you are incapable of doing. If there is a little red warning light or a little beeping warning sound, you are to awaken me at once. Understood?"

"Yes, sir. But I am capable of monitoring the equipment because I know . . ."

"Did I ask for your opinion? Did I order you to talk? Anything you have to say is just shit to me, mister. Understood? If you answer anything more than yessir that will be disobeying orders, and that will go into the charges against you. Now, what do you say?"

Jan was tired, getting angrier with every passing moment. He said nothing and he enjoyed the red glow that suffused the officer's skin with every passing silent second.

"I order you to speak!"

Jan slowly counted to five before he said "Yes, sir."

It was very small revenge for the verbal abuse he was taking. But it was enough for the moment. Jan took an Awake pill and tried not to rub at his sore and grainy eyes. Only the softest red glow illuminated the control room. Stars filled the viewport ahead; flickering readouts and displays from the detection apparatus monitored space in all directions. They were passing through the outer web now, and very soon their reports would be the only early warning in this particular portion of space. Although he had received no instructions from Thurgood-Smythe, Jan knew exactly what to do in this situation.

They were heading away from Earth, at full acceleration, into space, in the direction of the attacking fleet. The orbiting radio telescopes had detected objects out here, at maximum range, in a portion of space where nothing should be. The IP-256 was on its way to scout what could only be the rebel space fleet. Jan would control his anger and do nothing to irritate Captain Lastrup any further. He regretted losing his temper and speaking out of turn, then aggravating the offense by adding dumb insolence to it as well. As soon as the Captain came on duty he would apologize to him. After that Jan would do his best to be a good spaceman, and would work as hard as he could to do exactly as he was told. He would do this with all the effort of will that he could muster. He would keep doing this until they had pinpointed the attackers and were absolutely certain of their identification and position.

At that time Jan was going to use a one-meter length of thick electrical wire, he had it cut and ready, and would then experience the sweet and satisfying pleasure of strangling the military son of a bitch.

Fifteen

"Got them, look at the size of that fleet—is this going into memory, Tech? If it's not I'll . . ."

"Going in fine, sir," Jan said. "Onto disk storage with a backup on molecular wafer. I've replayed both and they're perfect."

"They better be, they had better be," Captain Lastrup muttered savagely. "I'm setting up a return course now. As soon as the main dish bears on Earth, squirt out the readings with maximum watts. Got that?"

"Absolutely, sir. This is the moment I have been waiting for."

There was true joy in Jan's voice. As he spoke he was carefully wrapping the ends of the thick wire around and around each of his hands. He snapped it tight and looked at it thoughtfully. About seventy centimeters in length; that should do nicely. Without releasing his grip on the wire he unclipped from his seat and kicked off towards the pilot, twisting neatly in midflight to approach head first with his arms extended before him.

Lastrup had a glimpse of the moving figure out of the corner of his eye. He turned and had just enough time for a look of shocked amazement before the stretched wire dropped beneath his chin and was locked into place by the swift crossing of Jan's arms.

Jan had given careful thought to this operation for a long time, planned every part of it precisely. A steady tightening now of the wire, not a sharp snap that might crush the man's throat. He did not want to kill him, just secure him. It was a silent struggle, punctuated only by Jan's heavy breathing. The Captain was of course not breathing at all. He struggled a bit but could do nothing. His eyes closed and his body went limp very quickly. Jan loosened the wire, ready to tighten it instantly if the man was shamming. He wasn't; he was deeply unconscious, breathing hoarsely but regularly, with a strong pulse in his neck. Perfect. Jan used the wire to lash the officer's hands securely behind his back, and then tied another length about his ankles. There was more than enough trailing wire from his wrists to secure the unconscious officer to the rear bulkhead out of harm's way.

First step done. Jan did not bother to waste a glance at the ship's controls. He had examined them closely during his time on watch alone and had very quickly determined that he was not going to become a deep space pilot by calling up the instruction manuals from memory. They took for granted too much previous knowledge. Therefore he had relied on the simple and archaic statement by Newton that any object in motion tends to remain in motion, in a straight line and at a constant velocity. That object now was the IP-256 and the straight line was pointed rather accurately at the approaching rebel ships. It was the pilot's decision to alter that course that had produced his abrupt lapse into unconsciousness. The course change he wanted had been computed and was ready for implementation. Which was the last thing that Jan had in mind. With the pilot secured and forgotten, he turned to his equipment panels.

It was too much to expect that their two courses would coincide and that this ship would meet the attackers head on. This did not matter at all if Jan could establish contact with them. He switched on the power and swung the largest dish antenna so it pointed at the fleet. Exact alignment would not be necessary; even the tightest signal he could broadcast would be far greater in diameter than the fleet by the time it reached them. He cranked the power to maximum, hooked a recorder into the line, then swung the bead microphone into position before his mouth.

"This is Jan Kulozik calling, from Earth scoutship IP-256 now closing upon your present position. This signal is highly directional and beamed at you. Don't, repeat don't, make any attempt to answer at this time. Please record this message. Message follows.

"I was resident on Halvmörk and left that planet with a food ship commanded by a man named Debhu. We were captured in orbit by Earth forces and made prisoner. Later all the prisoners were killed; I'm the only survivor. I will give you all the details later but tell you this now so you will understand who I am. Please do not fire on this ship when we get within range. This is a two-man scout and I have secured the commander. I do not know how to pilot this vessel nor do I intend to learn at the present time. The ship is not armed. Here is what I suggest you do.

"As soon as you have computed my course and velocity, dispatch one of your spacers on a closing course to match my speed. I will do nothing to alter any vectors, but I will open the airlock. I am familiar with spacesuit operation and will transfer to your ship. I suggest sending a pilot to take over this scout since it contains highly sophisticated detection gear.

"You have no reason to believe me, but also have no reason not to capture this scout. I also have information of highest priority about Earth defenses and coming operations there.

"I am broadcasting now on the emergency frequency. I am recording and this message will automatically repeat on the two main communication frequencies, then the emergency frequency again. It will be continuous until we meet. Message ends."

After this Jan could only wait. And begin to worry. He kept his receivers on and picked up a number of coded messages from Earth fleet command directed at the IP-256, all of which he cheerfully ignored. It would be best if the enemy forces thought that the scoutship had vanished completely. This could only cause dismay, and hopefully a good bit of confusion, perhaps even make them think about possible secret weapons that the rebels might possess. Yet Jan was still worried. His plan was a good one, the only possible one, but it required a great deal of patience. Since he had received no communications from the attacking fleet it could mean that his message had been received and that the instructions were being carried out. Or that everything had gone wrong, and they were heading swiftly into interstellar space. Or even worse, that there had been a mistaken identification of the ships approaching Earth, that they were defending, not attacking, forces. Once he had started to worry, he found a great deal to worry about.

Captain Lastrup did not make life any easier. As soon as he had regained consciousness he began a continuous and high-pitched description of what would happen to Jan after he had been returned to justice. Saliva ran down his chin, unnoticed by him in the intensity of his feelings, while his voice grew hoarse and rasping. Jan tried to stem the flow by threatening to get the throttling wire out again, but this had no effect. Then he warned that he would gag the Captain, and when this made not the slightest difference he actually put the threat into practice. But the sight of the bulging eyes, the face gradually turning from red to purple as Lastrup swung and writhed and bounced off of the bulkhead was too much, too inhumane. He ungagged the man and turned the radio on loud to roar counterpoint to the ravings.

Two days went by like this, with the Captain dozing off for blessed minutes in his bindings, only to awake and resume the tirade again. He would not eat, spat out the food that Jan tried to feed him, but did drink some water. Undoubtedly to keep his voice in good operating order. When Jan let him use the sanitary facilities he fought to escape and in the end Jan had to wire him to the apparatus. It was very uncomfortable for both of them. Therefore it was a tremendous relief for Jan on the third day when he found a weak blip at the outermost edge of the low-power radar screen he was broadcasting. It was approaching on what very well might be a converging course. He killed the recorded broadcast, dropped the power down to the weakest signal possible. And crossed his fingers.

"This is Kulozik on IP-256. I have a blip on my radar. Do you read me?"

The radio frequency rustle of the stars was all he heard. He sent the signal again, stepped up the gain on his receiver—then heard it, weak but there.

"Do not alter course, IP-256. Do not attempt to start your engines for any reason. Do not attempt any more broadcasts. If you do we will fire. Open your outer port but do not attempt to leave your ship or we will fire. Out."

Definitely warlike, Jan thought. But he would probably be doing the same thing if he were in their place. He killed his radar and radio transmitter, but left the receiver on, since it was well shielded and produced no detectable emissions. After that all he could do was evacuate the airlock and open the outer hatch. And wait.

"My friends are coming," he said, with more assurance than he really felt. This had not the slightest effect on his captive who described Jan's tortured future for the thousandth time. It was not pleasurable to hear and having the Captain removed from his earshot would be one of the major pleasures that would come with the end of this trip.

Something clattered in the airlock.

A moment later the cycling light flashed on and Jan could hear the air pumps laboring. He swung about to face the lock, floating there, waiting expectantly as the green light blinked and the inner door opened.

"Raise the hands. Don't move."

Jan did as he was ordered and two armed men kicked in from the lock chamber. One of them ignored Jan and swung on by him toward the Captain who turned his abuse in the newcomer's direction. The other man, his face obscured by the gold sputtering of his helmet, waved his gun toward the airlock.

"Get into one of those suits," he said.

While Jan was putting it on the first man came down from the control room. "Just the two of them," he said.

"And maybe a bomb wired to go off. This still could be a trap."

"Well, you volunteered for this mission."

"Don't remind me. Stay with the tied-up one, don't release him, while I shuttle this one over."

Jan was only happy to obey. Once outside the lock he saw the spidery form of a medium-sized deep spacer in orbit to the rear of the scout. His captor, with a jet pack on his suit, grabbed Jan by the arm and towed him over to the open airlock of the waiting ship. There were two other gunmen watching him as he came out of the airlock and stripped off his suit. A large man in a black uniform was looking at him closely. His hair was blond, melding into gray, his jaw large and pugnacious and thrust in Jan's direction.

"I am Admiral Skougaard," he said. "Now tell me what all this is about."

Jan was unable to talk, speechless, overwhelmed by a sense of deepest despair.

Because the Admiral was wearing the same Space Forces uniform that he was.

Sixteen

Jan fell back, as though struck a physical blow. The guns followed him and the Admiral frowned at the movement—then nodded understandingly.

"The uniform, is that it?" Jan could only nod wordlessly in return. The iron face cracked into a grim smile. "Perhaps I wear it as you do—if you are what you say you are. Not all men of Earth are traitors to mankind. Some of us helped, or there would have been no rebellion from the stars. Now I am going to have you searched, Kulozik, and then you will tell me your entire story in the finest detail that you can."

The Admiral was no fool and made Jan repeat the details over and over, checking on names and dates and many precise points that he seemed familiar with. They were interrupted just once when a report came in that the IP-256 had been searched for bombs and other devices and was clear. A pilot would take her to join the fleet. Finally the Admiral raised his hand and cut Jan short.

"Niels," he ordered. "Get us some coffee." He turned back to Jan. "I am going to accept your story—for the time being. All of your details about the food expedition are correct, including some that I doubt the Earth forces could know. I am aware of the true facts because I was the one who gathered the ships and arranged all the organization of the expedition."

"Did any of them get through?"

"Over half. Not as many as we hoped, but enough to ward starvation off for a while longer. Now we come to the new and interesting part of your story and frankly, I have just no way to evaluate it. You know this Thurgood-Smythe well?"

"Far too well. My brother-in-law as I said. He is a monster of cunning."

"And treachery. We can be absolutely sure of that. He is either betraying his trust and aiding the rebellion. Or has laid a complex and treacherous trap to destroy us. So it must be treachery either way."

Jan sipped the strong, black coffee and nodded agreement. "I know. But what can we do? At least one part is certain, the Israeli participation."

"Which could simply be a more deadly part of the trap. To lure us in and destroy us. The Israelis could very well be helpless pawns, doomed to destruction to further his ends."

"They might very well be. It is the sort of thing that would appeal to him. I hadn't thought about that. But what of his plan to seize the Mojave base? That sounded reasonable. It certainly would affect the outcome of the war."

The Admiral laughed, then blew on his coffee to cool it. "Not only reasonable, but the only possibility of victory for either side. We know it and they know it. We could capture the Lunar bases, the satellites, even all of the Lagrange colonies, and Earth could survive. Her fleet would be as strong. And we would grow weaker with every passing moment. Mojave is the key. The other shuttle bases are merely landing strips. Whoever controls Mojave controls space operations—and wins this war."

"Then it's that vital?"

"It is."

"What do you plan to do?"

"Analyze it and sleep on it before I see you again. In any case there is nothing to be done yet, not until we are closer to Earth's orbit. I'm going to lock you in a cell for a while. Sorry."

"Don't be. After Captain Lastrup's company I'll enjoy the solitude. How is he?"

"Under sedation. He is in a bad way mentally and will need treatment."

"I'm sorry about that."

"Don't be. This is war. In the same situation he would undoubtedly have killed you."

An aide interrupted with a printout which he handed to the

Admiral, who read it slowly, then raised his eyes to Jan. And smiled as he extended his hand.

"Welcome aboard, Jan Kulozik. This is the confirmation that I was waiting for. One of our ships is in orbit around Halvmörk, unspaceworthy after the fighting. But its communication apparatus is operational and they are hooked into the Foscolo net. They have checked your story out with the people there. What you have told us is the truth. There is an additional message here that they confirmed all of the personal parts of your story with your wife. She sends her love."

Jan seized the Admiral's outstretched hand. "It's my pleasure to serve with you, sir. I've had no part in the rebellion up until now . . ."

"You have done more than most people. You are the one who saw to it that the corn was waiting when the ships arrived—it would have burned except for your leadership. Do you realize how many lives that food saved?"

"I know, I realize that it was important. But it was a passive action that's over and done with now. The reason that I was arrested and transported in the first place was because of my activities in the resistance. Now that the planets are free, and the last battle is about to begin, you must understand, I want to take a part in that."

"And so you shall. Just as long as you make yourself available at all times for our intelligence people. They'll want to pick your brain. Then we may need you as well for liaison with the Israelis once the fighting starts. Satisfactory?"

"Yes, of course. I'll do whatever is asked of me. By training I'm an electronic engineer and I used to specialize in microcircuitry design. But it has been mostly mechanical maintenance the last years."

"That is first class—and there is a very good chance that you are just the man we need. I want you to meet another technician, Vittorio Curtoni. He is in charge of our armament, and has designed most of our defenses, including what everyone refers to as the secret weapon. I understand there are still some teething troubles with it, so perhaps you could be of help."

"That would be ideal."

"Good. I'll arrange transport to the *Leonardo.*" The Admiral raised his hand and an aide came hurrying over.

One of the scouts vectored to the flagship while Jan suited up again, then transferred to it. He stayed in the open airlock so he would not waste any time pressurizing and depressurizing. Through the open hatch he could see the arc of deep spacers that spread out and away on both sides. One of the ships was coming close, growing larger and larger until they killed their momentum just a few meters away. Jan kicked out and drifted across the gap to the waiting and open airlock of the *Leonardo*.

A lean, black-haired man with a great brush of a moustache was waiting for him inside.

"Are you Kulozik, the one who is supposed to help me?" he asked, with more suspicion than enthusiasm in his voice.

"If you're Vittorio Curtoni, then I'm the one. Yes, I hope that I can help. I know I can if you can use the services of an experienced microelectronic engineer."

Curtoni's wariness vanished instantly. "Can I use you? Can a starving man use a grilled pig? Let me show you what we have been doing." He led Jan deep into the ship, talking rapidly and scarcely stopping for breath.

"Jury-rigged, all of it, invented, manufactured and tested all on the same day. Sometimes. Admiral Skougaard, of course, a great help. Would have taken years instead of months if he hadn't turned over all the Space Forces blueprints and specs to us. He had been collecting them for a very long time, both the successful weapons and the proposals that were never carried through. What do you know about space warfare?" He lifted one quizzical eyebrow as he turned to face Jan.

"I've been in a space battle, but that was personal contact and hand to hand fighting. About battles between opposing forces—about all I know is what I see in the films."

"Exactly! Films like this, I imagine."

They entered a workshop, but Curtoni led Jan away from the machines and instruments to an ordinary TV set with a row of chairs before it. Curtoni keyed in a code and turned the set on.

"Sit, enjoy," he said. "This is an archaic film from the dawn of history that I found buried in the memory files. It is about a war among the stars, there—see!"

Music exploded from the loudspeaker, and on the screen a mighty spacer flashed by. It had turrets and windows, gun emplacements and energy guns. Close behind was its pursuer, an even larger spaceship. Mighty rays and beams lashed out from the ships, lights flashed and there was the constant roar of engines,

the zapping and crashing of the rays. There was a quick cut to a
man in a turret, wheeling it about to fire his ray guns as the other
ship swooped close. Luckily the smaller ship darted aside in time
and fled for safety behind a nearby moon. Then the screen went
blank and the roars and music died away.

"What do you think about that?" Curtoni asked.

"Very little. Seemed like fun, though."

"*Merda!* Fun for infants in arms perhaps. But technically it is a
monstrosity. Not one fact—not a single one—is scientifically correct. There is no sound in space, ships do not stop or turn suddenly, human reflexes are worthless in spacecraft maneuvering or
warfare, ray guns do not work . . ."

"I'll give you all that. I suppose I never really thought about it
before. But don't dismiss the rays so quickly. I've worked with fusion cannon. They turn rock to lava in a few seconds."

"Of course!" Curtoni held his hands out in the air, about a
hundred centimeters apart. "When the rock is this far away.
What about a hundred meters away? Would it set fire to a piece
of paper? Or a thousand kilometers, which is practically touching
in space, when it would probably look like a light bulb if you
could see it at all. The propagation of light, the propagation of
any form of energy . . ."

"Of course, varies in proportion with the inverse square of the
distance. I wasn't thinking."

"Exactly! No one ever does until they are face to face with the
problem. Which is why I show everyone my little training film
first. It makes a point. Another point is that space war is so close
to impossible that it can be called highly improbable."

"But we're fighting one now, aren't we?"

Curtoni switched on the apparatus on one long bench and
shook his head no. "We are fighting a rebellion, with Earth ships
standing up to Earth ships. A real war, with ships from different
civilizations coming from distant stars. Bunkum, like that thing
we just saw. Even Earth's Space Force never planned for a war.
When hostilities began only a few of their ships had weapons. Installed but never used since the Commonwealth had absolute control of space and all of the spacers. They thought one or two
might be seized some time, so prepared their weapons just in case.
And all of the same simple design. And what would that be?"

"Missiles obviously, adapted from those already designed for
use in the atmosphere."

"Perfectly correct. And how long do you think it would take us to design, develop and test our own missiles?"

"Years. Even if you captured some and copied them, the manufacture of circuitry, control systems, jets . . . probably just about as long."

"Perfectly correct. It is a pleasure to speak with an intelligent man—that is of course someone who agrees with me. So we dropped the missile approach, though of course we have some on the Space Force ships that we took over. It was more important to develop defenses first which we did by copying and modifying the Earth detection systems. We see the missiles coming, then generate electronic fields to mislead their guidance systems. For offense we have taken a more simple line. Like this."

He picked up a small finned piece of metal from the bench and bounced it in his hand.

"That's a slug from a rocket pistol," Jan said.

"Perfectly true. And a better weapon in space than it ever can be on a planet. No gravity to drop it, no air to slow it . . ."

"Or guide it. The fins are useless."

"Again you are right, Jan. It had to be redesigned with the thrust ahead of the center of gravity. Very simple. Even simpler to mount a number of firing tubes on a turret and have the whole thing controlled by the navigation computer. Put a flock of these things into space in front of a spacer and you have a wreck. Speed equals mass and a few grams of metal will impact with tonnes of force. Goodbye enemy."

Jan turned the tiny rocket over and over in his fingers. "I do see one or two problems. Distance and speed, or rather they're both the same thing. You can't pack enough thrust into something this tiny."

"Of course. These are mostly for defense. For attack we have developed this."

He turned to the work bench and picked up a small metal ball, then pressed a button on the control board. Jan could hear a faint humming sound, and when Curtoni held the sphere close to a vertical metal ring secured to the bench it sprang from his hand and hung, suspended, in the center of the ring. There were other rings mounted close together down the length of the bench. When Curtoni pressed a second button there was a whistling sound and a flash and the sphere vanished. A loud crack echoed from the other end of the compartment as it crashed into the thick plastic sheet, hung there and dropped to the deck.

"Linear accelerator," Jan said. "Just like the ones on the Moon."

"Exactly the same. The large Lunar models take containers filled with ore and shoot them right out of the Moon's gravity, to the Lagrange satellite colonies for processing. As you see a magnetic field is created in the first electromagnet ring. It suspends the iron sphere. Then, when the series of electromagnets are activated, they act as a linear motor, moving the sphere along faster and faster until it shoots out of the far end." He turned and picked up a larger sphere that nestled comfortably in his hand.

"This seems to be the most practical size we have discovered by trial and error. It weighs a little under three kilograms, which is almost exactly six pounds in one of the more archaic systems of measurement. When I was researching this project I was helped a good deal by early ballistic texts that dealt with muzzle velocities and like terms. I was fascinated to find out that primitive sea battles were actually fought with solid shot of just this weight. History has many lessons for us."

"How far have you gone with the project?" Jan asked.

"Four deep spacers have been converted to cannon ships. This is one of them. Named after one of the earliest theoreticians of the science who made such incredible drawings of his weapons. Leonardo da Vinci. We have loaded these ships with hundreds of thousands of cannonballs which have been forged in space from satellite iron. Most easily too. The specified mass of molten iron is released in free fall, whereupon its surface tension forms it into a perfect sphere. The secret weapons run the length of the ships and project from each end. The entire ship is rotated to aim the cannon, with aiming and firing controlled by the navigation computer. It all works well except for one small fault."

"What's that?"

"Bugs in the control circuitry. The spheres must be launched within microseconds of each other to be effective. But we haven't been able to do this yet."

Jan threw the cannonball back onto the bench and smiled. "Let me see your documentation and your diagrams and I'll do my best to get rid of your bugs."

"Instantly! You will win this war for us yet!"

Seventeen

"The fruit is ripe for harvesting," the old man said. "The longer we leave it the more we will lose."

"There are a lot more important things you can lose," his daughter said. "Like your head, maybe. Come on Tata, the others are all waiting."

The old man sighed with resignation and followed her out to the kibbutz truck. He was the last one to arrive and the others pushed over to make room for him on the crowded wooden benches. The firebox had been loaded with resinous pine logs an hour earlier so there was a good head of steam. As soon as he had the signal that they were all aboard, the driver opened the throttle and they moved out. Past the buildings where the lights still burned warmly and down the winding lane through the orchards and out onto the main road. They drove in darkness, but the smooth surface was easy to see in the dim light from the starfilled sky.

They crossed the Syrian border a little after midnight, the transponder in the truck answering the request from the detection circuits with its identification code; the computer in Tel Aviv made a note of its departure. Just before they reached El Quneitra the truck turned in to a deep wadi that wound back from the road. The darkness was intense between its high walls and the driver felt his way along, stopping suddenly when a light blinked ahead. There were camels waiting here and murmured guttural greetings as the passengers disembarked. The driver waited in the cab as they went by, some of them reaching up to pat his arm, others murmuring a few words. When they had all vanished in the darkness he reversed out and drove the truck back to the empty buildings of the kibbutz, reaching there just before dawn. He was the volunteer who was staying on.

"Like a city of the dead when I came through on the way here," the painter said. "A very frightening proposition to one of any imagination at all. Streets empty of children, only a few vehicles moving, one or two other pedestrians. It was dusk and the lights were coming on in the houses which at first I found very cheering. That is until I looked into the windows of one as I passed and saw that it was empty. It was the computers doing it, and I felt even more uncomfortable. Hold that corner of the stencil tight, if it's not asking too much, Heimyonkel." He swung the spray gun back and forth with practiced skill. "When do you go?"

"Tonight. The family is already out."

"Kiss your wife for me and tell her to think of a lonely bachelor in her dreams, alone and preparing for destiny among the shadowy hangars of Lod Airport."

"You volunteered."

"So I volunteered. That doesn't mean I have to be laughing with joy does it? All right, take it down."

The painter stepped back and admired his work. On both swelling sides, and the wings, of the Anan-13 heavy transport the six-pointed star of Israel had been painted over. In its place was a starkly black cross.

"Symbolic, and not too nice," the painter said. "If you read history, which you don't, because you're a *yould*, you would recognize that cross. Do you?"

Heimyonkel shrugged and poured silver paint carefully into the spray gun.

"It's the cross of Germany, that's what it is, obliterating the Mogen David of Israel. Which is not nice and also, I wonder what the hell it is supposed to mean. Does the government know what it's doing? I ask you but you don't know and, P.S., I don't know either."

Large sheets of paper were fastened into place with tape to cover the new insignia. After this had been painted silver there was nothing visible at a distance to indicate that the work had been done.

Amri Ben-Haim was very worried. He sat slumped in his favorite chair, staring at nothing, while the glass of lemon tea grew cold before him. Only when the sound of an approaching copter drew his attention did he sit up alertly and look towards the door. He sipped some of the tea and wrinkled his lips with displeasure. As he put it down Dvora came through the door with a package.

"Another one, and delivered by a Security policeman as well. Made my flesh crawl. He just smiled when he handed it over and wouldn't say a word."

"Reflex sadism," Ben-Haim said, taking the thick envelope from her. "He can have no idea of its contents. Those kind of people just enjoy making others suffer." He shook out the familiar sealed metal box and tapped out the combination. When it snapped open he took the disc it contained and put it into the computer. Thurgood-Smythe's unsmiling features appeared on the screen.

"This is our final communication, Ben-Haim," he said. "By now your troops and planes will be ready to begin the operation as instructed. The exact date will be given to you later this month, and you have your departure and flight plan. You will be flying in darkness all the way, so that will take care of visual and satellite observation. You have your instructions about the radar nets. Never forget that this is a coordinated attack and exact timing is the only way to prevent disaster."

Thurgood-Smythe glanced down out of sight of the camera and smiled very slightly.

"I have a number of reports here that inform me that you seem to be moving a great deal of your population out of the country at night. Very wise. There is always the chance of a nuke or two, even if things go perfectly. Out of spite you might say. Or perhaps it is that you don't trust me? Nor should you have reason to. Nevertheless you are taking the correct course of action and victory is its own reward.

"I hope to be at Spaceconcent in Mojave when you arrive. Do arrange with your troops not to have me shot, if you don't mind. Goodbye then, Amri Ben-Haim. Pray for success in our ventures."

The image vanished. Ben-Haim turned away from the screen shaking his head. "Don't shoot him! I'll flay him alive if anything goes wrong with this plan!"

Fryer panted heavily as he dragged his bad leg up the stairs, climbing a single step at a time. He carried the gun over his shoulder in order to leave one hand free to clutch onto the bannister. It was a hot, close day, and sweat cut runnels through the dust on his face. The boy struggled along behind him with the heavy case of grenades.

"In here," Fryer said, opening the door carefully and looking in first to be sure that the curtains were still closed. "All in order, my lad. Put them there under the window and go on about your business. I'll give you ten minutes to get clear. Go slow and don't get stopped at any checkpoints. If you do it will get into the London computer that you were in this area, and that will be the end of you."

"Can't I stay, Fryer? I could help, help you get away too with that bum leg."

"Don't worry, lad, they won't get the old Fryer. They got me once, right and proper, give me this leg and a tour of the camps in the Highlands. Once was more than enough of that, let me tell you. I'm not going back. But you're getting out, now, and that's an order."

Fryer sat down on the case with a wheeze of relief and listened to the footsteps retreating back down the stairs. Good. One less thing to worry about. He dug out a joint, thin and black and almost pure hash. A few good lungfuls had him feeling better so that he didn't even notice the pain in the leg. He smoked slowly and carefully, and waited until the roach was burning his lip before he spat it out, grinding it under his heel into the plank floor. Then he drew the curtains aside and carefully lifted open the window. A light breeze blew in from Marylebone, carrying with it the sound of heavy traffic. A military convoy was passing and he drew back against the wall until it had gone by. When the sound had dwindled and vanished he pulled open the lid of the case. Taking out one of the grenades he bounced the chunky cylinder in his palm. Made by hand from scrap metal, shaped and filed and loaded with care. When he had tested the gun out in the wasteland only one in twenty had misfired. And they had improved the things since then, he had been told. He hoped so. Holding the gun with the base down he let the grenade slide down the tubular barrel. It hit the bottom of the barrel with a solid chunk. Good. Fryer leaned forward and looked across the road at the gray cliff of Security Central.

Not a window broke the grim facade. The headquarters of Security in Britain, and now possibly the whole world. A prime target. If the calculations were correct the launching charge should be just enough to put the thing onto the roof of the first setback on the front of the building. Only one way to find out. Fryer put the gun to his shoulder, aimed carefully and squeezed the trigger.

The gun cracked and the butt smacked him hard in the shoulder. He saw the black speck arc up and over the edge. Perfect. Another grenade dropped down the barrel and when he fired this time he saw white smoke beginning to billow up from the roof of the setback.

"Well done, me old son," he said cheerfully, then put round after round as close to the same place as he could. The thermite in the grenades would burn through anything, that's what the boffin had said. He was absolutely correct.

Alarms were going now and armed men were beginning to appear in the street below. Fryer drew back from the window so they couldn't see him, then lay prone on the floor and continued to fire from that position.

The next time he pulled the trigger there was only an angry hiss from the gun.

"Bloody hell!" he muttered savagely as he rolled over and inverted the gun to bang the muzzle on the floor. The misfired grenade slid out and dropped free, smoking and sputtering. He clutched at it, grabbed it up cursing at his burnt hand, then threw it through the window. There was an explosion just below followed by screams of pain.

Serve the bastards right, he thought, getting too close. He scrambled to the door, ignoring the pain in his hand, and fired the next one down the stairwell. There were more shouts and a spray of bullets that passed over his head. That would keep them busy for a bit.

There were only two grenades left when they broke the door down. He fired one of them at the attacking men and was reaching for the very last grenade when the bullets tore through him. He died quickly, lying on his back under the window, looking up at the clouds of smoke blowing by outside.

Eighteen

Admiral Comrade Kapustin felt very secure, very secure indeed. He whistled lightly through his teeth while he pulled his high leather boots on, then stood and smoothed down his tunic before the mirror, pulling at it so it bloused out nicely above the wide leather belt. The rows of medals and decorations clinked gently when he strode to the door and threw it open. There was a clatter and a stamp as the marine guard outside drew himself up to attention. The Admiral touched his fingertips idly to the visor of his cap to return the salute as he strode by. The great day was here at last! His heels slammed into the deckplates even more heavily than usual so that his spurs jingled lightly. If anyone saw anything incongruous in boots and spurs in a spaceship, 200,000 miles from the nearest horse, they made no comment. The fate of anyone who dared to even smile in the direction of Admiral Comrade Kapustin was too awful to even consider.

When he entered the War Room the Admiral's aide, Onyegin, was ready as always. Clicking his heels and bowing slightly as he held out the silver tray. The Admiral downed the little glass of frigid vodka in a single gulp, then took one of the papirossi cigarettes; the aide produced a burning wooden taper to light it.

"Today is the day, Onyegin," the Admiral said, expelling a cloud of aromatic smoke. "The first space battle in history will be taking place soon, and I shall be the first officer to ever win one. A place in the history books. Any change in their course?"

"None, Comrade Admiral. You can see for yourself."

He snapped orders at the Tank operator who activated the

hologram field to show the course of the approaching enemy fleet. The Admiral stamped over to stand before the glowing display. It occupied a space of almost thirty cubic meters, taking up the entire center of the War Room. The display was of course three dimensional and could be viewed from any side. A group of glowing symbols sprang into view in the Tank, terminating in a dotted white line that ran up and out of sight.

"Their course so far," Onyegin said, "and the projection into the future." A second broken line of light, this time red, extended down from the enemy fleet to end at floor level.

"Good," the Admiral grunted. "Now where will this take them?"

The small blue sphere of the Earth snapped into existence, surrounded by her captive satellites and orbiting Moon. The line of the course passed them all by.

"That is the projection as of this moment, not taking into consideration any future changes," Onyegin said. "However there are still course alterations possible. Like this."

The red line fanned out into a number of arcs, each one of them terminating at one of the objects in space. The Admiral grunted again.

"Earth, the Moon, power satellites, colonies, anything. Well that's why we are here, Onyegin, learn that lesson. We defend Earth. Those criminals must pass us to work their mischief, and that will not be an easy thing to do. And my old friend Skougaard is leading them. What a pleasure! I shall personally execute the traitor when he is captured. Vodka!"

He downed another glassful, then seated himself in his command chair where he had a perfect view of the Tank, the pickup microphone beside his head swiveling automatically to follow his every move.

"The fighting so far has been sordid, just filthy stabs in the back. Bombs and mines and treachery. They have not only been traitors, but cowards as well who have fled our wrath, then sent us packing with missiles from planetary bases. That is all over now. We have had enough time to lick our wounds, to organize and regroup. Now we are on the defensive and they must come out and meet us. What a shock they will get when they do that. Let me see the latest photographs."

The astronomers on the Earth-orbiting 13-meter optical telescope had protested when ordered to photograph the approaching fleet. Their enormous metal reflecting mirror was designed for completely different purposes, they said. Shielded from the sun, with no atmosphere to dim its vision, it could penetrate the mysteries of the incredibly distant galaxies, examine closely the separate star systems thousands of light years beyond our own. Important research was in progress; this was no military toy to spy out invaders. Their attitude had changed abruptly when a score of Security men had arrived on the next shuttle from Earth. Ways were found to look at the attacking fleet.

The rebel spacers filled the Tank now. Fuzzy and gray, but still distinct, stretched out in a long arc.

"The flagship, the *Dannebrog*," Admiral Kapustin ordered.

The ship in the center of the attacking line swelled up until it was a meter across, fuzzy and unclear, just its outline distinct enough to see.

"Is this the best you can do?" The Admiral was displeased.

"We have been doing some computer enhancing," Onyegin said. He did not add that most of the enhancing had been done by letting the computer see a photograph of the flagship. The three dimensional image blurred, changed and cleared. An apparently solid image now floated there.

"Better," the Admiral condescended. He walked over and stabbed his finger into it. "I have you Skougaard, you and your precious *Dannebrog*. You shall not escape. Now, let me have a display of our converging courses."

The image changed again—with the symbols of the enemy fleet at one side of the Tank, the Earth forces on the other. First a broken line sprang across the Tank from the invaders, then one from the defenders. Where the two lines intersected sets of numbers appeared, one green, one yellow. The last digits flickering and changing constantly. Green represented the distance in kilometers to the intersection from their present position, yellow the time to get there at their present speed. The Admiral studied the figures closely. Still too far.

"Show me ten and ninety."

The computer made the complex calculation in microseconds and two arcs of light cut across their future course, less than a quarter of the way to the enemy fleet. The arc closest to the fleet was the ninety, a range at which ninety percent of their missiles could be expected to strike the enemy—if no evasive or screening action was taken. The ten was further out and represented ten percent of the missiles. There were hours to go before even this impractical range would be closed. Space warfare, like ancient naval warfare, consisted of long journeys punctuated by brief encounters. The Admiral sucked happily on his cigarette and waited. He had always been a man of infinite patience.

Skougaard's flagship, the *Dannebrog*, did not have an overly sophisticated War Room like its opposite number, the *Stalin*. Skougaard liked it that way. All of the information he needed was visible on the screens, and if he wanted a larger image a projection apparatus threw a picture that could cover the entire wall. It was all solid state, with multiple parallel circuitry, so there was very little that could go wrong. Any force strong enough to incapacitate the circuits would undoubtedly destroy the ship as well. The Admiral always felt that a complex hologram display, with its intricate circuitry, was just wasted effort and unnecessary complication. Since the machines did all of the work they only needed to show him what was happening in the simplest manner, then obey his instructions the instant they were given. He looked at the displays of the converging fleets and rubbed his large jaw in thought. He finally turned to Jan who waited quietly at his side.

"Then my heavy weapons are in perfect working order, ready for operation at any time. Good. I have a feeling of some reassurance now."

"The problem was not too complex a one," Jan said. "If the truth be known I applied some of the work I had done on automated production lines where we have had to speed up repetitive work. It is a matter of thinking mechanical and not electronic. Feedback cycles are fine in circuitry because the various operations happen so fast that they appear instantaneous in real time. But with mechanics you are moving physical objects that have both weight and mass. You can't stop and start them as easily, and when you do it takes measurable amounts of time. So I rewrote the cannonball loading program in units, so that each one of the cannonballs was constantly in motion and controlled by a file in the program all on its own. Therefore if there should be a mishap or a slowdown, that particular cannonball is shunted aside and the next one takes its place. There will be no complete shutdown and restart as you had in the past. It also means that the cannonballs can be fired at much shorter intervals, which will allow the interval between firings to be exactly regulated."

The Admiral nodded appreciatively. "Wonderful. And since time means distance in an orbit we can space them out exactly. How close together can they be fired?"

"The best we can do is one about every three meters."

"Your best is incredible. That means I can fire across the line of approach of a ship or a fleet and they will run into a solid wall of those things."

"Ideally. This will simplify the range function, leaving only aim to worry about."

"I have some surprises in store for my old friend, Kapustin," the Admiral said, turning back to the screens. "I know him very well, his tactics and his armaments—and his stupidity. While he has no idea what I am going to hit him with. This is going to be an interesting encounter. I think you will find it something worth watching."

"I don't imagine that I'll have much time to be a spectator. I thought I would be with the gunners."

"No. You will be more valuable here with me. If Thurgood-Smythe contacts us, or if there is any situation involving his presence, I want you here to evaluate it instantly. He is the only unknown factor in my calculations. Everything else has been allowed for. The computations made, the program written."

As though to drive home the point the numbers on the course screen began to flash and a horn sounded. "Course change," the computer announced aloud at the same time. The vibrations of the engines could be felt through the soles of their feet.

"Now we will see how fast Kapustin's computer is," Skougaard said. "Also, how fast he is himself. A machine can only supply information. He will have to make up his mind what to do with it."

"What's happening?" Jan asked.

"I am splitting my forces. For two very important reasons. This ship, and the *Sverige* over there, are the only ones that have sophisticated anti-missile missiles—for the simple reason that they are both deserters from the Earth Space Forces. Old Lundwall, who commands the *Sverige*, should have retired a decade ago, but he is still the best there is. He and I worked out this operation together. We will each head a squadron of ships lined up in a file behind us. There is a good reason as well for this. While I know that our people have worked very hard on electronic systems of missile avoidance, I would rather rely in the beginning on known technology. I am sure that these systems will work well and there will be plenty of opportunity to use them later on. But if I have a choice, there is something very satisfactory in having a screen of seeker missiles out in front to soak theirs up before they can reach our ships."

Jan watched the screens that displayed the positions of the various ships. They were slowly moving in relation to each other, in a complex pattern controlled by the computers. The flagship had drawn ahead, while half of the ships were moving into station behind it. The other half were doing the same with the *Sverige*—while at the same time both squadrons were separating as their courses diverged.

"That will give Comrade Kapustin something to think about," Skougaard said. "All of our ships are falling into line behind these two leading battleships. And that line will always be pointing at the enemy fleet. Which means that, as far as they are concerned, all of the ships except two will have disappeared. It's a good thing that the comrade does not read history. Have you ever heard of Admiral Nelson, Jan?"

"I have—if he's the chap who stands on top of the column in Trafalgar Square."

"The very one."

"Some early English hero, from the middle ages or something. Fought the Chinese?"

"Not quite. Though he would have probably enjoyed it. He must have done battle with every other navy. His greatest victory, a victory that killed him, was at the Battle of Trafalgar where he broke through the French line of ships just as I plan to do now. He had different reasons for doing so, though one result will be the same. The lead ship will bear the brunt of the fighting until the line is breached . . ."

"Missiles launched," the computer said.

"Aren't we out of range yet?" Jan asked.

"Very much so. But these are the anti-missile missiles. Their engines fire just a short blast then cut out. That means they form a protective umbrella out in front of us, to intercept the other missiles when they come. We also get some early warning that way."

A short time later a sphere of soundless fire blossomed and grew in space far ahead of them. Distant as it was it was still bright, and the visual screens went dark as they overloaded and the filters cut in.

"How very unusual," Skougaard said. "Kapustin is using atomic missiles in his first attack. A good idea, I suppose, if the tactic works. Very wasteful if it doesn't because I know just how many he carries."

Admiral Skougaard looked at the time, then at the screen that displayed the two squadrons now lined up in straight lines astern of the leading ships.

"An historical moment," he said. "The beginning of the first battle of the first war in space. May it end in a victory for our forces. The entire future rests upon its outcome."

Nineteen

"He's up to something," Kapustin said, concern but not worry in his voice. His trap was prepared. All that Skougaard could do was fall into it. In the Tank the ships of the enemy fleet were coming together, blinking out of sight one by one, until apparently only two remained. While the holograph presented a three dimensional image, all it had now was a two dimensional picture to work with.

"They are going into space drive!" Kapustin shouted. "Trying to escape me!"

"That cannot happen, Admiral Comrade Kapustin," Onyegin said, formulating his words carefully before he spoke. The hardest part of his job was giving the Admiral information in such a way that he could imagine he had thought of it himself. "You were the one who first explained to me that because of the interlocking gravity fields the Foscolo space drive could not be used this close to a planet. Something far simpler is happening. They are forming two lines astern . . ."

"Obviously. Any fool can tell that. Do not waste my time by explaining the obvious. But have you noticed that their courses have changed as well? Keep your eyes open, Onyegin, and you will learn one or two things."

It was hard not to be aware of the number of changes taking place as the flashing arrows rotated and changed positions, the displayed numbers changing as well. While this was happening the Tank operators took time to program in two lines of ships in the Tank. It meant nothing but would please the Admiral. Which was always their first order of priority.

"I want some predictions where these new courses are taking them. And fire some missiles, atomic ones. They'll be wetting their drawers when they arrive."

"A limited supply . . . rather early don't you think . . . perhaps other missiles . . ."

"Shut up and do as ordered."

The words were quiet and toneless and Onyegin went cold, knowing he had overstepped himself. "Of course, instantly, a logically perfect idea!"

"And give me some predictions where these new orbits are heading."

Curving cones of light appeared in the Tank, emanating from the two approaching squadrons. At first the cones engulfed great areas of space, including the entire Earth and a number of satellites. As further information came in from the radar sweeps the cones narrowed, shrinking to two lines again once the orbit changes had been made.

"Two separate strikes," Kapustin said, glancing back and forth from one to the other. "The first aiming at our Lunar bases. Fine. The missile batteries there will destroy them as they come close. And the other, where is it going?"

"Apparently towards geostationary orbit. There are any number of satellites out there. It could be . . ."

"It could be anything. And it doesn't matter. They'll be dead and dispersed into thin atomic gas long before they get there. We'll divide our forces as well. I want both squadrons to intercept, cut directly across the course of those ships. They will have to get through us to attack Earth and that will be no easy thing."

It was a battle of invisible forces, electrons in computers—light waves and radio waves in space. Neither of the opposing fleets could see each other visibly yet; this might never happen even after battle was joined. They were still thousands of miles from each other. Though closing rapidly, their tiny gleaming images would be invisible against the burning stars, even to a watcher in space. Only the explosion of the atomic missile could have been seen. These sailors of the starways were the true descendents of the first seagoing navies where large guns reached out over the horizon to destroy an enemy that was completely out of sight.

Closer the opposing columns swept, and still closer, until on as-

tronomical terms they had merged into a single object. They still
could not see each other. Only their optical telescopes, fitted with
electronic magnification, could produce visible images. Admiral
Kapustin looked at the enlarged outline of the *Dannebrog* that
now filled the screen; he nodded grimly.

"The second squadron will do as I do, fire when I do. There
will be no independent command. Nor will any other ships attempt to approach the *Dannebrog* after she is gutted. She's my
prey. Fire a scattered missile pattern. Shake them up."

Aboard the *Dannebrog* Admiral Skougaard smiled and slapped
his knee.

"Look at that fool," he told Jan, pointing to one of the displays.
"Spending his irreplaceable missiles like pocket money." The computer kept a running tally of all enemy missiles destroyed or
averted. "Basically he is just a stupid man with no idea of tactics.
I imagine he thinks that he can beat us by the use of brute force.
Which could be possible if he waited until we closed, then our defenses could be overwhelmed and beaten down by sheer numbers
of missiles. However we have a few surprises in store, so that tactic will not work either."

"Main cannon firing has commenced," the computer said.

Though the central axis of the line of ships was pointed at the
opposing squadron, it was angled toward the invisible track in
space down which the enemy was moving. The two big gun ships
were pointing at that track—and they now began firing. Two continuous streams of iron spheres hurtled outward toward the point
in space where the enemy would soon be. Stern jets flared on the
gun ships to keep them in position, to counteract the backward
thrust of the cannonballs. The speeding streams of metal looked
like pencils of light on the radar screen, moving so fast that they
were soon out of sight. Only the blips of the defensive missiles
remained, resembling a second and larger fleet moving ahead of
them. Their radar reflectors, gauss fields and heat sources were designed to lead attacking missiles astray.

On board the *Stalin*, Kapustin was not as pleased as he should
be.

"Are there technical errors? This cannot be true," he said, pointing to the set of numbers that displeased him.

"There are always errors, sir," Onyegin said. "But they would
be only a small percentage of the final figure."

"Yet this stupid machine keeps telling me that there have been no hits on the enemy fleet. None at all. Yet with my own eyes I can see the explosions."

"Yes, Admiral. But those are decoys to draw our fire. After each contact our monitoring missiles radar-sweep the area of the explosion for debris. They can tell by the mass of debris whether a ship was destroyed or another missile. But you must remember that with each explosion one of his decoys is destroyed. Since we have far more missiles than they have, we will win in the end."

Kapustin was slightly mollified, but not completely pleased. "And where are his missiles? Isn't the coward going to fire back?"

"Since he has a much smaller quantity, I imagine he will wait until the range has closed to exact the most value from them. But our defense screen is out there in front of us and will not be penetrated."

The timing of the remark was most unfortunate. A moment after the words had left Onyegin's lips the alarms sounded. OBJECTS ON COLLISION COURSE was spelled out in letters of fire and screamed aloud at the same time. Almost instantaneously after this damage reports began coming in from ship after ship. The Admiral stared, horrified, at the vision screen that showed debris spraying from his spaceships; one of them exploded in a gout of flame as he watched.

"What is it? What is happening?" he shouted.

"Meteorite field . . ." Onyegin said, though he knew that could not be possible.

The Admiral seemed paralyzed by the disaster, sitting gape-jawed in his chair. Onyegin called for a display of what had caused the damage. Although the entire encounter had been over with in less than a second, the computer had recorded the action and now replayed it at slow speed. The first sign of approaching trouble was a wall or a bar that swept in from space across their track. It was at least two kilometers long and speeding with great precision in a collision course. Then the impact. It had to be enemy action. When a section was enlarged he could see that the apparently solid bar was made up of discrete units of matter. Gaps appeared in it as defensive missiles exploded, but it made little difference to the overall strength. It struck.

"It appears that there is a secret weapon," Onyegin said.

"What is it?"

A *secret*, Onyegin was tempted to say, but not tempted very much since he greatly valued his life. "Inert material of some kind that has been launched into orbit to meet us. What kind of material it is and how it is projected to reach us is still unknown."

"Will there be more?"

"I would presume so, though of course we cannot know. They might have expended their effort in their single try . . ."

"More defense missiles. Launch them instantly!"

"They seemed to have no effect at all the first time, Admiral. If we expend them now we will not have them later when we need . . ."

He fell, struck to the floor by Kapustin's openhanded blow. "Are you disobeying orders? Are you interfering with my command of this fleet?"

"Never! I apologize . . . just advice . . . never happen again." Onyegin pulled himself to his feet; a runnel of blood twisted across his face. "Put out an umbrella of defense missiles . . ."

"All of them! This weapon must be stopped."

Even as the command was uttered the missiles were launched. Onyegin wiped his sleeve across his mouth, smearing his uniform jacket with blood, unaware of it. What else could they do? There must be some action they could take. The fool of an Admiral was incompetent, the officers and men too much in fear of him to make any suggestions that might draw his attention to them.

"Might I suggest evasive action as well, Admiral. It could be more effective than the missile defenses. Whatever the rebels' weapon is, it is unpowered, there were no radiations of any kind detected before it hit. Therefore it must be launched into its trajectory. If we altered speed there is a good chance the weapon would miss."

"What—slow down? Do you take me for a coward?"

"No, sir. Of course not. Speeding up would have the same effect. Hurrying forward into battle."

"Perhaps. Issue the order in any case. It can do no harm."

"Cease firing with the big cannons," Admiral Skougaard ordered. They've increased their speed so the last bombardment will miss, go behind them. But we made them suffer. Look at that screen. We seem to have hit a good quarter of them. The next barrage will finish them off. Are we in range of the small guns yet?"

"Coming up in thirty-two seconds, sir," the ranging and aiming operator said.

"Commence firing then. I want a wall of iron out there for them to run into."

The spiderweb turrets were in constant, minute and precise motion, pointing their tubular guns at the selected point in space. They were built of a simple array of girders upon which were mounted the launching tubes of the rocket guns. Flexible plastic tubes ran from the breech of each gun and back to the ship, carrying forward a continuous supply of the small steel rockets. It was a crude, fast but deadly efficient weapon.

When the measured point in space was reached, the firing circuits were actuated. Electronic ignition set off the rocket shell lodged in every breech. When these had hurtled away the next shells were moved into position, then the next. Since there was no need to lock and unlock the open breech, no shell casings to eject, the rate of fire was incredible, limited only by the mechanical speed of the loading magazine. In each gun an average of 60 rockets were pushed forward and fired every second, 480 from every turret. A total of 197 turrets had been built and installed in a feverish rush before the fleet had left, the final connections on many of them actually being completed en route. The effort had been worth it.

Every second 94,560 rocket slugs flamed out from the guns. Two and one third tonnes of steel. When the firing stopped at the end of one minute, over 141 tonnes of flying metal had been launched towards the Earth fleet. Corrections had been constantly made in the aim during the firing, including a computation that would allow for a certain amount of evasion by the enemy if they should fire their jets.

Outward, further and further the invisible mass sped, a sparkling fog on the radar screens that quickly vanished. The same computer that had aimed the missiles now counted down towards their moment of arrival. First the minutes, then the seconds, hurrying steadily backward towards zero. Now!

"My God . . ." Jan gasped as the optical screen lit up with the multiple explosions. All of the defensive missiles had been activated at approximately the same moment by the mass of steel. Space was on fire with atomic and chemical blasts, clouds of flame that expanded and merged as though to screen the destruction and tragedy that was happening behind it.

As the attackers sped past the still growing cloud they could see the enemy fleet. Admiral Skougaard had his guns aimed and missiles ready. After one glance he ordered them to stand down. He turned in silence from the screen; he had known most of the men who had died; they had been his comrades.

Where once a fleet of space ships had been there now existed only torn and jumbled metal debris. Mixed in with it was the exploded flesh of Admiral Kapustin along with that of every man who had sailed with him. The defensive fleet had ceased to exist, both squadrons destroyed in the same manner, within seconds of each other.

The two clouds of wreckage and fragments were quickly left behind.

Ahead lay Earth.

Twenty

"I should be getting to my plane now," Dvora said. "All of the others are aboard."

She had grown tired of sitting in the car and had climbed out to lean against its side. The night was warm, the stars flickering brilliantly in the rising air currents. Although the airport was blacked out, the dark silhouettes of the big transports were visible where they were lined up along the runway. Her ammunition bag, machine pistol and helmet were at her side. Amri Ben-Haim stood next to her, the bowl of his pipe a glowing spark in the darkness.

"There is no rush, Dvora," he said. "There are thirty minutes at least to takeoff. Your soldiers are grown men, no need to hold their hands."

"Grown men!" she sniffed expressively. "Farmers and university professors. How well will they behave when there are real bullets coming their way?"

"Very well, I am sure. Their training has been the best. Like yours. You just have had some field experiences that they have not. Rely on them . . ."

"Message coming through," the driver said as his radio beeped for attention.

"Accept with my code identification," Ben-Haim said.

There was a murmured interchange. The driver leaned out the window. "A two word message. *Beth doar.*"

"Post office!" Ben-Haim said. "They've done it. Taken out the Khartoum station. Tell Blonstein that the situation, to use his favorite expression, is go. Then get to your plane. You shouldn't be hanging around out here."

Dvora had her helmet on, her microphone activated, the message passed. "Yes . . . yes, General. I'll do that." She turned to Ben-Haim. "A communication for you from General Blonstein. He says to keep an eye on Israel for him. He'd like to find it here when he gets back."

"So would I. When you talk to him next say I told you that was up to him, not me. I'll be sitting on my porch waiting for results. That is just as long as I have a porch to sit on." Dvora gave him a quick kiss on the cheek and was gone, the sound of her running feet vanishing in the darkness towards the planes.

Ben-Haim watched quietly as, one by one, the engines of the massive planes burst into rumbling life. Exhausts spat tongues of flame that quickly died away as their throttles were adjusted. The first craft was already moving, picking up speed, faster and faster until it hurled itself into the air. The others were just seconds behind. Both runways were in use; a steady flow of rushing dark shapes that suddenly ended. The thunder of their engines diminished, died, and silence returned. Ben-Haim's pipe was dead; he tapped it against his heel to knock out the ashes. He felt neither sorrow nor elation, just a great weariness after the days of preparation and tension. It was done, the die cast, no changes were possible now. He turned to the car.

"All right. We can go home now."

Out of sight in the sky above, the flight of planes circled out over the ocean as they gained height; the airspace over Israel was too small for such a maneuver. There was no concern about radar detection here, but there were settlements and towns in the adjoining countries where people might hear and wonder what all the planes were doing up there in the night sky. When they crossed Israel again they were over six miles high, their engines inaudible on the ground below. In a formation of two stepped vees they turned southeast, flying down the length of the Red Sea.

Grigor looked out of the window of the plane and made tsk-tsk sounds with his tongue.

"Dvora," he said, "what I see is not strictly kosher."

"A drove of pigs?"

"Not even with my eyesight from this altitude." Grigor was a mathematician, very absentminded, possibly the worst soldier in Dvora's squad. But he was a sharpshooter who never missed his target no matter what the pressure; an asset to be relied upon. "It's where we are going. We're supposed to be attacking Space-concent in the western United States—I know, don't get excited. A big secret with the name removed from all the maps. A child could tell. Anyway, the North Star was very clear back there when we turned. So now we are going south so I wondered, something not quite kosher. Or these planes maybe have big fuel tanks to get to America by flying over the South Pole?"

"We are not taking the most direct route."

"You can say that again, Dvorkila," Vasil, the heavy weapons gunner, said.

They were leaning towards her from the seats in front and in back, listening.

"No secrets now," another soldier said. "Who can we talk to about it?"

"I can tell you about this part of our course," she said. "But no more until after we refuel. We are going south now, staying over the sea, but we'll be turning west very soon over the Nubian desert. There is—or rather there was—a radar station in Khartoum—but that has been taken care of. It was the only one we had to worry about since there is not another one all the way across Africa, not until we get to Morocco . . ." Her voice died away.

"And then?" Grigor urged. "Something maybe to do with the big black cross I found on the side of this plane when I helped to tear the paper off it earlier tonight. Sailing under false colors like pirates?"

"It's top secret . . ."

"Dvora, please!"

"You're right, of course. It can't do any harm now. We have, what you might call, agents placed high up in the UN government." Or maybe they have us, she thought to herself. No doubts now. Even if this was a trap they had to go ahead with it, right to the bloody end. "So we know that German troops are being sent to help hold the space center in Mojave. We have their identification and their markings on our planes. We intend to take their place."

"Not so easily done," Grigor said. "I assume that there are other things that you are not telling us . . ."

"Yes. But I can add just one thing more. We are flying just one hour ahead of the German planes. That's why the delay on the takeoff. Exact timing is very important, since once we're airborne we're out of touch with the ground. From now on everything happens by schedule. So—take some rest while you can."

The dark map of Africa moved past slowly and steadily beneath them. Most of the men slept in the blacked-out planes, only the pilots were alertly awake and watching their instruments, monitoring the operation of the automatic pilots. General Blonstein, a qualified flyer himself, was in the pilot's seat of the lead plane. From this height he could make out clearly the darkness of the Atlantic Ocean, coming into view beyond the pale deserts of Morocco. The receiver rustled.

"*Rabat tower to Air Force flight four seven five. Do you read me?*"

"Air Force flight four seven five. I read you, Rabat tower."

The radio contact was just a formality. The ground station had already activated the transponder in every craft, completely automatically, which had returned all the recorded data including identification, route and destination.

"*We have you cleared for the Azores, Air Force flight.*" There was the sound of mumbled voices for a moment. "*We have a flag on your flight plan that you seem to be running fifty-nine, that is five niner, minutes ahead of your filed flight plan.*"

"Strong tail winds," Blonstein said calmly.

"*Understood, Air Force flight. Out.*"

There were other ears listening in on the ground control frequency. A burnoosed man concealed from sight in a grove of trees close to the coast highway. Paralleling the highway were the columns of a high tension electricity line. The man had been following the conversation closely, frowning as he concentrated on making out the words through the crackle of static on his cheap radio. He waited a few moments to be absolutely sure that the transmission was over. Nothing else followed. He nodded and bent down to press the button on the box at his feet.

A bright white flame lit up the night; a few seconds later the sound of the explosion reached him. One of the pylons in the 20,000 volt line leaned over, faster and faster, until it struck the ground. There was a colorful display of large sparks that went out quickly.

So did half the lights in Rabat. It was not by accident that the radio beacon station was included in this circuit as well.

The duty staff at Cruz del Luz airport on the island of Santa Maria were all soundly asleep. Very few planes had been stopping recently for refueling in the Azores, so the night shift had quickly become used to staying awake during the daytime hours. Admittedly someone had set the alarm bleeper, but that wasn't really needed. The radio would wake them up.

It did. Captain Sarmiento was pulled from a deep and dream-free sleep by the amplified voice from the wall speaker. He stumbled over from the couch and banged his shins ruthlessly on the control station before he found the light switch.

"Cruz del Luz here, come in." His voice was rough with sleep and he coughed and spat into the wastebasket while he groped through the printouts on his desk.

"This is Air Force flight four seven five requesting clearance for landing."

Sarmiento's scrabbling fingers found the printout even while the voice was speaking; yes, the right one. "You are cleared for approach on runway one. I have a reading you are locked in to landing control." He blinked at a figure on the sheet, then looked up at the clock. "Your arrival approximately one hour ahead of schedule Air Force flight . . ."

"Tail winds," was the laconic reply.

Sarmiento dropped wearily into his chair and looked with disdain at his sleepy, shambling crew just entering the office. His temper burned strongly.

"Sons of whores! A major refueling, the first in six months, a most important wartime occasion and you lie around like swine in a sty."

Sarmiento continued enthusiastically in this manner while his staff hurried, hunch-shouldered, about their duties. This was good employment and they wanted to do nothing to jeopardize it.

The runway lights came on brightly as the fire engine raced along it to take position at the end of the runway. Out of the darkness the beams of landing lights speared in and the first of the arrivals thundered overhead to slap down to the runway's surface. One after another they landed, and once on the ground were guided automatically to the refueling points. Every bit of the operation was computer-controlled. Engines were cut and brakes applied at the proper spot. A TV camera rose up from each refueling well and scanned the undersurface of the wing above, locating the fuel access port. Once identified and pinpointed the smoothly articulated arm could open the cover and insert the hose so that pumping could begin. Sensors in each tank assured that there

would be no overflow or spillage. While this industrious robot activity was taking place all of the big planes remained dark and
quiet, sealed tight. Except for the command ship. The door on
this one opened, the entrance stairs ground out and settled into
place. A man in uniform came quickly down them and strode
firmly down the length of the refueling stations. Something drew
his attention to one of the pits, he bent over and looked close. His
back was to the tower, the underpart of his body in shadow, the
package that slipped from his jacket dropped into the well, unseen. He stood, brushed his clothing straight, then continued on
toward the illuminated control tower.

Sarmiento blinked up at the officer and felt slightly grubby.
The man's black uniform was pressed and smooth, the buttons
and gold braid gleaming in the light. A maltese cross hung about
his neck, there were decorations on his breast, a glass lens covered
one eye. Sarmiento climbed to his feet, impressed.

"*Sprechen sie Deutsch?*" the man said.

"I'm sorry, sir, but I don't understand what you are saying."
The officer scowled, then continued in thickly accented Portu-
guese.

"I am here to sign the receipted form," he said.

"Yes, to be sure excellency." Sarmiento waved in the direction
of the computer bank. "But that will not be ready until all of the
refueling is complete."

The officer nodded curtly, then strode up and down the office;
Sarmiento found important work to do. They both turned when
the bell rang and the completed form was ejected.

"Here, and here if you please," Sarmiento said, pointing out the
correct places, not even looking at the papers himself. "Thank
you very much." He tore off the bottom copy and passed it over,
happy to see the man turn and stamp away towards his waiting
aircraft. Only when he was safely aboard did Sarmiento pick up
the forms to file them. Strange names these foreigners had. Hard
to read the angular script. Looked like Schickelgruber . . . Adolph
Schickelgruber.

Urgent hands pulled the officer through the door, closing it
almost on his heels.

"How much time?" he asked, urgently.

"About twenty-eight minutes yet. We have to get airborne before they make radio contact."

"They might be behind schedule . . ."

"They could be ahead of it if our imaginary tailwind is real. We can't take any chances."

The first planes were already off the runway, vanishing up into the night. The lead plane was the last one to go, following the others out into the darkness. But instead of reaching for altitude it made a long circle out over the ocean and returned to the air field. Throttled back, flying low, making a pass down the runway.

"There's the fire engine, back in the barn already," someone said.

"And the rest of the men still in the building, no, there's one at the door, waving," General Blonstein said. "Let's give him a blink of our lights to say farewell." This time they continued out across the ocean to the west. Blonstein pressed the earphones to his head, listening, praying for time. Still all right, nothing, no other calls yet. "That's enough," he finally said, flipping up a red cover and thumbing the button beneath it.

Sarmiento heard the strange thud and looked up at the window just as the column of flame jutted high into the air. The aviation fuel burned brilliantly. Alarms sounded on all sides, the printers chattered, the radio burst to life with prerecorded emergency messages.

The German troop carriers had just cleared the African coast when the message came through.

"New course," the commander said, summoning up a map on the screen. "Some sort of accident, message didn't go into details. Anyway, we're cleared now for Madrid."

The commander was concerned about the new vector and the status of fuel in his tanks. He never thought to call through to Cruz del Luz airport; that was no concern of his now. Therefore the worried, frightened and tremendously upset Captain Sarmiento was spared one other problem in addition to the ones that now tormented him. He would not have to worry about how two flights that night had been scheduled to arrive with the same flight numbers and identical descriptions.

Twenty-one

"That is the first half of the job completed," Admiral Skougaard said with satisfaction as the debris of the enemy fleet vanished behind them. "It went far better than I had hoped. Did as well as Nelson did at Cape Trafalgar, better if you consider the fact that I am still alive. And we suffered not a scratch, unless you count the man with a broken foot where one of our cannonballs dropped on it. Course corrections?"

"Computed, sir," the operator said. "Engines will be firing in a little over four minutes."

"Excellent. As soon as we are in our new orbits I want the watches below to stand down and eat." He turned to Jan. "Privilege of rank; I'm having mine now. Join me?"

Food had been the farthest thing from Jan's mind up to that moment. But as the tension of the past hours drained away he realized that it had been a long time between meals. "I'll be happy to join you, Admiral."

The table was already laid when they entered the Admiral's private quarters, the chef himself putting the last of the food on the table. The Admiral and the chef exchanged some remarks in a guttural and incomprehensible tongue, laughing together at a throaty witticism.

"Smorgasbord," Jan said, eyes widening. "I haven't seen that since—why I don't remember when."

"*Stor kold bord*," Admiral Skougaard corrected. "The Swedish term has taken over in the popular mind, but it is not the same thing at all. We Danes enjoy our food. I always ship out with my

larder full. Growing empty now," he sighed. "We had better win
this war quickly. Here's to victory."

They toasted each other with tiny glasses of frigid akvavit,
downing them in a gulp. The chef instantly refilled them from
the bottle—frozen into its own cake of ice on the table. Thickly
buttered rye bread was heaped high with lashings of herring in
endless variety. Cold beef with grated horseradish, caviar with raw
egg, more and more and all washed down with bottles of cold
Danish beer. Theirs was the appetite of victory—of survival as
well. In defeating the enemy they had extended their own exist-
ences a bit more into the future. Eat and drink; the morrow
would come soon enough.

Over coffee, with just enough room left to nibble a bit of cheese,
their thoughts returned irresistibly to the final phase of the battle.

"Would you believe that I had the computer programmed for
at least two dozen future plans, depending upon the outcome of
the battle?" Skougaard said. "And of all of them I came up with
the best. Number one. So my next problem is how to keep that
plan a secret from the enemy's reserves. Let me show you."

He arranged the salt cellar, mustard pot, knives and forks upon
the table top. "Here we are, our squadron is the knife. Next to us
is the fork, the second squadron. Over here is Earth and that is
the way they are headed. The remaining enemy ships are in loose
groupings, here and here. They'll be on interception orbits by now
but they will be too late to interfere with what will happen next.
Before they can reach this spot our ships will capture and occupy
these spoons, the power satellites. As you know these big mirrors
turn solar energy to electricity and radiate it to Earth as micro-
waves. This energy feeds the electric grids of Europe and North
America, which means that they will be very unhappy when we
cut it off. All of the satellites, at exactly the same second. With a
little luck we'll start a blackout cascade. But all of this is really
just nuisance value. Earth has enough other energy sources that
they can cut in, so it won't matter at all in the long run. But the
present is what concerns us. Hopefully they will try and dislodge
our men. This will have to be done hand to hand because they
don't dare fire missiles or they will destroy their own satellites.
But we have no compunction about firing at their ships. It will be
an interesting battle. And totally unimportant. A diversion, nothing more. Here," he tapped the knife, "is where they should be
looking."

The knife moved out and around one plate and back towards another which had some small cream cakes upon it. "The Moon," Skougaard said, touching the first plate. "And Earth," pointing to the second plate, then taking one of the cakes. "Hopefully the diversion will pull off a lot of their defenses. The second part of the plan should make a big hole in what is left."

"This second part. This is where we coordinate with the attack on Spaceconcent in the Mojave desert?"

Skougaard licked a last bit of cream from his fingertips. "Exactly. My hope is that with the destruction of their main fleet, the attack on the satellites, blackouts and power failures, resistance sabotage, why they just might forget about Mojave for the moment. If your friend—our friend hopefully—Thurgood-Smythe is telling us the truth, why he will have a lot to do with increasing the confusion. In any case, win or lose, we go for the big one." He put a second knife beside the first one and moved them around the plate, to the back of the Moon.

"Here is where I divide my forces yet again. We will be out of sight and detection from the Earth stations when we are on the far side of the Moon. Also, when we pass this spot, here, we will be over the horizon and past the last remote detection station. That is when we fire our engines for a course change. A minor change for the main body of the squadron," he moved one knife slightly away from the other, "since we don't want it to come out into the waiting missiles of the defense forces, which will be in position by that time. But a major change for the remaining two ships. This one and the troop transport. We change orbit and pile on the G's. We whip around the Moon like a weight on a string— and come out here. Far from the defenses and on a precise orbit for Earth."

"An orbit that will eventually terminate over the Mojave?"

"Exactly. The *Dannebrog* will supply cover, a missile umbrella screen against anything coming up from Earth. That should be easy because they have to rocket up out of the gravity well. We should have plenty of time to pop them off as they come. And we have nothing to fear from the Moon bases behind us since they will have had a few bombs and iron cannonballs down their throats to give them something else to think about."

"You make it sound simple," Jan said.

"I know. But it isn't. Warfare never is. You plan as best you can, then chance and the human factor come into it to produce the final results." He poured a glassful of akvavit from the water-beaded bottle and threw it down his throat. "A few more of these, then a good sleep—and we see what is waiting for us when we come out from behind the Moon. I suggest you get some rest as well. And if you are the praying type, pray that this strange brother-in-law of yours is really on our side this time."

Jan lay down, but could not sleep. They were hurtling at incredible speed towards an unknown destiny. Dvora was mixed up in it; he should not be thinking about her, but he was. Halvmörk, all his friends and the rest of the people there. And his wife; they were light-years away. Light-years from his thoughts as well. This warfare, the killing, it was going to end soon. One way or the other. And Thurgood-Smythe, what about him? He was the deciding factor in the whole equation. Would his plan work—or was it just a convoluted and complex plot to betray and destroy them all? Warm flesh, dead flesh, guns, death and life, all swirled into a jumble and the alarm buzzer startled him awake. He had fallen asleep after all. The reason why he had set the alarm returned through the fog of sleep and a sudden knot of tension formed in his midriff. The battle was entering its final phase.

Jan found Admiral Skougaard in a philosophical mood when he joined him. Skougaard was listening to the muttered comments from the computers and nodding his head as he looked at the displays on the screens.

"Did you hear that?" he asked. "The big cannons are firing again at a target they can't see, that will be destroyed well before they reach it. Have you considered the mathematical skill involved in this little exercise that we take so much for granted? I wonder how many years it would take us to do these computations by hand. Look—" he pointed at the cratered surface of the Moon slowly moving by beneath them. "I supplied the computers with accurate photographic maps of the Moon. On these maps I marked the three missile bases that are located on the Earth side of this satellite. After that I simply instructed them to fire the cannon to knock these sites out. That is what they are doing now. In order to do this the Moon must be observed and our orbit, speed and altitude determined. Then the sites must be located in relation to this orbit. Then a new orbit must be calculated for the cannonballs, that will include our speed, their launching speed, and the precise angle that will permit their path to terminate on the chosen missile site. Marvelous." His elation vanished as he looked at the time, to be replaced by the studied calm he presented during battle. "Three minutes and Earth will be over the horizon. We'll see then what kind of reception is waiting for us."

As Earth's atmosphere slowly rose into view the rustling static on their radios was replaced by muffled voices that became quickly clearer as they moved into line of sight of the stations. The computers scanned all the space communication frequencies to intercept the enemy messages.

"A good deal of activity," Skougaard said. "They have been stirred up enough. But they have some good commanders left—all of them better than the late Comrade Kapustin. But if Thurgood-Smythe is doing his job there should be conflicting orders going out. Let us hope so since every little bit helps."

The blue globe of Earth was clearly in sight now; a web of radar signals filled space, followed instantly by more accurate laser detectors once the rebels had been found. As soon as this happened the invading fleet broke radio silence and began searching and ranging as well. Figures and code symbols filled the displays.

"It could have been better for us," Skougaard said. "Then again it could have been a lot worse."

Jan was silent as the Admiral called for course computations, estimates of closing speed, ranges, all of the mathematical details that were the essentials of space war. He did not hurry, although thousands of miles passed while he considered his decision. Once made it was irrevocable—so it had to be right.

"Signal to first squadron in clear. Plan seven. Then contact the second squadron, coded report."

Skougaard sat back to wait, then nodded to Jan. "The enemy has spread a wide web, which is what I would have done myself, rather than risking everything on covering a few orbital boltholes. They knew that we wouldn't come out from behind the Moon on the same orbit we were on when they lost contact with us. This is both good and bad for us. Good for the others in the first squadron. They are in tight orbit for two of the most important Lagrange satellite colonies, the manufacturing ones. Whether they attempt to capture them or not depends entirely upon how hot the pursuit is. We'll know soon when all of the enemy course corrections are completed. It will be a slow stern chase because our opponent's forces are so widely separated. That could be dangerous for us because they could mass more ships than I would like to intercept us. Let us hope that they get their priorities wrong."

"What do you mean?"

Skougaard pointed at the screen at the image of the troop carrier in orbit beside them. "At this point in time everything depends upon that ship. Knock it out and we have surely lost the war. Right now its orbit terminates in central Europe, which should give the enemy something to ponder over. But during braking approach its course, and ours, will be changed to put us down in the Mojave. Just one hour after the Israeli attack begins. With our aid the base will be secured, the missile sites captured. When they are secured we can fight off any attack from space, or destroy the base if attacked by land. End of battle, end of war. But if they knock out that transport, why then we don't take the base, the Israelis will be counterattacked and killed—and we will have lost the war . . . wait. Signal from the second squadron."

The Admiral read the report and grinned widely. "They've done it! Lundwall and his men have taken all three power satellites." The grin faded. "They fought off the interceptors. We lost two ships."

There was nothing to be said. Capture of these satellites, and the orbiting colonies, would be immensely important in ending the war quickly after Spaceconcent was taken. But right now both actions were basically diversions to split the enemy forces to enable the troop carrier to slip through. How successful these diversions would be would not be known until the Earth forces were established in their new courses.

"Preliminary estimation," the computer said calmly. "Eighty percent probability that three ships will intercept force one alpha."

"I was hoping for only one or two," Skougaard said. "I don't like the odds." He spoke to the computer. "Give me identification on those three."

They waited. Although the approaching space ships could be clearly observed electronically, they appeared just as points in space. Until they could be seen as physical shapes the identification program had to look for other identifying signs. Degree of acceleration when changing course gave clues to their engines. When they communicated with each other their code identities might be discovered. This all took time—time during which the distance between the opposing forces closed rapidly.

"Identification," the computer said. Skougaard spun to face the

screens as the numbers appeared there far faster than they could
be spoken aloud.

"*Til helvede!*" he said in cold anger. "Something is wrong, very
wrong. They shouldn't be there. Those are their heaviest attack
vessels, armed to the teeth with every weapon that they possess.
We can't get through. We're as good as dead now."

Twenty-two

There was never any uncertainty about the summer weather in the Mojave desert. During the winter months conditions varied; there could be clouds, occasionally even rain. The desert would be uncharacteristically green then, dusted with tiny flowers that faded and died in a few days. Beautiful. That could not be said about the summer time.

Before dawn the temperature might drop down to thirty-eight degrees, what the Americans, still valiantly resisting the onslaught of the metric system, insisted on calling ninety. It might even be a few degrees cooler, but no more. Then the sun came up.

It burned like the mouth of an open oven as it cleared the horizon. By noon, sixty degrees—one hundred and thirty—was not unusual.

The sky was light in the east, the temperature just bearable, when the planes came in to land. The tower at the Spaceconcent airfield had been in touch with the flight since they had begun to lose height over Arizona. The rising sun glowed warmly on their burnished skins as they dropped down towards the lights of the runway.

Lieutenant Packer yawned as he watched the first arrivals taxi up to the disembarkation points. Big black crosses on their sides. Krauts. The Lieutenant did not like Krauts since they were one of the Enemies of Democracy in the paranoid history books that he had been raised on. Along with Commies, Russkies, Spics, Niggers and an awful lot of others. There were so many bad guys that they were sometimes hard to keep track of, but he still managed to feel a mild dislike for the Krauts, even though he had never met one before. Why weren't there good American boys here, defending this strategic base? There were, his company among them, but Spaceconcent was international, so any UN troops might be assigned here. But, still, Krauts . . .

As the engines died the landing stairs slowly unfolded. A group of officers emerged from the first plane and came toward him. Soldiers clattered down behind them and began to form up in ranks. Packer had leafed through Uniforms of the World's Armies briefly, but he could recognize a general's stars without its help. He snapped to attention and saluted.

"Lieutenant Packer, Third Motorized Cavalry." The officers returned the salute.

"General von Blonstein. *Heeresleitung.* Vere is our transportation?"

Even sounded like a Kraut from one of the old war movies. "Any second now, General. They're on the way from the motor pool. We weren't expecting your arrival until . . ."

"Tail vind," the General said, then turned and snapped out commands in his own language.

Lieutenant Packer looked worried as the newly formed up troops quick-stepped off towards the hangars. He moved in front of the General who ignored him until he worked up the nerve to speak.

"Excuse me, sir, but orders. Transportation is on the way—here are the first units now—to take your men to the barracks . . ."

"Goot," the General said, turning away. Packer moved quickly to get in front of him again.

"Your people can't go into those hangars. That is a security area."

"It is too hot. They get in der shade."

"No they can't, really, I'll have to report this." He reached to turn on his radio and one of the officers rapped him hard on the hand with the butt of his gun. Then ground it into his ribs. Packer could only stare, speechlessly, and hold his bruised fingers.

"There is a silencer on that pistol," the General said, all trace of an accent suddenly vanished. "Do as I say or you will be shot instantly. Now turn and walk to that plane with these men. One word, a wrong action, and you are dead. Now go." Then he added in Hebrew, "Inject him and leave him there."

When the last engine had been shut down the computer in the

control tower disconnected the landing and taxiing program and shut it down as well, signaling that the operation was complete. One of the operators verified with a visual check using field glasses. All of the planes were wound down now. A lot of trucks and busses about; he wouldn't start clearing the ramps until they had moved out of the area. The convoy officer was going into a plane with two of the newcomers. Probably had a bottle in there. German soldiers were probably just like their American counterparts. Brawling, boozing and banging. Good thing they locked them behind wire most of the time.

"In the back, not here," the Corporal said as the soldier opened the cab of the truck and started to climb in.

"Ja, Ja, gut," the soldier said, ignoring the command.

"C'mon, Christ, I don't speak that stuff. In backski, fucking quickski . . ." He looked down in amazement as the newcomer leaned over and slapped him on the leg. Something stung. He opened his mouth to protest, then slumped forward over the wheel. The Israeli clicked the safety in place on the palm-hypo and put it into his pocket, then dragged the Corporal from behind the wheel as the door opened on the driver's side. Another Israeli slipped in, taking off his helmet and laying it on the seat beside him, then putting on the Corporal's fatigue cap in its place.

General Blonstein looked at his watch. "How much longer to go?" he asked.

"Three, four minutes, no more," his aide said. "Boarding the last coaches now."

"Good. Any trouble?"

"Nothing important. A few people asking questions have been put to sleep. But we haven't hit any of the guarded gates or buildings yet."

"And we're not going to until everyone is in position. How much longer to jumpoff?"

"Sixty seconds."

"Let's go. These last people can catch us up. We're not going to change the attack schedule for any reason."

Dvora sat next to Vasil who was driving the heavy lorry; her squad was jammed into the back. Her long hair had been tied into a bun and hidden under her helmet, her face was bare of any cosmetics.

"How much longer?" Vasil asked, his foot tapping the accelerator, the motor rumbling in response. She glanced at her watch.

"Any second now if they are keeping to plan."

"This is a big place," he said, looking up at the service towers, gantries and warehouses that stretched into the distance behind the wire fence. "We can maybe take it—but we can't hold it."

"You were at the last briefing. We're getting reinforcements to consolidate."

"You never said where they were coming from."

"Of course not. So if you're captured you won't be able to talk."

The big man smiled coldly and patted the bandolier of grenades hung about his neck. "The only way they'll capture me is dead. So tell."

Dvora smiled and pointed skyward. "Help will come from there." Vasil grunted and turned away.

"Now you sound like a rabbi," he said, just as her radio sounded a rapid series of high-pitched bleeps.

"Go!" Dvora said, but he already had his foot down on the accelerator. "Gunners ready?" she said into her radio.

"In position," the voice said inside her head. She tightened her chin strap to keep the bone conduction headphone secured in place.

The big truck rolled around the corner of the warehouse and stopped by the military police box there. The gate that blocked the entrance remained shut. The MP leaned out and scowled.

"You're going on report, buddy, because you are stupid and you are lost. That thing isn't cleared to come in here . . ."

The time for harmless drug injections had passed. Through a slit cut in the canvas cover of the truck the muzzle of a machine gun emerged, firing, sweeping back and forth. Because of the long silencer on the end of the barrel it only made a muffled coughing sound; the crash of broken glass and punctured metal was much louder. A second gun on the other side killed the MP there.

"Ram it," Dvora said.

The heavy truck lurched forward, crashing into the gate, pulling it down with a shriek of torn metal, drove over it. An alarm bell began sounding somewhere in the distance; there was the muffled sound of explosions.

Dvora had memorized their route, but she did not believe in taking chances so had the map unfolded on her lap. "Left at the next corner," she said, her finger on the track marked out in red.

"If we don't meet any resistance on the way this should take us directly to our target."

The service road they were on cut through an area of office blocks and warehouses. There was no other traffic. Vasil put his foot to the floor and the heavy truck picked up speed. The gearbox screamed as it shifted into top gear, the soldiers in back grabbing for support as they jarred through a pothole.

"That's the building we want, the big one . . ."

Her words ended in a gasp as the road surface ahead stirred and cracked, crumbled, then split from curb to curb. Vasil was standing on the brakes, the wheels locked, the tires screaming as they skidded, scarcely slowing, burning rubber. They looked on, horrified, braced themselves, unable to do anything else as they saw the concrete fall away in chunks and slabs as a meter-high steel plate levered up to block the road. The slide ended in a metallic crash as the truck drove headlong into the rust-splotched barrier.

Dvora plunged forward, her helmet cracking hard against the metal dash. Vasil clutched her by the shoulders and pulled her erect.

"Are you all right?"

She nodded, dazed by the impact. "This barrier . . . wasn't mentioned in the briefing . . ."

A hail of bullets tore through the metal of the truck, crashed through the windows.

"Bail out!" Dvora shouted into her microphone, raising her gun at the same time and putting a long burst into the doorway of a nearby building where she thought she had seen someone move. Vasil was already in the street and she dived after him. Her squad were dropping down and seeking cover, returning the fire.

"Cease firing until you see a target," she ordered. "Anyone hurt?"

There were cuts and bruises, no more. They had survived their first combat encounter and had all found cover, either under the truck or against the building wall. The firing started again and slugs screamed off the road, sending up spurts of dust and fragments from the sidewalk. At the same time there was the bark of a single shot from under the truck and the firing stopped. A metallic clatter sounded, loud in the silence after the firing, as a gun fell from a window across the main road; a man's motionless arm hung down across the frame.

"There was only the one," Grigor said, snapping the safety back on his rifle.

"We'll advance on foot," Dvora said, looking at the map. "But away from this main road now that the alarm is out. The alleyway across the road. Scouts out, proceed as skirmishers. Go!"

The two scouts, one after another, rushed across the empty road and into the security of the alley mouth. The rest of the squad followed. They double-timed now, aware of the quick passage of the minutes, Vasil grunting to keep up, running heavily under the thirty kilos weight of the big recoilless 50 calibre machine gun, his two ammunition carriers at his heels.

They crossed one other main avenue, in quick rushes, but met no more resistance. Steel barriers had also risen through the road's surface here; they could see more, at regular intervals, stretching away in the distance.

"One street more," Dvora said, folding the map and putting it away. "The building will be defended . . ." She raised her hand and they all stopped, guns ready, alert.

A man had stepped out of a large open entrance ahead moving cautiously, his back to them. A civilian, apparently unarmed. "Don't move and you will be all right," Dvora said. The man turned and gasped when he saw the armed troops.

"I'm not doing nothing. I was working in there, heard the alarms, what's happening . . . ?"

"Back inside," Dvora told him, signaling her squad to follow. "What is this place?"

"Quartermaster supply. I was servicing the forklifts, charging them up."

"Is there a way through this building?" Dvora asked.

"Yeah, sure. Stairs to the second floor, cut through the offices. Look, lady, can you tell me what's going on?"

"There has been trouble, fighting, rebel sympathisers. But we are stopping them."

The man looked around at the silent, armed squad, their uniforms bare of identification or marks of rank. He started to ask a question, then instantly thought better of it. "Just follow me. I'll show you the way."

They went up one flight of stairs and started along the hall.

"You said the second floor?" Dvora was suspicious, her gun raised.

"That's right, this one. The second floor."

She waved him on. Little details. She had forgotten that Americans called the ground floor the first. And who had forgotten the little detail about the barriers in the road? She wondered how the others were doing, but knew better than to break radio silence.

"That's the street door ahead," their captive said. "Where you want to go."

Dvora nodded and pointed to Grigor, who stepped forward and slapped the man on the back of the neck. He stifled the startled scream with one big hand, then eased the unconscious figure to the floor.

After unlocking the door, Dvora slowly opened it a crack and looked out, distant gunfire and explosions could be heard—then quickly closed it again. She set her radio on the command frequency.

"Black cat five to black cat one. Do you read me?"

The answer came instantly. *"Black cat five reading."*

"In position."

"Black cat two is in trouble. Pinned down. You're on your own. Effect entrance now. Out."

The squad stood waiting for instructions, weapons ready; Dvora looked around at them. Good people. But they knew next to nothing yet about combat. They were about to learn. The survivors would be experienced.

"The groups attacking the front of the target have been held up," she said. "They must be meeting strong resistance. So we're going to have to do the job. The building across the road should not be as well defended. We hope. The plan is to get in there, get to the rear where it backs onto the target. We go through that wall . . ."

She broke off as they heard a siren in the street outside, growing louder. She pointed to Grigor who ran forward and dropped flat, then opened the door slightly. "Car coming," he said. "It may be stopping at the doorway there—someone has come out and is waving to it."

"We go," Dvora said, making an instant decision. "Bazooka. Take it out as soon as it stops. Then put one through the doorway. We'll follow right behind."

After that it was a matter of training. Vasil rolled aside and the bazooka gunner dropped down in his spot, eyes to the sight, his weapon trained. His loader was beside him, pushing the rocket missile into the rear of the tube, slapping his shoulder to let him know it was ready. The rest of the squad moved to the sides, clear of the backlash of flame when it was fired. In the street the siren wailed down to silence as the car braked to stop.

A tongue of fire shot back from the bazooka and an explosion rocked the street outside. The loader was jamming in another rocket even as the glass from broken windows was crashing to the ground.

"Smoke, target obscured . . ." the bazooka gunner muttered, waiting—then the flame lanced out again. The explosion, inside the building this time, was muffled. Dvora threw the door wide and led the squad in a rush.

A smoking wreck of a car, bodies burning in the crackling interior. Up the steps and through the ruined doorway, jumping over the huddle of still more bodies here. One of them alive, raising his gun, soaked in blood. Two shots cracked out and he fell with the others. They were jammed in the entrance, fighting to get in. A long hallway, running, shouting soldiers coming towards them.

"Down!" Vasil shouted, standing spread-legged while they dropped, spraying death like water from a hose from the muzzle of his machine gun. Sheets of flame blasted from the recoilless ports behind his arm, empty casings bounced clattering from the wall. The big 50-calibre slugs tore the running men apart, spun them about, hurled them down, killed them all.

There was little mopping up to do. The speed and shock of their attack had carried the defenders before it. But time was running out; they were falling behind. They moved faster now, following Dvora's directions as she consulted the detailed floor plan she had been given. Thurgood-Smythe had supplied it of course. Along with all of the other information needed to launch the attack. She had forgotten the man, and her doubts, in the cold frenzy of the fighting. Nor could she afford to think about him now.

"This is the place," she said, when they entered the large room, one end filled with packing cases. "That wall, where the notices are posted. Six meters in from the lefthand edge."

And they had even remembered to bring the measuring rules. Three of them had been issued so at least one would get this far. Dvora got her breath back while they made the wall.

"Take cover," she said. "In the hall, behind those crates. When the charges go—we go. We should be in a wide corridor leading to the entrance that has to be unblocked. This is the big one."

Dvora checked the fuses herself; all secure. Then ran back to the hall, the wire hissing from the roller in her hand. Dropped through and hit the firing button at the same time.

For one instant as the charge blew she thought of Thurgood-Smythe, and if he had told the truth about what awaited them on the other side of the wall.

After that there was no time for thought. Coughing in the cloud of dust and smoke, scrambling through the ragged opening. Running. The surprise of the defenders as they were taken from their rear, heads turning, mouths opening even as they fell.

It was butchery. The heavy bunkers outside were open from the rear, had no defenses from that flank. Grenades and gunfire cleaned them out.

"Come on now . . . black cat . . . the door is open . . ." she gasped into her radio. Troops appeared through the thick smoke. General Blonstein was first.

"Final goal. Missile control room," he said. "Follow me."

They stopped outside the entrance to the complex, still out of breath from rushing up the three floors.

"Keep your weapons lowered when we go in there," Blonstein said. "We don't want any sabotage. I'll talk to them, explain, give them a story, while the rest of you filter through the control consoles. Remember, we want to capture this place, not destroy . . ."

His words were interrupted by the thud of a small explosion, apparently from a room across the hall from them; a dozen gun muzzles were trained on it as the knob slowly turned. It opened even more slowly and a man appeared, leaning back against the door jamb for support; his clothing drenched in blood.

"Thurgood-Smythe!" Dvora said.

"There has been treachery in high places," Thurgood-Smythe whispered as he slowly slumped down to the floor.

Twenty-three

"They knew," Admiral Skougaard said, staring fixedly at the identification of the enemy ships. "They had to know. There is no other explanation for the presence of that force to be there at this time."

"Thurgood-Smythe?" Jan said.

"You tell me." There was no warmth or humanity left in Skougaard's voice now. "You brought me the plan."

"I also said that I wasn't sure if it could be trusted or not."

"And so you did. We'll all pay with our lives for that mistake. At least we can see what is happening. I'm sorrier for the troops jammed into that transport."

"We can still fight, can't we? We're not giving in?"

Cold anger was replaced by a wintery smile on the Admiral's face. "We'll not give in. But I'm afraid we have no chance at all of winning. We are up against three times as many missiles as we can launch, probably more. They'll just overload our defenses then come through. About all we can do is separate from the transport, fight a holding action for as long as we can in the hopes that they will survive."

"Won't that work?"

"No. But we do it anyway. Orbital mechanics is too rigid a discipline for there to be any doubts. They will meet us, we will fight. We might injure them, probably not. They'll take us out. Then follow the transport and pick it off at their ease."

"We can change course."

"So can they. We cannot get away, only prolong the end. If

you have any personal messages put them through to the radio room for transmission for the second squadron to pass on . . ."

"It seems so unfair! After coming this far, after the battles for the planets, everything!"

"Since when has fairness had anything to do with winning battles? Armies and navies used to travel with priests—on both sides —each assuring the fighting men that God was on their particular side. One general said that God was on the side of the biggest battalions, which is nearer to the truth."

There was little to add to that. Three fighting ships against one. The outcome of this encounter could not be in doubt. Under the Admiral's direction their orbits were altered slightly and the two spacers began to drift apart; there was no change in the enemy's orbit. Skougaard pointed to one of the screens.

"They are risking nothing—and leaving nothing to chance. If we hit the atmosphere at this speed we will burn up. They know we must brake, and just how much, and they will be there to meet us just when we are most vulnerable, when our speed is lowest, just outside the atmosphere."

As the hours dragged by rage gave way to apathy; the numbness of the condemned man in his cell, waiting for the wardens. Jan thought about the road that he had followed that had led him to this spot, at this particular time. Although he had no desire to die, he could not see how he could have done anything differently, could have followed any other path, taken any different decisions. His life was what it was, he had no regrets other than that it was just being terminated a little earlier than he had planned.

"And now the last act begins," Skougaard said with grim Scandinavian fatalism as sudden explosions flared in space ahead. "They send their first missiles even though it is extreme range, knowing they can't hit us—but knowing that we have no choice, that we must expend our antimissile defenses. Attrition."

The steady attack by the enemy missiles continued relentlessly —then stopped as suddenly as it had begun.

"Our reserves are down to twenty percent," Skougaard said. "What kind of cat and mouse game are they playing at?"

"Radio contact is clear," the operator said. "On our frequency, but emanating from the Earth ships. They want to talk to you, Admiral."

Skougaard hesitated a moment, then shrugged. "Put them through."

A communication screen flicked on with the image of a full-bearded man in full dress Space Force uniform.

"I thought it might be you, Ryzard," the Admiral said. "Why are you calling?"

"To offer you terms, Skougaard."

"Surrender? I don't think I like that. You'll only kill us all in the end anyway."

"Of course. But you'll get a few more weeks of life. A trial, a military execution."

"Sounds charming, but not very attractive. And just what arrangements have you made for my ships to surrender?"

"Ship. Singular. They want you and your *Dannebrog* as a memorial to the failed rebellion. The other ship with you, which I assume is a troop carrier, we are blowing up. That is another kind of memorial for the rebellion."

"You can go to hell, Ryzard, you and the rest of your murderers."

"I thought you might say that. You always were stubborn . . ."

"One question, Ryzard, a last favor for an old classmate. You were informed of our plans, weren't you?"

Ryzard brushed his fingers slowly through his beard before answering. "It can do no harm now to tell you. We knew exactly what you were going to do. You never stood a chance. Our information came right from the top . . ."

Skougaard broke the connection with a slap of his hand. "Thurgood-Smythe. The galaxy would have been a better place if he had been smothered as an infant . . ."

A buzzer sounded stridently for attention, a red light began pulsing on one of the screens at the same time. Skougaard swung about to look at it.

"Earth-launched missiles," he said. "They are going to a lot of trouble to make certain of their kill. Those big ones have multiple atomic warheads. Can't be stopped by anything that we can put in front of them now. Must be a dozen of them. Launched in counter orbit, they'll be here in seconds . . . but no! That can't be possible!"

"What?" Jan asked. "What do you mean?"

The Admiral was struck speechless, could only point at the screen. Jan looked, seeing the plotted course of the new attack, the three enemy ships.

Distant explosions flared in space as the missiles pressed home their attack. But not at the rebels, not at all.

It was the three attacking ships had been destroyed.

The missiles had been aimed at them, not the two rebel ships, had punched through their defenses, had vaporized them utterly in the instant hell of atomic explosions.

It was unbelievable—but it had happened. In a single instant defeat had been turned to victory. In the stunned silence that followed the Admiral's voice bellowed out clearly.

"Make a signal," he said, an uncontrollable tremor in his voice. "Secure for retrofiring. And prepare for landing. Enemy forces destroyed. We're going in!"

Twenty-four

Down out of the clear blue sky the two great spaceships fell. There was no ground control, no contact with Spaceconcent control, so they were not being guided into the landing pits. They were aimed instead for the wide stretches of concrete of the airfield. Well clear of the transport planes, they dropped down on thundering spires of flame in a crushing five-G landing. Strapped to their bunks, fighting for breath where an 80-kilo man suddenly weighed 400 kilos, the crews and the soldiers waited. As the landing legs touched the engines were cut—and they were on the ground. The reinforced concrete buckled and cracked under their weight, but the computers compensated instantly for the difference and the ships remained upright.

As the engines shut down aboard the *Dannebrog* the shields snapped away from the outside cameras and the scene appeared on every screen inside the ship. The troop carrier, with smoke still billowing up around it, suddenly changed shape as all of its cargo doors and hatches were blown out at the same instant. Landing ramps reached out and crashed down into place, while folding ladders rattled down from the open ports. The attack was on. Light tanks hurtled down the ramps and out through the smoke while soldiers swarmed like ants down the ladders. There was no sign of opposition and the attackers spread out as quickly as they could, racing toward the buildings at the edge of the field.

Admiral Skougaard was listening in on the combat circuit. He nodded with pleasure then leaned over and switched the radio off.

"They're down and safe," he said. "Contact made with the Israelis and they have joined forces to knock out all of the remaining resistance. We've done our job. Now it's up to them."

Jan watched the troops fan out through the buildings until they had vanished from sight, his thoughts going around and around and refusing to settle down. Was this it—really it? Was the war over—or would the Earth troops continue the fighting? They could not be stopped if they did; the defenders would be overrun, wiped out. But the base would be destroyed. Was the threat of this great enough to prevent the disaster . . . ?

"Here," Skougaard said, pushing a waterglass towards Jan. "We will drink to success now—and victory to follow soon after."

It was akvavit not water that filled the glass and the Admiral drained his with pleasure, smacking his lips. Jan took a large swallow which was more than enough.

"Ground transportation on the way," the radio operator said. The Admiral nodded.

"Good. We'll use the engine room lock."

The combat car was braking to a skidding stop as they came out, the blue and white emblem of the Earth forces still marked on its side—although it was pierced by an ominous scatter of bullet holes. The Israeli driver threw the door open for them.

"They want you both at HQ," she said, and the vehicle hurled itself forward as soon as they were inside, squealing about in a tight turn and rushing towards the exit. They bumped through the debris where an opening had been blown in the fence and on into the streets beyond. Smoking wreckage marked the scenes of the worst fighting; crumpled bodies as well. There had been losses, heaviest around the control building that had been the prime target. A field headquarters had been set up in the ground floor. They entered it by the simple expedient of walking through the gaping hole that had been blown in the outer wall. General Blonstein was talking on the radio link, but he dropped the handset when they came in and hurried over to greet them.

"We have won here," he said. "The last defenders have just surrendered. But there are two enemy armored columns coming this way, as well as regiments of paratroops. We hope to have them stopped well before they arrive. Negotiations are going forward now and all the problems seem to be in hand." He made a gesture towards the adjoining desk, at the man seated there and talking on the phone. Even from the back it was easy to recognize Thurgood-Smythe. He disconnected and turned to face them.

"Welcome back, Jan, Admiral. Things are working according to plan as you can see." There were smears of blood on his face and his clothing was soaked and dark with even more blood.

"You've been injured," Jan said. The corners of Thurgood-Smythe's mouth lifted slightly.

"Don't sound so hopeful, Jan. The blood is not mine. It belongs to an associate, now dead, who attempted to interfere with my plans. Auguste Blanc the director—former director I should say—of this space center. He countermanded orders of mine to the defending fleet."

"The ships that were waiting for us?" the Admiral said.

"Precisely. Though I really can't blame him since all of the orders I had sent out were issued in his name. In case there were difficulties I preferred the responsibility to be his, not mine. He found out what was happening and chose to go along with the ruse instead of confronting me, only countermanding my orders at the last moment. This could have been embarrassing."

"To you," Jan said, his voice tight with anger. "We could have been dead."

"But you aren't, Jan, are you? The delay was not serious in the end. Poor Auguste was fool enough to face up to me, to brag about what he had done. After taking my gun away of course. Everyone seems to have a gun these days. I tried to move away from him, but had to do it slowly in order not to startle him." Thurgood-Smythe looked down and brushed at his blood stained clothing. "He was quite startled when my gun exploded. This is his blood. Stunned me a bit. Did worse to him. I was sure he would try to arrest me on his own, that is why I had the gun prepared. He was such a stupid man."

"Mr. Thurgood-Smythe enabled us to take over missile control without sabotage or damage," General Blonstein said. "He had the missiles fired that took out the ships that were attacking you. He is now negotiating the surrender. He has been invaluable to our cause."

The sub-machinegun was leaning against the wall. Jan turned away, no one even noticed, and walked slowly over to it. Only when he had seized it up and swung around to face them were they aware of what he had done.

"Stand clear of him," Jan ordered. "I'll shoot anyone who is in the way in order to be sure that he is dead."

The muzzle swung back and forth in a tight arc. The room was suddenly silent. There were guns on all sides, but no one was expecting this, no one was ready; they were motionless.

"Put it down, Jan," Skougaard ordered. "This man is on our side. Don't you understand what he has done?"

"I understand too well—not only this, but everything else that he has done. He is a liar and a murderer and he cannot be trusted. We will never know why he has done what he has done, but it doesn't matter. When he is dead we will be safe."

Someone moved, stepping forward, and Jan swung the gun in that direction. It was Dvora.

"Jan, please," she said. "He is on our side. We need him . . ."

"No we don't. He wants to take over again, I am sure of that. A hero of the revolution. And when he does it will be for his own benefit. He doesn't care about us or the revolution, or anything else other than himself. There is only one way to stop him."

"Would you shoot me as well?" she said, standing before him.

"If I had to," he said, slowly. "Step aside."

She did not move—and his finger was tight on the trigger. "Don't be a fool," Admiral Skougaard said. "You're dead yourself if you shoot him. Is that worth it?"

"Yes. I know what he has done. I don't want that sort of thing to ever happen again . . ."

Thurgood-Smythe walked forward and pushed Dvora to one side, coming on until he was just before the muzzle of the waiting gun.

"All right, Jan, here is your chance. Kill me and get it over with. It won't bring any of the dead back, but it will make you happy. So do it. Because if I live I might be a power in your brave new world, might even run for office in your first democratic election. That would be ironic, wouldn't it? Thurgood-Smythe, enemy of the people—savior of the people—being elected to power by a free choice of the people. So shoot. You can't have enough faith in your new freedom to permit someone like me to live in it, can you? So you, the one who has been so much against killing, will be the first to kill in the new republic. Why—you might even be the first one tried and condemned under the new laws."

There was irony in his voice, but he wasn't smiling as he spoke. If he had been Jan would surely have pulled the trigger. But he didn't. It would have taken just a touch, the slightest pressure and the problem of Thurgood-Smythe would have been ended forever. But matters involving Thurgood-Smythe were never so simple.

"Tell me the truth," Jan said, so quietly that none of the others could hear. "Just for once in your life. Had you planned it all this way, or did you just see an opportunity to change sides and make the most of it? Which was it?"

Thurgood-Smythe looked Jan fully in the eyes as he spoke.

"My dear brother-in-law, telling you anything now would be a complete waste of time. You would not believe me whatever I said. So you will just have to make your mind up on your own for I shan't help you."

He turned about when he had finished speaking, walked slowly away and drew out a chair and seated himself. Jan willed himself to fire. But he could not. Whatever Thurgood-Smythe had done, whatever his reasons had been, he had aided them in the end. The liberation of Earth would not have been possible without his help. With sudden insight Jan realized that the victory might have been won in another manner without Thurgood-Smythe's help; but once he had become involved the responsibility had shifted to him. All choice had been removed. Jan actually smiled as he engaged the safety with his thumb and let the gun slide to the floor.

"All right, Smitty, this round to you. You are free to go. For now. Run for office, do whatever you like. But don't forget that I am watching. Revert to your bad old ways . . ."

"I know. You will come and find me and kill me. I don't doubt that for a second. So we will just have to let the future take care of itself, won't we?"

Suddenly Jan wanted to get out into the fresh air, to be free of this man, of the very room he was in, to forget him and the past and to look forward to the future. He was not stopped as he turned about and left. He stood outside, drawing in breath after deep breath, wondering at the emotions that tore at him. Someone was next to him; he turned and saw that it was Dvora. Without thought his arms were about her, holding her very tight.

"I am going to forget him," Jan said in a fierce whisper. "I'm going to put him from my mind and go home to Halvmörk, to my wife, to my people there. There's work to be done."

"And here as well," she said. "And I'll go back to my husband . . ."

"You never told me," he said, surprised, holding her at arm's length.

L1

"You never asked." She was smiling, brushing the hair out of her eyes, smearing even more her beautiful but battle-stained face. "I told you that, remember? That between us, it was only chemistry. He's a rabbi, very devout and serious, but a very good pilot as well. He flew one of the planes here. I was very worried about him. The condition of the world has kept us apart too long. Now it is going to draw us together."

Jan found himself laughing, for no reason at all, laughing until tears rolled down his face. He hugged Dvora to him then released her for the last time.

"You're right. It's over and we have to believe that it is over. And we have to work to see that it comes out right for everyone." He looked up into the smoke-filled sky with sudden realization.

"And I'm coming back to Earth. I don't think Alzbeta will like it at first, but she will get used to it in the end. Earth is going to be the center of the worlds as it always has been. I can do the most for Halvmörk and its people by being right here . . ."

"You can do the most for everyone. You know Earth and you know the planets and you know what people must have."

"Freedom. They have that now. But it might be even harder to hold than it was to get."

"It always has been," she said. "Read your textbooks. Most revolutions are lost after they have been won."

"Then let us make sure that this one stays won." He looked up at the sky again. "I wish it were night now. I would like to see the stars."

"They are out there. Mankind has gone out to them once and did not do very well. We have a second chance now. Let us see if we can do better this time."

"We had better," Jan said, thinking of the power they had, the weaponry and the infinite ways of dealing death and absolute destruction.

"We must. I doubt if we will have a third chance if we don't get it right this time."